MW01039038

Also by Clayton Smith

Death and McCootie

Pants on Fire: A Collection of Lies

APOCALYPTICON

Dapper Press
www.DapperPress.com

Printed in the United States of America

ISBN 978-0-9898068-3-1 (pbk.)

For my parents, Randy and Denise, who have always been relentless in their support, and who are biologically responsible for this novel.

Acknowledgements

Goodness gracious, it took a lot of people to bring this book together and make it the *Apocalypticon* it is today. (And if you think it's bad now, you should have seen it before these wonderful people got involved.)

First and foremost, thank you to my wonderful wife, Paula, who didn't let me not finish this book. She's been an excellent sport about me locking myself in my office for hours on end, and her support has been absolutely crucial. She has also proven herself to be an extraordinary editor, and I can't thank her enough. For everything.

Thanks, too, to my dear friend Dave Bloom, for also not letting me not finish this story. He's also largely responsible for getting me to *start* this story. So basically, if you don't like this book, we can all blame him for making me write it.

I ~~stole~~ borrowed the personalities and/or physical characteristics of quite a few friends and acquaintances to populate the pages of this book with characters. Some of them gave themselves over willingly, others were borrowed in secret, and for all those who found themselves inserted into this story in one form or another, thank you, from the bottom of my heart. You gave these characters real life and depth, and you helped me to tell this story with a richness I'm fairly certain I couldn't have achieved on my own. All the characters' positive traits come directly from these real-world counterparts, and all the negative traits were completely invented by me. Here are the people whose lives I borrowed, and to whom I owe a debt of gratitude:

Patrick Dean and Ben Unglesbee. Thank you for "allowing" me to insert you as my main characters. You two are a couple of the funnest, weirdest, most adventurous people I know, and I couldn't have written this book without you guys. I apologize for the bumps and bruises along the way.

Dave Bloom. Thank you for providing an excellent foil for the aforementioned pair of goofballs. (Look, Dave! You got two acknowledgments!) Sorry I made you a villain.

Sammi Park Alexander, Shannon Boland, Ryan Briggs, Christine Colletti, Amy Dean, Tom Long, Sarah Miller, Millie Munshi, Libby Sallaberry, Kortney Seben, and a random Amtrak conductor I've had a few times on the Lincoln Service whose name I couldn't even guess. Some of you probably didn't even know you were in this book. Surprise! Don't sue me.

This book also went through a rousing editing process, and I cannot possibly thank Grace Austin or Patty Russell enough for their insights, suggestions, edits, and notes. The input you gave was obscenely helpful in turning this project from just a bunch of words into a real, live story. Thank you, thank you, thank you!

I'd like to thank Molly Reckman for designing the original cover for this book. I ended up going in a different direction with the style, but Molly's art is really fantastic, and you should go check it out on my site, www.StateOfClayton.com. Thank you for the wonderful work, Molly!

The art that now graces the cover of this book was done by a very talented gentleman named Octavian Todirut. It was a distinct pleasure to work with him in developing this concept, and I truly think it's the perfect cover for this book. Thanks, Octavian!

This book began as a National Novel Writing Month project (www.nanowrimo. org), and without the structure the Office of Letters and Light provides through this project, it's doubtful that I'd have ever written all the words needed to finish this book. OLL is a great non-profit that does outstanding work...please consider checking them out online and making a donation to their programs!

Lastly, I'd like to thank Hugh Howey, author of the WOOL series. Hugh, we've never met, but I attended your panel on self-publishing at SXSW 2013, and you gave me the courage and incentive to tackle the e-publishing beast head-on. Without your words, I might not have set my sights on self-publishing this work, and I thank you for that.

If there's anyone I've missed, I am very genuinely sorry, and I promise to make it up to you. Double promise.

APOCALYPTICON

CLAYTON SMITH

THE
RULES OF THE APOCALYPSE

An incomplete list taken from the journal of Ben Fogelvee

RULE #1: SURVIVE.

RULE #2: IF IT LOOKS HUNGRY, RUN AWAY FROM IT.

RULE #4: DON'T TALK ABOUT NICE THINGS.

RULE #7: MONEY IS NO LONGER MONEY. FOOD, WEAPONS, SHELTER, AND CLOTHING ARE MONEY.

RULE #9: EVERYTHING IS A WEAPON.

RULE #10: LITERALLY EVERYTHING IS A WEAPON.

RULE #12: ERR ON THE SIDE OF CRAZY.

RULE #14: WHEN FOOD IS SCARCE, EAT ANYTHING GREEN.

RULE #15: DISREGARD RULE #14.

RULE #18: FUCK TIME.

RULE #22: DYING IS BULLSHIT.

RULE #26: WHEN IN DOUBT, DEFER TO ENTERTAINMENT MEDIA.

RULE #31: NEVER FANTASIZE ABOUT FOOD.

RULE #33: VODKA IS DOCTORS NOW.

1.

Three hard knocks, two soft knocks, one long knock, three short knocks, two and a quarter rapid-fire knocks, one flat palm slap, four knuckle taps, one palm slap, seven knuckle taps, two long knocks, seven left hand-right hand alternating slap-pounds, three short knocks, one knuckle tap, two palm slaps, three hard knocks, two soft knocks, three hard—

"Wait. Shit." Patrick closed his eyes and ran through the latest sequence in his head. He raised his knuckles again. *Three hard knocks, two soft knocks, one long knock, three short knocks, two and a quarter rapid-fire knocks, one flat palm slap, four knuckle taps, another palm slap, seven knuckle taps, two long knocks, seven left hand-right hand alternating slap-pounds, three short knocks, one knuckle tap, two palm slaps, three hard knocks, four hard—*

"Dammit!" Patrick slammed his fist against the door, not quite hard enough to break it down, but hard enough to be able to claim later that he had. "Ben Fogelvee, you open this door right now, or I swear to all that is holy, I will rain down on you with blazing goddamn acid until you look like a Batman villain!"

He waited, huffing, out of breath, for a few seconds, but heard nothing from 24C. He had just decided to go find an ax when the deadbolt turned, the chain slipped back, the padlock clicked, the knob lock fell, and the door creaked open four centimeters. A suspicious eye with a crystal blue iris pressed itself to the thin opening and scrutinized the tall, razor-thin aggressor in the hall. Satisfied, the eye relaxed. Ben pulled the door all the way open. "Oh. It's you."

Patrick closed his eyes. "You make me so angry, you know that?" He pushed past him into the apartment. Ben shut the door and fastened the half dozen locks behind him.

"Don't project on me because your memory's going."

Patrick kicked through the wrappers and crusty spoons littering the marble-tiled floor and plopped down on the stained velvet duvet. "My fist is about to be going into your mouth."

"I used to pay eight bucks a month for a website that'd show me that." Ben picked up a can of Yankee beans from the floor, sniffed it, made a sour face, then tipped the can up and shook a few of the slimy legumes into his mouth. "You've got a lot of pent-up anger happening today. I don't think this yellow air agrees with you."

Patrick sighed. "You know it's me at the door. It's *always* me at the door."

Ben scoffed. "That Knock Code is the only thing keeping me alive," he said, channeling some long-dead Vietnam vet. "This is the apocalypse, Patrick. The enemy is everywhere."

"The apocalypse was years ago. If the universe wanted you dead, it would've put you down already. I think you're gonna live forever, Benny Boy."

"The code works," Ben insisted. "I haven't had a single breach."

"Because it's *always* me."

"Someday, it might not be."

"Yeah, and I can see why you'd be confused by who's at the door when you hear my voice coming from the other side of it."

"So what if it's your voice? How do I know you're alone? Jesus, for all I know, some desperate lunatic's got a window shard pressed against your throat 'cause you're his ticket in here. Did thirty years of Steven Segal movies teach you nothing?"

"No one wants to get in here," Patrick said, rubbing his eyes. Though, of course, there were plenty of reasons why someone actually *would* want to get into 24C. The previous occupant had been a loopy old widow with more money than Donald Trump (God rest both their souls) who had nothing better to spend it on than lavish comforts for herself and her mentally retarded Schnauzer. The old bat had been chronically paranoid, conveniently enough, which accounted for the attached panic room that had once been 24D. That little haven had certainly come in handy in the early days. Ben's apartment was a penthouse war bunker. And it had a killer view of the lake.

"*Everyone* wants to get in here!" Ben said smugly.

"No one knows you live here, no one *cares* that you live here, and if anyone *did* know and/or care that you lived here, they wouldn't care enough to climb through 24 stories of land mines to get here. Trust me. No one's coming for you."

"You come."

"I can be persuaded not to."

Ben studied the piece of paper tacked to the inside of the front door. "You know, you almost had it. Four hard knocks, the little knuckle thing, and two more slaps, and you were in."

"I feel like giving two more slaps right now. Bring me your face."

"It's not my fault they built this place with no peepholes. How hard is it to put in peepholes? Who doesn't have peepholes? She has a 1,500 square-foot safe room with 18-inch-thick titanium walls, she doesn't have a peephole?"

"Can we just stop talking about this?" Patrick frowned. "I haven't had my coffee grounds yet."

"Jesus, you're still on those?"

Patrick nodded. "I've sucked the stupid things so long, they're turning white. Ah, Benny Boy. Remember coffee?" He smiled and curled up on the duvet, his bony arms enfolding his bony legs.

"Stop it," Ben said.

"Steaming and black and always the start of a good 'Like I like my women' joke."

"I can't talk about it."

"Hot and sweet."

"Don't."

"Black and bitter."

"I hate you."

"With two big lumps."

"Yeah, yeah."

"Ground up and in the refrigerator."

"I got it, I got it. Now stop it, you're breaking Rule Number Four." He pointed to a large, handwritten poster taped above the fireplace. But Patrick didn't need to look at the Rules of the Apocalypse to be reminded about Number Four. He'd written that one himself: *Don't talk about nice things.*

"Sorry. I got carried away. Oh, but it's a special occasion!" He bolted upright. "I came over to tell you some very important news."

"I *thought* it was a little early for a social call," Ben said. "I mean, I didn't want to say anything." Rule Number 18: *Fuck time.* "But not speaking of time, it's breakfast time. Want some chili?"

"No, I'm good. I had some salt pork."

Ben's eyes grew wide. "Damn, Pat. You porked up?"

"I ate more pork than a fat kid who loves pork."

"Oh my God." Ben's face fell. "You're really doing it. You're committing suicide today. You've finally had enough, and you're jumping out the window."

"No. But my news is of similar gravity." Patrick smiled and waited for the joke to catch. It didn't. "Get it? Gravity? Come on. Get it?"

"I don't get it."

Patrick frowned. "I hate that you don't get things."

"I know you do. What's the news?"

Patrick smiled sadly. His eyes grew heavy at the temples, and for the first time since...well, since ever, probably, Ben thought he could actually see his friend's age. "Ladies and gentlemen, I regret to inform you that we have entered Code White."

Ben's heart fell past his ribcage. "Oh." He sank to the floor like a deflated bounce house, his legs splaying out crookedly. He looked up at Patrick with confusion. "Really?" he asked, which was a stupid question to ask, because of course it was *really.* You didn't joke about Code White.

"As of last night," Patrick nodded. "Sorry I didn't tell you then, but I thought you could use one more good night's sleep."

"Yeah," Ben said absently, a million thoughts buzzing like static in his brain. "Thanks. I *thought* the stores were getting a little low."

The two men sat quietly for a few minutes. They gazed out through the balcony windows into the bright yellow haze, each dwelling on his own memories, or fears. They were plunging into unchartered territory now. Code White changed everything.

It was Ben who finally broke the silence. "Does anyone else think it's weird that you have this bizarre Pudding Cup Death Coundown Clock going on? No? No one? Just me? Weird."

Patrick shook his head. "It's not a Pudding Cup Death Clock. It's a pudding cup *homage*."

"I don't care how French you make it sound, it's still dumb," Ben sighed. "So, Code White. Which is last? Vanilla?"

"Butterscotch."

"Ooooh, butterscotch. More yellow than white, isn't it?"

"Yeah, but Code Yellow sounds like a citrus shortage. Code White has more gravitas."

"Yeah," Ben agreed. "Man. I love butterscotch."

"Yeah, me too. So did she."

"Really?"

"Yep. Wasn't her favorite, but she liked it."

"I thought kids liked chocolate."

"Well, sure, she liked chocolate. She also liked butterscotch."

"Butterscotch is an old person flavor. You don't start liking it 'til you're, like, seventeen."

"Seventeen is old?"

"It was when I liked chocolate."

"Well, what can I say? She was a weird kid."

Ben sighed. His gaze floated through the decadent apartment, the Survivorman's Shangri La, and he was heartbroken. He really loved that goddamn condo. "Well, shit." He stood up off the floor and brushed the dust from his jeans. "Where we goin'?"

"Ah! That is the good news."

"I was hoping for some of that."

Patrick stood up and stretched. He had slept fitfully the night before, mostly from worry, but partially from excitement. They were going on an *adventure!* He grinned as he popped his joints into place. "I've put a lot of thought into this, and here's what I've decided. I survived M-Day. I lived on for three years in this crumbling urban wasteland. I beat the Monkeys, fought crippling depression, and learned how to eat canned tuna without vomiting all over myself. It's been a long, cold, miserable, broken-down, yellow-haze road, and, if I'm going out, then by God, I'm going out with some dignity. Benny, my boy, we are going to Disney World."

•

It didn't take long to plan the journey. Not because it was an easy journey to plan, but because there just wasn't much they could plan *for*. There was a time, not so very long ago, when getting ready for a trip meant typing a destination into Google Maps and loading up the Santa Fe with three more suitcases than were necessary, most of them filled with shoes. All one really needed to "be prepared" was a full iPhone battery and a spare tire. But M-Day had made things a bit more unpredictable. For starters, the Internet was little more than a smoldering pile of melted tubes. And cars! Ha! Cars were *completely* impractical. The vehicles of the dead choked the roads, at least in the city. Sure, the interstates were probably a little less crowded, but even if Patrick and Ben *could* weave a car out through the city limits, they'd be out of gas before nightfall. If the charred remains of the BP down the street were any indication, there would be no fuel along the way. Bodies of would-be gas thieves with dried blood caked from their slit throats? Sure, plenty of those. But gas itself? No way.

Since Patrick was the marginally more responsible one and Ben was the King of Food Mountain, it seemed natural that Ben should handle the canned goods and Patrick should be in charge of pretty much everything else: can openers, utensils, rope, blankets, his Leatherman, pens, pencils, notebooks, first aid kit, and anything else he could get his hands on. They would each carry their own clothing, of course, and any weapons they could scrounge together. Also, one of them needed to be the expedition leader. They were certain to face extreme dangers outside the apartment building--murderers, thieves, treacherous landscape, starvation, inclement weather, maybe even a few surviving Jehovah's Witnesses--and if they were going to survive all that, they would need to think and act as one person with one brain. "And I will be that brain," Patrick explained.

"Wait, wait, wait. Why do you get to be in charge?"

"Because this is my trip. It was my idea."

"So? Maybe that puts you too close to the situation. Maybe you're too invested in this trip to make logical, objective decisions. Maybe the fact that it's your trip means I should be the one in charge."

"No, it absolutely does not mean that, and I'll tell you why."

Ben crossed his arms. "Fine. Why?"

"Because Disney World is south."

Ben snorted. "So?"

"So why don't you show me which direction that is."

Ben hesitated. Patrick had leveraged his greatest weakness. *Damn.* He had to make a confident decision, and he needed to act quickly. He took a chance and pointed firmly toward Lake Michigan.

Patrick nodded. "That's why I'm in charge." The point was conceded with no further objection.

"So Disney World. That's where we're going. That's it," Ben said.

"That's it," Patrick agreed. "If by 'it' you mean 'everything.'"

Ben tented his fingers and shook them at his guest. "Okay, now I'm not saying Disney World is a dumb destination. But listen, Pat. Disney World is a really dumb destination. Seriously."

Patrick reached across and grabbed Ben's hands in his own. "No, Ben. Disney World is the best possible destination. Decades of snappy marketing tricks have made it so."

Ben yanked his hands out from under Patrick's. "Let's make a list of destinations that are less dumb than Disney World. Ready?" He spread his hands wide, as if he were offering a magnanimous gift. "Las Vegas. Grown-up Disney World. Let's go there."

"Pass!" Patrick slapped the coffee table with both hands, his eyes growing wide and bright. "Disney World or bust!"

"No, don't do that," Ben said, shaking his finger at Patrick's crazy-eyed face. "This is your trip; it's your decision. All right, I get that. I understand. If you want to go to Disney World, well, shit. I guess we'll go to stupid Disney World. But Disney World is for babies and honeymooning Christians. Not for real life grown-ups. And do you know the only thing lamer than Disney World? Burned out, rusted up Disney World full of charred baby skeletons."

Patrick leaned back in his chair and crossed his arms. "I once knew a Ben Fogelvee who would have thought a burned out, rusted up Disney World full of charred baby skeletons sounded *awesome*," he challenged.

"Yeah, you know, it *does* sound pretty bad ass," Ben mused. "I'm warming to the idea. But try this option on for size. Old Cliff in 13B says he knows a guy who knows a guy who hosts a *battle fucking royale* once a week in this dirt circle arena in his backyard somewhere in Detroit. These guys, they come from all around with sticks and knives and bats and iron pipes and just wail on each other for three hours until everyone's dead."

"Hmm." Patrick pressed a finger to his lips and thought carefully. "Now, that sounds like something I would certainly like to play a video game about. But are you *sure* everyone dies? What about the last guy? He lives, right?"

"Hell no, he doesn't live! First place is the quick, painless release of death from this stupid post-apocalyptic life. Everyone dies, one just less painfully than the rest."

Patrick squinted and pointed a suspicious finger at his host. "Are you sure this is a thing?"

Ben pointed back and met Patrick's squint. "Here's what I think. I think we find you a stick, and we make you a *champion*. If we're going Code White, make it the bright, blinding white of nuclear self-destruction."

"I appreciate where your head's at, Ben. I like your thought process. And it's tempting. Don't get me wrong, it's extremely tempting. But we're going to Disney World."

"Why?" Ben sighed. "Do you at least have a good reason?"

"Of course I have a good reason. Because I've never been. And I read somewhere that you should go before you die."

•

Patrick stood at the bank of windows in front of his balcony. These days, 24E was considered a river view apartment. The 30-story skyscraper at Grand and Wells toppled a week back, falling mostly east, thank God, where the HVAC roof units plunged to the depths of the lake. The base of the building still smoldered, meaning someone must've gotten ahold of some top-shelf explosives to do the job. This type of destruction wasn't exactly uncommon, though things had certainly quieted down a bit after the Great Chicago River Bridge Explosions a couple years back. Still, buildings got bombed pretty regularly. As far as Patrick knew, the latest victim building was just another apartment bloc, and its destruction didn't make a whole lot of sense, but sense wasn't exactly the prevailing theme these days. At any rate, the building's collapse gave Patrick a straight shot to the Chicago River, which he could sometimes actually see, when the wind whipped a clearing through the thick, and ever-present, yellow smog.

He funneled a handful of pale, sort-of-brownish coffee grounds into his mouth and chewed thoughtfully. The last dredges of caffeine had probably soaked through weeks ago, but the placebo effect made him feel instantly more focused. He checked his watch. 9:57. Any minute now. He hoped.

He shoveled the wet grounds from one side of his mouth to the other with his tongue and paced over to the dining room table, a battered antique made by Annie's great-grandfather almost one hundred years before. Darkly stained scrollwork trimmed the strong oak plinth. Patrick fingered the carefully carved rivets, tracing his fingertips around the smooth, knobby curls. For the first time ever, he actually considered the table and marveled at its presence. One hundred years old and showing no signs of weakness. It would be there long after he left. Depending on how things went with the world, it could very well be there until the end of recorded time.

He thought of Annie, and of all the meals they'd eaten in front of the television all those years, the stupid, goddamn worthless television, when they should have gathered around this heirloom that was so much a piece of her. The blood of the man who made that table ran through Annie's veins. It had, before the blood spilt and pooled, before it seeped out in viscous globs and dried and turned to rust, before it flaked and drifted away in the wind.

He wiped the tears from his eyes and shook his head, forcing the image back under. He pushed up onto the tips of his toes and looked out the window. Still nothing. He looked back at his watch. 10:03. Any minute now.

The butterscotch Snack Pack sat innocently in the center of the table. Patrick smiled and picked up the little two-pack. Butterscotch. Sure, most kids wanted chocolate, Ben had that right, and Izzy did adore chocolate. Just like her mother, she'd have eaten her own hand if it were made of chocolate. She just liked butterscotch more. She was such a weird kid, so imaginative and bizarre and confusing, and so completely, undeniably his.

Izzy's pudding in Patrick's hand on Annie's table. *The gang's all here.*

Patrick tore the cardboard holder and tossed it aside. He set one pudding cup down on the table and hefted the other. He tossed the pudding cup up and down as he paced back over to the windows. Still nothing. He checked his watch. 10:07. Any minute now. *Come on.*

He turned to continue his pacing when a glint of light on the horizon caught his peripheral vision. He spun back to the window, pressing his nose against the glass. For a moment he wondered if he had imagined it, but there it was again, a sharp glint on the horizon, barely visible through the yellow cloud, but unmistakable. He pulled open the door and stepped out onto the balcony. For nearly three minutes he strained his eyes against the smog, trying to verify the moving shape, when a sharp wind from the lake ripped a hole in the cloud, and he could see it suddenly, the entire train moving slowly down the tracks a few miles away. He smiled a big, lopsided grin as the engine disappeared into the underground station.

He ran back through the door and slammed it shut. He tore the foil cover from the pudding cup and smiled down at the smooth, creamy surface. He grabbed a spoon from the kitchen counter and plunged it into the butterscotch. Three years, four months, and thirteen days had passed since the Flying Monkey attack, and every second of that time had ticked its way down to this pudding cup. He thought maybe he should say something, so he said, "The second-to-last of many." It sounded stupid, and he wished he had said something a little more historical, for the sake of his own personal record and the biography that he assumed Ben would probably want to write about him someday, but there was no time for revisions. He had to hurry. The train left in just twelve hours. They would need every bit of it to reach the station.

He finished Izzy's butterscotch in three bites.

●

Ben had a serious dilemma. He glanced at the oversized knapsack, crammed almost to the brim with canned food and bottled water, then over at the weapons cache, his very own carefully cultivated collection of cutlery and bludgeons.

Decisions, decisions.

He could carry the knife in his belt, the bat in his hand, and the machete in the bag, but then he'd have to leave the hammer and the baton behind, and both of those were light, which would make them good in a surprise attack. He might be able to fit the baton in the bag with the machete and the food, but it'd be a tight fit, if it fit at all. Or he could put the baton on his belt, if he could find the nylon case, put the knife in his pocket, and maybe carry the hammer, but then he'd have to leave either the bat or the machete behind. He could put the machete in the bag and carry both the hammer *and* the bat, but the proportions were all wrong, it'd make him feel stupid. He could switch out the hammer for the machete, since the machete and the bat were roughly the same size, but then he'd have one weapon in each hand that really required two hands to use it effectively, so that'd be pointless, and, besides, he was liable to cut his own leg off walking like that. The stupid machete was *sharp*. He could leave the machete and put the bat in the bag, or maybe put the hammer in the bag and carry the bat, but then he'd have all blunt weapons, except for the knife, which was handy, but too small to really be useful for large, fast-moving targets, and you never knew when you'd come across a mutant bear. He could leave the bat behind, since he'd always kind of swung like a girl anyway, but something about the idea of a blood-spattered bat really spoke to him, probably due to all the B-movie horror flicks he'd watched in the break room years ago as a Blockbuster clerk, and, besides, what if he found a huge spike lying on the ground somewhere? He'd definitely want a bat to drive it through, *Warriors*-style. But it didn't make sense to leave the hammer, the knife, or the baton behind, seeing as how they didn't take up a whole lot of room. What if he carried both the baton and the hammer on his belt? Then he could put the knife in his pocket, the machete in the bag, and the bat in his hand. *Perfect!* It was settled.

Then he remembered the pipe wrench. *Oh dammit, the pipe wrench!* How could he forget? He couldn't leave the pipe wrench! He'd been sitting on a great Clue joke for *months* now, just *itching* for a chance to say it after braining someone with the wrench. He had to bring it. But, damn, it was heavy and pretty bulky. He'd have to sacrifice the bat and carry the wrench. Or maybe tie it to his belt, but three weapons down there would get heavy, and they'd probably make his pants sag, which would make it impossible to run like hell if any of the weapons failed. He could leave the machete, but dammit, no, never mind, he couldn't leave the machete; he'd already been over this.

He felt like crying. *Shit*, he thought. *The apocalypse is hard.*

He had just decided to dump out all the food and stuff the bag full of weapons when someone knocked at the door. Three hard knocks. Ben froze.

"Ben, it's me," Patrick called from the hall. "Can I come in?"

Ben stood rooted to the floor and listened. It didn't sound like there was anyone else out in the hall with him, but, hell, the apartment door was 24-gauge with a steel frame and ultra-high-density foam insulation. Who knows what he wasn't hearing out there?

What he *was* hearing was Patrick muttering a muffled string of expletives. There was a loud thud near the bottom of the door (a kick, probably). Then, with no small amount of perverse delight, he heard the sequence begin...

Three hard knocks, two soft knocks, one long knock, three short knocks, two and a quarter rapid-fire knocks, one flat palm slap, four knuckle taps, another palm slap, seven knuckle taps, two long knocks, seven left hand-right hand alternating slap-pounds, three short knocks, one knuckle tap, two palm slaps, three hard knocks, two soft knocks, four hard knocks, one rippling knuckle tap, two palm slaps.

Ben double-checked the sequence against the sheet tacked up by the door. His jaw fell open in surprise. *Holy shit, he got it right.* Ben shrugged and reached for the top chain lock, but stopped short. He leaned back over to the code sheet and looked at the date at the top. *Huh*, he thought. "Sorry," he called through the door. "That was *last* week's code."

This time, the string of curses was not muffled.

"Ben, if you don't open this door, I will leave you here to die alone, I swear to God. And I will not give you the rights to my biography."

Against his better judgment, Ben threw back the series of locks and cracked open the door. Patrick's face burned a deep crimson. He'd never seen the poor guy so angry. "What makes you think I want to write your biography?"

"Don't act like you don't." Patrick pushed the door open and stepped inside. "If you don't knock off this Knock Code nonsense, I'll have no choice but to—oooo, weapons!" he cried, pointing at the arsenal splayed out on the living room floor. "*Bemme. Bemme! Bemme* weapons," he said, making quick open-and-closed grabby hands.

"Are you speaking a language?" Ben asked.

"*Bemme!*" Patrick pointed frantically at the pipe wrench. Ben shook his head, but picked it up and handed it to his gaunt friend. "Ooooo! Pipe wrench!" Patrick swung the heavy tool wildly, freezing in various (and completely off-balance) ninja poses. "Yes! I like this. This shall be my wrench, and I shall call him Rusty." He swung it around his head, and the weight of the wrench carried him straight back into the wall. The head blasted right through the drywall. "It works!" Patrick cried.

"Okay, two things," Ben said, swiping the wrench out of Patrick's hand. "One, the wrench is mine. Two, everything here is mine."

"Aww, come on! All I have is a putter. Holy cats!" he cried, eyes bulging. "Is that an extendable baton?"

"Yeah. It is. Don't touch it."

"Where did you get that?!"

"The U-Spy Store."

Patrick gasped. "At Fullerton and Western?"

"Yep."

"No way."

"Yes way."

"You went to the U-Spy Store without me?!"

"Yeah. I did."

"Unbelievable! When did you go all the way to Logan Square?"

"Last year, in the fall."

"What the hell! Where was I? Why didn't I get to go? I love the U-Spy Store! I introduced you to the U-Spy Store!" And then once again, for good measure, "I *love* the U-Spy Store!"

Ben shrugged. "You were off on one of your dumb pudding hunts. Er, wait, no," he said, thinking. "That wasn't a pudding day. That was a food-to-pudding *calculation* day. You stayed inside all day and did math."

"Oh, don't you dare hold math against me, don't you dare! I had to maintain a very specific food-to-pudding ratio to get the timing to work out for us, involving an extremely precise algorithm, and the whole formula was constantly in flux because I kept finding more pudding, you know that. *You know that!*" Patrick crossed his arms and huffed.

"Oh, don't be a baby," Ben said, slapping Patrick on the arm. "If it helps, I almost died."

"That does not help. It only makes it more exciting!" Patrick cried.

"Yeah, that's true. It was pretty bad ass. We got jumped by this band of hipsters at the Milwaukee-Damen six-point."

"Who's we?" Patrick cried.

"Me and Harold, the guy from 3B."

"You brought the guy from 3B?! You didn't bring me, but you brought the guy from 3B?!"

"Don't get too excited. He got shot in the face."

Patrick gasped. "The guy from 3B got shot in the face?"

"Right in the face."

He shook his head in awe. "I always wondered what happened to the guy in 3B."

Ben nodded. "Shot in the face. So, really, I saved your life by not taking you. You're welcome."

"You are a true friend."

"It was pretty crazy. He got shot by the ringleader. The fucking kid was trying to fire a warning shot in the air, but he was too damn lazy to lift the gun all the way."

Patrick scoffed. "Goddamn hipsters."

"Right?"

Patrick sat down on the floor and crossed his legs, completely enraptured, forgetting momentarily about the exciting weapons just to his left. "How'd you get away?"

"Oh, the one guy totally lost his shit when he shot Harold. He just sat down and started crying in the middle of the street. I took off, and a couple of the guys chased me, but one guy's jeans were so tight he couldn't lift his stupid legs, and the other one got his summer scarf caught on a piece of scaffolding."

"Fucking hipsters," Patrick said.

"Fucking hipsters," Ben agreed.

"It's amazing to me that they've survived this long."

"Not me," said Ben. "Makes total sense. They don't eat anything, they don't get physical, and they always travel in herds."

"So you're saying the hipster is the post-apocalyptic cockroach."

"I'm saying the hipster is *every* era's cockroach."

"Fair." Patrick rocked back and forth slowly on his tailbone, trying to remember what he had come to tell Ben in the first place. "Oh! Right! We have to hurry." He leapt up and dusted himself off. "Our carriage awaits. How's the food?"

"It's good. I was just about to dump it all out."

Patrick frowned. "Out?" he asked.

"Yeah. Out."

"What, like...out of the bag?"

"Yeah, Patrick, out of the bag." He picked up the knapsack and turned it over, dumping the contents onto the floor. Patrick watched, horrified.

"No, you clod!" he yelled. "The food goes *in* the bag!"

"I'm making room for the pipe wrench!"

Patrick smacked his palm against his forehead. "No, see, this is *exactly* why I'm in charge. We need food to survive. We do not need the pipe wrench to survive. A pipe wrench is cool...it's very, very cool, I'm the first to admit, and if *Grand Theft Auto* has taught me anything, it's that cool weapons are extremely important in gratuitously violent situations...but we don't need it. Now. I applaud your enthusiasm for carnage, but, please, put the food back in the bag, and we'll take only the weapons we can carry."

Ben looked hopelessly at the metal cans strewn about the floor. He sighed. "Yeah, you're right. I'm sorry. I just had, like, *The Warriors* playing on loop in my head, and it all just looked so cool, you know, the bat with the wrench and the machete sticking out of the bag, but yeah. Okay. We'll bring the food. I'm sorry." He began scrambling after the cans and stuffing them back in the bag.

"It's okay, Benny Boy. We all get excited about *The Warriors*. But you do need to be punished, so I'll be taking the baton. And the hammer." He hefted both, one in each hand, and swung them crazily through the air. "Yes, these will do nicely." He stuck them in his back pockets. "Think you'll be ready to go in twenty?"

"Sure," Ben said, slipping the wrench into the knapsack and zipping it shut. "Hey, which do you think looks better?" he asked, grabbing the machete with his left hand and the bat with his right. He held them out in a defensive stance.

"You'll kill us all if you use the machete. Bring the bat."

Ben frowned. "Well someone should bring the machete," he said.

"True," Patrick mused. "It may be useful for cutting our way through jungles and murderers."

"You want to carry it?" Ben asked, holding it out, blade-first.

"Good Lord, no, not like that," Patrick said, raising his hands and taking two steps back. "I'd be an amputee in three minutes flat. But I *do* have an idea." He tapped a finger knowingly to his nose. "You leave it to me. I'll be back here in twenty minutes, and we're off."

•

Patrick stalked through the rooms of his condo, a living shade among memory ghosts. Here, in Izzy's room, an angry, pink baby the size of his left hand once screamed and screamed, her fists clenched in newborn rage. There, in the laundry room, was where Annie used to slap his hand and say, "Get out of here! Let me do this. You'll turn our clothes pink and midgety." He walked through the living room, past Izzy's coloring table, where she had held up so many proud drawings and explained; "This is Mommy, this is Daddy, this is Elvis, this is me." He passed the kitchen, where Annie stirred a boiling pot and sang softly to the baby in her belly, *Well we got no class, and we got no principles, and we got no innocence, we can't even think of a word that rhymes.* He peered into the office. Just after they moved in, he'd caught Annie hanging a Bruce Campbell-signed *Bubba Ho-Tep* poster over his computer. She'd huffed at him, pretending to be mad. It was supposed to be a surprise. The poster was still there.

He sat down at the desk and pulled open the top drawer. Inside, resting on a mess of pens, stamps, and rubber bands, sat a small, folded piece of paper. It had yellowed slightly with age and with the oils from Patrick's hands. He lifted it out of the drawer and unfolded it gingerly, careful not to tear the sharply creased folds. The writing was barely legible after all this time, but he could have recited the entire thing by heart. He traced his fingers over the words thoughtfully, then re-folded the paper for the millionth time and slipped it into his front pocket.

Ben was waiting outside his door when he stepped into the hall. "Well don't you just look like something out of a Stephen King novel!" With the pack of food on his back, a duffel of personal belongings slung across his shoulders, the knife sticking out of his pocket, the wrench in his belt loop, a bat in one hand, and a machete in the other, Ben looked like G. I. Joe-pocalypse. Adding to the overall effect was the fact that he had just freshly shaved his head, and a nick above his left eyebrow trickled a thin line of blood slowly down his brow.

"I'm ready to go all *Desperation* on this city. What do we do with this?" he asked, hefting the machete.

"Ah! Yes." Patrick slipped his backpack off and pulled at a piece of rope that crossed his chest. It was tied to something long, flat, and brown behind his back at either end. He lifted the whole contraption over his head and held it out for Ben to see. "Holster!" he declared.

Ben eyed the thing suspiciously. "Is that cardboard?"

"*Corrugated* cardboard," Patrick corrected, "yes. Fastened with flush hinges along this end and metal clasps on this end, see?" he asked, indicating the two long edges of the holster. "If the blade gets stuck, you just pop up the clasps, the top piece falls open, and the machete comes free. *Voila!*" With a flick of his wrists, he unsnapped the sheath. The top flat piece of cardboard flopped over and hung from the bottom piece, swinging lazily.

"If the blade gets stuck inside, couldn't you just cut your way out?" Ben asked. "Sharp metal beats cardboard."

"First of all, Ben, this is *corrugated* cardboard, please get it straight, and, second, no, you cannot just cut your way out because that would dull the blade, and, besides, a hinged machete holster is a lot of fun to play with, so that's how I made it. And, now, guess what. Because you questioned it, you don't get to hold it." He snatched the machete from Ben's hand and fit it carefully into the cardboard envelope. He closed it, locked the clasps, and swung the piece back over his shoulder.

"You're gonna kill someone with that thing," Ben pointed out.

"Let's hope it's neither one of us." Patrick shouldered his backpack and twirled the baton in his hand. "Well. We should get going." The baton spun out of control and clattered to the ground. "I am *excellent* at this."

Ben nodded. "All right, look, before we head out, I have to ask. Are you *sure* you want to do this? We can keep scrounging. We've become excellent scroungers. Just because we're almost out of food now doesn't mean we have to be almost out of food forever."

Patrick shook his head. "We'd just be delaying the inevitable. We're going to hit empty eventually, unless you're planning on starting a farm, and I refuse to believe you'd look decent in a mesh hat. Besides, don't think of this as certain suicide! Think of it as an exciting adventure that's only also certain suicide."

"That's a great thought, thanks."

"Hey, who knows what the world is like over the horizon? I haven't been farther than North and Halsted since the Monkeys hit. And, Jesus, I haven't been south at all, not a single block. Besides, even if we stay holed up here, it's only a matter of time before the scavengers rip through the building. I'd rather take my chances out there, in the unknown, than to die a miserable death at the hands of Cubs fans. Do you understand me, Ben? *I will not die in Cubs territory.*"

Ben tapped the bat nervously on the ground. "You know, you just said some variation of the word 'death' about thirteen times. I want to lay all my cards on the table here before we leave. Frankly, Pat, I don't want to die. I'm starting to think that this trip is some sort of subconscious death wish for you, and that worries me because I'm also going on this trip, but *without* a subconscious death wish. So it feels like a conflict of interest."

Patrick sighed. No, this wasn't a death wish trip, but it wasn't exactly *not* a death wish trip either. "Ben, if you don't want to go, you should absolutely stay."

"Ooooh, no," he said, shaking his head. "I've never turned down an ill-advised, dangerous adventure in my life, and I'm not about to start now. Besides, you're my best friend and also pretty much the only person I know who's still alive. If you went alone, I'd be bored out of my mind. I'm not backing out, but I'm just saying, if you're going to be making all of the decisions, you need to make them for both of us. You need to make decisions that keep us alive, no matter how fucked up your heart cavity is from losing your family. I'm your family now, so we keep each other alive," he finished too gruffly, awkwardly covering his rush of emotion with a thin, pocked veneer of testosterone.

Patrick shoved the baton in his pocket and put both of his hands square on Ben's shoulders. "Benjamin Alice Fogelvee. Listen to me." He stared directly into the shorter man's eyes. "I do not have a death wish, subconscious or otherwise. I'm going to die sometime, whether it's forty years from now from old age or from falling down the stairwell in two minutes on our way down to the street. But I promise you, I will do my dead level best to arrive safely in Orlando. I have no plans beyond Disney World, but that's only because I have no idea what the world is like anymore. I can't plan for it, other than to see it through. Stop worrying about me drowning myself in the lake, and start worrying about the best way to brain someone with the bat, 'cause it's a long road to Union Station. Okay?"

Ben patted Patrick's hand. "You had me at 'brain someone with the bat.'"

2.

Blowing up the other bridges had been a good idea, Violet reflected as she swirled the wine in her glass. The C4 had cost her five cases of Louis Jadot Chablis, but, hell, it was worth it. The La Salle bridge was prime real estate, and now it was the only crossing point into the Loop, excepting, of course, the Adams Street Bridge on the south branch. The Amtrak fuckers had that one locked up. Oh, and the Lake Shore Drive Bridge. The very idea of Lake Shore made her bristle with anger. She spat in its direction, willing the flames of her hatred to spread down the river to whatever slinky bitch Mommar was letting run his business these days. She turned to the west and sipped her Screaming Eagle Cabernet. It was decent, but it wasn't French.

She let her eyes wander over the wreckage of the other bridges. Most of the debris had sunk to the bottom of the river, but here and there a riveted trellis rose from the water, its jagged edges stirring pale green foam against the swirling water. Where each bank abutment had been, now only twisted, stubby steel arms stretched for their mates on the other side.

It had taken a full six days to rig up and detonate the explosives. The maître d' in charge wanted to destroy the bridges one at a time: rig the explosives, detonate the charges, destroy the bridge, repeat. He said it would save confusion and minimize the potential for error. "Bullshit," she'd said. "I want every last survivor within five miles to know who owns this river. They blow at the same time, all of them. Give 'em fireworks from hell."

And fireworks from hell they'd been. Twenty-one bridges in all, from Chicago Avenue in the north to Harrison Street in the south, and all the way east to Lake Michigan, including the 290 Interstate bridge over the south branch of the river. The three river branches exploded into furious balls of orange and yellow heat like the devil's trident. Thick, black smoke pooled in the air, choking out even the ever-present yellow fog, while the staggering heat melted cars below. Just think of it. *Melted cars.* The explosion shattered windows in buildings for a quarter mile radius, and when the smoke and flames finally died, Adams, Lake Shore, and La Salle were the only bridges left standing for 5,000 feet in any direction.

People still talked about that operation. It was a glorious orchestration.

More importantly, it made Millard's control over the Loop all but absolute. He controlled everything from Congress in the south to the Chicago River in the north and west. He hadn't bothered extending his dominance to the lake, for obvious reasons, but Violet knew if he ever decided to set his mind to it, he'd control the water too. Millard was like that.

Violet snapped her fingers. The bus boy sitting on the edge of the bridge jumped to his feet. She shook her nearly empty glass at him. He ran to the center of the bridge, picked up a red flag from the ground, and waved it high in the air. After a few seconds, he dropped the flag and ran back to her side. "Anything else right now?"

"No, that's fine," she said. She shooed him away.

She drained the last of the Cabernet from her glass and brooded over the Lake Shore Bridge. The Adams Bridge didn't worry her. The Amtrak rail men guarded it like it was made of diamonds, so while her people couldn't get through, neither could anyone else's. The Lake Shore Bridge was different, though. She'd protested...passionately...to Millard about destroying it along with the rest, but Mommar had already dug his claws in, and he had made some sort of deal. Millard let him not only keep the bridge, but 50% of the tolls. In exchange for what? Millard was guarded about the specifics. She'd done everything she could think of to worm it out of him. She'd put on her slinkiest black strapless, gotten him slobbering drunk, done things with her mouth that would make most men cry. But all he would tell her was that LSD was off-limits to her crew. The fact that he, for whatever reason, felt he couldn't trust her was absurd. It was insulting. That he had stripped her of a bridge that was rightfully hers was enraging enough; his blunt dismissal of her was salt in the wound.

But, ah, *que sera, sera*. Things could be worse. Three years and counting since M-Day, and she'd never lived so well.

A waiter in a white tuxedo appeared in the doorway of Fulton's Restaurant carrying what Violet knew was a perfectly room temperature bottle of red. He walked slowly, so as not to bruise the wine, but his nervous discomfort was obvious. Sweat shone high on his brow despite the chilly temperatures. Since M-Day, the yellow cloud blocked most of the sun's heat. Even in the dead of summer, the temperature rarely rose above 60. In this world, sweating was for the belabored.

He approached the bridge and was allowed passage by Holly, the Hostess on Duty. He crossed to the center of the bridge and presented the bottle to Violet. "2005 Harlan Estate The Maiden, ma'am."

Violet smirked behind her sunglasses. It wasn't really bright enough to justify sunglasses; it never was anymore. But these were $4,000 Moss Lipow Round Cut frames, and she looked like a goddess. "Taking me on a cult tour this afternoon?"

"Yes, ma'am," the waiter said, keeping his eyes low as he began working the cork.

"How fun," she purred. The waiter (she'd forgotten his name, they all looked the same) pulled the cork and held it out for her to examine. She lifted the Lipows to get a better look. The majority of the so-called "silk merchants" passed almost nothing but counterfeit wine these days, the truly valuable selections had grown so rare. No one dared try to stock Millard's cellars with schlock, but even so, it was prudent to be sure. She peered at the Harlan Estate logo stamped into the cork above a dark blue "2005." She nodded, satisfied, and the waiter poured her a taste. She dipped her nose into the glass and inhaled deeply. Cigar tobacco and coffee. Delightful. She swirled the ruby wine, inspecting the legs, then sniffed deeply a second time. Crème de cassis as well, she noted, and asphalt. A touch of asphalt. She poured the wine into her mouth and swirled it around on her tongue. Dark fruits, spicy oak, light minerals. "Thank you," she said to the waiter. He poured her a full glass, set the bottle next to her, and returned to the restaurant.

Another day, another inspection of the troops. After this glass, she'd take the bottle and check in on the Lower Wacker Guard.

She suddenly noticed movement to the north and craned her neck in anticipation as two figures turned the corner of La Salle and Hubbard. The rest of the bridge crew had noticed them too; the small army of bus boys and waiters rose from the concrete where they spent most of their days lounging and trading stories. Someone whistled down to the naval unit in the boat below the bridge. The men in the boat scrambled to find a square white flag with a blue cross reaching to all four sides. They waved it high above their heads, the rippling flag well below the field of vision of the two figures standing two blocks away at street level, but perfectly visible to the gunmen in the third story of the old Britannica building.

Business had been slow all day, and, according to the morning report, it'd been a slow week, rounding out a slow month. This was partially due to the post-M-Day timeline, Violet knew. Survivors were dying every day, and she personally didn't know anyone attempting to reproduce (willingly, at least). The lack of epidurals alone was enough to make a trash bag seem like a solid contraceptive choice. The world population was dropping steadily, and Chicago was feeling the pinch.

Another issue was the bridge's location. It was on the north side of the city, but most refugees flooded in from the south. A northern rim entry point had been necessary in the early days as a means of traffic control. The Congress Barrier had gone up in the first weeks out of necessity. It was just too dangerous to leave the city open from the south. Anyone begging entry had to hoof it back down to Roosevelt, pay off whatever crew was running it that week, head north along the river, past the Loop, up to Halsted and Division, then circle back down to approach from La Salle. Most of the refugees gave up or died somewhere along the way, which was fine with Millard, and with Violet. They had as much business as they needed to stay flush. The ones who made it to the bridge paid well, especially after the treacherous journey through Cabrini Green, which had been reclaimed by psychopathic hoodlums who were still finding drugs God knows where.

But as time wore on, refugees from the south grew fewer and fewer, and those who made it to the Congress Barricade often gave up and threw down their packs at the wall. Violet had visited the Barricade last week and found a tent city sprawling for more than six blocks south.

It made things on the bridge pretty slow.

So it was no wonder the entire army took an active interest in the two men approaching the bridge. The pair moved quickly, and Violet could soon make out their features. One was tall and skinny, the other short and fit. The tall one had a head that, while not exactly bulbous, seemed a little too big for his thin frame and was covered with dirty blonde hair that flopped from side to side as he walked. His features were swollen and curved, despite the somewhat sunken nature of his cheeks, and the overall effect made him appear affable and charming, in a bumbling, I-might-fall-over-at-any-moment sort of way.

The shorter man was more blunt in appearance. He was like a sports car that's been modified into a family sedan; plenty of power, but with a compromise on looks. Not that he wasn't attractive, in his way, Violet decided. It was more an issue of the looks not fitting the stature. His brow was overly sharp, giving him a permanent scowl, but his eyes were crystal blue, and the juxtaposition between dark brow and light eye made him look confused. His shaved head, which would have given an edge of danger to any other man, instead made him look like a child who's been punished by an alcoholic mother with a straight razor.

Both men were laden with packs and seemingly well armed, the hallmarks of the M-Day refugee. Refugees were always so *exciting*. Violet hopped down from the bridge railing and sauntered over to the hostess's station. She teased out her tightly curled chestnut hair with a few quick finger twirls as her stilettos clicked against the cold concrete. She pushed her breasts up in their Victoria's Secret Bombshell cups and unbuttoned another button in her dark red blouse for good measure. A little action this afternoon would do her a world of good.

Patrick and Ben sidled up to Holly's podium at the entrance to the bridge just as Violet arrived. The cute, blonde hostess greeted them with her flashiest smile. "Good afternoon. How can I help you gentlemen today?"

Violet stepped up to the podium just as the taller one opened his mouth. "Thank you, Holly, I'll take it from here," she mewed, gently guiding the younger woman away from her station. Holly pouted dramatically and gave the boys a slow, sad little wave. *Oh, she's good,* Violet thought. Then she whirled around to face her guests.

"Hello, gentlemen, welcome to the Loop. Your names, please?" she asked sweetly.

Patrick tilted his head, confused. "I'm sorry?"

"Your names, please," she repeated, more firmly, though still with a smile.

"Um. Well. I'm Patrick, and this is B—"

"Bradford," Ben quickly interrupted. "My name is Bradford." Violet caught Patrick raising a quizzical eyebrow at his colleague. *Hmm. Shady.*

"Patrick and Bradford, Patrick and Bradford, let me see, now." She flipped open a black, leather-bound notebook to a page marked with a thin, red ribbon and pored over a long column of names written in small, formal script. She scanned down the page twice with a finely manicured finger before shaking her head. "No, I'm sorry, I don't see a reservation here for you. Can I ask when you made your appointment?"

"I'm sorry?" Patrick asked. "Our appointment?"

"Yes, your appointment. You do have an appointment, don't you?" she asked, leaning over the podium to give them a decent look at her cleavage.

"Bradford, did you make an appointment?" Patrick asked his companion, hands on his hips. "I distinctly remember telling you to make an appointment. Did you make an appointment? Bradford? Bradford!" Patrick kicked the shorter man in the shin.

"Ow! What?!"

"I am obviously talking to you, *Bradford!* Stop staring deeply into this woman's breasts and answer me!"

Ben's face took on a decidedly grape-like hue. "I'm not--I wasn't--no! I wasn't looking at her--lady, I wasn't looking at your, uhm—" He cleared his throat and made an awkward circling gesture with his finger in the general direction of her chest.

Violet tossed her hair and laughed. "Oh, honey, they've been stared at by worse than you," she said. "Your friend was asking if you'd made an appointment with us."

"An appointment? For a bridge? No, why would I do that?" He turned to his companion. "Patrick, why would I do that?" Patrick had no idea.

He shrugged. So did Ben. *A couple of real shruggers, these two,* Violet thought.

"I see." She made a great show of looking confused and conflicted. "We usually don't show people in without an appointment. It's city policy." She glanced at the tall one through her long eyelashes. He had a strange cheery, yet apathetic vibe about him. She liked him instantly. "Buuuuuut I think I can probably make an exception for two weary travelers such as yourselves. Tell me," she said, leaning down again and squeezing her breasts in tight with her elbows. "What's your pleasure?"

Patrick's eyes narrowed. "Are you asking if--what are you asking right now?"

Violet grinned demurely. God, she was good. Aphrodite reincarnate. "I mean what are your plans for your stay in the Loop? A hotel, of course, and we have several posh high-rises with available rooms. All six of our restaurants are 4- and 5-stars (post-M-Day criteria, of course), and for entertainment, well, we're full to the brim. We have shows running in the Goodman and the Oriental, if live theatre is your thing, and we're currently running a breathtaking Russian Postmodernism exhibit at the Art Institute. Aside from the restaurants, we have four fully stocked bars, and while drinks do go for a premium, I assure you, you won't find a drop of schlock in the Loop." Here, she leaned even closer and lowered her voice a few decibels. "And if you're in the mood for something a little spicier, we've just recently opened the New Admiral Theatre over on Monroe, and, gentlemen, let me assure you, the no-touch rule is not, and will not, be in effect in post-M Chicago." She straightened up over the notebook and clicked her pen open. "So. What'll it be?"

Both men eyed her suspiciously, which wasn't exactly the reaction Violet was used to receiving after this spiel. Wolf-eyed, tongue-lolling, hand-rubbing desire was much more common. "How do people pay for that?" Ben asked.

"Excellent question!" She reached into the podium and retrieved the menu. "The first few pages offer the prices of some of our more popular services in Loop Units. And if you flip to the back here, the last two pages show the common currencies we accept and how they translate into those Units."

"A pack of cigarettes is one Unit?" Ben asked.

"A whole carton is worth ten," she pointed out. "It's really a fantastic deal."

"Vodka, 750ml, 20 units."

"Liquor is big business," she said sweetly. "So tell me, boys. What'll it be?"

Patrick took a step forward and laid his forearm on the podium. "Right. About that. This all looks very nice, really, you've obviously outdone yourselves. All of you! Nice work, everyone!" he called out to the army on the bridge, giving them a round of applause. A few confused busboys raised a hand in gratitude. "But here's the thing. We don't really need any of this. We just need to pass through."

"Oh. Travelers," she said, disappointed. "Well. We can provide you with the best escorts."

"Do we need escorts?" Patrick asked.

"I don't think we need escorts," Ben said.

"Of course you need escorts. We retain majority control over the Loop, of course, and I assure you, all of our fine establishments are quite safe. But the streets can be another matter. Our escorts are guaranteed to provide you with safe passage. For a very nominal fee."

"Of course," Ben muttered.

Patrick waved a hand through the air. "I'm sure we'll be fine on our own. Look! Bradford has a hammer!" Ben plucked the hammer out of his belt loop and held it up.

"Yes, I see that. Of course, you're free to take your chances, but we require the fee either way, so really, you should take the escort."

"How nominal is this fee?" Patrick asked.

Violet leaned in close so he could smell her perfume. "How nominal is your destination?"

Patrick nodded slowly and wagged a conspiratorial finger in the air. "I don't think that makes any sense, but I see where you're going with it. We need to get to Union Station."

Violet's smile flattened into a straight, thin line. *Those Amtrak sons of bitches.* She forced herself to smile again, but dammit, she hated losing business to the Red Caps. "Of course. An escort to the Adams Street Bridge. Fifty Units."

Ben sputtered incredulously. "Fifty? Did you say fifty? Or fifteen?"

"Fifty. Five-oh." Of course it was a ludicrous fee, but there was a steep Amtrak spite tax.

"Oh, come on. Fifty of your dumb Units just to walk ten blocks? No way!"

Patrick raised his hands. "Now, hold on, hold on. Look. Miss Violet—"

"Just Violet," she said, her tongue dripping with honey.

Patrick smiled. "Sure. Look, just Violet. I understand your need for compensation. This is a very fine bridge, namely in that it hasn't been blown to bits, and we're happy to give you something for safe passage across it."

"Like a fist to the mouth," Bradford mumbled. Patrick kicked his shin again, hard. He screamed and hopped away from the bridge, cursing and howling.

"It's just that fifty Units does seem a little unreasonable," Patrick continued, "and I can't help but notice that there's another bridge right over there." He nodded toward Lake Shore Drive. "Surely we can reach some sort of agreement that allows us to use your bridge instead of that other, probably much cheaper, bridge."

Violet was ready for this. "Please do feel free to use the LSD Bridge, if you prefer. Our guests are free to use whichever option appeals to them. But you should know that the LSD Bridge is run by contractors, not by members of my team, and the authority of those contractors extends only until the southern end of the bridge. Once you cross into the city, you're once again under our jurisdiction. And while of course you're welcome to cross using their bridge, it's possible that some of my busboys won't take too kindly to that sort of slight. They're very sensitive, they are. They don't like it when people use the contractors' bridge. Sometimes they act up and lash out, sometimes through physical violence. And since you won't have paid for our safe passage escorts, well, there's not much to be done to protect you, I'm afraid. So I do hope you'll reconsider." She beamed at him with her kindest smile.

Patrick sighed. "Can I see the menu, please?" Violet reached into the podium and produced another booklet. He flipped to the last page and ran down the list of currency calculations. He muttered to himself as he read. "No...no...no...no...oh! A pound of coffee, six Units. What'll you give me for this?" He reached into his pocket and produced a Ziploc bag full of light beige crystals.

Violet examined it suspiciously. "What on earth is that?"

Patrick looked at her like she was handicapped. "It's obviously coffee."

"That is not coffee."

"Oh yes it is. Smell it." He peeled the bag open and held it under her nose. She took a cautious sniff. It smelled like mushrooms and used dental floss.

"Jesus," she sputtered, gagging. "Get that away from me."

He looked hurt as he zipped the bag and held it close to his chest. "How many Units? Four?"

"None. It's repulsive."

"First of all, it is not repulsive, it is delicious, and it is the only thing that keeps me going! And, second, that's just fine, because I wouldn't trade it to you for all the Units in the world because you're not worthy to chew it!" Just then, Ben dove onto the scene from out of nowhere and snatched the bag of off-white granules from Patrick's hand.

"Excuse my friend, he's an idiot. How much for his drugs?"

Violet raised her eyebrows. "Excuse me?"

"His drugs. This." He shook the little Ziploc bag. "How much?"

"Don't you dare!" Patrick cried. "She's not worthy!" He grabbed for the gritty powder, but Ben pulled it back, out of reach.

"These are drugs. It's...what do you call it. Not crack. What's the other thing? Made from that flower."

"Opium?" Violet suggested.

"Opium! Opium? No. That's white. This is different. This is, um... what do you call it...this is...Patrick, what do you call this very rare and expensive drug?"

Patrick stood, open-mouthed and staring. A thin trickle of spittle spilled over his lip and dripped to the ground. "Erm. Yes. That is called... croke. That's the street name, anyway. It's a crack/coke hybrid."

"Right. Croke," Ben agreed.

Violet crossed her arms. "Crack *is* coke," she said. But she wasn't quite sure if it was true. She thought she remembered reading it somewhere, a few years back, when Newsweek did some major cover story on street drugs. But she couldn't remember.

Patrick, however, did seem sure. He shook his head back and forth, hard. "No, no, no, that's different. This is different. This is croke. And...I need it." He made a half-hearted attempt to snatch the bag.

"Sorry, Patrick, but we need to get to the train," Ben said, a little too loudly. He held the bag up a little too high. He avoided Violet's eyes for a little too long. Everything about all this new development was a little too *something*. Violet mulled things over carefully. She had a hunch she was being swindled, but on the other hand, the big-headed one certainly acted like a drug addict. And if the claim were true, she could make a mint cutting the stuff and unloading it on the Loop refugees. She'd never heard of croke, but that wasn't particularly surprising. People were always finding new powders and chemicals to shoot into their veins. Who could keep up?

She had an idea. "Okay," she said to Patrick. "Do a line."

Patrick turned his head so his ear canal pointed at her nose. "I'm sorry?"

"Do a line. Of your croke."

He opened and closed his mouth like a fish. "So...right here?"

"Yes. Right here." She put her hands on her hips and gave her best sassy snarl. "If it's really a street drug, prove it. Do a line."

"You don't want him to do that; one line is worth, like, 80 Units. You should just take it all," Ben said.

"It's true," Patrick chimed in. "I mean, I'm happy to do it. Obviously. I *need* to do it. Give it to me now, Bradford! Ha, ha!" He playfully reached for the bag. "We have a lot of fun with that. But it's really in your best interest to just take the whole thing."

"Do a line right now, or you can count yourselves shit out of luck and kiss the train goodbye. But, hey, if you jump in the river and swim, maybe you can reach Lower Wacker. We don't control the underground, you could take your chances there." She jerked a thumb over her shoulder at the southern riverbank. The River Bridge Explosions had ripped away chunks of the retaining wall, exposing dark sections of Lower Wacker Drive. Patrick peered over her shoulder, squinting through the fog and into the gloom.

"Oh, those two men are dancing!" he said. Violet reached into the Hostess's podium and handed him a pair of binoculars. He pointed them at the two men in question, and his face went pale. "Oh, no. No, they're not dancing. One of them's beating the other one to death with a pipe."

"But, hey," Violet said with a smirk. "You have a hammer." Patrick looked at Ben. Ben looked at Patrick. Violet looked at her French-man-

30

icured nails. "You want to use my bridge? Sell me on your drugs." She stepped around the podium, snatched the baggie from Ben, and shook out a little pile of the tan dust. "Well?" Patrick bit his lip and eyed the powder. Beads of sweat popped up on his brow. His skin became almost translucent. His nervousness was palpable. *Nice try, hobo*, she thought. Who did they think they were dealing with?

But then he took a step up to the podium, and Violet couldn't help but wonder if the sweat and the shaking and the paleness really were nothing but a drug addict's reaction to fix he knew would be his last for a long, long time. He smoothed the pile down with a gentle, trembling finger and formed it into a long, low line. Then he spread his legs, took three deep breaths, cracked his neck, put a finger to one nostril, and sucked the crystals into his sinuses, into the bloodstream that would carry the chemicals straight to the nerves in his brain.

Something red and sparking exploded in Patrick's cranium. It was like a drunken fairy dust fireworks show in there. He gasped for air and clamped on to the edge of the podium to keep his hands from grabbing the bridge rail and ripping it right out of the concrete. "Wow!" he yelled. "Wow!" He shook his head a few times, then wiped a bit of beige powder from his nostrils. "Oh, yeah, that. Yeah. That feels good," he sputtered, his eyes welling up with tears.

Violet was impressed. The drugs must be pretty good. "Okay. 50 Units. For the whole bag."

"Whoa, whoa, whoa," said Ben, waving his hands, "no way. That's at least 85 Units worth of crack. Croke," he quickly corrected himself. Wait, hadn't he already said a line was worth 80? *Shit.* He was horrible at math. Well, it was too late now. "You want 50 Units worth, you can take 50 Units worth, but if you want the whole bag, *you* owe *us* 35 Units."

"Ooo, good math," Patrick choked.

"Thank you."

Violet hesitated. She wasn't in the habit of haggling with short men, but Patrick was already tripping over himself, swaying this way and that through the middle of La Salle, holding his forehead in both hands and moaning. This croke was some sort of next-level narcotic, for sure. She could unload that amount for 5,000 Units, easy. She decided not to push her luck. "Fine. 35 Units. We'll settle up on the way. Grab your friend before he falls into the river."

Downtown was a train wreck, mostly metaphorically, but in some cases, literally (the El hadn't fared well in the apocalypse). As they followed a few feet behind the self-proclaimed Concierge of Chicago, Ben couldn't help but notice how crummy it all was. Every single building along the river had its windows blown out; some of the buildings themselves had toppled over, ripping huge gashes into other skyscrapers on the way down. Trash littered the roads, which wasn't uncommon, but it was all so indicative of high-spirited people; empty wine bottles, clean pig ribs, broken Champaign flutes, used condoms, soggy lace underthings. He wondered just how many people were holed up in this part of town.

Violet led them down Wacker Drive, which curved south along the Chicago River where it forked, not too far from the La Salle Bridge. The gang of teenage waiters in tuxedos watched them go. There were probably two dozen of the young employees on that bridge, and they looked like they hadn't eaten nearly as well as their mistress. Their eyes were yellowed and dripping mucus, their cheeks sunken and hollow, their hair thinning to gray wisps...it was unsettling. Violet was up ahead now, speaking in quick, hushed tones to a muscular man in his mid-30s trying way too hard to look like Wesley Snipes, circa *Demolition Man*. As far as Ben could tell, the woman was completely off her rocker, so in hindsight, it wasn't too surprising that she'd fallen for the coffee grounds. Off her rocker or not, though, she had a terrific ass, one that made his throat make weird sounds as it twitched along in front of him.

By the time they reached Washington, he was sick of carrying Patrick's dead weight. "Come on, you idiot," he said, easing himself out from under his companion's arm, "walk yourself."

"Ben!" he hissed. "I did it!" He pumped a shaking fist straight into the air. "I snorted coffee!"

"You did. And it was hilarious," Ben admitted. "But now I need you to walk, because if I have to carry you one more step, I'm probably going to just hit you with the bat and leave you to die."

"Eh, that's okay," Patrick said, straightening up and smoothing down his shirt. "The effects wore off three blocks ago. You really stuck it out there for a good couple hundred yards, though. You're a great friend." He raised his hand to high five.

"I hate you," Ben muttered.

"Yeah, well, you made me snort soggy coffee grounds, so we're even."

"Yeah, and that got us across the bridge, so you owe me."

"Yeah, but with my help, you were able to have a conversation with a pretty girl, so we're even."

"Speaking of...what's her deal?" Ben asked. "What the hell was all that 'do you have an appointment' shit?"

"Benny Boy, I have no friggin' idea. But I've long since learned that when you're dealing with the crazies, it's best to just play along."

"Smart."

"Yeah. Marriage taught me that one."

"Hiyo!" This time, Ben returned the high five. "Hey. Look over there." He nodded toward a small group of heavily armed men dressed in all black up ahead. They milled around at one of the ramps leading down to Lower Wacker. Violet raised a hand in greeting as they approached.

"How is everything today, Captain?" she asked one of the men, who had a red bandana tied around one bicep.

"No problems, Miss Boland. Everything's quiet."

"Had a little skirmish earlier, but nothing to be worried about," piped up a younger looking kid on the other side of the ramp.

Violet frowned. A skirmish could mean just a little dust-up. It could also mean a bomb threat. "What kind of skirmish?"

"Nothing big," said the captain, his voice nonchalant. "A few bums tried the ramp."

"They got wood instead!" the younger kid boasted, hefting the wooden club in his hand.

"You men are heroes. Keep up the good work," Violet said as she reached out and touched the captain's muscled arm. "What is it about a man in a Lower Wacker Guard uniform?" she winked. The captain blushed, and they were off.

"So wait, is she a concierge, or a prostitute?" Patrick murmured once they'd put a bit of distance between themselves and their escort.

"A constitute?" Ben suggested.

"Ah, yes. The elusive constitute. A favorite among post-apocalyptic skeezes."

When they reached the Civic Opera House, Violet and Simon Phoenix's doppelganger stopped short. "Wait here," she said.

"Why? Where are you going?" Ben asked.

"To get your Units," she said, "as promised."

"Oh! We'll take coffee. Ben, tell her to bring coffee!" Patrick said, jumping up and down.

"Coffee? Is that his word for drugs?" she asked. Ben nodded. "Hm. He's pretty far gone."

"Croke ain't no joke," Ben said solemnly. Patrick exploded with a laugh and covered it with a cough.

"I'll be right back. Don't move." She went in through the revolving door, leaving the man with the dyed blonde Mohawk to watch them. But he grew immediately bored with that task and wandered off to go talk to a group of Lower Wacker Guards, leaving Patrick and Ben alone under the massive Opera House overhang.

"What was all that 'Bradford' stuff?" Patrick asked.

"You think I'm gonna give her my real name? Are you nuts?"

"What was she going to do, write it on a voodoo doll and stick needles in your junk?"

Ben's face grew serious. "You never know."

"*Pffft*."

"How about you stop worrying about my self-preservation and start worrying about how we're gonna manage our way onto that train?"

"I imagine we'll climb the steps."

"Har, har. We're gonna be climbin' the stairs to Nowheresville if we don't figure out how to pay our way."

"Nowheresville? Is that walkable? Is it south? We're headed south."

"Don't think I won't kill you. I will, I'll kill you."

"Relax. We're going to be fine."

"How do you know?"

"Because we have something to trade for passage."

"What's that?" Ben asked.

"A white slave," Patrick said.

Ben opened his mouth to speak, but stopped. Had he heard that correctly? "I'm sorry, did you say a *white slave?*"

"Hmm?" Patrick asked.

"Did you just say we would trade a white slave?"

"Just now?"

"Yes. Just now."

"Is that what you think I said?"

"Yeah, it is."

Patrick shook his head and cleared the tension with his hands. "Look, I don't want you to worry about this. I have a plan, and all I need from you is trust. Which you're contractually obligated to give me, since I am, in fact, in charge."

"That's true, you're in charge," Ben conceded, "but if you recall, I'm the one who got us across the bridge."

"Yeah, and in doing so, you lost us my coffee, didn't you?" Patrick demanded.

"I don't think you can call that coffee anymore. Chemically speaking."

Patrick sighed and placed a hand on Ben's shoulder. "You've proven to me that, if all else fails, I can rely on you to come up with a somewhat mediocre plan. That's a skill that may come in handy before we're done, but until I give you the sign, just leave the plans to me."

"What's the sign?"

"You'll know it when you see it," Patrick said. "But it'll most likely involve screaming and running, and probably the flailing of limbs."

Just then, the revolving door spun, and Violet reappeared holding a paper bag. "Gentlemen, your Units." Patrick snickered. Violet rolled her eyes. She pulled out a fifth of Smirnov vodka. "20 Units."

Ben grabbed the bottle and inspected it sadly. "No Grey Goose?"

"And 15 Units," she said, ignoring him completely. She reached into the bag and produced a one-pound bag of ground Sumatra. "*Actual* coffee." Patrick instantly burst into tears.

"Oh my God!" he blubbered. "How did you--you can't possibly even--I don't know how to--oh my God, coffee!" He sank to his knees and lurched forward, grasping for the bag. Violet, startled by his sudden, awkward movements, dropped it. It fell to the sidewalk and burst open at the corner, sending coffee spilling across the cement. Patrick fell to his face and began scooping the coffee into his mouth, rubbing it into his gums.

"My God," Violet breathed. "I've never seen someone so far gone! Does he realize it's not even croke?"

"It's hard to know *what* he realizes," Ben said. "Listen, I don't want to be a girl about this, but I'm pretty sure your menu said a pound of coffee was six Units. Not fifteen."

Violet frowned, her face turning an angry shade of red. "That was for

Folger's. This is Kona. Take it or leave it." She snapped her fingers, and her fellow escort trotted back over toward them.

Ben glanced down at his companion, who was patting the spilled coffee grounds onto his tongue. "Looks like we're taking it."

"Good choice. Well, gentlemen. We hope you enjoyed your brief stay in the Loop."

"Aren't you escorting us to the train?" Ben asked. "That was the deal."

"Cumo will see you the rest of the way. I'll be taking my leave here. The next block is the Mercantile Exchange. Those Day Traders give me the creeps."

•

Patrick literally could not be happier. Maybe it was their quick progress, maybe it was the three grams of snorted coffee grounds setting off his brain cells like Pop Rocks, but everything felt right with the world. He had fresh coffee in his mouth and half a plan in his head. He was going to get them on that train, and while he had started the day gravely concerned about the missing half of that plan, his fear was melting away like nuclear snow on a smoking pile of rubble. Nothing would stop them now.

Then he got smacked in the head by a rock.

"Ow! *What the shit?*" he screamed, plastering a hand to his temple. Blood began oozing through his fingers. "What was that?"

"Oh my God," Ben said, pointing to a building on the right. His eyes grew wide in horror. "Patrick. Look. It's douche bags."

Patrick whirled around and squinted through the fog. Sure enough, up ahead, a few dozen twenty-something men and women in once-trendy (but now torn and ratty) business suits hung from the windows of a pair of massive towers. The men all wore their hair spiked up in front with some sort of stiff but pliable product, and some of them appeared to be wearing brown shoes with black suits. Most of the women seemed to be clad in tight skirt suits and thick-rimmed black glasses. Ben was right. These people were douche bags. "Day Traders," he muttered.

Word of the Day Traders had spread north some time ago; Patrick had first heard about them just a few months after M-Day. Rumor had it they had once been hot-blooded up-and-comers on the financial floor, once considered demigods among their own kind, but they were now disillusioned husks who still clung desperately to the old ways. One of the stories said that they had a generator in the CME building that they used to watch *Boiler Room* on loop, a very *Clockwork Orange*ian practice that had twisted their perceptions of reality in untold, dangerous ways. Money was their deity, despite the reality that legal tender was now worth less than the paper it was printed on. Supposedly they hassled everyone who walked through their turf for money, but they weren't beggars. If you had cash, they didn't ask you for it, and they didn't murder you to get it. If you had money, they *worshipped* you. They brought you into their towers and made you their king. They begged you to toss them some leads, tried to impress you with their cold calls. But if you were broke, you were less than nothing to them. You were target practice.

Clearly, Patrick and Ben weren't even being given the benefit of the ask. The Traders were just assuming that they were penniless, probably going off the way they were dressed. The Traders *always* judged someone by the way he was dressed. Confirmation of their opinions came in the form of a second rock, which went whizzing only inches from Ben's nose.

"Wesley Snipes! Do something!" Patrick hissed.

The large man only turned and shrugged. "I got no beef with the Traders," was all he said. The feeling was reciprocal. A flurry of stones flew toward them, but only at the *them*. Cumo just watched from a safe distance, looking bored.

"You're supposed to protect us," Ben said, shielding his face with his hands.

Cumo shrugged again. "They're not *murderers*. They ain't gonna *kill* you," he said, as a small piece of concrete pinged off Ben's shoulder.

Patrick let loose a string of expletives and dove for shelter behind a piece of building rubble lying in the middle of the road. Ben followed suit, diving headfirst over the concrete pylon as rocks pelted it from the west. "Well, fearless leader?" he said, scrabbling back toward the cover of the cement, his gigantic knapsack making him look like a turtle who had survived a horrible, mutating nuclear accident. "Got a plan?"

"As a matter of fact, I do," Patrick said. "Let's just hope I can still speak the language." He peered over the rubble and waited for an opening in the rock barrage. When it came, he jumped up, threw up his hands in surrender, and shouted, "If you're not inside, you're outside!" Every Trader with a rock froze, wondering if they'd heard him right. They mumbled to each other up there in the windows. "It's working," he whispered down to Ben. "Keep your mouth shut and follow me." He took a step away from the concrete shield, hands still raised, and shouted, "I look at a hundred deals a day! I choose one!" The mumbling overhead increased, and some of the Traders started nodding their heads. Patrick continued. "I mean, it's easy to get in. It's hard to get out. Am I right?" A few of the Traders shouted their agreement. Patrick took a few more steps down the road. Ben followed closely behind, using Patrick as a human shield. Cumo followed at a distance, amused. "'Cause money is a bitch that never sleeps!" Patrick cried. A couple of soft cheers went up in the windows. He was on a roll. "Bulls make money! Bears make money! Pigs? They get slaughtered! And parents are the...the...what are they? The...oh! Bone on which children sharpen their teeth! Huh? Huh?" One of the women on the third floor shouted, "It's true! Only the strong understand!" Several of her fellows agreed.

Patrick and Ben were almost down to the halfway point between the two towers. There was still half a city block to go. "That's the one thing you have to remember about WASPs. They love money and hate people! Hell, I don't throw darts at a board. I bet on sure things! Read Sun-Tzu, *The Art of War*. Every battle is won before it's ever fought. A fool and his money are lucky enough to get together in the first place. Because what's worth doing is worth doing for money! It's a zero sum game! Money itself isn't lost or made, it's simply transferred from one perception to another!" Random cheers of "Yeah!" and "He's right, he's right!" echoed along the otherwise empty street. Farther and farther down the block they crept, Patrick now pumping his fists in the air triumphantly. He was screaming the words now. *"I'm talking about liquid! Rich enough to have your own jet! Rich enough not to waste time! Fifty, a hundred million dollars, buddy. A player, or nothing! Because greed captures the essence of the evolutionary spirit. Greed is right, greed works! The point is, ladies and gentlemen, that greed, for lack of a better word, is good!"* The entire Chicago Mercantile Exchange burst into wild applause. The men high-fived in excitement, the women fanned themselves with phone message sheets. The roar of the Traders was deafening. Patrick had never felt such a rush. Now they weren't throwing stones, they were throwing money, *their* money. "Teach me how to spot a ripe IPO!" "Show me impressive

38

returns!" "Help me roll my IRA!" "Take me down to nothing and rebuild me!" The cries of delight and need fell upon them, on and on, until Patrick and Ben reached the next block. Then they turned tail and ran like hell, Cumo ambling casually after them.

"What the hell did you just do?" Ben asked, incredulous.

Patrick beamed as he ran. "I gave them every Gordon Gekko quote I could remember."

"That was genius."

"And we didn't lose the coffee," Patrick said, hefting the bag in his hand. "That's why I'm in charge."

3.

Horace toed at the gore stuck to the plow shield. Here and there, small clumps of hair matted together in dark red clots fell from the blade, exposing tiny white bone fragments that peppered the bloody spray. Jesus, those lumps of brain matter were really stuck on there.

"Christ. I hate when this happens."

"When you hit someone with the train, or when they get stuck?"

Horace glanced sharply at his second-in-command, a grave young man with somber grey eyes, a gristly black beard, and a bald head under his Amtrak cap. He was an able conductor, but often spoke too freely for Horace's taste. "Both," the older man muttered. "Find someone to clean this up. I want it sparkling by the time we pull out."

He turned and strode toward the station, noting with disgust the blood and grey matter that had exploded onto the engine windows. Christ, this was a messy route. You wouldn't think it--most of the last 300 miles of rail ran through open space, what used to be farmland--but between the suicides, the goddamn loose cattle, and the occasional near-sighted refugee, the entire Lincoln Service was a bloodbath.

The Monkey piss didn't help matters. Visibility in the fog was never any better than half a mile, and it wasn't safe to blast the horn. It'd be like calling starving children to Thanksgiving. A train, even a train as stripped down as Bertha, would still be considered a cornucopia of resources for the average survivor. Horace's men were capable of protecting the train to a point, but it's not like they could beat a retreat if they were swarmed. Best not to draw any unwanted attention, which meant no horn. Oftentimes, between the fog and the silence, people just didn't see the train coming, unlikely as it sounded. A lot of refugees followed the tracks when they had no compass. Maybe they didn't figure the train was still running. But they didn't know Horace Stilton.

He stopped halfway down the platform and pulled an antique gold watch from his pocket and examined the time. Most people weren't concerned with time these days, but a railroad man knew better. There was always a schedule to keep, even if the world had given up its timetable. He watched the second hand make three complete rotations, and when it struck the 12 on the fourth time around, the time was precisely 3:00pm, Central Standard Time. He tugged on the chain around his neck and drew the long, thin whistle from inside his shirt. He blew four short, sharp blasts. "Departure in four hours!" he hollered.

Horace had been with Amtrak for almost thirty years. He had started as a lowly part-time ticket clerk at a time when low gas prices and a good economy meant the near death of the passenger train industry, and slowly moved up the ranks, to full-time clerk, then Service Assistant, then Lead Service Attendant. Then, around 2008, the economy tanked and things really picked up at the Blue Lady. Horace rocketed up to the coveted position of Assistant Passenger Conductor Trainee and completed the training program in record time. Somewhere in D.C. there was still a plaque with his name on it. But for all the promise he'd shown, Horace had stagnated in that position. He'd shown decades of dedication to the company, but when all was said and done, it was still an Old Boys' Club, and Horace didn't fit the profile. He wasn't well connected. He wasn't a blood relative of anyone on the Board of Directors, he hadn't knocked up the company president's daughter, and his father hadn't gone to school with the VP of This or That. He was stonewalled at every Lead Conductor position that came available. He jumped service lines, from the Acela Express to the Texas Eagle to the Pacific Surfliner to the Illinois Zephyr to the Empire Builder back to the Texas Eagle, leaving his family, friends, and any semblance of a normal life behind in a desperate attempt to show his worth in the right place at the right time. But for every Lead Conductor opening, there were six less deserving "friends-of-a-friend" winking at each other in the bullpen. Horace lost traction, his resentment festering within his heart like an open sore.

Until M-Day, that is. The apocalypse marked a significant turning point in Horace's life. The Flying Monkeys wiped out over 80% of Amtrak's staff, including all but three commissioned Lead Conductors, all three of whom abandoned their posts after the Great Genocide. As far as Horace was concerned, that was just the latest proof that they had no right to be called conductors in the first place.

The day after the apocalypse, no one showed for work. No one except for Horace. He arrived at Los Angeles Union Station as if it were any other day. In truth, he hadn't quite grasped the enormity of the attack. With no friends or close relatives to worry about his safety, his phone hadn't rung once, and there wasn't a single person he could think to call to get more information on the rumblings outside. He knew there had been a serious, multi-target attack on the United States, of course. It was on every channel. L.A. had even been one of the twenty-six targets, and he could see the yellow dust drifting by his window in thick clouds. It had scared him at first--it was early spring, the first truly hot Californian day, and he, like so many others across the country, had his windows open for the first time that year, giving the mysterious yellow plague easy entry into his apartment--but it hadn't affected him, and though he heard screams and sirens out in the streets, he thought what most Los Angeles survivors thought at the time: another impotent terrorist threat. His apartment was located only a few blocks from the station, and, sure, there was chaos in the streets on his way to work the next morning, but, Christ, this was L.A. When *wasn't* there chaos in the streets? To top things off, most of the news broadcasts had gone off the air sometime the night before. He thought the attack must be clouding the airwaves, obstructing the signals, something like that. How was he to know that 99% of the anchors, producers, writers, cameramen, make-up artists, and interns were lying dead with their bodies half melted in pools of their own excrement, pus, and blood, with that crazy, viscous yellow gel oozing out of their pores?

Looking back on it, there were probably dead bodies littering the sidewalks, but how would a few dead bodies look any different from the litter of hobos he passed every day? It wasn't until he'd reached Union Station that he realized something was seriously wrong. There was no mistaking the previous evening's passengers rotting on the terminal floor.

Most people would have screamed and fled. But Horace saw an opportunity.

It didn't take long to confirm that the conductors scheduled for the next Texas Eagle were either dead or no longer bothering with the 9-to-5. Amtrak needed a new conductor. Horace finally had his promotion; the murder of 95% of the U.S. population had made it so.

Now, more than three years later, he was thriving. An operational transportation service was incredibly lucrative in post-apocalyptic America. Refugees were willing to pay everything they had to escape the stench of death and the disappearing rations in their hometowns. Everyone thought somewhere else would be better. It was so stupid. Horace had directed his train all over the country. No city was any better off than any other.

After a time, the refugees became fewer and far between. It meant fewer fares, but that was okay, because Horace was nothing if not adaptable. Bertha's main focus shifted from passengers to cargo. Survivors were willing to pay top dollar (figuratively speaking, now that the dollar was worthless) for cargo transport. Traders paid him to move large amounts of wares to some post or other a few hundred miles away. Railroad towns paid him to take loads of trash away from their newly erected city walls. Farmers paid to have food shipped to arid regions across the country. He'd hauled everything from carrots to corpses; anything people needed moved or removed.

The years had made him rich and powerful in the eyes of the weak and struggling. He had a legion of Red Caps, a full, capable train staff, an enterprising if not affable Assistant Conductor, complete reign of the entire Amtrak rail system, and a series of strategically placed food and supply depots situated across the country. And sweetest of all, he was acknowledged by everyone he met as Lead Conductor. These had been a good three years, and Horace wasn't sure what he would do with himself if the well ever went dry.

He entered Chicago's Union Station through the empty sliding glass door frames, sidestepping to avoid the pickets of glass stabbing out of the black metal. He flagged down one of the Red Caps, an earnest young man named Louis, who came hustling over. "Yes, sir?"

"Take Stevens and find our cargo. Two clients today; we got twenty-four full-size waste containers and a load of scrap metal coming in from that Loop woman's people, and a pallet of books coming in from the library. Don't know what the library man'll look like, but shouldn't be too hard to spot the cargo. Violet's paying us in red, six cases, make sure it's not schlock. As for the books, I want you to pay him from this." He grabbed a small linen bag from his pocket and tossed it to Louis.

"What are they?" the young Red Cap asked, hefting the light pouch in his hand.

"Bone fragments, from saints. Taken out of church altars, apparently. Seems disrespectful to me, but I guess desperate times and all that. Elsewise, they're extremely valuable. Rome's not sending any more of 'em stateside, so don't give away more than you have to. Use your best judgment based on the number and quality of the books. Not looking for any specific titles, but you know what I mean. I'd say one fragment for thirty decent books sounds about right. Be fair with the price, but not generous. We only got those ten fragments, plus sixteen more. You got all that?"

Louis nodded. "Waste barrels and metal from the busboys, books from the library."

"Good boy. Run along." Louis turned and scampered off in search of Stevens. Horace checked his pocket watch. As always, he was right on schedule.

•

"Now, this bridge looks especially well guarded," Patrick said, stroking his chin thoughtfully. "And everyone on it is wearing a red hat. I received no memo about a red hat."

"Haven't you ever taken the Amtrak?" Ben asked. "Those guys are Red Caps. They help old people with their luggage and stuff."

"Ah, yes! Now I remember. They're like big Boy Scouts."

"Sort of. But they don't sell cookies."

"Cookies?" Patrick shook his head. "Oh, Ben, your formative years must have been such an incredible train wreck," he said, patting him on the shoulder. "So! Do you think we just...*cross*...?"

Ben shrugged, looking at the legion of men and women in red caps swarming the walkway. There was a line of them spread out along the entrance to the bridge, with maybe three dozen more spaced out along the road behind them. Another twenty or so surrounded the Adams Street entrance to the Amtrak platforms. "Sure. There's a lot of them, but they don't seem particularly violent." He approached the Adams Street Bridge and took a step toward a gap in the line of Red Caps. A heavily bearded guard one on his left drew back a fist and smashed him in the mouth with a right cross. Ben went toppling over backward, landing in a daze on his pack and looking more like a mutated turtle than ever. Patrick rushed up to him and helped him to his feet. "Nope. Nope," he said, wiping blood from the corner of his mouth. "I was wrong. They are particularly violent."

"Huh," Patrick said. "That guy just punched you right in the face." He gazed in awe at the Red Cap, who had resumed his formal posture and gazed into the distance, like a British Queen Guard. "That was really nice form," he said admirably. Ben shoved him away.

"Thanks for the recap. I don't think they're going to let us through."

"Sure, not if we try to just barrel on through. That was a stupid plan. A stupid plan, Ben. Sometimes all it takes it a little honey. Follow my lead." He turned and approached the line of Red Caps. He picked out a woman who looked especially small and pleasant, and said, "Excuse me, but I was wondering if you would be so kind as to let us pass." Or that's what he would have said, if she hadn't interrupted him by bringing her boot hard into his groin before he could finish the word "excuse."

"Crip on a crutch!" he shouted, holding a hand to his throbbing genitals and stumbling away from the Red Cap Guard. "They can't be reasoned with!"

"Seeing your pain actually lessens my pain," Ben observed.

"Criminy Christmas," Patrick swore. "I haven't been kicked by a girl like that since grad school."

"Probably deserved it then, too."

"Oh, I definitely deserved it *then*. I did *not* deserve it just now."

"Well," Ben said, crossing his arms in frustration. "Now what?"

Patrick patted his testicles and made sure everything was in order before craning his neck to see Union Station on the other side of the river. So close, but so far. There didn't seem to be any easy entrance points into the river, and even if there were, they'd just run up against more Red Caps on the other side. Besides, he knew they couldn't swim loaded down with all their gear. And he doubted Ben could swim at all, with those stubby legs. He looked downriver and saw what looked like a bridge far in the distance. Roosevelt, he guessed, or maybe Harrison. Whichever street it was, it was located south of a massive wall, easily thirty feet tall, that seemed to stretch from the river across the Loop, probably to the lake. If the train ran true to form, they only had a few more hours to get to the station and talk their way on before it departed. There just wasn't time to try to go around. "Okay, I have a plan," he said finally. "But I have to warn you. It's not a very good plan."

"I hope it involves you going first."

"Unfortunately, it does." Patrick said, taking a deep breath. "Okay. Follow my lead. And watch out for fists." He shook out his hands and cracked his neck. Then he turned back toward the bridge and approached once more. When he got close, about ten feet from the first guards, he pointed to a random Red Cap milling around just behind the line. "Hey!" he shouted, loud enough to get the attention of everyone in a thirty-foot radius. "It's you!" He gave his best look of amazed bewilderment and jogged up closer to the line of guards, but out of arm's reach. "Oh my gosh, I can't believe it's really you! It's been ages, how are you?" The Red Cap stopped milling and stood rooted to the ground, absolutely dumb-founded by this apparent stranger who suddenly seemed to know him. He wasn't quite sold, Patrick could tell by the way his eyebrows twitched uncertainly. He pressed on. "You look amazing! God, I never thought I'd see you again! I'm so glad you survived, I thought for sure the whole gang was dead. And here you are, of all places! If that isn't the craziest--and you're a Red Cap now!" He put both hands on his hips and gasped in wonder. "Good on you!"

The Red Cap had a crucial decision to make--lie, or risk personal embarrassment in front of his peers. So, of course, he lied. "Oh. Yeah! Hey! Wow! Look at you!" he said, trying to sound convincing. "This is so crazy! What has it been--gosh, I don't know how long." Then, brave soul that he was, he took a real chance. "Has it been since...Arkansas?" he tried nervously.

Patrick jumped on the opportunity. "Arkansas!" he cried. "That's ex-actly right! My God, the times we had, huh?" he beamed.

"Oh, yeah," the Red Cap nodded. "I still get...just...chills. Thinking about it."

"Yeah! Wow! Just...just wow," Patrick said, giving a low whistle. "Isn't it crazy that after all these years, it took the apocalypse to get us back together?"

"Sure. When all it would have taken was a phone call," the Red Cap said, laughing uncomfortably.

Patrick clapped his hands and rubbed them together. "Wow, yeah, so, we need to catch up, we--actually, may we?" he asked, taking a careful tiptoe step into a gap in the line of guards.

The Red Cap looked conflicted, but now that he'd committed, it was better for him to embrace it. A lot of people were watching. "Oh! Yeah, yeah, come on through. Guys, let them through. These are old friends. From Arkansas!"

"Go Razorbacks," Patrick said with a little fist pump. He slid between two stern looking guards. Ben followed close behind. "Go Wal-Mart," he murmured.

"So," Patrick said, clapping the Red Cap on the shoulder and bobbing his head encouragingly. "We should catch up. What've you been up to? What're you doing now?"

The Red Cap nodded. "Right, right, well, you know, I work for Amtrak," he said, pointing to the patch on his shirt.

"Oh, yeah, right, of course. Sounds like a great gig, great...you know... side benefits...and stuff."

"Yeah, it's good. It's good. Yeah."

"Yeah."

"Yeah."

The three men stood awkwardly, Patrick rubbing the back of his neck, Ben trying to look uninterested, the Red Cap rocking back and forth on his heels. The other Amtrak employees were no longer paying them any attention, and the Red Cap seemed desperate to get out of the situation. He smiled and continued to nod. "Yeah," he said again.

Patrick cleared his throat. "Ahem. So. What do you think we—"

"Stevens!" came a loud cry from across the bridge. The Red Cap snapped around at the sound of his name. A young, reddish-haired Red Cap was jogging in their direction. Stevens looked mightily relieved.

"Louis! There you are! Great! Louis, these are, ah...my friends," he said, indicating the other two men.

Louis nodded politely, but he was obviously in a rush. "Horace wants us on cargo duty, stat."

Stevens let out a massive breath of relief. "Oh! Right! Cargo duty!" He turned to Patrick. "Listen, I am *so* sorry, but I have to run. It was so good running into you, I've got to go, ah...will you two be all right finding your way out? I'm sorry, I have to go."

"Oh, it's fine! That's fine, we'll be fine," Patrick said, waving him off. "Not a problem. Go on. We'll be fine."

"Okay, great. Well. So good to see you!"

"Oh, you too!" Stevens reached out a hand to shake. Patrick misread the gesture and moved in for a hug. By the time he realized his mistake, it was too late; he was committed. He embraced the Red Cap slowly and stiffly. Stevens shouldered nervously away, but patted Patrick on the back three times quickly. Then he turned and ran off with the other Red Cap.

Patrick turned to Ben and tapped his finger against his nose. "Just like I planned it."

"Not bad," Ben admitted. "I thought I was going to have to go fielder's choice on these sons of bitches." He swung the bat lazily for emphasis.

"That's not--you don't know baseball, do you?" he asked. Ben shrugged. "Well, what say we go find ourselves a train!"

Now that they had breached the security line, they found the way basically free and clear. A few of the patrolling Red Caps gave them suspicious looks, but most had seen them talking with Stevens, and if some of them hadn't, well, the fact remained that these two strangers had made it past their defenses, so there must be a good reason for it. It wouldn't do to question the front line's abilities before the whole squad. The two travelers hurried across the bridge and up the concrete stairs to the left, to the northeast corner of the 222 South Riverside Plaza building. They nodded politely to the Red Caps guarding the door and were allowed to pass through the doorway. Patrick thought back to a time when he and Annie had ridden the train to St. Louis, back before Izzy was born. They'd used this very entrance, and the doors had slid open at their arrival. Now, those doors were gone, replaced by a huge, ragged hole blown out of the wall. They stepped through gingerly, avoiding dusty, charred rubble, and found themselves on a short landing with four flights of steps directly ahead. The middle rows of stairs were technically escalators, though they weren't doing much escalating these days. "Pffft," Patrick said, shooing a hand at the broken escalators. "They didn't work last time I was here either. I don't know why I pay my taxes, nothing changes."

They descended the steps slowly and carefully. The landing was at ground level, so the farther down they went, the farther underground they were. There were no skylights in the station, save a few fist-sized holes that had been blown into the ceiling. A handful of Red Caps scampered through the halls, running errands and paying no attention to the two strangers in the corridor. Every hundred feet of so, a candle burned on the floor along the wall, throwing dim, orange halos and long shadows. Patrick lifted the hammer from Ben's belt loop. "Hey!" Ben cried, swatting at Patrick's hand. But Patrick was adamant.

"You're holding the bat, you can't use it anyway." Ben grumbled his assent. Patrick held the hammer in his left hand and took the baton from his pocket with his right, popping it open with a quick flick of the wrist. Behind him, Ben gripped the bat with both hands, ready to swing like Mike McGwire. Or was it Matt McGwire? Pat was right, Ben didn't really know baseball.

They crept along the hall, passing between a ransacked McDonald's counter on the right and the black, burned out husk of a Corner Bakery on the left. Something rustled across the McDonald's linoleum. Patrick swung to the right and raised the hammer, his heart thudding in his chest. A rat raced out of the darkness and stopped three feet from where they stood. It raised its head and screamed at them, then turned and skittered around the corner.

"Jesus hell," Ben cursed, breathing hard. "What are we *doing* down here?"

"It's the only way I know to the platform," Patrick said. "The train boards underground."

"Shit, then let's *walk* to Disney World. Above the underground, where there's light."

"It's not far. Just be ready."

"For what?"

Patrick shrugged. "For anything."

They crept farther down the hall, coming to another set of stairs and broken down escalators. A huge advertisement for Chase Bank covered the steps and the escalator rails. Chase had been Patrick's bank. "Hey,

Ben," he said, easing himself down the stairs. "Remember money?"

"I remember people *talking* about money. I don't remember ever seeing any for myself. Also, Rule Number Seven." *Money is no longer money. Food, weapons, shelter, and clothing are money.*

At the bottom of the stairwell, they made a U-turn to the right. Through the gloom, Ben could just barely see the outlines of doorways. The hallway candlelight illuminated thin wisps of Monkey fog on the other side, making the dark air glow yellow. They nearly collided with a Red Cap as they turned the sharp corner. "Watch where you're going, jackass!" she whispered, before taking off around the corner and up the stairs. Patrick turned to Ben. "Was she talking to you, or me?" Ben shrugged.

They moved cautiously down the hall. Patrick wished, not for the first time in his post-apocalyptic career, that he had an emergency survival flashlight. There was one in the emergency kit in the trunk of Annie's car, the kind of flashlight that you powered with a hand crank, but it had gone up in flames like everything else. He'd searched everywhere for a replacement, but to no avail. Emergency flashlights were worth their weight in pre-M-Day gold.

"Which track is it?" Ben asked, nodding to the column of train tracks beyond the doors on their left.

Patrick shook his head. "A: How the hell should I know? And B: Those are the Metra rails. We're not taking the Metra. I am *not* going to the suburbs." He spit on the floor for emphasis.

After about thirty feet, they came to a hallway on the right. It, too, had once had electronically sliding doors, but they seemed to be in short supply these days.

They could hear voices now, faint voices coming from somewhere up ahead. The darkness looked a little less complete up there, and Patrick realized there must be light around the corner at the far end of the hall, maybe a hundred feet ahead. They crept toward it, their sneakers crunching over wrappers and magazines scattered around the floor. They passed a newsstand that had been smashed to bits. The Coca-Cola case now rested on its side, along with the magazine racks and snack shelves. Patrick noticed with some amusement that someone had bashed in the glass top in the center of the checkout counter and stolen the Illinois Lottery scratch-offs from their cubbies.

Immediately after the newsstand, the hall opened up into a high-ceilinged lobby. A tall set of staircases rose off to the right, leading back up to street level, where dim, yellow light filtered in through more busted doors. Farther to the right, Union Station continued underground, beneath Canal Street and over to the original Union Station building. Patrick peered down the long, dark hall and saw sparks in the distance that might have been fires burning on the station floor. To their left was the entrance to the Amtrak waiting rooms. Here, too, the sliding doors had been ripped from their tracks and tossed haphazardly aside. There were loud shouts coming from the waiting room, and they decided to bypass it. They continued straight down the hall.

"Need help with your bags?" a voice rasped from the stairwell. Ben jumped and swung his bat in the general direction of the voice. He swung so hard that the momentum carried it around in a full arc, missing Patrick's skull by centimeters. "Need help with your bags?" the voice asked again in a ragged, choking tone. Patrick peered into the darkness. A lumpy figure crouched on the stairs, swaying gently back and forth. "Need help with your bags?"

"I don't think he's talking to us," Patrick whispered. He took a cautious step closer, hammer raised, poised to strike. The man on the stairs wasn't facing them. He crouched on the balls of his feet, back against the railing, staring at the opposite stairwell.

"Need help with your bags?"

Patrick lowered the hammer and quietly backed away. "Come on. Let's go."

"My God, this is so creepy," Ben whispered. "Hey. Let me hold the machete."

"Jesus, no!" Patrick hissed. "That's literally the only way this situation gets more terrifying."

The hall terminated at the Amtrak platforms. They could just barely see the straight outlines of the train tracks in the darkness ahead. The glow of light grew brighter to the left. They turned the corner and found a group of Red Caps surrounding a short man in a blue hat. The man in blue hovered over some papers splayed out on the floor, the Red Caps illuminating them with old-fashioned oil lamps.

Patrick had been on enough Amtrak trains to know that while the Red Caps might be the muscle, the Blue Caps were the brains. A blue cap signified a member of the on-board train crew, the servicemen, the ticket-takers, and the conductor. The Blue Cap was his man.

He pulled Ben back around the corner, into the darkness. "Okay," he whispered. "It's game time. Are you ready?"

Ben nodded. "What's the plan?"

"Do you trust me?"

"Not really, no. What's the plan?"

"I can't tell you."

"Why not?"

Patrick hesitated. "Because you won't like it."

"Why am I not surprised?" Ben asked.

"No, I mean you *really* won't like it."

"Fine, then just tell me what it is so I can refuse to go along with it."

"No, see, that's why I need you to trust me."

"Patrick, tell me the plan."

"Do you trust me?"

"I'd trust you a lot more if you told me the plan."

"I want you to look me in the eyes and say, 'Patrick, I trust you.'"

"Okay, okay, I get it. Patrick, I trust you."

"Is that true?"

"Yes."

"No matter what?"

"Yes, no matter what."

"Do you mean that?"

"Of course I mean it!" Ben hissed. "I trust you, okay? I trust you, I trust you, I fucking trust you!"

"Okay. Remember you said that."

Ben furrowed his brow. He was about to ask why, but before he could make a sound, Patrick hauled off and whacked him in the face with the hammer.

Ben's howls of pain brought the Amtrak crew running. Patrick slipped the hammer into his belt loop as the Red Caps skidded around the corner, weapons brandished. They held their lanterns up to the scene before them. Orange light flickered over Ben's writhing body on the ground. Patrick stood over him angrily, his fists planted firmly on his hips.

"I demand to know who's responsible for this!" he cried. The Red Caps looked from one to another, confused. "Well? Speak up!"

The man in the blue hat shouldered his way through the mob of Red Caps, which was no easy feat, given his diminutive stature. He stood no taller than 5'5", more than a full head shorter than the shortest Red Cap. A long, brown mustache bushed from beneath his nose and tapered to drooping points below the corners of his mouth. His eyes were lost behind a pair of small, circle-rimmed glasses that would have been a better fit for a United States Postmaster, circa 1883. Though he was on the husky side, he must have lost at least a little weight since the apocalypse, because he kept hitching up his pants as he moved. "What is the meaning of this?" he demanded, huffing in consternation.

"That is precisely what I'd like to know!" Patrick said. "One of your Red Caps attacked my poor friend here with some sort of blunt instrument. I demand to know why, and I demand justice! Where's the conductor of your train?"

"I am the conductor," the little man said, puffing his chest out. "Now what's this about an attack?"

"One of your men came tearing through here with some sort of weapon and smashed it directly into my friend's face! I mean, just look at him! He's hideous now!" He indicated Ben's crumpled form with both hands. He was moaning loudly, cursing with angry nonsense.

"You say one of my men did this?" the conductor asked, raising an eyebrow in suspicion.

"I most certainly do! He ran right by; there was no mistaking that red hat. And here, I thought the Red Caps took pride in their professionalism." He crossed his arms in a huff.

The conductor glared around at his men. "They're meant to, that's for sure. Can you describe the man for me?"

"Well, it was dark, of course," Patrick said, rubbing his chin. He thought back to the bearded Red Cap guard who'd clocked Ben on the bridge. It seemed like a good time for poetic justice. "But I know he had dark hair, it looked jet black, and he a beard about this long." He held a hand six inches below his chin.

"Sounds like Rodgers, sir," piped up one of the Red Caps in the back.

"Rodgers is supposed to be guarding the bridge," the conductor said. "What on earth would he be doing down here?"

"Smashing people with hammers, apparently!" Patrick said, exasperated. "Or mallets, or nightsticks, or whatever it was! Look at poor Ben!"

He crouched next to his friend and patted his head gently. Ben began to say something, but Patrick furtively covered his mouth. "I think he's lost the ability to speak! My God, I think your man knocked him voiceless!"

"Voiceless?" said the conductor.

"Yes, voiceless! We'll be lucky if he ever speaks again!" He took Ben's hand and helped him to his feet. A few of the Red Caps gasped as he stepped into the light. Already, a huge, purple welt was forming just under his left eye.

"Holy Lord!" the conductor swore, stepping forward for a closer look. "He really got you."

"Yes, he did," Patrick said firmly. "We demand satisfaction!"

"And you're sure it was one of my men who did this."

"Of course I'm sure! Who else could it have been? Do you think I did this? Is *that* what you're suggesting? Why would I smash my own friend's face in? He's all I have left in this world, the only tether to my former life, the only link that still exists between what is now and what used to be!" Patrick willed himself to cry. It didn't work. He wiped at his eyes anyway, hoping the darkness made it impossible to see that there were no tears.

The conductor looked agitated. He pulled a watch from his pocket and frowned at it. "What sort of satisfaction? I don't have much time."

"Well, we came down here to watch the train pull out. Ben's a simple-minded person, and he loves to watch the trains." Patrick patted him on the head. Ben lurched away and swatted back. Patrick slapped at Ben's flailing hands. "Behave, sweet, simple Ben!" he cried. Ben threw a mighty kick at his supposed friend, but with his eye swelling shut, his depth perception was off, and he whiffed by a good three feet. "*Mrrraugh!*" he growled. He stalked off to sniffle and sulk in the shadows. Patrick continued: "We just wanted to watch the train, but now I suppose, given all that's happened, well...Ben, how would you like to ride that train?" Ben waved his hand angrily from the corner.

The conductor frowned harder. "We don't do much passenger transport anymore," he said.

"If you don't do much, then you must do some."

The Blue Cap continued to frown. "I only say that because we have one passenger right now, a journalist. But she paid her way, handsomely."

"Don't tell me Ben hasn't paid the ultimate price!" Patrick replied.

The conductor scowled. "How far would you want to go?"

"Where are you headed?"

"South."

"Hmm," Patrick said, feigning surprise. "I suppose we could see our way to letting this incident slide for a ride as far as...what, St. Louis?"

The conductor stroked his mustache. As he stood there thinking, a low rumbling rose from down the hallway. Patrick turned to see two Red Caps pushing a flat, metal cart loaded down with barrels. "First load of waste," the man named Louis said. "Stevens'll be along shortly with the rest." The conductor nodded, and the Red Caps parted to let the cart through. As it passed, Patrick glanced down into the open barrels. A thick, syrupy liquid sloshed around inside of them. In the darkness, the stuff looked black as tar, but the smell in the air said differently.

"Is that vegetable oil?" Patrick said.

Louis shrugged as he rolled. "Some kind of waste. We're dumping it," he said, pushing through the crowd.

"Our work doesn't concern strangers, Louis," the conductor said sharply.

"Sorry, sir."

A light bulb clicked somewhere in Patrick's brain. "You could be using that for fuel, you know."

The conductor whipped around, his eyes narrowed. "What did you say?"

"You can use that to fuel the train. I mean, you can if it's cooking oil. It smells like it is."

The conductor grabbed him firmly by the elbow and looked up at him. "Is that true?" he asked.

"Sure it's true."

"How do you know that?"

"I'm a mechanical engineer," Patrick said proudly. "Or, you know, I was. Before M-Day."

"Louis!" the conductor cried. "Hand me the cargo sheet." Louis stopped and fished a folded piece of paper from his pocket. He handed it to the Blue Cap. The conductor unfolded it and held it up next to one of the Red Caps' lanterns. He raised an eyebrow. "Corn oil."

"That'd do it," Patrick said.

"You're suggesting I take that stuff and dump it into my gas tank?"

Patrick shrugged. "If you're in a pinch for fuel, sure. I mean, it'll make things volatile as hell, but yeah, you could power a train on that. If you have enough of it."

"We have twenty-four barrels of it coming on board right now." He refolded the paper and handed it to Louis. "Get that cargo on board, keep it safe. Put three barrels in the engine, we'll see what's what. The rest goes in the cargo hold." Louis nodded and pushed the cart off toward the platform. The conductor turned back to Patrick and stuck out his hand. "Name's Horace Stilton, Lead Conductor of the Texas Eagle. Welcome aboard."

•

Ben was in a bad mood. His cheek was tender where his supposed best friend had smashed it with a hammer because that was the best dumb fucking plan he had been able to come up with. The worst part was, the dumb fucking plan had actually worked, which meant similarly dumb fucking plans were going to be encouraged in the future.

A rational voice somewhere deep inside suggested that all of this really was for the best. After all, they *had* managed to get on the train, something Ben had been pretty sure they'd never be able to do. But that small, rational piece of his brain was completely drowned out by the much larger, much stronger emotional piece, which wanted to claw Patrick's face, swig the vodka, derail the train, and set fire to Disney World. *That's what I'll do. I'll burn that fucking Disney World. If we make it there, I swear to high heaven, I will set fire to anything still standing.*

They headed toward the platform, surrounded by Red Caps, Patrick smiling his goofy smile, happy as a clam to be headed south. The train loomed before them, each car tall and silver with the blue Amtrak logo still perfectly visible along the side. It was a modest train, only six cars long, including the engine. The conductor led them to the second from the rear and gestured up the stairs. "Passenger car. Don't go wandering between cars. My men have instructions to take out anyone who tries to cross without my expressed permission. You don't have it."

"You mind if I go up and take a look at the engine?" Patrick asked, genuinely interested.

Horace peered at him over his glasses and sighed. "Guess that's fine, seein' as how I'm headin' that way myself. Come with me. Your friend gonna be all right?"

Patrick examined Ben's face carefully. "Ben, are you okay? Blink once for yes, twice for no."

"And blink how many times for, 'If I get my hands on the son of a bitch who hammered my face, I'm going to strangle him with his own intestines'?"

"Four, I think." Ben blinked four times. "Yep, he's fine." Patrick followed the conductor down the platform. Ben rolled his eyes and launched himself up the steep set of stairs. He was more than willing to take a short reprieve from his "friend." One of the Red Caps followed him and took up a position at the entrance to the car, his hands clasped at his waist. A guard, apparently. Besides Ben and the Red Cap, the passenger car was empty.

It had been a while since Ben had been in an Amtrak car, and his very private, very special love for the Harry Potter series had encouraged him to hope against hope that the company had upgraded to exclusive, wood paneled sleeping compartments at some point over the last decade. But what awaited him at the top of the stairs looked more like the inside of a Greyhound bus. A center aisle separated a long column of four-seat rows, two seats on the right, two seats on the left. They were covered in blue pleather that was literally coming apart at the seams. The upholstery was ripped, torn, and scratched so badly, it looked like someone had locked a swarm of feral cats in the car for a week. Some of the seats had been removed altogether, and some faced the wrong direction. A couple of the rows swiveled freely, apparently unable to be locked into place. Each side of the train had a luggage rack suspended above the seats, running the length of the car. These racks had once held suitcases and duffels; now they held canned goods and bottled water.

Ben sulked past the restrooms, the doors of which had been removed, and found a reasonably comfortable looking seat two-thirds of the way down the car. He leaned his bat against the aisle seat and slipped the knapsack from his shoulders, tossing it onto the seat next to the window. He caught his reflection in the darkened glass, and for the first time realized that lights were on inside the car. They were dim, but they were on. Rope lights set into the ceiling ran the length of the car, giving off a soft, orange glow. He crept into the row and examined himself more closely in the window. "Holy shit," he muttered, touching the puffy purple lump under his eye. Pat had really clocked him good. Other than that, though, he seemed to be okay. His lip wasn't really swollen from the Red Cap's punch, and the shaving cut on his head had stopped bleeding. Hammer wound aside, he looked pretty good, and now that he was actually on the train, he was feeling a little better, too. He was still pissed at Patrick, but at least they were on track (ha, ha). And there were plenty of armed Red Caps on the train, so he'd even be able to get a decent night's sleep without waking up in terror every time he thought he heard a sound. He reached into his knapsack and pulled out a few energy bars. He tore into one and chewed thoughtfully, almost happily. Hell, this wasn't so bad. All in all, it'd probably be a pretty restful ride.

●

"Oh, yeah, I can see why you get so much splatter," Patrick said, examining the plow blade fixed to the front of the train. "This design is all wrong. You must get enough blood sprayed up there to cover the whole damn windshield."

"We do," Horace admitted with a sigh. "And not just blood. Brain matter, bone fragments, pieces of internal organs. Got a whole lung stuck up there one time."

"Yeah, I'm not surprised," Patrick nodded, running a hand over the plow. "Looks like the weight is right, and the steel is solid, I bet those bodies shit both ways on impact if you get up to 70." He looked to Horace for confirmation. The conductor nodded proudly. "It's good construction, but the angle is the main problem. The proximity to the engine is an issue too. See, if you had the right v-plow instead of this straight plow, and it came out another eight feet or so, the bodies would slip right off to either side, and most of the gore would be outside the windshield radius by the time the engine arrived."

Horace tugged at one corner of his mustache. "Huh. Guess you're right. The other big problem is heavier materials in the tracks. Dump trucks, water towers, things of that sort. We lose a lot of time stopping the train and moving those obstacles by hand. Hard as hell to see 'em in the fog, too, we've had more than a few close calls."

"I bet." Patrick rubbed his chin, wishing, not for the first time, that he was capable of growing a full beard worthy of stroking. "You know," he said slowly, "you could rig up a system that pushed the plow forward when you wanted to crash through something bigger. A dump truck would still derail it, but it could handle something between that and a human body. It'd be like a high-velocity battering ram. Add that force to the initial force the moving train gives the plow in a resting position, and you could blow your way through all kinds of barriers."

"You could design that?"

Patrick drummed his fingers against his chin, so as to appear deep in thought. "I suppose I *could...*"

"...But you'd need to be compensated," the conductor finished. Actually, Patrick was just fishing for a complimentary plea of desperation, something along the lines of, *But we need you, you're obviously a brilliant engineer, we can't do it without you!* But hey, yeah, compensation was good. Much better than a compliment.

"Yes," he said, "I could probably design something for the right amount of compensation."

"Two bottles of red wine and a sack of rice?"

"How about three bottles of red wine, a sack full of canned chili, two bladed weapons, and a corkscrew?"

"Two bottles, six cans of food, one blunt weapon, and a bent nail."

"A bent nail?"

"Closest thing we got to a corkscrew."

"Hmm." Patrick tossed the offer around in his head. "Three bottles, five cans of food, one bladed weapon, and hell, I'll take the nail." He stuck out his hand. Horace considered the offer, then grasped it.

"Deal."

•

Lindsay was frustrated in pretty much every way imaginable. The Red Caps wouldn't allow her to cross the bridge into the Loop, where she could plainly see dozens of people milling about. "Let me over there!" she screamed, shaking one of the Caps by his lapels. "I need to interview those people!" But the Red Cap just looked at her as if she were speaking an alien language and brushed her aside. Lindsay huffed.

This trip just wasn't panning out. She was more prisoner than passenger on Horace's train, and she had quietly borne the brunt of the crew's collective rudeness because she knew Chicago would be worth it. Surely there would be survivors swarming the "Second City." With over four hours to pounce on a few subjects and ask her questions, she'd be halfway to her Pulitzer by the time they pulled back out of the station. If there still was a Pulitzer. But there *had* to be a Pulitzer. There were still journalists left in this world, and that meant there was journalism, even if there were no more live wires to send the stories around the world. M-Day provided an extraordinary opportunity for a hungry news hound like herself because not only was it the single most destructive and globally-affective event in the history of the human race, but if the rumors were true, 99% of her competition had been wiped out, including, she presumed, that smug bitch Tillie from Bloomberg, who'd scooped her on the Peruvian copper mine emergency story and snagged the goddamn Livingston Award. Publicly, of course, Tillie's passing due to inhalation of the Flying Monkey chemical was personally devastating, as well as a grave loss to the journalistic community. Off the record, she was glad the slut was gone. That was *her* Livingston Award, goddammit.

And here she was, risking life and limb for the story of her career, hell, of *anyone's* career, with dozens of potential interviewees just falling over themselves on the other side of the river, and she was being stonewalled by baggage handlers! Unbelievable. Un-fucking-believable! She stamped her foot on the ground so hard, her kitten heel snapped off, and her ankle twisted painfully beneath her. She screamed at the top of her lungs, shaking her fists at the sky, cursing the bridge, cursing the Red Caps, cursing Nine West, and cursing whatever god that would let her life fall to shit without giving her a single fucking break. She screamed until she ran out of breath.

"Something wrong?" a voice whispered in her ear. Lindsay jumped and gasped.

"Jesus, Bloom! What the hell are you doing, sneaking up on me like that?" she asked the train's assistant conductor, a hand pressed to her thudding chest.

"Just stretching my legs," he said, his voice soft and level, as always. "You didn't hear me walking?"

"Clearly," she said, rolling her eyes. "Hey, I need to get across the river. Will you tell these bozos to let me cross?"

He stared out over the river with his flat, grey eyes. Ever expressionless, Lindsay could only guess what he was thinking. "No," he finally said, his gaze locked on something across the way. "It's for your own safety."

"Bullshit. I don't want to be safe, I want a story!"

"It's not worth dying over."

"Those people are playing bocce ball!" she cried, pointing to a group of middle-aged men and women gathered in an old parking lot overrun with weeds. "I don't think they're serial killers."

It was meant to be hyperbole, but Bloom shrugged his shoulders. "Maybe they are, maybe they aren't. Who knows. John Wayne Gacy was a Jaycee and volunteered at children's hospitals." Bloom slipped his hands in his pockets and breathed deeply of the pale yellow air. Finally, he turned to Lindsay and met her eyes. "Horace ordered them to keep you on this side of the bridge. You may not like it, but he's responsible for you, and while you're under his care, his word is law."

"I am under no one's care," she insisted, sticking a finger in his face. She harrumphed and turned from him with a flick of her head, her short brown hair snapping behind her. She hobbled to the rail overlooking the Chicago River and waved her arms frantically at a pair of women in a rusty boat below. "Hey!" she screamed. "Hey! You, there! Where are you originally from? Did you come to Chicago before or after M-Day? Hey! You! Come on, I'm talking to you! Hey! Tell me what a typical day is like for you! Hey! Do you hear me?"

Out of the corner of her eye, she saw Bloom check his wristwatch. "Better wrap this interview up," he said, with only the hint of a smile. "We pull out in thirty."

•

Patrick plopped down in the seat next to Ben just as Horace blew the whistle for last call. "What'd I tell you, Benny Boy? Stick with me, and it's smooth sailing." He zoomed his hand through the air to show just how smooth their sailing could be.

"Yeah. Real smooth." Ben finished his second energy bar and tossed the wrapper on the floor.

"Sorry about your face," Patrick frowned. "It was for the greater good."

Ben waved him off. "Whatever. It's done. I mean, I owe you a swift kick to the teeth when you least expect it, but it's done."

"You won't feel that way when I tell you what I just did," he said with a grin. Ben raised an eyebrow. "I traded my services for some goods."

Ben snorted. "And how *was* sex with a man?"

"No, no, no, not that. I mean my smarts." He tapped his forehead. "The ones that live in my brain space."

"Do tell."

"I'm designing a battering ram for our conductor, and in return, he's agreed to ply us with wine and food. And a nail."

"You realize that nothing about what you're saying is sounding one bit *less* sexual, right?"

Patrick sighed. He shook his head and cleared the air with his hand. "Okay, let me start over. I'm going to design a hydraulic smashing apparatus for the train, and they're paying me three bottles of wine, some food, a bladed weapon, and a bent nail."

Ben's ears pricked up. "A bladed weapon? What kind of bladed weapon?"

"He didn't specify, but I'm hoping for a broadsword," Patrick said, crossing his fingers. "We can go all *Game of Thrones* on Arkansas."

"I've always hated Arkansas," Ben considered.

"We all do, Ben. We all hate Arkansas."

Just then, they heard a sharp clomping on the metal stairs. They both turned to see a short, angry brunette storming unevenly past the posted Red Cap guard and into the car. She cursed under her breath as she peeled off her shoes and hurled them into the last row. She plopped down across the aisle, her arms folded tightly across her chest, fuming and muttering to herself, staring straight ahead and seeing nothing, except, presumably, some reddish sort of anger. She argued with herself for a full three minutes before she realized there were other people in the car.

"Oh!" she exclaimed, jumping to her feet. "Hi."

"Hey," said Ben. Patrick waved.

The train lurched forward, and she stumbled backward, crashing down on the hard plastic armrest and slamming to the floor in the middle of the aisle.

"Oh!" Patrick cried. He jumped up from his seat and rushed back to help her to her feet. "Are you okay?"

"As relative to what?" she demanded, brushing off her jeans and straightening her sweater.

"As compared to, say, Ben over there," he said, jerking his thumb over his shoulder. "He recently got hit in the face with a hammer." Ben raised his middle finger. Patrick waved.

"Okay. Yeah. Better than that." She smoothed out her clothes and shook a hand through her hair. "Let's try this again. Hi! I'm Lindsay."

"Patrick," he said, shaking her hand. "And that's Ben. He's cranky. Are you the journalistic spirit whose presence was foretold to us?"

"You guys mind if I sit with you?"

"Not at all." They walked back to where Ben sat with his arms crossed. Patrick plopped back down beside him, and Lindsay took the row directly in front of them, kneeling in the seat, facing them with her arms on top of the headrest. By the time they were situated, the train was pulling out of the tunnel, and watery yellow light poured into the car. With all the darkness in the station and on the platform, Patrick had forgotten it wasn't quite nighttime yet. "And we're on our way," he said quietly. He learned forward and reached back to his rear pocket, felt for the slight outline of the folded piece of paper. It was still there, safe and secure. He fell back, closed his eyes, and smiled.

A speaker hidden somewhere in the ceiling crackled to life, and Horace's voice came through in a series of pops and clicks. "Good evening, ladies and gentlemen, this is your conductor speaking. This is train 315, southbound Texas Eagle to Los Angeles, making scheduled station stops in Bloomington/Normal, Springfield, St. Louis, Little Rock, Texarkana, Dallas, Temple, Austin, Tucson, and Yuma. If this is your first time riding with Amtrak since M-Day, please note several changes to our policies. There will be no food or beverage service on this train. There is no luggage steward. Guests are not free to walk between cars without the expressed permission of the conductor or his assistant. You may disembark the train at our scheduled station stops; however, if you are not back in the train car when we pull away from the station, you will be left behind. We'll give you fair warning before we pick up and move on. It may become necessary to stop the train between scheduled station stops. If this does happen during our trip, please remain in the car. There is no smoking aboard Amtrak trains. Please be sure to disembark the train at the agreed upon station. You are also free to disembark the train earlier, at your convenience, if it is convenient for you to jump from a moving train. On behalf of the Red Caps, the Assistant Conductor, and myself, thank you for riding Amtrak. Next station stop is Bloomington/Normal, Bloomington/Normal up next, approximately two hours." The speaker fizzled into silence.

Ben snorted. "Is that really necessary? I mean, he does know it's just us and his crew, right? He could just come back here and...you know... tell us."

"He does this every time we leave a major station," Lindsay said, rolling her eyes. "But, hey, he's a railroad man. That's how they used to do it. Old habits die hard. I mean, look at you two. It's hardly ever warmer than 50 degrees outside, a shaved head is *insanely* impractical. And your watch there. Self-winding? When's the last time you needed to know the time? It comes in handy for Horace the Tank Engine here, granted, but really? You don't need that. And me, I just snapped off a half-inch heel outside. Why in God's name am I wearing heels? It's dangerous out there, everything's fight or flight, and I'm a reporter. I'm a writer, not a fighter." She grinned, and Patrick could tell this wasn't the first time she's used that line. "I'll take flight every time, and how far am I gonna get on a half-inch heel? Not too far. We're all creatures of habit, all of us."

"Or sentiment," Patrick pointed out.

Lindsay, for whom sentiment was an afterthought at best, looked confused. "What do you mean?" Patrick held up his watch so she could inspect it more closely. It was a cheap kid's watch, something you used to be able to buy at Wal-Mart, with a purple plastic band, clasped near the very tip through a handmade hole. A Disney princess in a flowing yellow gown curtsied on the watch face. The plastic jewel was cracked, but Lindsay could still make out the digital time. As far as she could tell, it was accurate. She looked at Patrick quizzically.

"It was my daughter's," he explained. "You're right, it's not really practical, and it breaks the hell out of Rule Number 18, but it's a good memento. And hard to lose." He shook his wrist; the watch held strong.

"Has it always kept the right time?"

"Ever since we bought it, a few months before M-Day. You'd be surprised how much of something you can find when you're the only person looking for it," he said.

"Like watch batteries."

"Or Snack Packs," added Ben.

Lindsay threw back her head and moaned. "Oh, God, I miss Snack Packs!"

Ben's face soured. "Not me. They taste like chemical toilets."

"Delicious, delicious chemical toilets," Lindsay mused. "God. What I'd give for a Snickers stuffed inside a Twinkie dipped in a Snack Pack."

"Rule 31," said Patrick. "Never fantasize about food."

"Ugh. You're right. Now I'm depressed." She lowered her chin onto the headrest. "Where you guys headed?"

"Disney World. By way of St. Louis."

"Two very similar destinations," she said sarcastically. "Why the lay-over, what's in St. Louis?"

"An arch," said Ben.

"Maybe," Patrick pointed out.

"Maybe," Ben agreed. "If it hasn't keeled over."

"Busch Stadium," Patrick said.

"Budweiser."

"Schlafly."

"Lemp Mansion."

"Forest Park."

"Soulard."

"The Hill."

"Ooo, the Hill. Toasted ravioli."

"Imo's."

"Ted Drewes."

"Oh, *dios mio*, Ted Drewes!" cried Patrick.

"Rule 31," they both sighed.

"Is it safe to assume you're both from St. Louis?" They nodded. "Well, then, what about your families?" Lindsay asked. "Any idea if they're, uh..." She didn't need to finish the sentence. Patrick shook his head.

"No. No clue. For all I know they're living the good life, feasting on the neighbor's cows. Or the neighbors, for that matter. Or they could be liquefied on the love seat. I don't know. I'm not sure I want to know."

"Are you kidding me?" Lindsay bounded up out of her seat, fiddled underneath it until she found the lever she was looking for, and spun it around so she could face the two men. "I'd want to know. I'd really want to know. You know, for closure."

"*Do* you know?"

She nodded. "My parents are dead. Oh, but not from the Monkeys! They died a couple years before, in a gas leak."

"Oh, I'm so sorry," Patrick said. Lindsay smiled.

"People always say that when I tell them. Isn't that weird? There's not a single person in the country who didn't lose dozens of family members, friends, loved ones, co-workers, acquaintances...they all died really, *really* painful deaths. Everyone living in America, maybe the whole *world*, experienced excruciating loss on M-Day, yet everyone's first response when they hear my parents passed away painlessly and got spared the apocalypse is, 'I'm sorry.'"

"Old habits," Ben muttered.

"I'll drink to that," said Lindsay.

"Ooo! Yes, let's!" Patrick dug out his backpack and retrieved the bottle of Smirnov. "How do you feel about Russian white?" he said, handing the bottle to Lindsay.

"Well, normally I'd hold out for a sloe gin fizz, but hell, if vodka's all you've got..." She cracked open the cap and took a short swig. Her face twisted up in pain, and she fought to swallow the harsh liquor. "Gah!" she gasped, shaking her head. "I used to be a lot better at that." She handed the bottle back to Patrick, who took a shot before passing it on to Ben.

"So! You're a journalist," Patrick said, crossing his legs casually. "There a big market for that?"

"Ha! Less than ever. Man, I thought we were a dying breed *before* M-Day."

Ben took a thoughtful drink of the vodka. "But it has to exist in some form, doesn't it? News still happens, people still need to communicate, word has to spread. Journalism still exists if there are people to record events."

Lindsay looked at him in surprise. "Did you study journalism?"

"'Study' is one word for it. 'Enrolled in classes, then decided never to attend them unless blitzed out of my mind on Old Crow' is another one."

"That's at least, like, 87 words," Patrick pointed out.

"And here I thought you were probably just a racist, homophobic skinhead, but, in reality, you're an almost somewhat partially educated man!"

Ben leaned closer to Patrick. "Is she making fun of me?"

"Yes, that is absolutely what's happening right now," he nodded. Ben frowned.

"No, you're right. I'm sorry. You're totally right. I've met people who've gone back to handwritten newsletters. Five years ago newspapers were on the brink of extinction; now the Internet is dead and the printed word reigns supreme. It's really glorious, in that whole end-of-the-world-irony kind of way."

"Did any of the major publications survive?" Ben asked. "I mean, obviously they're not powering printing presses or anything, but I don't know...is TimeWarner still ruining peoples lives from Columbus Circle? Is CNN still making wildly incorrect statements in 140 characters or less? Is the Associated Press playing telephone with correspondents on horseback?"

"You want to know if there are any big stories being covered?" she asked.

"Well, that's nothing at all like what I asked, but sure. We'll go with that. Are there?"

She smiled confidently and traced her finger in little circles on the armrest. "There may be one or two especially enterprising young writers out there working on extremely vital news stories."

Patrick slapped his own armrest and said, "Okay, I'll bite. Lindsay, are you one of the enterprising writers working on vital news stories, and, if so, what vital news story are you working on?"

Lindsay looked up at them and grinned. "I thought you'd never ask.

"I'd lived in Manhattan for a few years before M-Day. Well, technically I was in Astoria, but it was the same thing, especially as far as my family in Dubuque was concerned. I definitely worked in Manhattan, though, eeking out a living at the *New York Post* as an entry-level beat writer. It was a stupid beat, really, covering the ridiculous world of American collectibles (yes, there's a beat for that), and the pay was laughable. Still, I was the only collectibles reporter in the galley, so I never fought for inches when there was a story worth covering, which, yeah, okay, didn't happen often. A feature story every time a new stamp was printed, fluff pieces on idiotic muscle head car shows on Coney Island, the occasional actual news coverage of a rare coin heist, God, at least those were engaging. The comic cons, ugh, they were the worst. All those fat nerds dressed up in latex and slobbering over Lucy Lawless. Let's just say it wasn't the investigative life I'd fantasized about at J-School.

"The beat did give me an opportunity or two, though. The editorial powers that be noticed my knowledge of antique pennies when they needed a new angle on the Peruvian copper mine disaster a few years back. Remember that? I'd written a story, okay, an admittedly mediocre story, about the potential impact on the penny, but that story had led to some *really* good inside info about the mine collapse itself, and when the rumors started flying that maybe the owner had set charges to bring down the mine, guess who they wanted to go investigate! Me! Well, me and three other writers, and two interns, but whatever! I was one of them! They even flew me to Peru, can you believe that? To some jungle village, and I had a translator, a photographer, the whole shebang. I'd written one hell of a piece on the disaster, one *hell* of a piece. I'd actually gotten a source to confirm that the owner was a documented shyster and amateur explosives enthusiast. It was a hell of a piece! Maybe you guys read it?" Patrick and Ben shook their heads. "Oh. Well, it was practically nominated for a Peabody." *Goddamn that Tillie.*

"But anyway, most stories weren't like that. Most were about obsessive introverts who couldn't give quotes for shit. Still, it was the *Post*. It's not like I was working for some art house basement press in the Bronx. Journalism was a tough nut to crack, and I cracked it. Maybe not wide open, but a little, around the edge. With hard work and determination and blah blah blah, I'd be hitting the editorial desk by middle age. Not too shabby!

"Then M-Day happened, and of course, everything changed."

"Of course."

"Of course!"

"Of course. I was in the newsroom when word of the Flying Monkeys started zipping around the office. At first we thought it was another stupid, baseless terrorism threat, 'Oh my God, we're bombing you, America, blah blah blah,' and no one really paid much attention. We got those calls all the time. But just after 3:00, Jimmy Wilson, this old, connected pro, received confirmation from a source in Washington. 'Confirmation' is a word you didn't just use in the newsroom. There was an attack coming, and, worst of all, it wasn't just imminent, it was literally happening *at that moment*. There were airborne missiles on their way. So we did what everyone else probably did. We lost our shit."

Patrick raised his hand. "I lost my shit."

Ben nodded. "I scattered my shit all over the place."

"There's no shame in lost shit. Please continue."

"Well, someone flipped the main newsroom monitor to ForceFeed, it's the Armed Forces Data and Information Feed, this pretty direct broadcast of info from joint military chiefs, right? They only used it to transmit information about national safety, but it was so damn censored, we usually didn't bother with it. I'd actually never seen it live before; the last time they turned it on was 9/11. I was still in Iowa then. It came through now, though; they were just broadcasting this huge mess of info.

"We couldn't believe it! The satellite video feed was literally *full* of these streaking white lines. Tens of thousands of missiles screaming through the air on their way to the U.S., all launched from Jamaica. Fucking *Jamaica*! Everyone knew it had to be a mistake, right? Some anonymous hackers playing hell with the live stream. No one had expected Jamaica to funnel its tourism funds into chemical weapon research and development, and, Christ, the sheer number of missiles! After everything was over, I talked to this one guy, this uptight military analyst, kind of a jackass, but anyway, he said Jamaica's biological warfare program must have been initiated in '63 or '64, right after they won their independence. How they found the resources to build a world-ending arsenal of chemical weapons, where they stored them, how they kept them secret, hell, why in God's name they designed them to look like fucking *monkeys*, who knows? No one knew *anything*, we just couldn't believe it!

"The *Post* building didn't take a Monkey, but I saw one slam into Rockefeller. They were small--I don't think many people remember that. Did you guys see any? Up close, I mean?" They both shook their heads.

"Not really," Patrick said. "I didn't know what was happening 'til the rockets had hit, and our building was clean."

"They were these small little rockets, so it's not like they took entire buildings down, obviously. The one I saw ripped a hole in the Rock big enough to drive a dump truck through, but it's not like the city was gonna get leveled. So we're watching, just totally open-mouthed, and this rocket slams into the side, and we're all scared shitless, and no one thinks, 'Hey, I should duck and cover,' but we should have, 'cause, shit, they could have been nuclear for all we knew. Not that ducking and covering would have helped much then anyway, but still. You'd think that would be your reaction, right? But we just watched, and when it hit the building, that giant yellow cloud just exploded right out of it. We thought it was fire smoke, 'cause fire makes yellow smoke, right? Yeah, I know. Real brilliant. But we didn't know *what* to think. And rockets were screaming across the sky, you could hear them slamming into buildings all down Fifth Ave. Once we heard this massive shattering sound, like someone had just broken a window over our heads. I think that was Times Square.

"Then the yellow clouds were everywhere, thick and bright and weird, like a nuclear Big Bird was molting dust. So weird. Then it was in our ventilation system, and the whole newsroom was covered in Monkey dust. I should've been terrified, I don't know why I wasn't, I guess it was more confusing than anything. What did I know about chemical warfare? I mean, I know it *now*, you see a puff of weird-colored dust puff out from a bomb, you get the bejesus out of Dodge. But back then, I remember thinking, 'Huh. This is so weird.' Like I was numb, you know? I was covered in this dust, and I sneezed a few times, but otherwise, I was fine. What the hell, right?

"Remember how no one screamed? From the Monkey dust, I mean. People screamed their damn heads off when the bombs came, or just out of sheer confusion. Manhattan was a fucking nightmare, cars piling up in the streets, and eight million people jamming the sidewalks. It was trash day in midtown too, so you had all these people walled in by garbage bags, trying to shove their way through. I saw it all from the window; there was this one woman who got trapped under a garbage avalanche. I don't know if she got smothered or if the dust got her, but she didn't get up. It was awful," she said. She paused, chewing on her bottom lip. "What was I talking about?"

"Screaming," Ben said. "Specifically, the lack thereof."

"Oh! Screaming. Yeah, remember that? I guess the chemical ate through the vocal chords too quickly. It all acted so fast. So I'm standing at the window, watching the chaos outside, just in total awe, you know? I didn't notice people around me were dropping dead; they weren't making any noise. It was probably three or four whole minutes before I turned to say something to my friend Nikki. I'll never forget that, that milky blood goo pouring out of her nose and her ears, then just out of her pores, all of a sudden, like someone had dumped a bucket of Big Mac sauce on her head. Her eyes, geez, they just *popped*, and she was clutching her stomach, it got all distended, started sloshing around. What kind of powder liquefies a person's organs? Who would *make* something like that? It makes me sick, just thinking about it. And no one screamed. They just...melted.

"Anyway, later, when the smoke cleared, so to speak (not literally, of course), there was practically no one left in New York. I mean, *no one*. They say 95% of the U.S. population died as a result from the attacks. In New York, it was easily over 99%. *Easily*. Manhattan was a ghost town. I stayed there for three months after M-Day, three whole months, and I literally saw seventeen other survivors. Seventeen, out of eight million. I'm sure there were more around the island and holed up in their apartments, but you get the idea. I doubt there were more than a few thousand, citywide.

"Which leads me to my story. I came across it by accident, really. So much had happened, and work was the furthest thing from my mind. The entire world had ended." She snapped her fingers. "Just like that. Just 90 minutes, and it was over. I remember on my way out of the *Post* building that day, I passed this huge office full of Internet servers, and there was smoke just pouring out from under the door. Not Monkey dust, legitimate fire smoke. Turns out the super ventilating fans actually helped suck the dust *into* the server room. Brilliant, right? The servers got jammed, overheated, and basically melted, just like the people. And the streets were jammed with cars and rubble, there were sticky remains everywhere, you couldn't take a step without having to pull your shoe free of the goo, it was awful. So I wasn't thinking about work, not at all.

"I joined this little survival camp of eight other people. I didn't know any of them, we just came across each other, but we figured it was smart to stick together. Hell, we didn't know what was going on, if we were about to be invaded by Jamaicans, or attacked by zombies, or who knew what else? Safety in numbers, though, right? So the nine of us stuck together for a few months. You get in a group of strangers like that, it's not long before you're making the old small talk...old habits...and someone started asking where everyone was from. There was this middle-aged couple, Jan and Harlan, they were from La Crosse, Wisconsin. There was an actress from Baton Rouge, a stock broker from Sikeston, Missouri, a PR guy from outside Davenport, a musician from Memphis, this woman from Hannibal, Missouri, I'm not sure what she did. Then there was a waitress from Eudora, Arkansas, and I'm from Dubuque. So what, right?

It was all polite nods and 'Oh, I've heard nice things about Baton Rouge.' Three months passed, and I didn't think any more about it, 'til some of us decided to split off and venture out of New York. It was pretty obvious by then that no one was coming to get us. The waitress made some joke about all of us visiting each other in our hometowns 'when this is all over.' It's a stupid idea, but you find encouragement in the dumbest things sometimes. So we all said sure, it's a date. I even scrounged up an atlas from a newsstand and marked the towns. When I was done, we all looked at it, I even had to double check with everyone about the geography, it was so weird. All eight towns more or less lined up in a straight vertical line running the length of the Midwest. We were all originally from the same longitude. And I'm like, what are the odds?

"I set out the next morning, headed I don't know where. West, mostly, to try to see if I could make it home. Out of curiosity, I asked everyone I met along the way where they were from. Where they were born. They'd tell me, and I'd mark it on the map. St. Louis. New Orleans. Quincy. Cape Girardeau. West Memphis. Every single person I met was from the exactly same vertical line on the map! I mean, geez, look at this thing!" She pulled a dirty, torn booklet from her bag and flipped it open to a heavily marked page. Small red dots covered the entire Midwest. "There's a river of red running from Minneapolis to the Gulf! You guys, I think that every single survivor of the apocalypse was born and raised along the Mississippi River."

"Oh, come on," Ben said. "That's ridiculous. Every single one?"

Lindsay nodded. "Every single one."

Patrick turned to the Red Cap who was still standing at the rear entrance of the car. "Say, chief! Where are you from? Originally?"

"Dakota, Minnesota."

"I like it. It rhymes. Is it near the Mississip?" The Red Cap nodded. Patrick slapped the armrest. "Proof! Irrefutable proof! We're all from Big Muddy."

"How does that even make sense?" Ben asked.

"Exactly! And that's the focus of my story! I've spent the last year working my ass off to find one single survivor who *didn't* grow up within fifty miles of the Mississippi. I've met thousands of people. *Thousands.* They're *all* from the river area. The train has been great, I've ridden out to L.A., and there's another operational line there that goes up to Seattle.

The farther you get from the Midwest, the less people there are, and all transplants."

Patrick looked deep in thought. "So what, something in the water made us all immune?"

Lindsay clapped her hands together in delight. "Exactly!"

"It would've had to have been something that made it through the various filtration systems," he said, his eyes starting to come to light. "Let me take a look at that map." Lindsay handed it to him, and he traced his finger to the northern-most dot of red. "What's this place?"

"That's Maiden Rock, Wisconsin."

"So the survivors start there," Patrick murmured. "Whatever went into the water must have dumped in just upriver."

"If that really is the northernmost origin of survival," Lindsay pointed out. "Who knows how many survivors are out there, I've only met so many." She was testing him, but she couldn't help it.

"Yeah, but if you go too far, you hit Minneapolis-St. Paul. That's a pretty big metropolis, odds are, with your sample size, you'd find *someone* who grew up in that region."

She beamed. "You know, it took me almost a whole week to reason that out. I mean, it's just a theory, but it makes sense."

"You could say it holds water," Ben said, grinning. Patrick and Lindsay did not grin. "You know. 'Cause it's about a river. Holds water? Whatever, screw you guys." He took another slug of vodka.

"Quiet, Ben, the grown-ups are talking." Patrick handed the map back to Lindsay. "Have you been up there yet?"

"Yep, last month."

"What'd you find? Please tell me there's a hunched over bald man in a black cloak who dumps toxic green waste into the river once a day and periodically gets his ass kicked by a green mulleted superhero," Patrick said, his fists clenched in excitement.

"Did you just mash up Smurfs and Captain Planet?" Ben asked.

"I did! You got it! High five!" They slapped hands.

"You guys are so weird," Lindsay observed. She shook her head. "Anyway, there are four big industrial buildings on the river between Maiden Rock and St. Paul, a plastics factory, an ironworks, a computer hardware factory, and a freakishly large undertaker operation."

Ben started. "An undertaker 'operation'? What, like a death factory?"

"Sort of."

"They dumped their bodies in the river?"

"Not bodies. Ashes. The cremation chambers emptied into the septic system." Patrick and Ben both stuck their tongues out in disgust.

"We grew up drinking human body ash water?" Ben asked.

"Oh, that's the least of it. You don't even want to know what I found in La Crosse."

"How old are they?" Patrick asked.

"Who?"

"The factories, how old are they?"

"I don't know. I guess judging by the looks, I'd say the ironworks and the undertakers have been there the longest, the other two seemed relatively newer. Why?"

"If you were finding middle-aged survivors in New York, whatever was pumping our salvation into the river must have been doing it when they were small, decades ago. Have you seen any small children on your travels? Not newborns, but say, three- or four-year-olds?"

"Yeah, I have," she said. She began to see a few more pieces of the puzzle start to drift together. "So...the source of immunity has been dumping steadily for at least the last several decades..."

"...Which rules out any older factories that went out of operation before M-Day," Patrick finished. "Given what we have to go on, it looks like either the ironworks or the undertakers are responsible for immunizing us all."

"So we're smelted people drinkers," Ben groaned, slumping back in his chair. Lindsay did the same.

"I wonder what chemicals they use to prepare bodies for cremation," Patrick mused, stroking his chin. "Who would've thought? Cannibalism might have saved our lives."

4.

Bloom stared out the window at the cold, empty fields, his view curtly blunted by the fog. At sunset, the sickly yellow hue became flushed with bright pink. It was like passing through cotton candy. The train whipped through the smog, sending it swirling off over the stubbly, hard ground as they raced past. The Illinois landscape was a cruel beauty. He gripped the curtain and slid it shut.

Bloom spent less and less time in the engine these days. More often than not, there wasn't much point. Horace only handed over the controls when he needed to sleep or shit. He could be a real prick like that. Bloom spent most of his time in the Business Class car, surrounded by the same six or seven Red Caps, his personal coterie.

The Business car suited him fine. He was actually starting to prefer it over the engine. The seats were comfortable, the company was better, and the bar was only a few steps away. He swirled the whiskey in his glass. The clink of the ice cubes soothed him, helped him focus on the upcoming job. By his estimation, they had just over an hour until the Bloomington/Normal station. The job would probably take another two hours, and, hell, by the time they loaded the cargo into the secure car? It'd be after midnight before it was all said and done, so Bloom would need to moderate his drinking. But a couple glasses never hurt anyone. "Who's our contact in Bloomington?" he asked the Red Cap across the aisle.

The lackey had his cap pulled low over his eyes and his legs slung over the armrest, dangling out into the aisle. He grinned his perpetual grin, his sharp teeth flashing in the watery orange interior light. "Man named Simms," he said in his thick Southern drawl. "Bradley Simms."

"Simms," Bloom repeated, slowly and thoughtfully. He sipped from his glass, letting the warm, smoky alcohol evaporate on his tongue. "Have we done business with him before?"

Calico shook his head. "Nope. Horace found him. He don't know him, though. Just got connected up with him someways."

This wasn't surprising to Bloom, though he wasn't exactly happy to hear it. Horace liked to act on every tip he got, if he thought the train could benefit. Greedy fucker. Except he wasn't the one doing the acting; he left that for Bloom and his men. It was far easier to send others into the darkness than to lead the way yourself. "We'll need the cavalry, then. Bulaski, you stay here and keep an eye on things. The rest of you will come along. I want everyone fully armed. Let Horace's Caps handle the cargo. I want each of you stepping out of here with weapons in hand." The Red Caps nodded. Bloom nodded back, surveying them all with his calm, expressionless eyes. "Head back to the cargo hold. Make sure we're all set. Calico, you stay here. The rest of you, get moving." The Red Caps stood and obediently filed out of the car. Bloom shifted his gaze to the man stretched lazily across the seats in the back. "We've got some things to discuss," he said. Calico flashed his teeth from under the brim of his cap.

•

It was full dark by the time they reached the first station. Patrick had dozed off, but the sudden, jerking halt of the train shook him awake. "Mm? Pizza?" he asked, rubbing his sleepy eyes. He looked around and remembered where he was. "Mm. No pizza," he said sadly. He stretched his arms back over his head and yawned hugely. He cracked his neck with a few quick flicks of his head. Through his slowly focusing eyes, he saw Ben standing at a window a few rows down. "What's going on?" he asked.

"Station stop," said Lindsay from the other end of the car.

"Horace is talking to a sad looking guy with a beard," Ben explained. He could do without the sadness, but he secretly yearned for a beard of such wonderful proportions.

"That's Bloom," Lindsay said, "the Assistant Conductor."

Patrick joined them on the other side. He peered down through the windows and gasped. "Campfires!" He pressed his hands and face against the glass. Six low fires burned brightly against the inky darkness. It had been ages since he'd seen a controlled fire! "Ben! Quick! Grab some chili and meet me outside! Bring ghost stories!" He tripped over his own feet scrambling out of the seats and sprawled into the aisle. "Ow," he whined.

"Pat, you *might* not want to go out there."

"Of course I want to go out there! They have fires! You know I love a good fire, Ben. You *know* that."

"Yeah, but look who's sitting *around* those fires."

Patrick glowered. He had a strong foreboding that Ben was about to ruin fires for him in a big way. He edged his way back over a pair of seats to a window and looked more closely down at the flames. He gasped again. "Oh my God," he breathed. "Hippies."

"*Lots* of hippies," Ben corrected.

Patrick turned from the disgusting sight and slumped back against the glass. "Why did it have to be hippies?" he mourned.

Lindsay rolled her eyes. "They're not hippies. They're just really dirty college students." She grabbed her notebook and hustled past Patrick. "Really dirty college students who are gonna spill their guts to me." She disappeared down the metal stairs.

Ben started. "College students? Oh God, it's even worse than I thought." He looked over at Patrick. "What do you think?"

Patrick weighed his options. On the one hand, he hated both hippies *and* smug college students, especially the dirty ones. They smelled like sweat, patchouli, and constant disappointment. On the other hand, he really loved fires, possibly more than he hated hippies and college students, and he suddenly remembered that he hadn't eaten since the Snack Pack that morning. His distaste for opinionated young gadabouts was a matter of preference, but his need for hot chili was bordering on survival necessity. He begrudgingly kowtowed to Rule Number 1: *Survive.*

"I guess we go out there," he said miserably, "'cause I don't think they're gonna let us start a fire in the train. But I tell thee this, Benjamin Judith Fogelvee. I am taking my machete, and if I hear one of them, just *one* of them, complain about the one percent, so help me, I will butcher those hippies like it was *Mercenary Christmas.*" *Mercenary Christmas* was the title of the video game he and Ben had developed a few years earlier. Neither of them was a video game developer; thus far, it was a "concept only" piece.

"Fine. But remember, this is your idea. If they dreadlock my hair and make me play Hacky Sack, I'm holding you responsible, and I will personally urinate in your food." Ben crossed his arms. He'd done it before. He'd do it again.

"You don't have any hair to dreadlock," Patrick pointed out.

Ben scowled. "Don't you play dumb with me, Patrick Deen," he warned. "Don't you dare."

They each grabbed a can of chili from Ben's pack. Ben armed himself with the bat. He gave it a few practice swings, preparing himself, just in case. Patrick swiped the can opener from his own bag and slung the machete over his back. On his way toward the exit, he glanced back out the window and did a quick headcount of all the dirty hippies mellowing around the fires. "Holy Lord, they outnumber the Red Caps." He ran back to his bag and pulled out the hammer and the baton and tossed the knife to Ben. "Can't be too careful," he said. Then they lowered themselves from the train car and ventured forth among the unclean.

•

There was something coldly beautiful about an abandoned college campus. The silent stately architecture, the ghostly statues, the open Quad, littered with trash and debris but largely unmarked by human tread. When full of hormonal teenagers, a university was a ludicrous place, a hovel of fornication and desperation. Institutions of higher learning ought to be revered as hallowed bethels. Instead, they became little more than expansive toilets for lazy, drug-addled children of privilege. It was precisely this saturation of immoral self-indulgence that drove Bloom from formal education so many years ago. University life had deteriorated the university, but now, with scores of college students scoured from the earth, academic institutions had regained some aspect of their stolen grandeur. *One could actually learn in this place*, Bloom thought, striding purposefully across the Illinois State University campus. But then again, what was there left to learn?

They crossed the Quad, Calico at the point, Bloom's remaining six Red Caps fanned out behind him, weapons brandished. They formed a well-armed wedge around Bloom and Horace's Red Caps, Louis and Stevens, who struggled with a rolling cart tied down with piles of books. The wheels kept rolling off the paved path, into the soft earth. The ground was still slick with the stubborn coating of melted bodies, even after all these years.

"That's DeGarmo, straight ahead," said one of Bloom's lot, a promising new recruit named Hammock.

"Yes. The sign was a dead giveaway," said Bloom dryly.

Promising, but not quite there.

DeGarmo Hall loomed above them, an unassuming block of a building. Four brick pillars served as the building's four corners, supporting what had once been solid walls of glass. Most of the panes had been shattered, and DeGarmo looked more like an oversized pavilion than an academic building. A fire flickered inside, throwing long shadows that pricked at the Quad. Calico gave the signal to halt, and the party stopped and listened. The only sound was the occasional pop of the fire. Calico turned to Bloom.

"How ya wanna handle this, boss?" he grinned.

"Hammock and Ryan, you stay outside, guard the entrance. Louis, Stevens, keep the books out here until we give you the okay. The rest of us go in, staggered. Understand?" There were nods all around. "The man we're meeting is named Bradley Simms. It should be a straight transaction, but we don't know anything about him. Be on your guard." Bloom pulled his sabre from the scabbard at his waist. The long, curved blade glowed orange with firelight. "Let's go."

They stepped cautiously into the building. Blackened metal bookshelves littered the ground, covering piles of charred, paperless spines and mounds of ashes. They crunched over the burned rubble toward the fire that crackled in the center of the room. A solitary man sat before it, the flames reflecting brightly off his round glasses. He had thinning brown hair but a boyish face, despite, or perhaps because of, the uneven stubble that sprouted under his cheeks. He wore what appeared to be pressed corduroy pants and a white collared shirt under a dark quarter-zip sweater. He turned and stood at the sound of their approach.

"Mister Bloom, I presume?" he asked, his enunciation crisp, his tone mellow.

"Simms?" Bloom asked.

"Professor Simms, yes. Please, have a seat, join me." He indicated a circular clearing around the fire.

"We'll stand," Calico said, his sharp teeth flashing in the firelight. He tapped his bludgeon against his thigh, to the tune of "Camptown Races," if Bloom wasn't mistaken.

"If you'd rather. You brought my books?"

"They're outside," said Bloom. "And you have our weapons?"

"Of course. Could I see the books, then?"

Bloom didn't take the man to be much of a threat. He was skinny, and he didn't appear to be armed. Which was ironic, given the number of weapons he was trading for the books. "Are you alone?"

"Blissfully so," Simms mused. "There's a small group of janitors who sometimes hole up in the recreation building, but if you didn't pass anyone on the Quad, then I'm the only one for several hundred yards. As requested," he added sharply. "Which is more than I can say for you and your armed guard."

"Hold up your end of the deal, and it won't matter how many we are," Bloom said simply.

Simms seemed to be growing uneasy. "Show me the books, please." Bloom turned and signaled toward the door. He sent Hammock back to clear a path through the fallen bookshelves. Metal scraped metal as he heaved the twisted wrecks out of the way. Louis and Stevens struggled with the wheels to get them to move through the piles of ash.

"What happened to this place?" Bloom asked as his men fought with the cart.

"Yeah," said Calico with a leer. "You like books so much, you shouldn't burn 'em,"

Simms glowered. "The library was sacked by students after M-Day. Ungrateful Philistines. They took some sort of perverse pleasure in destroying the books they'd been required to read during their time here. This library once held more than half a million books. Less than 30 survived the fire intact."

"And you sleep in the ashes." Calico smiled under his cap.

Simms turned his sharp eyes on Bloom's second-in-command. "I do not. But it seemed a fitting place to make the exchange."

"A fitting place would have smooth floors," Bloom said as Louis and Stevens rolled the cart to a stop behind him, sucking air.

Simms seemed not to hear him. He rubbed his hands together as he stepped forward to examine the books. He ran his finger down the spines of each stack. "Kraszewski...Judson...Updike...Dumas...Spinoza..." he read, his voice now calm. "An eclectic collection, at least." Bloom raised his eyes to Calico.

"Weapons," Calico said.

"Yes, of course, of course," Simms mumbled, leafing through a small hardcover. "Right over there. Under that shelf," he directed with a nod. Calico crossed to a bookshelf lying flat on its face. With a surprisingly graceful strength, he tossed the metal structure off to the side, revealing a small arsenal. Bloom sheathed his sabre and stepped in to examine the weapons. They were old, some probably even older than this great state of Illinois. There were heavy wooden clubs worn in at the grip, spears fitted with hand-cut arrowheads, and over a dozen hatchets and toma-hawks with chipped blades.

"This is everything?"

"It's all that's left of the museum's collection. I trust they're up to your high standards," Simms said.

"If they're good enough for Indians, they're good enough for us," Calico said, picking up a tomahawk. He chopped it through the air. "It'll do," he grinned.

Bloom nodded at his Red Caps. "Load them."

They loosed the knots and unpacked the stacks of books from the cart, tossing them carelessly in a heap despite Simms' loud and angry protestations. Then they gathered up the weapons, tossed them onto the platform, and tied them down.

"Let me ask you a question," Calico said. He lifted the brim of his cap, and even in the darkness, Bloom could see the grave distinction between his crystal blue left eye and his dark brown right. So could Simms; he blanched when he saw the unnerving discoloration. Calico showed his teeth and flipped the tomahawk in his hand. "Why you givin' up these weapons? These days, most people would kill for a blade like this," he said.

Simms lifted his chin in a show of calm superiority, despite his sudden pallor. "The sharpest weapon in the world is no match for a sharp mind," he answered, hugging a book to his chest with one hand and tapping his forehead with the other.

"Oh, I don't know if that's true," said Bloom. In one fluid motion, he slid the sabre from the scabbard and slashed it through the air. A thin red line appeared across Simms' neck. His eyes widened in shock. The cut split open, and a thick spray of blood burst from his throat, black and steaming in the cold night. His lips worked soundlessly. Blood gushed as he crumpled to his knees. His eyes rolled up in their sockets, and he collapsed face-first into a pile of ashes.

"Jesus, Bloom," Louis cried, "what did you *do*?"

Bloom stepped forward and wiped the blade clean on Simms' sweater. "I didn't have a choice. He attacked me." He slid the blade back into the scabbard and turned to face Horace's Red Caps. "Then his men attacked you."

Calico moved like lightning. He leapt into the air, ramped off a fallen bookshelf, and brought the tomahawk down on the crown of Louis' head. It split the cap and buried deep into his skull with a soft *thunk*. In the same motion, he whirled around to the cart and slipped a heavy club from beneath the ropes. He spun back, club held high, and brought it down hard into Stevens' cheekbone. The Red Cap screamed in pain and crumpled to the ground, legs thrashing, hands covering the gushing would on his face. Calico stood over him, grinning, and took the club in both hands. He raised it high over his head, then smashed it down on Stevens' face, again and again. After the third swing, Stevens stopped screaming. Calico pounded the man's broken hands into his own sinus cavity, gore and chunks of bone shooting through the air and sticking to the wooden club. With a final blow, he caved in Steven's forehead, sending brain matter squelching out of the eye sockets. Calico stood up tall, covered in blood, breathing heavily and smiling. "Weapons win," he said with a wink.

Bloom signaled to Hammock. "You. You're off the train. This stop is yours. Stay here, secure the campus. Start with the recreation building. Put down anyone who gets in the way."

Hammock beamed at the honor. "Yes, sir! And what do we do with these books?"

Bloom lowered his calm gaze to the little pile. "Burn them."

•

Ben felt pretty damn good. He had a full can of chili and almost a third of a bottle of vodka in his belly, and between the hot food, the booze, and the fire, he was warm, inside and out, for the first time in years. The company wasn't so bad, either. Lindsay was right, the hippies weren't really *that* hippyish, mostly just even-tempered college kids. No one seemed interested in discussing their favorite obscure Swedish indie band, and not a single one of them owned a Hacky Sack. They'd dodged a bullet there. A few of the kids at their fire were actually pretty funny, and it was nice to be outside, looking up at where the stars would be if they could see through the fog. Even a dark haze was better than the stucco condo ceiling. The air outside was fresh, by post-apocalyptic standards, and the way people laughed and told stories around the fire, hell, it was almost like old times. Just a few square miles from normal. His face still hurt like a mother, despite the alcohol, and he was still going to kick Patrick squarely in the balls as soon as he got a clear shot, but, all in all, things were good.

The kids around their fire called it a night. They wished the travelers well, then scooted out into the darkness, toward the campus. Ben passed the vodka to Patrick, who took a long swig. He was turning red in the cheeks, a good sign that he'd had almost enough to start making a fool out of himself. That made Ben happy too. No one made a drunken fool out of himself like Patrick made a drunken fool out of himself. Patrick turned to hand the bottle to Lindsay, but she was suddenly gone. "Hey. Where'd she go?" he asked.

"She's over there, talking to the Ruby Slipper Gang," he said, pointing to a group of girls around the fire, each one of whom wore her hair in braided pigtails.

"Man," Patrick said, blinking hard. "She talks a *lot*."

Ben nodded vigorously. "Yeah, she does. I thought journalists were supposed to be good at listening."

"I know, right? I mean, don't get me wrong. She's totally nice." Patrick tipped back the bottle, then handed it to Ben.

"Oh, yeah, sure, no, she's nice," Ben agreed wholeheartedly. "I just don't really want her to talk anymore. Is that a mean thing to say?"

"No-no-no-no-no," Patrick said. "It's the right thing to say, you know why? You know why? 'Cause it's the *truth*. And the truth is always right."

"Yeah," Ben slurred. "We're right." He gazed thoughtfully into the fire, blowing across the mouth of the bottle. The low *wooooooooooo* carried across the platform. Someone with another bottle at another fire answered with a higher-pitched *woooooooooo*. Ben raised the bottle to toast his new friend. "The Red Caps seem to like her," he observed.

"Who?"

"The Red Caps."

"No, they seem to like who?"

"Whom."

Patrick sighed. "They seem to like *whom*?"

"Lindsay."

"Ah!" Patrick slapped his knees with his hands. "Yes. They do. You know why? Because she is a female who does not ignore them. That's a Red Cap's kryptonite."

Ben pondered this for a moment. "That sounds like *my* kryptonite," he said.

"It's *all* men's kryptonite," Pat admitted. "If it looks like a woman, and smells like a woman, and talks like a woman, and is a woman, we like getting attention from it."

"Until we get too much attention from it," Ben added.

"Yes. There's a fine line there. Not many women can walk it."

"I should date a tightrope walker," Ben mused. "That would be stupid hot."

"Are you sure you're not thinking about a contortionist?" Patrick asked, squinting into the fire. "That's the hot kind of circus performer. Tightrope walkers are just regular people who can walk a straight line. They're like sober versions of me. But contortionists! *Ooo-wee!*"

"What do you think it would be like to date a fire eater?" Ben asked. "Do you think she would taste like gasoline?"

Patrick squinted at his friend. "Why would she taste like gasoline?"

"Because that's what they put in their mouths. To spit fire."

"Wow, no, that is extremely wrong. *Extremely* wrong. Gasoline is definitely not what they use."

"Yes, it is," Ben insisted. "It's flammable."

"Yes, it is flammable. Highly flammable. If they put gasoline in their mouths and spit it onto fire, their heads would literally explode. They use paraffin."

"How do you know that?"

"How *do* I know that?" he frowned. "Oh! I learned it! In Coney Island, at the freak show."

"I want to go to Coney Island," Ben complained.

"No, you don't. No one wants to go to Coney Island."

"Well, whatever. Do you think she'd taste like paraffin?"

"You mean...in the mouth? Or...?"

"Yes, you moron, obviously, in the mouth," Ben said. "Unless... hmm..." He sat back and sipped thoughtfully.

Patrick shrugged. "She probably would. Unless you kissed her while she was spitting fire. Then it would still taste like paraffin, but really *spicy* paraffin."

Ben snickered. He didn't know why that was so funny. It was probably one of Patrick's least funny jokes. And the man told a *lot* of unfunny jokes. Still, Ben laughed. It just felt so good to be sitting outside, drinking by a fire. It reminded him of grade school.

"Why do they let her move through the train?" he asked.

"Who? The contortionist?" Patrick made grabby hands for the bottle. "*Bemme.*" Ben obliged him.

"No, Lindsay. How come she gets to move around, and we don't?"

"I don't know, Benny Boy, but I tell you what. That train car is *boring.*" Ben nodded. That train car *was* boring. He was glad they were only taking it as far as St. Louis. He wasn't sure exactly how they were going to transport themselves the rest of the way to Orlando, but he was glad it wouldn't be in the train.

"Last time I rode Amtrak, they let you move around all you want," Patrick said. "This new Amtrak is bullshit. No food service? Really? I demand my microwavable cheeseburger in a bag!" he cried, stomping his foot. A few kids from the other fires glanced their way, concerned. Patrick smiled and waved to them. He pointed to the bottle, then made the universal hand sign for *Oh, it's fine.*

Ben picked up a twig from the nearby woodpile and held it into the fire. When the tip caught, he pulled it out, blew out the flame, and waved the ember-tipped stick through the air, making streaking light patterns in the darkness. "It's weird that we can't move around. Do you think they're hiding something from us?"

Patrick crossed his legs and leaned forward. "I'm glad you asked. The thought had crossed my mind. Exhibit A. Did you see the load of books those Caps carted off when we stopped? Where did those books come from?" Ben shrugged. "I'll tell you where. They came from that train." He pointed dramatically to the engine behind them. "Do you know what that means?"

Ben thought hard. The edges of his brain were starting to go soft, and reasoning was becoming a chore. "Amtrak employees are really well read?"

"No. Well, maybe. Yes. Possibly. Also, one of these cars is being used to store things. Wonderful things, like books. And who knows what else."

Ben beckoned for the bottle. "What's your point?"

Patrick threw up his hands in exasperation. "My point is, our fearless leader has a car full of treasure, and he's actively trying to keep us away from it. And if spending several years as a child who anticipated Christmas taught me anything, it's that if someone's trying to keep you out of a storage closet, it's because there's a very wonderful present inside."

Ben sat up straight. "You think they have something wonderful inside?"

"I do," Patrick said smugly, crossing his arms.

"Like a helicopter or something?"

"Well, not that wonderful. Something a little more modestly sized."

"What do you think it is?"

"I have no idea. But I think we've earned the right to find out."

Ben took a sip and realized that he thought they should find out, too. It wasn't fair, their being quarantined to the one railcar, when literally everyone else on the train got to roam around as they liked. Even Lindsay! Why did *she* get to visit the storage car? She was a journalist, someone whose career was built upon being nosy and pushy and expository. But she could be trusted with the storage car, and they couldn't? Absurd! It had to be an oversight. He said as much to Patrick. "Maybe we should just ask Horace if we can look around."

"No way!" Patrick shook his head so hard it practically fell off. "That's a sure way to make him think that we want to take a look around."

Ben was confused. "I know. That's what I'm saying. If he knows we want to look around, maybe he'll let us look around."

"No, you clod! If he knows we want to look around, then he'll try even harder to make sure we *don't* look around. We'll have a full-on Red Cap army guarding our seats. Is that what you want? To bring the entire Red army into our car? To ride to St. Louis in the Communist country of train cars?"

Ben had to admit that nothing about that sounded particularly fun. He was having trouble remembering specifics about Communists at the moment, but he had a vague recollection that they wore military lapels and beat people about the face with large automatic weapons. "No," he said, "I guess not."

Patrick closed his eyes and tipped his round head back. With his legs crossed and his thin hands on his bony knees, he looked like a disproportionate yogi searching for enlightenment. He inhaled deeply. In doing so, he sucked down a lungful of wood smoke and convulsed into a fit of coughing and choking. Ben jumped up and started *whapping* him on the back. Patrick's face turned bright red. His eyes streamed water. He pointed to the bottle of vodka. Ben handed it to him. He took a huge gulp and stopped coughing immediately. Lindsay craned her neck from across the platform and looked over with a combination of concern and pity. Patrick gave her the thumb's up.

"Jesus, are you okay?" Ben asked.

Patrick wiped his eyes with his sleeve. "I'm more than okay, Ben. I just had a spirit vision."

Ben looked around. He didn't see any spirits. "What, just now?"

Patrick nodded. "It came to me in the smoke. It was the spirit of the Illinois."

"The state?"

"The culture."

"Did he smell like corn?"

"She, Ben. It was a she."

"Did she smell like corn?"

"No, she did not. She smelled like glory."

"What did she say?"

"She told me that the last train car is the storage car, and that within that storage car, there are great wonders to behold. She told me I would see inside that storage car because it is my destiny. And she told me how I would do it."

Ben had to admit, he was impressed. "She said all that?"

"Yes."

"So how do you do it?"

"First, we get our hands on that cooking oil in the engine. You'll need it to create a diversion."

•

Horace flipped the page on his clipboard and continued down the list. Seven four-ounce containers of salt. *Check.* Two cases of 20 ounce red Solo brand plastic cups. *Check.* Five walkie talkies, sans batteries. *Check.* 57 packets of DeKalb corn seed. He counted 54. He counted a second time and got 55. He counted a third time. 55. He counted a fourth time. Satisfied, he made two red marks next to the line item on his sheet. Hopefully, the two missing packets had slipped off the shelves at a lurch. He'd check when he was done with the inventory. If he couldn't find them, they'd have a round-up in Springfield, and that would put the train behind schedule.

He moved to the next shelf. 15 used pocketknives, varying sizes and conditions. *Check.* One coil of wire, 7 feet long. The coil was present, but there was no way to measure its length without unspooling it. He picked it up and examined the tip. It showed a clean cut and was still black from where he'd burned it when he first entered it into the list. If someone had snipped off a length, he had done so with a sharp pair of wire cutters, the likes of which didn't exist on the train, as far as Horace knew, and had duplicated the burn mark, something almost no one would even think to check for in the first place. The odds of it happening were slim. Satisfied, he scribbled a checkmark on the list.

Horace enjoyed doing inventory. It calmed him. He didn't need to think in order to check their stores, and that lack of mental machination was exactly what he needed right now. Because if he started thinking, he would think about his frustration with Bloom, and the more he thought about his frustration with Bloom, the more likely he would be to blow up at him in front of the men when he returned, and one thing a conductor does not do is belittle his Assistant Conductor in front of the Red Caps. He and Bloom would have a calm, civilized, and, most importantly, private chat when he returned.

Horace checked his watch. Bloom and his men should have been back twenty minutes ago. It was a simple exchange, and the campus practically bordered the train station. His temper flared. He took five deep breaths, his heavy exhales fluttering the handles of his mustache. He still had a little over ten minutes before Bloom's inattention to time would put them behind schedule. With time to load the new weapons, gather the passengers, secure the train, and fire the engine, they would be cutting it close. They could probably make up some time on the way, but you never knew what was waiting for you on the tracks these days. Not having a safety cushion annoyed him to no end.

He moved on to the next shelving unit, standing on the tips of his toes in order to peer over the top shelf. He continued marking his marks but found himself idly wondering about the new passenger's progress on the hydraulic battering ram. He'd hoped to sit down with the young man and have a chat during this stop, but he was so irritated by the argument he'd had with Bloom before he and his men headed to the campus that he decided to do an inventory instead. It was in need of doing anyway, especially if there were two seed packs missing. He'd grab a few minutes with Patrick--was that his name? Patrick?--during the Springfield station stop. If they could still *afford* a Springfield station stop.

He finished the inventory quickly and methodically. He hung the clipboard on the hook by the front car entrance, then he returned to the middle row of shelves and lowered himself to all fours. He peered under the shelf but could see nothing in the darkness. He stuck his hand underneath it and wiped it along the floor, brushing away grit and dust bunnies and--ah! There! He slid the two rogue seed packs out and replaced them on their rightful shelf. He walked back to the list by the door and scratched out the two marks next to the seed entry. Satisfied, he crossed to the back of the car, where his cap rested on the stack of milk crates that served as his desk. He pulled out his watch once again and checked the time. His insides boiled, but he fought to retain his calm. One of the men might be watching him from the platform. But Bloom was far past the point of unacceptable tardiness. Horace had half a mind to leave him behind, him and his entire entourage, the handful of Red Caps that followed him like puppies wherever he went. He didn't trust them, not a whip, and especially not that Calico. The Devil's Eye, his grandmother would have called his ocular condition. When he was a boy, Horace's nana kept goats on her farm, and one of them had the same mismatched irises. "The Devil's Eye," she'd said, "a demon incarnate." The goat had seemed calm enough, but Horace could see more than a bit of the devil's work in Calico. Oh, he had half a mind to leave them behind, all right. He might do it, too, leave them all here to rot, if it weren't for Louis and Stevens. They were good men, loyal to the train, and he wouldn't leave them to the same fate.

Besides, for all his thoughtlessness, Bloom was a capable Assistant Conductor. The train was safe in his hands, as long as Horace was around to keep an eye on him. He'd have a hell of a time replacing him from the current stock of Red Caps. Not that they weren't able workers, but there was no conductor spirit about any of them. *Wouldn't hurt to start looking for a man to groom, though,* he thought, staring at the watch. *Just in case...*

He picked up his cap and fitted it snugly on his head. He checked his reflection in the mirror and straightened the brim. He was just about to button up and head back outside to prepare the platform crew for departure when a sudden spark of light flickered in the dead cornfield outside the window. The spark instantly roared into a full-fledged fire that spread across the stubbled ground with lightning speed. The flames flared into a billowing wall of orange and yellow heat that engulfed the entire window. The flames were close enough to the train car that he could already feel the window warming under his fingertips. He stared dumbfounded at the roaring fire for almost ten full seconds before one tiny sentence clicked in his head.

The cooking oil.

Uncontrolled fire was always a serious threat to the train; there was enough diesel fuel in the engine to blow the thing to pieces. That was why the supply car was the last car, out of range of any serious explosions that might flare up front. But now there were 25 sealed barrels of combustible cooking oil in the supply car. If the fire got close enough to heat the fuel to its flash point, all their cargo, the entire train, Christ, the entire *station,* would go up in flames! He didn't know the combustible temperature of cooking oil, but he sure as goddamn wasn't going to sit here and find out.

He hustled to the door, glancing off the corner of a shelving unit in his rush. He paused between the cars and assessed the fire. It wasn't as close to the train as it had seemed from inside the car. That was good. But a stiff wind could change that in a second. If he could pull the train up a few hundred yards, they'd clear the danger zone enough to buy them the time they'd need to get everyone on board and lock up the train. *Dammit, Bloom, where are you?*

He was just about to hop down from the cars and run to the engine when something snagged in his brain, something about the way the fire had grown. He looked out again, more closely. The flames had spread in a straight wall parallel to the train tracks. But now, looking carefully, he could clearly see breaks in the wall. Every fifty feet or so, the flames disappeared for a few feet, then started back up again, stretching another fifty feet. He could also see several lines of flames shooting back west, almost perfectly perpendicular to the main wall before him, but the field wasn't completely engulfed in flame. The fire was burning in high, wild, but *controlled* lines.

Horace's eyes narrowed behind his lenses. He turned and climbed up the metal footholds stamped into the outside of the car. He pulled his way up to the roof of the train, cursing his poor physical condition. He scrambled to his feet when he reached the top and turned to look out over the field.

He was right. The fire was controlled. Extremely controlled. Below him, spelled out in walls of fire eight feet high and stretching the length of an entire football field, was the word *HELL*.

•

Patrick watched the conductor's feet disappear over the top of the train car. He looked around to make sure no one was watching. There were people everywhere, but they were all in such a panic over the fire, no one was paying him any attention. Red Caps and college students alike ran around calling for water and shouting orders and expletives at each other. *Well done, Benny Boy. Well done.*

He leapt up onto the coupler and slipped into the last car. He quietly slid the door shut behind him, testing it to make sure he wasn't locking himself in. Satisfied, he brushed his hands together and smiled confidently. *James. Effing. Bond.*

"Ooo-wee," he said, giving a low whistle as he walked through the car. It was built like the other passenger cars, but the inside carried some serious modifications. The seats had all been removed and replaced with stacks and stacks of metal shelving units, which lined both sides of the aisle. They were bolted firmly into place at the floor, the ceiling, and the outer walls. Patrick grabbed the edge of one and shook it with all his might. The metal didn't budge.

The shelves were all labeled on the aisle side like library stacks, A to K on the left, L to V on the right. Each unit held six shelves, and each shelf was divided into two compartments. Each compartment was numbered, 1 through 12. He inspected the shelves immediately to his right, M1 through M12, and instantly realized why Horace didn't want them traipsing around the train. The M shelves were loaded with cases of alcohol. On further inspection, he found that the same was true for shelves N, O, and P. They were crammed full of booze. The cases were separated neatly according to type and, in some instances, subdivided by brand. He let his eyes wander over the shelves, involuntarily emitting soft, dreamy sighs as he reached out and touched sealed cases of Johnny Walker Black, Johnny Walker Red, Buffalo Trace, Bulleit, Early Times, Knob Creek, Gosling's, Captain Morgan, Belvedere, Three Olives, Beefeater, Smirnov, Bombay Sapphire, Sauza, 1800, Casa Noble--he stopped when he felt his eyes getting wet. He scrubbed at them with the hem of his shirt, embarrassed to be getting so emotional over liquor. It's not even that he wanted it that badly (though he did want it all, pretty badly), but he was just so glad a stash like this existed. Regardless of who would enjoy them, there were completely full, unbroken, unsmashed, unopened bottles of quality alcohol in this post-apocalyptic shithole of a country, and, dammit, that was worth a tear or two.

Just then, a loud, panicked voice floated past the car, and Patrick realized that he was standing right in front of a window. "Cripes!" he said, diving to the floor. So much for James Effing Bond. More like Mr. Effing Magoo. He lay still on the floor, his ear pressed against a heap of hard dirt crystals. He screwed up his mouth in disgust. It was official; vodka still didn't make him any smarter. But, hey, it had gotten him into worse scrapes, hadn't it?

He pushed himself slowly off the floor and crouched under the window. He peeked out through the bottom corner. He was facing the platform opposite the fire, and he guessed most of the people who had been sitting there around their friendly little fires had scampered around the train to watch the huge, terrifying, dangerously exciting fire on the other side. The platform was almost empty, save for a small group of Red Caps approaching from the north. He shied away from the window and whispered, "Shhhhh!" to no one in particular. He deduced that these Red Caps were Bloom's men, mostly because he saw Bloom bringing up the rear. One of them was pulling the cart, now full of sticks and axes instead of books. Patrick began to turn back to the shelves when one of the Red Caps stepped into the light of a campfire. His white shirt was covered in blood. From the way he carried himself, it wasn't his own. And was Patrick misremembering, or was the party smaller now than it was when they left? The vodka made his memory cottony, but he was pretty sure there should be more men out there. Something had happened on the campus. It probably had something to do with hippies.

By the time he realized they were about to enter his car, they were already climbing the stairs. He cursed under his breath and dove across the aisle. The rows were darker on that side of the train, if only slightly. He kept himself low to the ground and disappeared as far into the shadows as the space would allow. One of the Red Caps entered just as Patrick pulled his legs up under his chin. "Let's get them things stowed 'fore that fire takes flight," the man said. Patrick heard a scraping sound and several grunts. A second man was bringing up an armful of weapons. Patrick squeezed a hand over his mouth to keep his breathing quiet. The two men walked past his row without looking in. They walked down to row H. Patrick could just make our their movements through the spaces in the shelving units.

"Put 'em there for now," the first Cap said. "We'll inventory later. Between that fire and the clock, Horace is likely to shit." The second Cap dropped the clubs and axes to the ground. There was a shuffling sound, then the first Cap said, "Leave it. We're pulling out." They walked back to the door, passing Patrick once again without so much as a hesitation, and closed the door behind them. Patrick exhaled. *Thank God. Now I can get back to breaking and entering.*

He took stock of the shelves around him. They seemed to contain quite the *mélange* of cargo. Some of the items were impossible to make out in the dark, but he definitely recognized a bag of clothespins, half a dozen jars of either jelly or candle wax, a box of University of Miami - Ohio apparel, a first aid kit, an antique mantle clock, a fax machine, three blenders, a black bearskin rug, and...holy shit, was that a *flamethrower*? "This place is the world's best, crappiest flea market on wheels," he muttered.

He got to his feet and explored the rest of the car. Most of the shelves contained items that made sense--stores of food, bottled water, handheld weapons, maps--but he couldn't figure out why on Earth they were traveling with a *Smurfs* movie poster, or why a St. Alphonsus 1987 yearbook inhabited a place of apparent honor just one shelf above the red wine. Then, of course, there were the barrels of oil, 25 sealed drums that the Caps had somehow crammed into the back corner of the car. There were no shelves for the last twenty feet or so, just two restrooms and a stack of milk crates bolted to the floor in front of the only pair of seats left in the whole car. The cooking oil barrels filled both bathrooms and almost all of the open space in the back of the car.

Having conquered the cargo hold, Patrick decided he might as well jump to the second-to-last car to see if any secrets lay hidden there. He started back down the aisle, but stopped dead in his tracks when he saw a dark silhouette approach the car door. The Red Caps were back! He panicked and ducked up and to the left just as the door slid open. By some divine providence, the scrape of the opening door covered the sounds of his scuffling into the corner.

He closed his eyes and hoped for the best.

•

As always, Bloom appeared calm, even bored. It only made Horace's anger boil all the more.

Horace pulled Roland, the senior Red Cap, aside and told him to secure the train and pull out. The Red Cap looked justifiably confused. "Sir?" he said, not quite understanding.

"Secure the train, get us moving," Horace said again, through gritted teeth. He knew the Cap was capable of moving the train, at least for a little while. Besides, he only needed ten minutes, he told himself. It would take Roland longer than that to get the train secured. Ten minutes, and he'd be rid of Bloom, and they'd be on their way. He'd resume his conductor duties before they moved an inch. And if not, well, Bloom could sit down and shut the hell up until they got to Springfield. As far as Horace was concerned, Bloom was done.

Roland gave a quick salute and ran off to round up the other Caps. Horace didn't even look at Bloom; he couldn't. He beckoned with one finger and stalked over to the cargo hold. He wanted privacy for this.

He stepped up and into the dark car and stormed straight past the shelves to his desk. Bloom followed him in at an easy pace. Horace thought he saw a smile on the man's face as he emerged from the shelves and took up a post against one of the oil barrels. God, he'd never wanted to brain anyone so badly in his entire life. He crossed his arms and tried to focus on the best way to approach the subject. Finally, he said, "Well. What do you have to say for yourself?"

Now Bloom did smile. "Are you my father now?"

"I am your conductor!" Horace shrieked. Christ, didn't that *mean* anything anymore? "You tell me what the fuck happened out there! Start with what happened to Louis and Stevens and end with why the hell Calico is covered in blood!"

The smile disappeared from Bloom's face. His lips became razor thin. "I should be asking *you* what happened," he said, his voice taking a cold, ringing edge.

"How the hell should I know?" Horace cried.

"Because you're the one who sent us out there, undermanned against an entire goddamn army!"

Horace was exasperated. "What the hell are you talking about? Simms was one man, *one man*, and a philosophy professor, for Chrissake! What in God's name happened out there? I won't ask it again!" He smashed his fist on the milk crate, probably breaking his little finger in the process.

Bloom placed his palms calmly on the lid of the barrel he was leaning against. His knuckles turned ghostly white where he gripped the edge. "He had us outnumbered five to one. We made the trade, and his men jumped us. They took off Hammock's head and stuck it on a pike. A *pike*, Horace. Like Neanderthals. I saw them slit Louis nearly in half. They cut out Stevens' heart and set it on fire. Do you understand what I'm saying to you? They savaged us. It was sheer luck the rest of us made it out alive. Your crew will mutiny when they hear. Fortunately, I'm prepared to take control of the train."

Horace literally shook with his rage. "Five to one?" he spat, his voice trembling. "They savaged you? *They* savaged *you*? Why don't you tell me how it's your men who came back covered in other peoples' blood, and how you managed to get away with the full load of weapons, and why not a single one of you has a goddamn scratch!" He leapt up from the bench and flew at Bloom. The Assistant Conductor was easily ten inches taller than Horace, and in much better shape, but Horace's fury surged through him. He grabbed Bloom by the lapels and shoved him backward over the barrel. "What did you do to them?" he screamed. "What did you do to my men?"

Bloom grabbed Horace by the wrists and twisted. The two men went tumbling over the barrels, knocking them over as they kicked and thrashed. One barrel tipped off its perch atop another and slammed to the ground, missing Horace's skull by three inches. Bloom punched the conductor in the mouth and used his loss of balance to throw him to the floor. Horace pushed himself to his feet just as the train lurched forward. Roland had gotten it moving faster than he'd expected.

They faced each other across the car, both breathing heavily. Horace's hands were balled into tight little fists at his side. He was ready to fly at Bloom again, but his assistant merely rolled his head on his shoulders and straightened his lapels. "Here's the real truth, Horace, whether you'll hear it or no. It was your contact, your deal, your ignorant shortsightedness that got our boys killed," he said calmly. "I've got a team of Red Caps who'll swear to it. I pray to whatever gods are left that the fact that your avarice sent those men to that meeting unprepared rips you apart. You'll live with that knowledge, Horace, and someday you'll die with that knowledge. Who knows when that day will be," he added. "Personally, I hope you live forever, you self-righteous, pathetic, insignificant little dwarf, and I hope you see Louis' weeping, bleeding face in your nightmares. It goes without saying that you're no longer fit to conduct this train. I want you off before we hit Springfield."

Horace snorted. "Mutiny, is it? You think you can take the train by force? I'd like to see you try. The men know who keeps them fed. You can stage all the massacres you want, cry foul as hard as you can, you're still nothing more than a shiftless, murdering coward! The men know it, and they'll never follow you. You're no more than a common cutthroat!"

"You'd do well to remember that," Bloom hissed through clenched teeth. Then he changed tactics, his voice once again becoming flat. "Let me tell you the reality, Horace. You've already lost the train. Two out of every three Red Caps are mine. I've got men controlling every station stop from here to Dallas. The stations are mine. The route is mine. This train is mine."

Horace guffawed. "The Red Caps don't follow you," he sneered. But even as he said it, memories of the past year flashed in his mind in machine gun-style rapid fire. They'd started the year with more than forty Red Caps, but along the way, they'd lost men, a lot of men, to attacks, to sickness, to accidents, to runners...he remembered those men clearly.

Goddammit, how hadn't he seen it? Right under his nose, for God knows how long, Bloom had been carrying out his coup. He relaxed his fists. He suddenly felt old and tired. If the men sensed a shift in power, their allegiance would flip quicker than the wind. Power was everything in this world, and Horace's had just evaporated.

Bloom smelled his victory. He smiled again, though his eyes remained flat and dead. "Time to disembark, Captain," he said. He gripped the hilt of his sabre and took a step toward Horace, and Horace had no strength to object. Just as Bloom reached for him, they heard an "Ahem" from the stacks. They both whirled around to see that passenger, Patrick, standing in the aisle.

"Er...sorry, am I interrupting something?"

•

Bloom hadn't planned on the coup happening quite so quickly, but what the hell? Horace gave him an opening, so he charged through it. He had enough men in place both here on the train and along the route to make it happen. And, hell, if he had to put up with the conductor's goddamned condescension one more day, he'd just kill the bastard and be done with it. He couldn't wait to throw him off the train. He hoped Roland was bringing her up to full speed.

But suddenly, out of nowhere, was the stowaway. What was he doing back here? Who was guarding the door? Fredrickson? Whoever it was would be off the train with Horace. Bloom could not abide incompetency. On second thought, he should make an example of the guard, really cement his place as Lead Conductor of Horace's men. He made a mental note to do so, but first he had to deal with the stowaway.

"What do you want?" Bloom asked coldly. Was that a *blender jar* in the stowaway's hand? If he was here to cause trouble, he was the least threatening figure Bloom could imagine, all bony arms and legs, and a head that looked like it would pop if you pricked it with a pin. And armed with a blender jar.

"I need to talk to you about the battering ram," he said to Horace.

"Oh," Horace said dumbly. "Uhm. Okay. What about it?"

"I've worked out a few different possibilities for the trajectory infusion system, and I need to know which you want installed. They each have their own benefits, but it really depends on if you want focus on power, or quickness, or durability, or efficiency. Can I show you what I have in mind?"

Horace looked at Bloom. "I don't know," he said. "Do we have a second for that, Bloom?" Even now, on the brink of his demise, he was concerned about appearances in front of the passengers.

Bloom considered the stowaway's request. He'd been briefed on Patrick's project, a hydraulic puncture shield to replace the current static plow. Supposedly he could design one that kept the blood off the windshield. If he could really manage that, it'd be a boon for Bloom and his men. He realized that as much as he just wanted to toss the passengers off and get on his way (except that journalist...she had a potential use, on a train full of pent-up males), he stood to benefit from the stowaway's plans. Plus, he was offering Bloom a chance to make a decision on how the plow worked. Horace would probably opt for efficiency if he had his druthers, but Bloom wanted it to focus on raw force. "All right. Show us," he said.

Patrick looked around doubtfully. Half of the barrels were knocked to their sides, rolling gently with the swaying train. "We'll need a little more space. Can we go out to the next car?"

Bloom hesitated. His Red Caps outnumbered Horace's, but still, if Horace made it past Fredrickson and into the Cap car, things could get messy, and Fredrickson had already proved useless at guarding the way. Then again, the train was fairly confining. If Horace tried to run, he'd have to thread the bottleneck between cars, and Bloom was quicker than the little conductor. "Fine," he said, to Horace's apparent surprise. "Make it quick."

What a thrilling night this is turning out to be, Patrick thought. Camp-fires, then a break-in, then narrowly avoiding detection, twice, then a fight between two ridiculous men, and now this. *The apocalypse can be so exciting!* He never saw this much action back in Chicago. This trip was officially a good idea.

He hoped he wasn't swaying too much. Launching yourself into a fight between two ridiculous men isn't something you do sober. Luck-ily, the cache of Kahlua on the bottom shelf, along with the vodka he'd already downed, had helped kick his confidence into gear. It had also sparked his brain receptors, because now he had what was colloquially known as "a plan."

He led them out the door into the coupler area. Fredrickson, who was pretty decent at counting, looked confused when Patrick burst through the exit. Patrick clapped him on the shoulder. "Good work here. Can we get you to move across the way, there?" The Red Cap looked over Patrick's shoulder to Bloom, who nodded curtly. He went through the narrow connection and stood at the far door. "Perfect!" Patrick cried. "Now. Let's see." He paced the width of the opening. The connector was open on both ends, and a cold wind whipped through the space. He held his hands about three feet from each other and did some quick estimat-ing and measurements. "Hm. Yes, okay. Good. This will work. Horace, can you come stand here, please?" He took the conductor by the arm and led him to the edge of the metal platform, just above the steps. Roland was really building up some speed in the engine; stubbly cornstalks and sharp gravel patches flashed past just beyond Horace's feet. "And now, you hold this," he said, handing him the blender jar. "And then...let's see..." He got on his hands and knees and traced imaginary lines on the floor with his finger. "Calculating the trajectory," he mumbled, "depend-ing on the kinetic force of the pinion...hmmm..." He rocked back and forth on his knees and studied the invisible markings. Finally satisfied, he nodded and climbed back up to his feet. "Okay. So the first option will give us more efficiency. Bloom, if you could stand over here, please." He ushered Bloom to the opposite edge of the metal platform. "All four options involve the same basic set-up. We install a reservoir at one end, fixed to the engine," he said, indicating Horace and the blender jar, "with a cylinder of some sort leading to the plow. That's you, Bloom. You're the plow." The man's face remained expressionless. "Okay, perfect. Excellent plow face. Now, for efficiency's sake, we'll use a shorter cylinder. Bloom, if you take a few steps in. Perfect. The water boils in the reservoir, steam builds up in the cylinder, and we release the valve at the end here..." He mimicked opening a valve. "...and by opening it halfway, the plow moves out at a slightly reduced rate of speed, but we conserve water and steam energy. But see, what we can do, if you want more power--let me see that blender, Horace. What we do for more power, okay, is a different kind of valve, and we cap it, like this." He turned the blender jar on its side so it represented a hollow cap. "Bloom, will you hold this, please?" Bloom reached out and took hold of the jar. "Perfect," Patrick said. "Thank you. Now, when the force builds up in the cylinder, we throw the quick valve, and the cap explodes forward." Then he planted his feet, lowered his shoulder, and heaved forward, connecting hard with Bloom and sending him flying from the train. Bloom smacked into an old crossing post as it whizzed past, splintering his ribs and snapping his right arm in half. He fell, unconscious and head-first, onto the gravel siding and slid down into a shallow pool of trackside muck. The train's Assistant Conductor drowned in four inches of muddy standing water.

Patrick turned to the astonished Horace. "Conductor," he said, making a low bow, "the train is yours."

5.

"Sorry we can't drop you closer," Horace said with a frown. "Not sure what happened to the bridge. It was there two days ago."

Patrick looked grimly out the train window at what used to be the MacArthur Bridge. Now it was the MacArthur Chasm. Strangely reminiscent of the bombed-out Chicago River bridges, the MacArthur was blackened at its ragged iron edges on either side of the bank. By leaning right up against the window, Patrick could peer over and see a few of the splintered railroad trestles caught against an anchored barge in the yellow foam-crusted river below. "It makes crossing tricky," he admitted.

"I can jump that," Ben said.

Horace's bushy mustache twitched. He flipped open his pocket watch and sighed. "This is gonna set us back an hour at least. We'll need to backtrack up to the interchange north of the MLK and reroute to the secondary track there," he said, pointing to another line of tracks far below them, at ground level. "I can let you boys off at the MLK or at the Poplar, but you'll have to hoof it from there."

"That's fine. We can take the Poplar," Patrick said. "We have a stop to make on 40 anyway."

Horace nodded. "Then we'll drop you above the bridge." He hustled out of the passenger car and disappeared into the engine.

"The man loves his schedule," Ben observed.

"Which is odd, considering he hasn't been able to keep to one the entire time we've known him."

Before long, the train lurched backward and moved at a snail's pace back up the tracks. Patrick and Ben loaded up with their weapons and packs. Ben struggled under the weight of his knapsack. "How is it that we set out for a probable suicide mission into the barren post-rapture Earth, yet, two days later, we have more food than we started with?" he groaned.

"The Mother Spirit of the Illinois works in mysterious ways, Ben," Patrick said, patting him on the shoulder.

"So the Indian spirit told you to push Bloom from the train?"

"I believe my hands were guided by higher powers, yes," Patrick said. "He's in a better place now."

"Where?"

"Not on this train. Thanks in part to your excellent fire-spelling abilities, I might add."

"Not *that* excellent," Ben said.

"What do you mean? You spelled 'HELL' beautifully."

"I was trying to spell 'HELLO.' I ran out of oil."

"Well, regardless, it did the trick. And in return for securing Bloom's expulsion, the least we can do is accept an extra thirty pounds of provisions."

"That I'm stuck carrying," Ben added.

Patrick shrugged. "You're a strong person, built for might. I am frail and built for kindling. But if it's any consolation, it we ever need to survive some sort of physical attack, you're at least five times more likely than me to succeed."

"Not weighed down, I'm not."

"Don't think of it as being weighed down. Think of it as leveling the playing field."

"So we agree, then. I'm *not* five times more likely to survive."

"Not laden down with all that weight, good Lord, no."

They secured the last of their weapons and nodded goodbyes to the few Red Caps Horace had allowed back on after the Springfield stop. Most had been tagged as Bloom's men and had been cast off the train.

Calico, the one with the mismatched eyes, hadn't been found at all. He'd somehow managed to slip off the train sometime between Bloom's untimely death and the Red Cap Roundup, though not without leaving them a message. They'd found a note that read COMING FOR YOU pinned to a seat cushion in the business class car with a dinner knife. Which was a strange threat from someone who'd apparently jumped the train that was carrying them far, far away. Wherever Calico had gone, he'd moved fast; two minutes after Bloom's untimely departure, Horace had the entire train secured, and the Red Cap was already gone, the ink on his note still fresh.

Lindsay stood up from her seat and gave Patrick and Ben each a quick hug. "Good luck, you guys. Thanks for everything."

"Good luck with your story," Ben offered.

"Thanks!" she beamed. "I've made some really great progress, thanks to your help! I mean, Patrick helped, you just kind of glowered a lot, but it was great to be able to talk through my notes with you two. A few more interviews along the trail, then I'll head back up north and see what else I can dig up in Maiden Rock, and I think I'll be ready for some final edits and--"

"No," Ben interrupted, "I mean good luck finding someone to publish it. Media is dead."

That was pretty much it for the goodbyes.

Horace slowed the train to a stop over Highway 40. "Wow, he wasn't kidding when he said he'd let us off above the bridge," Patrick said. The tracks ran high over the pavement below. The highway was choked with cars that had stopped or crashed at awkward angles. Horace reappeared in the passenger car as Patrick and Ben were on their way out. "I don't suppose you have a ladder," Patrick said.

"Sorry to say we don't," Horace said. "Think you can make the jump?"

Patrick peered out the window. "Eh. It's only bone crushingly solid pavement. We'll be fine." He shook Horace's hand. "Thanks again for the ride."

"Please, believe me, the pleasure's been all mine. You boys really saved my bacon, I hope you know that. There's always room for you on my route. Oh, thanks also for the cooking oil tip. We've been close on depleting the Amtrak fuel supply, the drums along our route, anyway. This was going to be our last full run on these tracks. Looks like we'll be able to keep at it for a while longer now, thanks to you."

"Thanks to the miracle of modern science," Patrick corrected him. "Just keep the oil warm; it'll gel up in the cold faster than diesel. Oh! I almost forgot." He pulled a folded piece of paper from his pocket. "Here's the design for your battering ram. I made it pretty detailed. You and your men should be able to put it together easily enough once you find all the materials. You'll need a reservoir. You could use a big propane tank or an industrial sized boiler, if you can rig it to the engine. Aside from that, a quick-release valve and a long steel tube. You should be able to dig all of that out at a junkyard somewhere."

"Or a bombed out Home Depot," Ben added.

"Fit the pieces together like this, put water in the tank, use your engine fires to heat it up, and release the valve when ready to blow the hell out of something."

"This is great. I owe you a debt of gratitude."

"You can repay me by not blowing yourself up. With a barrel of cooking oil boiling in the engine, this thing's gonna be volatile as hell."

•

They stood on the trestles and waved as the train pulled slowly away. Horace blew the whistle in two short bursts and saluted from the engine. When the train had cleared the highway, Ben turned to Patrick and said, "Please tell me you remembered to pack an elevator."

"Yeah, I did pack it, originally, but then there wasn't any room for my Little Orphan Annie decoder ring, so I took it out. But fear not, young traveler, for I have the next best thing. Rope!" He pulled the nylon rope from his bag triumphantly and let it uncoil over the side of the bridge. It dangled just over the edge of the tracks.

"Brilliant. You brought a really useful three-foot rope."

"Well, I'm going to find a use for it somewhere," Patrick said, hurriedly stuffing it back into the bag. "You just wait."

"You think we could jump it?"

"Sure. It's only twenty feet or so."

"Are you being sarcastic right now, or serious? I can never tell."

"This time, I'm being serious, mostly. Twenty feet isn't *that* many feet. It'll probably hurt like hell, but we'll live. Probably."

"Words every man wants to hear in a world without doctors," Ben muttered.

"There are doctors *somewhere*," Patrick reminded him. "They're just not you or me." He pulled off his backpack and let it drop into the bed of a truck below. The machete and the hammer went next. "I think our best bet is to aim for one of these car roofs. It spares us a few feet, and they have more give than the asphalt."

Ben took a deep breath. "Is it going to be a problem that I have horrible aim?"

"Nah. Even if you miss the car, you'll be fine if you hit the pavement. Just try not to break anything."

"Thanks."

"Just tuck and roll. Oh, and do *not* glance off a car, get twisted up mid-air, and slam head-first into the pavement. *That* might kill you."

"Please stop talking."

"Okay. Sorry."

Ben tossed his knapsack and weapons down as well. "All right. I'm aiming for that Windstar."

"Good choice. Lots of surface area. I'll shoot for the blue Expedition." He bounced on the balls of his feet and swung his arms like a swimmer preparing to dive. Ben rubbed his hands together. "You ready for this?" Patrick asked.

"Let's just get it over with," Ben said miserably.

"Okay. One...two...oh, by the way, this probably goes without saying, but be careful not to actually miss the highway itself. It's another thirty feet or so down the gap between the eastbound and westbound lanes."

"Why would I miss? The highway's forty feet wide, I'm aiming for the center of it, how would I miss?"

"I don't know! I'm just saying. Don't."

"Well dammit, Patrick, now I feel like I'm going to!"

"You won't, you've got forty feet to land it, you're fine. Really. It's impossible to miss."

"Then why did you say to make sure I don't miss?"

"I don't know. I just thought it was important to note that there's an extra thirty feet of air over there because a twenty-foot drop is fine, but a *fifty*-foot drop will absolutely kill you."

"Goddammit, stop talking about it!"

"I'm just trying to save your life."

"You're making me want to end it!"

"Then by all means. Miss away."

Ben let out a scream of frustration and threw himself over the side. His arms flailed, windmill-style, and he screamed the whole way down. He belly flopped on the roof of the minivan, arms and legs splayed out at all angles. The roof crunched inward on impact. Luckily, his forehead struck before the rest of his face, and he slammed into the car without breaking his nose. He looked all-in-all like a face-down urban snow angel.

"Ben? You, uh...you alive down there?" Patrick called.

It took a minute or two, but Ben eventually convinced his arms to move. He pushed himself out of the Ben-shaped crater and rolled over. Why was the sky pink? And why was he able to see sky? Where did all the fog go? "Patrick," he groaned. "When did your teeth grow wings?"

"Oh, boy. Hang on, Benny Boy, I'm coming." Pat launched himself off the trestle. He was five feet into his free-fall when it became very clear to him that he was going to miss the target. He screeched in terror. He slammed into the Expedition's frame just above the rear window, ricocheted headfirst into the hood of a Taurus, and crumpled to the asphalt in a heap.

"Patrick? Are you a comet?"

•

"Now what did we learn from this little episode?" Patrick asked, limping across the bridge.

"Find a longer rope."

"Yes, that's one thing."

"Did we learn anything else?"

"I can't speak for you, but I can say with confidence that I learned to never trust a Ford."

The two of them were an awful sight. Ben had received a mild gash in his forehead, and his right eye was now just as purple as his left. His right arm hung limply from its socket, though admittedly, that was mostly for show. Patrick's arms were covered in asphalt burns, the back of his head already had a knot the size of a baby's fist, and his left ankle had misplaced its ability to support weight. "Ben, lemme see that bat," he said.

Ben held the weapon close to his chest. "No. This is mine."

"Come on, I need it. *Bemme.*"

"What for?"

"I need a crutch."

"Use your machete."

Patrick scoffed. "Use the machete."

"Yeah."

"As a crutch."

"Yeah, why not?"

"Why don't I use it as a bat-getting tool instead?" he asked, drawing the blade from the sheath across his back.

Ben's mouth fell open. "Wow," he whispered.

"What? What happened?"

"Hold on, keep holding it up like that." He hobbled to the other side of the bridge and turned back to look. "Awesome," he breathed.

"What? *What, what, what?*" Patrick cried.

"You're standing amid a jungle of wrecked cars on a deserted bridge holding a giant blade over your head with a curtain of greenish-yellow fog behind you."

"Yeah? And?"

"You look like an anime hero."

"I do?!" Patrick squealed.

"Seriously. I'm gonna call you Patku from now on."

"That is so awesome."

"I know! Let me try."

"Let you 'try'? No, I will not let you 'try' the machete."

"Come on. I'll trade you for the bat."

Patrick considered this. His ankle really hurt, and the person Ben was most likely to injure with the machete was himself. "Fine. I will let you *borrow* the farmer sword. And I will *borrow* the bat. When I don't need it anymore, we trade back."

"Okay."

"No questions asked."

"Okay, okay!" It was Ben's turn to make grabby hands. Patrick handed him the machete and snatched the bat. He put his weight on it and hobbled away across the bridge. Ben held the machete in the air. "Pat!

Patku! How do I look? Huh? Pat, look! Come on, Pat, seriously. Seriously! How do I look? Pat? Pat! Goddammit."

Because of the fog, they couldn't make out anything of downtown until they were almost across the bridge. Like the gloomy, wiry outline of a gray ghost, the St. Louis Arch slowly emerged from the brume. It was still in one piece, though it now leaned precariously out over the river. A missile crater at the southern base evidenced the likely cause.

"Tough old bastard, isn't it?" Ben remarked.

"Like the president for which it is named," Patrick said.

Ben blinked at him. "President Arch?"

"Yes, President Rory Arch. He freed the carnies and passed the historical Clown Neuter Act of 17-aught-4."

"Okay, this time I'm almost positive you're being sarcastic."

Patrick sighed. "The Arch's proper, Christian name is the Jefferson National Expansion Memorial. It's named after Thomas Jefferson."

"He was a tough old bastard?"

Patrick shrugged. "I actually never met the guy."

The skyline slowly phased its way into view, and Patrick was surprised by how intact it all was. Many of the buildings had visible scars and holes from the Jamaican missiles, but unlike Chicago, where buildings were still being toppled with alarming regularity, most of the St. Louis skyscrapers still stood tall. Maybe the exploded bridge was an anomaly.

"What's our Highway 40 errand?"

"It's more of a tribute than an errand," Patrick said. "And it's right there." He pointed straight ahead to a massive brick wall that ran the perimeter of an entire city block. The corner of the wall closest to them was a series of high brick pillars that came together above the highway in gracefully curving arches. Fixed to the top of the wall were two giant red birds; between them, a sign bearing dark red, heavy-block letters spelling BUSCH STADIUM. Well, technically it read B SCH TA I M, but Patrick's brain didn't register the missing letters. In his mind's eye, the sign, and indeed the entire stadium, was as pristine as the day it was built. It was here the St. Louis Cardinals dug in and made their stand against incredible odds in 2006, and again in 2011, winning the two World Series championships that, in a way, had given shape and definition to Patrick's adulthood. Busch was the stadium of heroes and legend.

"Patrick, are you crying?"

"No," he said hurriedly, wiping his eyes. "I got some Monkey dust in my eye."

"Uh-huh."

Patrick was prepared to walk down the eternally long Clark Street ramp and double back to approach the stadium from street level. But providence, it seemed, had other plans. Some desperate fan (or thief, more likely, Pat thought sadly) had lain a wide plank from the highway's edge across to the open-air walkway inside the stadium, a distance of about sixty feet. "This is the Bridge of the Gods," Patrick said, confident that it was true. "It is meant for our passage."

"Yeah, that--that doesn't look stable."

"The Spirit of the Illinois put it here for our safe passage."

"The Spirit of the Illinois is a Cubs fan," Ben pointed out. He pushed his hand down on the edge of the board. It bounced and nearly fell off the ledge. Patrick grabbed it just in time and struggled to keep it in place.

"It's perfectly safe," he insisted. "Just don't bounce on it."

It took very little discussion to determine that Patrick would go first, or they would not go at all. He hoisted himself onto the plank, steadying his weak leg with the bat. "See?" he said, once he had gained what only a paraplegic might refer to as "footing." "It's fine." He shuffle-stepped across the chasm, inching his way slowly toward the stadium. The board began to sag and creak. Patrick didn't hear it over the sound of his determination.

"Pat, seriously. We'll go around. This is insane."

"It's not insane. Stop talking to me."

"It is insane. The board is cracking. Can't you hear it?"

"All I hear is Jose Oquendo waving me in. Please stop talking. I'm concentrating." He sank into the middle of the plank, arms out like a tightrope walker. Ben pushed down on the board with all of his weight. He closed his eyes. He couldn't watch. And yet somehow, miraculously, when he opened them again, Patrick was stepping over the other end of the board and into the stadium. "See? Piece of cake. Okay, your turn."

Ben looked over the edge of the interstate. Then he looked back at Patrick. He shook his head.

"What?"

"I'm not coming. I'll wait here."

"Oh, come on, it's fine!"

"Screw off. I'm not coming."

"But, Ben, you love baseball!"

"I hate baseball. I've *always* hated baseball, I don't know anything *about* baseball, and there's no baseball happening in there anyway."

Patrick conceded these points. "Okay, fine. Don't move. I'll be back in ten minutes."

Forty minutes later, Ben began to worry.

•

It wasn't exactly the field of his dreams. The grass was dead and brown in the few patches where it hadn't burned away. The bases had all been removed, stolen, most likely, by early M-Day looters who still thought they could sell valuables for a few bucks, or maybe by transients looking for makeshift shields or pillows. The scoreboard was battered and broken, maybe by the wind, maybe by hoodlums, probably a combination of the two. A missile had landed in left field, another in the third base line upper deck. Wind-borne trash covered the dirt and the stands, and the fog had settled so heavily in the basin of the stadium that he couldn't see the lights above. The most disturbing sight, though, was the jerseys.

The apocalypse had occurred during a home game. It was a fact Patrick hadn't thought about for years, but he clearly remembered it now, furtively checking in on the score from work, sneaking the Internet radio broadcast via earphone under his desk, quietly cursing the MLB for scheduling a rare mid-week afternoon game. The Giants had been in town. Strictly speaking, the Giants were still in town. Their jerseys littered the infield and the visitors' dugout. A few of the jerseys were still wrapped around skeletal fragments; they hadn't liquefied completely, meaning it went slower and more agonizingly for them. Most of the uniforms rested flat on the ground, stained a horrid rusty brown from their internal fluids, stuck to the ground with globs of dried intestine and marrow. Then he remembered something else he'd heard during the broadcast. His heart leapt with anticipation, but he didn't want to rush the discovery. He wanted to savor it. So instead of heading to the dugout, he took a lap around the bases.

There were no Cardinals uniforms in the field. Apparently even the rookies had consumed enough cremated cadaver during their time in

St. Louis to survive the chemical blast, at least long enough to get off the field. Halfway between first and second he found number 48, Pablo Sandoval. Stuck to third base was number 29, Hector Sanchez, and at home plate, short sleeves fluttering in the wind, number 58, Andres Torres. All as dead in life now as they had been in Patrick's heart after the 2012 NLCS.

He stood on home plate and looked into the stands with grave sadness. Most of the fans seemed to have gotten out safely enough, but there were still several hundred red shirts fluttering around in the seats. Probably trampled in the initial panic, he thought. Or else maybe the relatives or loved ones of die hard fans, not from the area, but tagging along for support.

He hopped the low brick wall and climbed the stairs behind the third base line to the Infield Box section. He didn't remember exactly where they'd sat when they brought Izzy to her first Cards game, but this was about right. He chose a row at random and sat down in the aisle seat. As a St. Louis expatriate living in Chicago, he'd missed the chance to raise his daughter on the family team, and they'd only made it to one game. He'd promised more, but life was so busy, trips were too short, they'd be back another time, it would work out better later. They had shared one game, Patrick, Annie, and Izzy, just after her fifth birthday. These were their seats, or they were close enough. This was his memory. He looked out over the field, at the tacky brown remains of the players and fans who had been. He was glad that she wouldn't see it like this.

He allowed himself a few minutes to remember. Annie yelling, "Put in Todd Worrell!" and "Mark Sweeney, hit a home run!" despite the fact that neither had been a Cardinal for over a decade. Izzy wrestling with a souvenir soda cup as big as her head. Annie picking a fight with the Cubs fan two rows over, because what the hell was a Cubs fan doing at a Cardinals/Mets game? Izzy's sheer delight at throwing peanut shells on the floor without getting scolded, Patrick's sheer delight at not having to scold.

He slipped the weathered note from his back pocket and unfolded it carefully. He sighed back his tears as he read, and remembered.

After a few minutes, he returned the note to its protective pocket, slapped the plastic armrests of the stadium chair, and got to his feet. He had one more stop to make.

He'd saved the most satisfying for last.

The year before M-Day, in a somewhat controversial move, the Giants brought Barry Bonds onto the staff as the hitting coach. He only traveled with the team part-time, despite his sizable paycheck. But he had traveled to St. Louis. Patrick hopped down into the visitors' dugout, and a goofy smile spread across his face. Laying in a heap next to the steps was a jersey with the name BONDS stitched across the shoulders. "All the steroids in the world can't save you from the apocalypse," he said.

Under normal circumstances, Patrick found himself repulsed by the idea of anyone taking pleasure in someone's mortal demise. But this wasn't someone. This was Barry Bonds.

Patrick dug through his bag and pulled out a lighter. The Great Chicago Chaos had taught him that the puddled remains of M-Day victims burned like kerosene, quickly and furiously.

"I've waited a long time for the chance to set you on fire," he said, clicking the lighter and holding the flame to the jersey. It caught instantly, flaring up in a low *whoosh*. Liquefied Barry burned bright. The flames consumed the entire uniform and reduced it to ashes within seconds. Patrick gave a curt nod as he watched the number 25 char into oblivion. "You'll never hurt baseball again."

When the fire died, he toed the ashes into the shape of an asterisk. Then he stuck his hands in his pockets and wandered off the field.

•

"Yours or mine?" he asked as they finished up a meal of cold beans and energy bars on the roof of a Land Rover overlooking the river.

"What do you mean?"

"Whose family do we check in on first? Yours or mine?"

Ben snorted. "Yours." He stabbed at the bottom of his can, turning the last few beans to mush. Then he hauled back and threw it over the side of the highway.

"Geographically, it makes more sense to do yours first. Mine's on the South Side; it's on the way out. We should hit up Maplewood while we're up here."

Ben shook his head. "Nah. Let's go do yours."

"No, seriously. I don't want to backtrack. We'd have to go up 270, and

Momo's probably wreaking havoc on the corridor."

"Who's Momo?"

"Momo! Momo the Monster."

"What the hell are you talking about?"

"You've never heard of Momo?"

"No," Ben said flatly.

"Pull out your iPhone, look it up."

"Har, har."

"He's a sasquatch! Lives in the woods! Eats babies and Reese's Pieces!"

Ben shot Patrick a suspicious glare. "Are you kidding me with this shit?"

"Not at all. Well, maybe the babies and Reese's Pieces part. I think that's E.T. But he definitely lives in a cave."

"Then we'll stay away from caves."

"What about the Cave of Wonders? Can't stay away from that one, huh?" Patrick planted his feet and went up for another high five.

Ben just stared at him. "Is that a euphemism?"

"Heck yes!" Patrick pushed at the air, waiting for the second half of his high five. It didn't come. "Momo lives along 270. I'm not circling back that way. We go see your family now."

Ben waved him off. "Forget it. Let's just see yours and go."

It was Patrick's turn to look suspicious. "You don't want to see your family?"

"What's the point? So I can see them living in post-apocalyptic suburban hell?" He hopped off the Land Rover and began pacing on the asphalt. "My mom's always sick with something, the flu, or shingles, or what she thinks is jaundice but turns out to be kidney stones, or what she thinks is kidney stones but turns out to be rickets. She's spent half her life hooked up to machines and taking pills. If she's survived this long without electricity or reliable food supplies, she's paper thin and probably crying her eyes out every night for my sister and me, when she's not in too much pain to think from whatever new-world super virus she's probably caught. And my dad, Christ, he's such a stubborn asshole. He won't take help from anyone. The man has no survival skills. He's probably holed up on the living room floor, shitting himself and eating rats. Literally, eating rats. He couldn't keep a house clean with all the marvels of modern technology. I grew up with cockroaches in the kitchen sink. I can't even imagine what the house is like now. If they're alive, they're in horrible shape. Best case scenario, they're dead, and that's a shitty best case scenario. I don't want to know."

He wandered off down the highway, kicking at tires as he went. Patrick let him get a good distance before climbing down off the Land Rover and following at an easy pace. By the time he caught up to his friend, Ben was lying down on the center stripe, arms crossed on his chest. Patrick stood awkwardly by his head. "You okay?"

"No."

Pat tossed his bag down and sat against a truck tire. "What if they *are* okay? Most of the people around here must've survived, right? Maybe someone is taking care of them, maybe someone beat your dad into submission. With giant logic fists. Or a reality hammer. Men in your family like getting hit with hammers, if I recall correctly. Or maybe your sister made it back? She was only, what, four hours away? What if they're fine, and it's killing them not knowing what happened to you? What if seeing you alive and well, or, you know, alive and beaten with bats and car parts, what if that's the thing that completes the whole picture? Makes the circle of life move one jump ahead of the breadline, and all that?"

Ben dug the heels of his palms into his eyes. "Why would I want to do that to them? Show up, 'Hey Mom, I'm fine, great to see you, going to Disney World now, so long.' It's a lose-lose game. Like fucking Battleship."

"You could always stay," Patrick suggested. "If they're fine, I mean. You could stay. Damn, what do you want to go to Disney World for anyway? You hate children; it would just make you depressed."

"Are you kidding me? I'm in this 'til the end. I'm still pretty sure you're gonna try to off yourself sometime in the next three days. I'm not letting you out of my sight. Besides, what am I gonna do, stay here and rebuild a life in the new frontier? Who am I, Charles Ingalls? I left the 'Lou for a reason. I'm an adventurer, and so far this has been about the dumbest adventure I can think of, and I'm not gonna bail now that we're finally getting to the good part. We're headed into the creepy South. I *love* the creepy South."

Patrick smiled. "I know you do, Ben," he said, giving him a little kick in the arm, "I know you do."

"So fuck it. Let's not go down that road."

"Literally."

"Literally," Ben agreed. "Let's go to the Deen Ranch." He wiped his eyes and jumped to his feet. He offered Patrick a hand to help him up. But Patrick just sat there, looking down and twirling the wedding ring on his finger. For nearly five minutes, he sat in quiet contemplation.

"Hell," he finally said. "We should probably just go."

"Yeah. I know. That's what I just said."

"No. Not go. *Go*."

"Oh." Ben raised an eyebrow. "You sure?"

Patrick nodded. "I've never said this before, and I don't plan on every saying it again, but Ben, you're right." He allowed himself to be hauled to his feet. "Any way you look at it, the best case scenario is a lose. I mean, I don't get the Battleship analogy, but the rest of it makes sense."

"Are you kidding me? You lose Battleship, you lose Battleship. You win Battleship, you realize you just spent twenty minutes of you life playing Battleship. It's lose-lose."

Patrick shook his head and clapped Ben on the back. "You're a weird little person, but I love you."

They started back east across the Poplar Street Bridge. "How many days to Disney?" Ben asked.

"On foot? Maybe...a month?"

"A month?! Good God."

"Yeah," Patrick agreed. "I really wish we'd sorted this out before we got off the train."

"At least you got to piss on Barry Bonds' ashes," Ben said. "There's always a bright side."

"I didn't piss on them. I just reduced him to them." He stopped short in the street. "Do you think I should go back?"

"No," Ben said, squinting down into the river below. "I think you should flag down that boat."

They skidded down the bank, waving their arms and hollering at the girl in the gray and orange speedboat. "Hey! Stop! Please! Hey! Heeeeey!" Ben shouted.

The girl looked up, dazed and doubtful, as if she expected these two yahoos rolling down the hill to be a mirage. But when Patrick tripped and skidded face-first into the water, the splash snapped her into reality. "Oh my God!" she cried. She jumped up, sending the boat rocking precariously. She slipped from one side to the other as it shifted under her feet. "Hey! Help! You guys, help me!" she cried, bobbing up and down like a human buoy.

"No, *you* help!" Ben shouted. "Come over here and pick us up!"

"I can't!" the girl wailed. "I don't know how to drive a boat!"

"Use the steering wheel!" Patrick said, shaking the water from his face.

"It's broken!" she cried. "Help!"

"See if there's a wide, flat object in the boat you can use to drag on the port side to set your drift eastward," Patrick hollered.

"I don't know what you're talking about!" she sobbed.

"Okay," Patrick shouted, slowing his words down. "Do you see a wide, flat object in the boat?"

Ben didn't wait around to hear it all a second time. The current was pulling the boat quickly now, and soon the girl would be past them and too far downriver to catch. He sprinted down the bank toward the destroyed MacArthur Bridge, losing ground as the speedboat cut rapidly through the water. It pulled even with him just as he reached the submerged trestles. He leapt onto the floating barge, losing his footing for a second, righting himself as the boat skimmed past, and with one last surge of power, he sprinted across the barge and vaulted into the air. He landed in the rear of the boat with a hard crash that nearly capsized the whole thing.

Ben groaned in pain as he sat up. He looked around the boat and grabbed a small Rubbermaid cooler from under one of the seats. He thrust it into the icy, yellow-capped water on the eastern side. Slowly, the nose of the boat began to drift to the left, until they ran up gently on the bank. Ben fell over the side of the boat, scrambled his way to the prow, and heaved the thing up the sandy gravel. When it was secure, he let go and collapsed backward onto the rocky beach, wheezing heavily.

"Holy cow!" Patrick cried as he ran open-mouthed down the bank, clapping his hands. "Ben! Are you okay?" he shouted downriver. "That was amazing!"

The girl peeked over the edge of the boat, shaking visibly. "Mister?" She reached out with one finger and prodded his kneecap. "Hey. Mister?"

Patrick arrived, skidding to a halt near Ben's shoulder. "Stand back!" he cried, throwing his hands up as a barrier. "I know CPR!"

"Patrick," Ben said weakly, his chest heaving, "don't touch me with your lips."

They gave him a few minutes to catch his breath. "That was amazing!" Patrick said again, once Ben began showing positive signs of life. "You were like Batman!"

"That's because I *am* Batman." He squinted up at the girl. "Don't tell anyone."

"I won't," she said seriously. Ben examined the girl. She had nuclear blonde, almost white hair down past her shoulders, with dark brown roots nearly an inch long at the base. She was small, probably no more than 5'3", with a remarkably tiny waist. She had large, cartoon character green eyes and wore tight, fashionable jeans with a v-neck t-shirt under a gray cardigan and dark purple scarf. She was easily the trendiest girl he'd met since the apocalypse. "My gosh, you saved my life!" she gushed. "I would've *died* in that boat, I *know* it!"

"How long were you floating?" Ben asked.

"Two days!"

"Really?" Patrick asked. He looked inside. There was no sign of food, no weapons, no provision of any kind. "Where are you going?"

"New York," she said.

Ben raised an eyebrow. "New York, like...*New York*, New York?" She nodded.

"You're trying to get to New York from Missouri by boat?" She nodded again. Patrick squinted at her. "I have to tell you, I think there's a serious flaw in your plan."

"What?" she asked, her big eyes confused and searching.

"For starters, New York is that way," he said, pointing northeast. "This river goes in for all intents and purposes what we're going to call the exact opposite direction."

"Oh," the girl laughed, "I know that! I'm not an idiot." Patrick shot Ben a look. Ben shrugged. "I'm taking this to the ocean, *then* I'm going *up* the ocean to New York. I looked on a map. It all connects."

"Yes, I guess technically, that's true," Patrick said.

"Man, that is a dumb plan," Ben decided. The girl's face fell.

"Why?"

"Well, for starters, you don't have the keys to this boat," Patrick said, examining the console.

The girl slapped her forehead. "*That's* what they key was for!" She reached into her pocket and produced a little orange floatable keychain with a grimy key dangling from the end. "I found this on the floor of the boat, and I was like, 'Someone dropped their car keys!'" She laughed. "I'm an idiot!"

Patrick did his level best to keep his face from falling into a hard grimace. He pushed on bravely and tapped the gas meter. "And, um, for seconders, you're out of fuel."

"I know, right? The stupid thing doesn't work!" She gave the hull a good kick. "You guys saved my life!"

"Some of us more than others," Ben said.

"I didn't know boats needed keys, too," the girl continued. "I mean, they're not cars."

Patrick nodded. "That is absolutely true. Boats are not cars."

"Gosh, I got in, and the boat started going, and I was like, 'Perfect! Next stop, New York!' But then I couldn't steer it, and the motor wouldn't go, and I was like, 'Oh, my God, I'm gonna get to the ocean, and I'm not gonna be able to stop! I'm gonna float all the way to *China*!'"

"Your views on geography are fascinating," Patrick murmured. "Can I ask why you're going to New York?"

"I need to get out of here. Everyone is so...weird! I can't take it anymore. I need to go back to New York, where things are normal."

"Back? Are you from New York?" Ben asked, surprised. "I *knew* that journalist was a nut job!"

"Yeah. I mean, not originally or anything. I'm originally from Hannibal. But it's so, ugh, *stupid* there. I moved to New York when I was, like, eighteen."

Patrick clapped Ben on the back. "Cannibalism, Ben. It's all about the cannibalism."

"I was back home visiting when all the stuff happened. You know? That bombing?"

"Yes, we're familiar with the large-scale event that nearly extinguished life on the planet. Please continue."

"I need to go back to New York. I miss my goldfish."

Ben cleared his throat. "Patrick, can we sidebar for a second?"

Patrick jumped to his feet. "Capital idea! A sidebar on the sandbar!" They walked down the bank a hundred feet or so and turned their backs to the girl sitting by the boat.

"Do you think we should tell her about New York?" Ben asked. "Specifically, that everyone in it is dead?"

"I'm not sure it'd do much good. I don't think she knows what words mean."

"Stop it. I'm serious. I mean, she can't take a boat to New York anyway." Then he added, uncertainly: "Can she?"

"Again. More proof of why I'm in charge." But Patrick rubbed his chin and thought carefully. "*Technically*, it's possible, yes. But in that boat? It's not built for distance. It'd probably break down before she got to Myrtle Beach. And I don't know where the hell she thinks she's going to find gas. Of course, if we could dredge up some cooking oil--"

"What is it with you and cooking oil?" Ben hissed.

"What? It's an incredibly versatile product! It fries potatoes, it softens bunions, it repels hippies, and it powers gas-guzzling locomotives! It's the wonder product of our generation! We could probably find enough of it to send the boat back up to Hannibal, but definitely not to New York."

"And she obviously doesn't want to go back there."

"Obviously."

"So tell me if I understand you correctly," Ben said. "She can't go upriver, because she could only go as far back as the place she's trying to get away from, and she can't go to the ocean, because a whale would eat her and her broken boat somewhere in the Atlantic."

"I don't think those are the words I used, exactly, but that's the general idea, yes."

"So it's really in her best interest to start a new life somewhere between here and New Orleans."

"I would not presume to know what's in her best interest," Patrick insisted. "But looking at it from our perspective, it's safe to say that yes, she would be better off resigning herself to a new life in a reasonably populated city along the Mississippi."

"So what you're saying is that it's basically our moral duty to commandeer both her and her boat and steer them safely into port at Memphis."

"I--oh, I see what you're doing," he said, wagging a finger at his friend. "I definitely did not say those words. I'm pretty sure 'commandeering a person' is the literal opposite of moral duty."

"Shut up, you know what I mean."

"We shouldn't try to 'commandeer' anything. If we want her to take us to Memphis, we should just ask her to take us to Memphis."

"I know, but it feels weird asking her to do that. It feels like tricking her."

Patrick blinked at him. "Tricking her?"

"Yeah."

"We're not *tricking* her if we're *asking* her. Once again, one is pretty much the exact opposite of the other."

"Then why do I feel bad for asking her?"

Patrick put his arm around Ben's shoulder and jostled him. "Because she's a pretty girl, and you're not used to pretty girls doing anything nice for you because they're usually drawn to much taller, handsomer men, so any time one does do something nice for you, you subconsciously think you must be tricking her into being nice to you."

"She is pretty, isn't she?" Ben asked.

"And you are short," Patrick said, "and not terribly attractive. But, hey, you saved her life. She probably would've drifted into the ocean if it weren't for you. And gotten eaten by a whale, or whatever dumb thing you said. Did you notice there's no food in the boat? No blankets, no tent, no fishing poles, no survival gear of any kind? She couldn't even figure how to steer the boat when given clear instructions."

"Those weren't exactly clear instru--"

"You literally saved her life," Patrick interrupted. "And you did it by leaping into a moving boat from a barge! You were like an especially un-coordinated flying squirrel!"

"I thought you said I was like Batman."

"The clarity of time has shown me that it was really more like an es-pecially uncoordinated flying squirrel. Either way, it was heroic. You've at least earned the right to ask for a ride."

Ben brightened a bit. "That's true."

"It is true! There's no harm in asking for a little ride."

"No, it's just a little ride."

"A very little ride! You know what? You know what? It's not even a ride. It's a *drift*. We're asking for a little *drift*."

"Yeah, a little drift down the river. And when we get to Memphis, she can fuel up and go wherever she wants."

"Sure she can."

"There's still one problem."

"What's that?"

"I'm no good at talking to girls. You do it."

"Heck no. You're the shining hero here. She's much more likely to say yes to you."

"I'm going to screw this up."

"Probably," Patrick agreed.

"My hands are already sweating," Ben said, wiping his palms on his jeans. "What if she says no?"

"Then we brain her with the hammer and commandeer the boat."

"I've really enjoyed this little pep talk."

Patrick winked. "Go get 'em, Tiger."

They walked back up the bank to where the girl was sitting. Ben sat down on the gravel next to her while Patrick wandered up the bank, trying to be inconspicuous. "Listen," he asked. "Do you think we could... uhm...catch a ride? Maybe to...uhm...Memphis?"

"Oh, totally!"

"Really?"

"Sure. You saved my freakin' life! The least I can do is give you a ride. Which way is Memphis?" she asked.

"That way," he pointed, looking to Patrick for confirmation. Patrick nodded.

"Oh! Awesome, it's on the way!" she said excitedly. "We don't even need gas to get there!" She slapped her knees and popped up to her feet. "Let's do it!"

Ben nodded smugly. *Conversation domination.*

6.

With the help of two makeshift paddles, they ran aground in Lee Park a few hours before dawn. "Are you sure this is it?" Ben yawned, squinting into the gloom. More fires burned here than anywhere else along the river, it's true, but there wasn't exactly a flashing neon sign welcoming them to Memphis.

"Either Memphis or Giza," Patrick said, pointing just northeast of the park. A river breeze thinned the fog near the shore, and in the glow of early morning fires they could just make out the outline of a giant pyramid, its point lost in a low, sickly brown cloud.

"What is that thing?" asked the girl, who had given her name as Lucy.

"The first structure ever built in Memphis," Patrick answered. "Completed by the ancient Egyptian settlers in 1237 B.C."

"Wow," she whispered, her eyes big as half dollars.

Ben shook his head at Patrick. "There's something wrong with you," he muttered.

They secured the boat, then fell into a somewhat heated debate. Patrick wanted to head off east immediately and get a few miles under their feet before sunrise, but Ben desperately wanted sleep. They had rested poorly on the train, he argued, and paddling for the last 18 hours under Patrick's sadistic command had earned him very few winks. Patrick insisted that the river was a dangerous place to stay, too open and strategically poor for a retreat if they happened to be attacked on land. They had no way of knowing what sort of terrifying hellmouth the Mississippi River coastline had descended into since M-Day, and without the relative safety of the train with its armed guards, they needed to start being smart. Getting away from the river would be safer.

"You think downtown Memphis at 3 am is the *safe* option?" Ben asked, incredulous. Patrick set to work trying to formulate a logical response to this, when suddenly they heard a gentle snore coming from the boat. Lucy had settled the argument by falling asleep.

They set up what little camp they could, draping their two blankets across the top of the speedboat and tying one end down with the short length of rope. They each chose one blunt weapon to cuddle through the night, in case of attack, then laid the rest of the armory out just behind the boat on the shore so they would be easily accessible in an emergency. They pulled on their extra layers of clothes to ward off the cold and hunkered down in the makeshift fort, Ben in the stern, Patrick in the bow, and the snoring bottle blonde in between. Ben noticed her shaking in her sleep. "You have anything else in your bag you can cover her with?" he whispered. Patrick hesitated. "What? What is it?"

"Well...technically, yes."

"Okay. So. Go get it."

Patrick frumped. "I don't want to."

"Why not?" Ben hissed.

"Because it's not meant for sleeping in!"

"Oh, for crying out loud. It's forty degrees, if you have something to cover her with, cover her. Look at her, for God's sake." She shivered harder now, her hands instinctively rubbing her thin shoulders in her sleep. Patrick sighed. He crawled over to his bag and pulled out a large, white shirt with two red birds perched on a bat embroidered on the front over the word Cardinals. He unbuttoned it and draped it over Lucy's shoulders. Even in the darkness of the covered boat, the scarlet letters spelling out MOLINA were eminently visible.

"You stole a jersey?"

"Well he wasn't wearing it!" Patrick hissed. "It was in the locker room.

I think if he wanted it, he would've stopped by the stadium at some point in the last three years!"

"No wonder you were gone so long. What else did you take?"

"Nothing!" Patrick cried. He crossed his arms and rolled over, facing away from his bunkmates. He clutched his bag angrily and shoved it under his head, punching it with his ear to dig a comfortable divot among the supplies inside. "That jersey is extremely important to me, Ben Fogelvee, and if Ditzy Darla drools on his uniform, you're paying with your kidneys."

•

Patrick awoke to the cold, hard slap of steel across his face. "Wake up."

"Ow!" he cried, rubbing his cheek. A long, wide welt had instantly started forming. "What's the matter with you?" He looked up and saw a tall, thin African-American man standing over him with Patrick's machete in hand.

"Wake up," the man said again.

"I'm awake! Cripes. Give me back my machete."

"No."

Patrick sat up. The blankets had been tossed back from the boat, and Ben and Lucy were already awake. They were being secured by more newcomers, their arms pinned sharply behind their backs. There were six assailants in all, and each one of them held at least one of Patrick's and Ben's weapons. *Note to self*, Patrick thought miserably. *Hide weapons while sleeping.*

"You come with me," the man with Patrick's machete said. "Madame Siquo is expecting you."

Patrick shook his head, trying to wake up his brain. "I think you've got the wrong guy."

"No," the man said again. "You are Mouse Hunter." His voice was surprisingly deep, especially for how thin and frail he looked. He wore a gray knit cap with a long tassel and an olive green vest with no shirt underneath, despite the chill in the air. He was skinny, but lean and ropy, and therefore much more than a physical match for Patrick, who was skinny, and just skinny. Plus, the man had the machete. And Patrick seemed to have misplaced his hammer in his sleep.

"I'm the what?" he asked, wiping his bleary eyes.

"Mouse Hunter," one of the other men piped up.

"Mouse Hunter," they all agreed, bobbing their heads.

"You are Mouse Hunter. Madame Siquo waits."

"There's been a misunderstanding, here. I'm not Mouse Hunter. I would never hunt mice. I'm scared to death of 'em. Ben, tell him."

"It's true," Ben admitted. "He's a pansy."

"A pansy," Patrick confirmed. "See? Sorry for the confusion. If I could just—" He moved to take the machete from the thin man. The man slapped his hand with the flat blade.

"Madame Siquo says you come with us, or I cut off your head." He placed the sharp end of the blade against Patrick's neck.

"Ah...I think I should discuss this with Madame Siquo in person," he said, gingerly pushing the blade away from his windpipe. "Not because you threatened me, mind you. But because I want to, for the sake of diplomacy." The man grunted and stood back, allowing Patrick to climb out of the boat. His right leg had fallen asleep, and he stumbled on his way over the side, crashing face-first into the dead grass. He wanted to stay down on the ground and die. This was just the most humiliating morning of his life.

The tall man grabbed him by the arms and lifted him easily to his feet. *Yes, I shan't be challenging this man's strength*, thought Patrick, who could barely heft his own backpack. "What about the boat?" he asked. "Who's staying with the boat?"

"All will stay. You and I will go alone."

"Oh good. A blind date from the Eighth Circle of Hell." He shot Ben a pleading look that said, *Get me out of this*, but Ben only shrugged and motioned with his eyes toward the men and their weapons. "I was right," Patrick said, glaring. "You, sir, are no Batman."

The thin man led him silently across the park and up the hill to Riverside Drive. They turned left and stalked along the quiet road. The fog was still thin, allowing a better panoramic than Patrick had seen in months. It was just a pity that all there was to see was Memphis.

He'd been to Memphis a handful of times in his life, and it seemed like every time he visited, the town was just a little worse -- a little poorer, a little more rundown, a little less appealing. The M-Day catalyst had sped up this devolutionary process exponentially, and now the home of blues and rock 'n' roll was little more than a burned out pile of building-sized litter. Everywhere he looked, windows were broken out and boarded up. Some buildings had fallen over, covering the streets with bricks and sheet tin for blocks. Broken glass crunched underfoot at every step. Trash fires burned in barrels, some unmanned, others warming crude derelicts with long, dirt-matted hair and ripped clothes stained with their own waste.

All in all, it was pretty much the Memphis he remembered. Just more so.

They turned right onto Beale Street and had to climb over a pile-up of rusty clunkers stacked nearly as high as the railroad bridge overhead. In a dusty field to the right, a gang of teenagers took batting practice at a line of broken bottles and the occasional ambler-by. They scattered when they saw the thin man trudging up the street.

"I must be pretty intimidating," Patrick said.

"They know I walk with Madame Siquo. They respect her power."

"Seems a little more like fear," Patrick observed.

The thin man nodded his gaunt head. "They are the same."

Patrick sighed. He was really not looking forward to this meeting.

A few blocks down, they passed the Orpheum. Its fire escape had been torn from the brick wall and now lay dead in the street. They climbed over the rusty brown staircase, avoiding sharp corners and thick bolts. "I saw The Pixies here once," Patrick mused aloud. "The bassist fell off the stage and gave some girl a concussion."

"It is home to Reverend Wharton's congregation now."

"Oh. Baptists?"

"Satanists."

Patrick shrugged. "Same thing."

They reached 2nd Street, the western edge of the Beale Strip, which was hilariously still cordoned off from vehicular traffic with broken and battered plastic white barriers. Surprisingly, fewer fires burned along the street beyond 2nd, and the occasional passerby became more and more rare. Either the darkened lights and the missing music made this a dead zone to those who remembered its heyday, or else the Strip was still what it had always been, a hovel for tourists to be largely avoided by the locals.

Patrick noted with sadness the dead and broken neon lining the street. Beale had once been so alive with color and light, even when the rest of the city cowered in the darkness and gloom of poverty. Now, most of the neon signs had been smashed, their glass tubes paving the street in tiny shards. The sign for B.B. King's had half broken off its brick building and hung ominously over the street at a 45 degree angle. The skull of Tater Red's leered darkly beneath his top hat. The brick and plaster guts of Beale Street Tap Room were blown across the middle of the street, apparently expelled from the old brick building by way of some explosive or other. The entire Strange Cargo building tilted precariously over the hole left by the explosion.

The thin man led Patrick up over the loose mound of bricks in the road. Pat nearly stumbled on a twisted bar stool but caught himself by grabbing a doorframe jutting up from the brown brick mess. He slid down the other side and followed the man to the entrance of Pig. Up above, the large, round sign of a flexing hog was mostly intact, as was a plywood board next to the entrance that read, "BIG ASS BEER TO GO." Most of Pig's windows were boarded up, but one of the doors was accessible and even retained unbroken plates of glass in its metal frame. A bald, muscular man in jeans and a tight black sweater sat on a stool outside of the door. He stood when he saw Patrick and the thin man approach. "Mouse Hunter?" he asked. The thin man nodded. The guard opened the door and ushered them in.

Another guard sat just off to the left, picking at his fingernails with a rusty nail. Patrick nodded politely. The guard spat a stream of thick, brown juice onto the floor.

"You wait here," the thin man said. He disappeared behind a curtain in the back of the room.

Patrick looked around. The windows were all blocked up, and candles provided the only light, but there were enough of them scattered around the room to see. Most of the restaurant was still in good shape, all things considered. The floor was grimy with years of grease and tread, but most of the black linoleum tiles remained, and the bare, scored concrete was only visible through a handful of squares. The tables and chairs had been pushed up against the northern wall as a barricade against the boarded windows and second entrance, leaving the majority of the seating area completely open. Posters and tin signs still hung on the walls, showing the rich history of Memphis and teasing the viewer with yellowing photographs of steaming barbecue.

The curtain rustled, and the thin man reappeared. "Madame is ready for you," he said, gesturing beyond the curtain. Patrick took a deep breath. *What the hell*, he thought. *Memphis is as depressing a place to die as any.*

He stepped through the curtain. The thin man let it fall behind him, cutting him off from the main room. Patrick climbed three rickety stairs to a raised platform that might have served as a stage at one time. Now it was a sitting area; four mismatched chairs surrounded a small, round, wooden table. In the furthest chair from the stairs, a high-backed piece of furniture with red velvet upholstery, sat an old woman. Thick ropes of hair the color and consistency of steel wool draped down her back and around her long, oval face. Her skin was the color of burned wood. She had sharp, bony features, weathered and hardened with age. A trio of candles burned low on the table, their dim light reflecting off the woman's milky white eyes.

"Welcome, Mouse Hunter," she said in a voice as dry as sand. She gestured to the armchair opposite her own. Patrick sank cautiously into it. He was almost certain the woman was blind, yet she seemed to be following him with her chalky white eyes.

"About that," he said. "I think you have me confused with someone else. I'm not exactly what you'd call the hunting type. More of the casually observing type. With intermittent color commentary."

The old woman reached into the folds of her dress and retrieved a shallow clay cooking pot covered with a lid. She shook the pot roughly. Something inside rattled like dice. "You do not seek truth. But truth has sought you out." She opened the lid and set it on the edge of the table. Then, taking the pot with both hands, she quickly flipped it upside-down. "The bones foretold your coming, Mouse Hunter. I am the channel of that which has found you." She pulled the pot away and revealed a pile of off-white pork rib bones, boiled clean of their gristle. Without taking her dead eyes from Patrick's, she felt about the pile with her gnarled hands, brushing her fingertips lightly along the edges, reading their positions. "Do you know why you are here?"

"Because black Skeletor brought me?" Patrick tried.

"Marimbo is Fate's escort," the old woman whispered, waving her gnarled old hands over the bones. "Our paths have converged; you have come to this place to learn the truth."

Patrick furrowed his brow. "I don't really know what you're talking about, ma'am. I'd really like to get back to my friend and move on."

"What is it you seek?" the woman asked.

"Disney World, mostly."

"Yes. You hunt the mouse. The mouse, you will find." Patrick shifted uneasily in his chair. The old woman began to chant over the bones in a language he didn't understand, which meant it was neither English nor very poor German. With a quickness belying her age, she plucked a bone from the top of the pile and held it high. "Your path is broken by peril. The light bringer." She laid the bone down in the center of the table. She plucked a second and held it aloft. "The running man." She laid this bone parallel to the first, then drew a third. "The butcher. The mummer. The demon's daughter. The siren. The fire drinker." She laid each new peril in line with the others. Then she took two bones from the pile, one in each hand. Her breath came shallow and quick, and her hands began to shake. Lines of worry creased her temples. "Ubasti Tom and the hollow man." She lay these two bones with the others and presented them to Patrick. "Your path lies broken. The bulldog is the mortar, the mouse hunter, the trowel." She scooped the bones and cupped them in her hands. She held them out to Patrick. "All may be, or none may be, or one may be. Choose."

Patrick raised an eyebrow. He had no idea what in God's name was going on. "You want me to...choose a bone?" he asked uneasily.

"All may be, or none may be, or one may be," she repeated. "Choose, Mouse Hunter."

He leaned forward cautiously. "This doesn't seem very sanitary," he muttered. He reached into her hands and picked up a bone, but when he touched it, he must have caught a jagged corner, because he felt a sharp sting in his finger. He cried out and yanked his hand back. The middle finger dripped a trail of blood across the table. He sucked the finger dry and shook out his hand. He was about to say something about third-world swine infections when he noticed something strange. The entire pile of bones in the old woman's hands was drenched in blood. It had only been a quick prick to the finger, but the bones dripped red, and the blood poured through the old woman's fingers.

Her brow furrowed, and when she spoke, her voice was sharp as glass. "All are chosen."

Patrick started. "What do you mean, all are chosen? All aren't chosen! I didn't choose all!"

"All are chosen," she repeated. "You do not seek truth, but truth has sought you out. You do not seek peril, but peril will find you." She placed the bones back in the clay pot and covered them with the lid. Then she stood up slowly and walked around the table to where Patrick sat. He instinctively leaned away from her. She caught his hands in her own. He tried to pull away, but she was surprisingly strong. When he looked into her eyes, he saw milky white tears running down her cheeks. "You chose all and so must choose again," she whispered. "The bulldog or the mouse hunter must fall. You will choose."

Something flipped in Patrick's stomach. Her hands were wet and warm with blood, but he couldn't pry away. Her words seemed to echo around his skull. "What do you mean?" he asked, suddenly desperate. "What does that mean? The bulldog or the mouse hunter, who's the bulldog?"

"The bulldog is the mortar. Mouse Hunter is the trowel. Without the bulldog, the mouse hunter is powerless."

"What, you mean Ben? Is Ben the bulldog?"

"The bulldog or the mouse hunter will fall. You will choose, but you will not know the choice."

"What the hell does that mean?" Patrick cried, panicked. "Please, let me go!"

She pushed her face to within centimeters of his own. He could feel her hot breath on his cheek. Her tears dried, and her voice became brittle once more. "The light bringer. The running man. The butcher. The mummer. The demon's daughter. The siren. The fire drinker. Ubasti Tom. The hollow man. Perils, all, and one must fall. Do not forget." A stale wind rushed into the room and whipped out the candle flames. The stage plunged into total darkness. Then the curtain parted, and the thin man stood in the opening. Orange candlelight filtered into the darkness. The old woman was gone.

The thin man beckoned. "You have upset Madame Siquo. You must go."

•

"So wait. Why pudding?"

Ben shrugged. "Something to do with his kid, I think. It was her favorite food."

"Oh, he had a daughter?" Lucy asked, her eyes wide with intrigue. "What happened to her?"

"The same thing that happened to everyone. She just...you know... melted."

"Oh my gosh, that is so sad. So he ate pudding in, like, her memory?"

"Well, it sounds kind of stupid when you put it like that. I don't know. All I'm saying is, he worked it out so he had exactly one Snack Pack for each day's worth of his food. So he ate a pudding every day, and when he ran out of pudding, he ran out of food."

"So why didn't he...you know...get more?"

"There *were* no more Snack Packs," Ben said. "Trust me. He looked."

"No, why didn't he get more food?"

"Because there were no more Snack Packs."

"I'm confused."

"I know you are," he said, patting her shoulder.

Lucy sat back against the boat, biting her top lip. "That is so weird."

"Tell me about it."

"Did he have a wife? What happened to her?"

"Yeah, Annie. We all went to college together."

"Did she melt too?" Lucy asked, her lip quivering.

"No," Ben said, his face falling with the memory. "She got pinned between a couple of SUVs."

"Oh my gosh," Lucy said, covering her mouth with both hands.

"She was a teacher. When the bombs started falling, I guess the kids in her class started melting, so she called Patrick. He was at work across town. There was just mass chaos, and Pat told her to stay there, but she wanted to go to the day care and find Izzy. She ran out into the parking lot, and some driver had liquefied at the wheel. His car went careening over the bushes and smashed Annie into the hood of another one. I guess it was going fast, it--well, Patrick eventually made it across town, hours later, and she was still there, and I guess--I guess half of her was caught, and the other half...it was...well...it wasn't." Tears streamed down Lucy's face. She rubbed frantically at her cheeks.

"That's so horrible," she wailed.

"It gets worse," Ben said miserably. "Pat was still on the phone with her. When it happened. He heard the whole thing."

Lucy wiped her nose with her sleeve. "My God," she said, her voice thick with mucus. "What do you do for someone who's been through that?"

Ben shrugged. "You pack up and follow him to Disney World."

Just then, Patrick and the thin man reappeared at the top of the hill. Ben cleared his throat and picked himself up. "Not a word about this to Pat, okay?" She nodded.

They stood up as the pair drew near, as did the rest of the thin man's party. They had huddled near the river, keeping watch over their captives from a few dozen yards away. "Everything okay?" Ben asked. Patrick met them by the boat and slid his recently restored machete into its cardboard scabbard. "Dude. You look pale. -Er. Paler. Than usual. What happened?"

Patrick rubbed a hand over Ben's bristly scalp and said, "Something extremely odd happened. I'll fill you in when I figure out what it was."

The thin man beckoned his crew, and they joined them at the boat. "Return their weapons," Marimbo said. "He has spoken with Madame Siquo. Violo," he said, motioning to a short, stringy man with curly hair, "*le carburant*." Violo removed his pack and produced from it three small metal canisters. He handed them to Lucy, who took them suspiciously.

"What is it?" she asked.

"Fuel," said Marimbo.

"For my boat?"

"For you to do as you will," he responded. "Madame Siquo sees your path. It is not the path of Mouse Hunter. She offers a gift of fuel, so that you may fulfill your destiny."

Lucy looked at Marimbo, then down at the canisters, then back at Marimbo. "So...I should use it for the boat?"

"You don't have to—" Ben started to say, but Patrick stopped him.

"Ben. She shouldn't come with us."

"Why not?"

Patrick sighed. "There's blood on the bones, and the path is broken with peril."

Ben furrowed his brow. "What the hell are you talking about? Oh my God. Are you high?" He leaned it to check Patrick's pupils. Patrick swatted him away.

"Like I said. Processing. Just...trust me."

"Oh my God," Lucy gushed, "I can go back to New York!"

Ben rubbed fiercely at his temples. "That much fuel is not going to get you to New York," he said. Christ, was he the only one thinking like a rational person? *And why did this woman's hair smell so much like honey and lilies?*

"I say this for the second and, God willing, the last time, but Ben's right. You won't get to New York. But it may be able to take you home. You should think about heading back to Hannibal."

Marimbo raised a hand in farewell. "To each, his path." He reached into his pocket and pulled out one of Madame Siquo's rib bones. Patrick hadn't seen him go anywhere near the pile of bones, yet there one was, curved and clean but for the reddish brown dried blood. He placed it in Patrick's hand and closed his fingers around it. "Remember your path, Mouse Hunter. Remember your choice."

7.

"Are we really going to go through Memphis without seeing Graceland?"

"Yes. But keep your chin up. If we get just the right amount of lost, we'll wander straight into Tupelo."

"I can't believe we're skipping out on Elvis. Look! That sign says ten minutes away!"

"By *car*, Ben. Ten minutes by *car*. That's two and a half hours by foot, which means three hours for us."

"Why three hours for us?"

"Because I'm lost in thought. I walk much more slowly when I'm lost in thought."

"Then stop thinking, and let's race to the King's house."

"We're not going to Graceland," Patrick insisted. "It's already nearly noon. If we go to Graceland, it'll take three hours. Then you'll want to go in, then you'll probably sit and cry like a poodle skirt fan girl, then you'll come up with some stupid scheme to steal a gold record or something, and by the time we get back on the move, it'll be dark, and we'll be spending the night in the Memphis metro, which means we probably won't wake up." The tinkling sound of breaking glass echoed in the distance, punctuating his point. "If we keep along 78, we'll be well into Mississippi by the time we set up camp."

"Oh, like Mississippi's going to be a safer place to camp. They're all brigands and thieves in Mississippi, every last one of them."

"Says who?"

"Says my infallible gut instinct."

Patrick stopped in the middle of the road and literally put his foot down. "I didn't want to have to play this card, Fogelvee, but you're forcing my hand. What was the one rule I gave you about this trip?"

Ben glowered. "If I'd known how awful your decisions would be, I wouldn't have given you the power to make them."

"You'll thank me tomorrow, when we wake up not dead."

They climbed the ramp onto Highway 78 and continued on southeast, dodging cars when they could, climbing over them when they couldn't. Patrick slipped the hammer from his belt and absently knocked the hoods of vehicles as he passed. The mindless repetition helped him think. After a mile of sulking, Ben finally gave in and broke the silence. "So who was Madame Sexpo? What'd she say to you to make you all pissy?" Patrick swung the hammer and dented the hood of a Hummer with a satisfying *thunk*. "Come on," Ben pressed, "I can help you process. I have a degree in English. I'm practically a human word processor."

"And to think, I kept you around, even after the tech boom of the mid 90's," Patrick said.

"Huh?"

"Never mind." He drove the hammer through the left headlight of the Hummer for good measure. "Okay, fine. Pull up a chair."

"I'll take that to mean a metaphorical chair."

"Whatever's comfortable." He described the old woman as accurately as he could, given the darkness of the room where they'd met. Apparently Ben had eaten at Pig once on a previous visit to Memphis and had at least a foggy memory of the restaurant. Patrick told him of the old woman's dark, weathered skin and her spooky white eyes. He nodded when Ben asked if she was a fortuneteller. "She definitely dabbled in fortunes."

"Did she have a crystal ball? That's the telltale sign."

"No. She had bones."

"Bones?" Ben asked, raising an eyebrow.

"Yeah, bones. She read bones." He held up the pig rib Marimbo had given him. "Like reading tea leaves. But, you know. Bones."

"Human bones?" he asked hopefully.

"Does this look like a human bone?"

Ben frowned. "Yes?" he asked.

Patrick sighed. "It's pig, I think."

"Oh."

"She threw them on the table and did this weird hand waving thing." Patrick flopped his hands through the air, mimicking the old soothsayer. "Then she told me our path would be fraught with peril."

"Seriously?"

"Fraught, or maybe broken. Broken with? Does that make sense? No, it must've been fraught. Yeah, fraught with peril."

"Well. That doesn't sound good."

"No, it was fairly troubling."

"Did she say what kind of peril?"

"As a matter of fact, she did." Patrick closed his eyes and tried to remember the scene. He wanted to repeat the perils accurately. In doing so, he stepped straight into a pothole and stumbled down onto the pavement with a loud curse.

"That looked pretty perilous," Ben observed. "Did she warn you about that?"

"Shut up. I'm trying to remember it all." He stood up and shook out his ankle. They continued down the highway. "Let's see. There's the light bringer. The siren. The running man. The demon's daughter. The mummy. No, wait, not mummy. The mummer? Is that a thing?"

"Of course that's a thing. I thought you read *Game of Thrones*. Hold on, I want to write these down."

"I was wondering when you were going to start chronicling my journey. You'll need good notes for my biography."

"I'm not chronicling your journey, you narcissist." He retrieved a notebook and pencil from his backpack and began scribbling. "Okay, start again. I got the mummer."

Patrick ticked them off on his fingers. "The mummer, the light bringer, the siren. The running man. The demon's daughter. What else? I think there were nine. Umm...oh, the butcher! That was one. And Umbro Tom and the hollow man. Was it Umbro? No, that's not right. Umbros are

136

shorts, not Toms." He tapped his finger against his chin. "The something Tom and the hollow man. Those two were together. And one more, I think. It was...oh! The fire drinker."

"The fire drinker?" Ben asked, scribbling. "That sounds badass." Patrick agreed. Ben read back down over his list. "The mummer, the light bringer, the siren, the running man, the demon's daughter, the butcher, the something Tom, the hollow man, and the fire drinker. Jesus, this list is intense."

"It really is," Patrick said.

"Do you think we met any of these perils yet? Maybe we're, like, almost done."

"Sadly, no. I got the very distinct impression that these were perils yet to come. But on the bright side, she told me I'd make it to Disney World, so they can't be *that* bad."

"Mm," Ben said, studying the list. "So what do all these mean?"

"They mean I'm really bad at solving riddles. Can your brilliantly English-degreed mind make heads or tails of any of it?"

"Yes, obviously." Ben studied the list as he walked, barely noticing the road. Several times, Patrick had to warn him of obstacles to keep him from injuring himself. He moved his lips silently, trying to make some semblance of sense from the words. Finally, after another half mile, he tapped the notebook with his pencil. "I think I've got it!" he exclaimed.

"Really?" Patrick asked.

"No, of course not. It's all gibberish. Who am I, Robert Langdon? Why did you give me this, take it back." He shoved the notebook into Patrick's hands.

"Really? Nothing? Not even the fire drinker?"

"*Especially* not the fire drinker."

"Hmm," thought Patrick. "My money's on a reverse dragon. Let's keep an eye out for Renaissance faires."

•

It was still light out when they reached the Mississippi state line. The state welcome sign still stood next to the highway, though someone had spray painted an X through Mississippi. It now read, *Welcome to HELL.* "That's a good sign," Ben said sarcastically.

"Ha. 'Good sign.' Get it?"

"Yeah. I do. 'Cause I said it.'" They crossed over the invisible state line and left Tennessee behind. "Hey, remember that one time when we went to Memphis, probably for the last time ever, since we're likely to die, and you didn't let me see Graceland?"

"Yeah. I do. I also remember the time when you complained about it like a little girl for eight days."

As they crossed over to The Magnolia State, it was immediately apparent why the sign had been adjusted. It wasn't because Mississippi had been completely blighted by the apocalypse, though it certainly had been. On either side of the highway, the earth was scorched where it had been cleansed with fire. What buildings had once stood were now no more than destroyed foundations and piles of charred wood. The trees that had somehow managed to survive the fire had been stripped of their leaves by the flames, and clumps of yellow dust clung to the hollowed trunks. But they had expected that sort of ruin.

No, what made Mississippi a hell on earth were the human bodies nailed to the tree trunks.

"Oh, dear God," Patrick breathed, his eyes wide with horror. "Are you seeing what I'm seeing?"

Ben didn't respond. He was too busy puking in the ditch.

Dozens of rotting, yellow-crusted corpses had been hammered into the charred trees along both the sides of the road. The bodies perched high above the ground like grotesque scarecrows. Each victim's arms had been broken at the elbow and at the wrist so the hands could be bent back around the curve of the trunk and nailed in from behind. Most of them had been hammered through the feet as well.

"Jesus Christ," Patrick whispered. "What happened down here?"

Ben shook his head, wiping spittle from his pale lips. "This trip just took a turn."

They walked on in silence. As the sun fell toward the horizon, the fog took on its pinkish twilight glow. The crucified remains turned a deep, reddish hue through the layers of rosy clouds, like streaks of blood in the brume.

"Maybe we should take a different road," Ben suggested after almost an hour of silence.

"Might be worth a shot," Patrick quickly agreed. They'd have to make camp before long, and he didn't want to sleep beneath a canopy of corpses if he could help it.

They left the highway at the next exit and headed east on what a rusty green sign told them was New Craft Road. The cars were fewer on this lower street, and they covered ground quickly. But the corpses kept pace, ushering them deeper and deeper into the heart of the state.

"Who would do something like this?" Ben asked.

"Anyone on our list fit the bill?"

"For all I know, *everyone* on our list fits the bill."

The deepening darkness brought a reprieve from the sight of the bodies hanging from the trees, but it did little to settle their imaginations. Every rustle in the woods was a creeping killer; every gust of wind was the breath of a psychopath with a hammer and a handful of nails. Patrick's anxiety was so bad that even he, the paragon of rationale that he was, began to see things in the night. A scorched bush was a crouching madman. A low-flying bird was an arrow loosed from a hunter's bow. A swaying tree was a hulk with a knife. A trick of the moon against the fog was the flare of a bonfire.

"Hey. Is that a bonfire?" Ben whispered. Patrick stared at him, incredulous.

"Are you in my mind?"

"What?"

"Do you really see a bonfire?"

"Do you?"

"Yeah. But I'm imagining it."

"I don't think you are."

The phantom light flickered off to the right, several hundred yards from the road. They glanced at each other. Then Ben took a step off the pavement and began creeping toward the fire.

"Ben!" Patrick hissed. "What are you doing?"

"I want to see what it is."

"Are you insane?!" he asked, slapping Ben's arm. "We have to go! Now!"

"It could be another survivor. We should find out."

"No! We should not find out!" Patrick spat. "You know who lights a huge, completely visible fire in a serial killer's forest? *The serial killer!*"

Ben thought about this. Okay, yes, it made sense. But he still wanted to know for sure who was camping in the forest. If it *wasn't* the person responsible for the crucifixions, they'd have an ally for the night. And if it *was* the murderer, well, they'd just run like hell. Or throw a hammer at him or something. "I'm going in. Better the devil you know than the devil you don't." He took another step into the woods, then stopped and turned back. "You should probably take out the machete."

"Ben!" Patrick hissed. "Benjamin Marjorie Fogelvee! Get back here! The rule of the road! *The rule of the road!*" But Ben was gone, stepping lightly toward the flames in the hazy distance. Patrick cursed aloud and followed his idiotic friend to their mutual death.

He caught up about 20 yards in. Ben was crouching behind a wide tree, one that was not acting as a support for a pierced body, thank God. Patrick crouched close behind him and slapped him on the back of the head.

"Ow!" he hissed.

"You're gonna get us killed," Patrick hissed back. Ben held a finger to his lips to signal for quiet. Together, they peered around the side of the tree. The fog cleared for a moment, and they could see plainly through the night air. An older man in a black shirt and black pants stood near the fire, holding up a small book. He seemed to be speaking adamantly, though they couldn't make out any of the words. He faced a group of people, maybe 20 or 30 of them, who crossed themselves and folded their hands tightly across their breasts.

"It's a preacher," Patrick said, surprised.

"*That's* the kind of person who starts a fire in the middle of a serial killer's forest," Ben said. "The kind with irrationally strong belief in supreme protection." He shifted his weight and stepped on a brittle twig. It cracked loudly and echoed around the woods. The man with the book stopped and peered out into the darkness.

"You've made your presence known to us," he called into the darkness in an easy southern drawl. "Be you friend, we welcome you to our fire. Be you foe, the devil will welcome you to his."

"Shit," Patrick muttered. "What do we do?"

Ben shrugged. "We could make a run for it."

"The two of us outrunning God's army? Dammit, Ben." He slapped the back of Ben's head again. "This is *precisely* why we have the rule of the road." He drew his machete from its sheath and held it tightly in his right hand. He pulled out the baton, too, and flicked it open with his left. "If we survive the night, I'm killing you in the morning." He stepped out from behind the tree and approached the fire. Ben took a firm grip on his bat and cut out after his friend. Together, they pushed through the fog, weapons at the ready.

One of the women in the congregation saw them first. "There!" she gasped, pointing at them. The man with the book whirled around to face them. He was unarmed. He spread his hands wide in a sign of peaceable innocence and took a step into the darkness.

"We are unarmed," he said, his voice booming through the woods. "You are welcome to our fire, but with weapons sheathed. My flock is peaceful, and we welcome peaceful sheep alone." A few cries of *Amen!* went up from the congregation.

Patrick looked at Ben. Ben looked at Patrick. "He looks unarmed," Ben whispered. "And old. I think we could take him."

"They outnumber us by a thousand percent."

"But they're mostly old women. I think we can take them, too."

Patrick weighed their options. It was unlikely an old preacher and his unarmed, elderly followers had climbed dozens of trees and nailed living (and presumably fighting) people there. And they had a fire, and a good number of people. He decided to go along with it, at least for the time being. "Here goes nothin'," he whispered. "Out of the frying pan..."

He slipped the machete back into its sheath and pocketed the baton. Ben followed suit, flipping the bat over and grabbing it by the thick end. "Sorry if we caused any alarm," Patrick said, walking toward the group with his hands spread wide like the preacher's. "We saw the bodies in the trees, and we thought—"

"Abominations," the reverend said sadly, shaking his head and clicking his tongue. "A sign that God has abandoned this world, to be sure. But we hope, and we pray, and we believe that He will return." There were more cries of *Amen!*

"You're not concerned about the fire?" Ben asked. "That it might draw attention?"

"We built the fire for warmth. We will not be scared off God's great gift of earthen providence by the likes of sinners."

"But the bodies—" Patrick started, but once again, the preacher interrupted him.

"There is a great strength in numbers. We are stronger now than we were before you arrived. The evil man does evil deeds, but evil finds him, too, in the end. If we must be that end, so be it." A young man in dark trousers and a dirty white shirt whooped joyfully from the other side of the fire. "Amen, brother," the preacher told him. He turned back to the newcomers. "I'm Reverend James Maccabee, and this here's the New Herald Christian Church. You boys are welcome to stay for the night, or longer, if your souls are at peace here."

"We really appreciate it," Patrick said. "We won't be a bother. We have our own blankets and food."

"Dirty, thin blankets and canned food, I reckon?" the reverend asked with a smile. "Nonsense. You boys keep those things for the road, where life is hard. In our church, our guests are part of the flock. If you'll allow, we'll put you up in a tent, and you'll share our meat tonight."

"Did you say meat?" Ben asked.

The reverend nodded. "These woods are plentiful, for those who know where to look. The good Lord, in His mercy, has provided us with deer for tonight's meal." He gestured across the fire, and, indeed, two women were hunched over a deer, trimming its hide from the red flesh, preparing it for the fire. "With the Lord's guidance, we never want for food."

Tears welled in Ben's eyes. He hadn't eaten a morsel of real meat in over two years, and even that was a rotting pigeon that had been dead under the El for at least two days. The memory of dysentery still made his stomach turn. Fresh meat was a miracle. Surely these people were God's own chosen ones. "Thank you," he said, his voice trembling. "Just... thank you."

The preacher clapped his hand on Ben's shoulder. "Thank the Lord, son. Thank the good Lord."

Dinner that evening turned into a great feast in honor of the new guests. The church's gatherers dug roots and wild onions from the earth and softened them together in a pot of boiling water. There was even a type of flatbread, made from ground wild grass and edible flowers set on a flat rock over the flames. The grease from the deer soaked into the crude, crisp dough and made it a pliable, earthy wrap. Patrick and Ben were given seats of honor in the inner circle around the fire, just to the right of Reverend Maccabee. The man said grace over the food, thanking

God for his provisions in these dark times, and he prayed for their safety and protection. With a rousing *Amen!* the congregation began to eat. Patrick could not remember a more satisfying meal.

The congregation was in high spirits. Reverend Maccabee laughed and shared stories with Mrs. Goodson, an elderly woman Patrick assumed would be the administrator in a normal, pre-M-Day brick and mortar church. When they'd licked the last of the grease from their fingers, the reverend settled back against the log he used for a bench, and the conversation gradually became more solemn. A handful of the church members, the younger and stronger among the group, wandered off and began linking together a wooden scaffold off to the side of the little clearing, right next to the biggest tree in sight. Fire had left the burned earth hard and dry, and two young men struggled with a set of stakes that refused to be driven into the ground.

"Our altar," Maccabee explained, seeing Patrick's wondering gaze. "We'll have an evening service before bed." Ben offered to help the two men, and Maccabee reckoned that they'd be glad for the assistance.

"Do you have a service every night?" Patrick asked as Ben trotted off to struggle with a dull stake.

"Every night, and every morning. We build our altar where we can, if the Lord provides us with the means for Eucharist. Otherwise, we have a simple prayer service."

"That's nice," Patrick said. He had never been much for structured religion (or unstructured, for that matter), but it was comforting to know that even in times like these, organizational worship could still exist. It was something left over from the time before. So much had burned away or died in the Jamaican attacks; there was little left to carry over into this scorched new era.

"It makes life worth fighting for," the preacher agreed.

Patrick wondered if the people nailed to the trees had fought for their lives. He looked up at the blackened trunks above. There were no crucified bodies, at least not within sight. He was thankful to the fog for that much. "Do you know who did that to those people?" he asked, indicating the trees.

"The same one who is the source of all evil thoughts and deeds."

"Miley Cyrus?" Patrick asked. The reverend didn't smile.

"The devil himself. That Lucifer."

Patrick started. "Lucifer. Light bringer!" he breathed, barely above a whisper.

The reverend nodded. "So he is called. A strange name for the Prince of Darkness. But then, he *is* the Great Deception."

Patrick pulled out the notebook and circled "Light Bringer." *Cripes,* he thought, *this first peril is a doozy.* He wasn't sure how to word his next question without sounding like a loon. But, he reasoned, if there was one person who would take it seriously, it was a man of the cloth. "So... how would one go about...you know...fighting the devil? If one were so inclined?"

Maccabee spread his arms and raised his eyes heavenward. "With prayer."

"That's it?"

"It is our best weapon against the darkness."

Patrick frowned. "I was hoping for something a little more actionable. Like, 'with a crossbow.'"

"Well," said the older man, a sly gleam in his eye. "Prayer is the best weapon, but that machete might just be second best."

The preacher got up to go check on the altar progress, leaving Patrick alone at the fire. He reached into his back pocket and pulled out the worn piece of notebook paper. He unfolded it carefully and held it down to the firelight. *We're going to make it,* he thought, reading the scribbled print. *God knows I don't know how, but we're going to make it to the Magic Kingdom.*

•

Lucy shivered against the river wind. It was dark, and cold, and she was so tired, she just wanted to stop at the nearest bank and go to sleep. But that one guy, the skinny one, he had told her not to stop for anything, 'cause it was so dangerous. But boy, was she miserable. Cold, and wet with river spray, and tired, and aggravated, and headed straight back to stupid freaking Hannibal with its stupid freaking Tom Sawyers and Becky Thatchers. Whose idea was it to keep *that* little tradition alive, anyway? Dressing up those kids was so freaking stupid.

She had passed the Arch about an hour ago, so she couldn't be that far from home. But jeepers, she was *tired.* She could almost close her eyes and drift off...

She jerked back awake just before the boat crashed into a heavy wooden dock. She jerked the wheel, just like the boys had shown her, and she zipped back out into the center of the river. "Holy hell!" she cried aloud. *That was close.*

She was thirsty. She needed a Red Bull. Whatever happened to Red Bull? They probably went out of business when everybody died. People probably spent all their money on funerals and stuff. Not on Red Bull.

Poor Red Bull.

She saw a light flicker up around the next bend. She squinted through the foggy darkness and continued on toward it. Not like she had a choice. She scuttled around the bend and saw it wasn't just a light; it was a torch. A full out fire torch, just like in *Indiana Jones*! She instinctively ran a hand over her whole body, clearing any snakes, spiders, mutant millipedes, or monkey brains that might be crawling around on her. *Ugh.* That movie was so gross.

The guy holding the torch was waving at her. *Oh, yeah, like I'm gonna stop and pick up a hitchhiker,* she thought. *Nice try, rapist.* She was glad she'd been directed not to stop. She tried not to look at the man as she sped past. Maybe he would think she hadn't seen him. But dammit, trying not to look at something you really wanted to look at was impossible, because that made you want to look at it even more, and the fire drew her eyes, so she *did* sneak a peek, and she gasped when she was close enough to see his face. She turned the tiller and sped across the river at a diagonal, away from the man on the bank. She knew he couldn't jump into the boat from where he stood, but still. She wanted to get far away. Even in the firelight, she could tell something was wrong with him. It was just a small discoloration, but it scared the bejeebers out of her. He had what her grandma called the Devil's Eye.

•

That night, Patrick dreamed of fire demons on horseback chopping off the heads of crying children with axes of brimstone. The rotten egg sting of sulfur poisoned the air as the heads spun in the wind. When each head landed on the scorched earth, it burrowed deep into the ground, and a tall, gnarled tree exploded from the soil. The trees had human faces etched into their trunks, and they screamed and wailed as the fire demons galloped through them, slaughtering more fodder. The trees cried tears of yellow blood that spilled down their trunks and pooled at their roots. The yellow goo rose into a tide that washed over the forest and soaked everything with its bitter metallic stink. A great hole ripped open in the center of the forest, and the yellow blood began a quickening spiral into the core of the Earth, pulling and sucking the screaming trees and decapitated bodies down with it. The Earth sucked the forest dry, revealing an entire army of fire demons, armed now with sledgehammers and red-hot railroad spikes. Each demon turned to the creature on his left and drove the hot spike through its brain. Somewhere, beyond the plain of massacre, from deep within the hole in the Earth, their prince laughed.

Patrick opened his eyes with a gasp. Two dark eyes stared down at him from above. He lurched up in his bedroll and scooted back into the corner of the little tent. "Easy, son, easy," said Reverend Maccabee. "You're all right now. You was havin' a nightmare." Patrick looked around uncertainly. Ben was still asleep under his blankets. He heard the easy crackle of the fire outside. He exhaled heavily through his mouth.

"Sorry. Was I shouting? Did I wake you?"

"It's all right," the reverend said, a queer look of concern on his face. "Friend Patrick, I have to tell you; nightmares are one of the tools of the devil."

Patrick rubbed at his eyes. "I think you have nightmares confused with FOX News."

The reverend did not laugh. "I'm as serious as the grave, son. The devil works in many ways, all of them terrible. One of those ways is through our dreams. Our nightmares. A soul burdened with nighttime terrors is a soul in the grasp of Satan."

"Uhm--I think I maybe just had a bad root last night or something. Could be the deer. I've never really had venison. I'm not sure how my body reacts to it." He thumped his chest and belched. "'Scuse me."

The preacher took Patrick's hand in his own and squeezed it gently. "The only way to be bathed in His light, to shut out the Darkness, is to be saved. Do you want to be saved, Patrick?"

Ooooh boy, he thought. *Here we go.* "Do *you* think I should be saved?" he asked, trying his hand at diplomacy.

"I think those among us who are not saved are doomed to an eternity in the fires of Hell."

"So that's a yes, then." Patrick examined his current options and discerned the path of least resistance. He decided that the simplest road was the sidewalk to salvation. Besides, Madame Siquo's list made him uneasy, and one more layer of protection against the devil couldn't hurt. "Okay. Then saved I shall be. Do we do this in the morning, or...?"

Maccabee shook his hand in excitement. "Once you decide to be saved, there's not a second to lose! We must bring about your salvation. The devil may enter you at any time." Patrick fought harder than that very same devil to keep at least six inappropriate jokes from escaping his mouth. Now just wasn't the time. "If you're ready, we'll do it right now."

Patrick shrugged. "Sure. What about Ben? Should we wake him up? We should probably save him too. He's got all *kinds* of blights of the soul."

The reverend glanced over at the sleeping figure. "Your friend is untroubled in his sleep. No signs of Satan have been made manifest to me. The New Herald Christian Church believes a pure soul is already saved and needs not the cleansing."

"Oh, trust me, that soul's not pure. The devil's been entering that one for years. Let's wake 'im up." Patrick tapped Ben on the crown of his head. "Hey! Wake up! We're gonna get you baptized!"

The trio stumbled out of the tent, eyes bleary with sleep. Reverend Maccabee approached the three night guards and explained the situation. Two of them broke off and began waking up the congregation in their tents. "You really don't have to wake everyone up," Patrick said.

"Oh, just me?" Ben sneered with a yawn.

"Salvation is a joyous occasion, brothers!" the reverend said with a broad smile. "Your brothers and sisters shall witness your cleansing and be heralds of the Lord's joy."

In ten minutes, the whole party was assembled. The members of the church seemed tired, but happy. They swayed and clapped in the night as the old would-be administrator led them in an uplifting hymn. Reverend Maccabee threw on a purple cloak over his black pants and shirt, then mounted the wooden altar and motioned for Patrick and Ben to do the same. "I hate you," Ben whispered as they climbed the stairs. "I just want you to know that."

"Those are the devil's words coming through you, Ben. Soon, you won't mean them anymore."

Two of the men from the watch climbed the steps after them; the altar was plenty spacious for the entire group. Reverend Maccabee held up his hands, and the people below fell silent. "Brothers and sisters!" he boomed. "Tonight, we have in our midst two poor sinners. Two decent human beings, two good-hearted boys, who have found themselves plunged into the devil's well. These two young men, like so many others, crave the forgiveness of the Lord. And, brothers and sisters, the Lord is good." Cries of *Yes he is!* and *Amen!* peppered the crowd. "Our God in Heaven is a kind God. He is a *merciful* God! He is a *forgiving* God! He is the Way, the Truth, and the Light, and it is through our God that *we shall be saved!*" *Amen!* "And so it is with great joy that we, His pure flock, offer salvation to the lost. It is with humility and awe that we are able to cleanse these young men here tonight." He turned and stepped over to Patrick and placed his open palm on the sinner's forehead. "Son of our Lord Jesus Christ, brother to all men and women, do you reject Satan and all his evil works?"

"All of them. Even the little ones," Patrick said.

"Is it your wish to accept the Lord Jesus Christ into your heart, and to purge the demon from your soul, to free your worldly body and eternal spirit from his clutches?"

"That is my wish, yes."

"Do you cry out for forgiveness from our Heavenly Father and beg him for his mercy?"

"I do. I do cry out." He leaned forward and whispered, "Should I cry out now, or...?" But Maccabee continued.

"Is it your wish to be saved?"

"Yes, being saved is a priority," Patrick nodded.

"Then. By your own admission and acceptance, you ask us, the holy flock, to cleanse you of your desire to do evil." Patrick opened his mouth to say that he never really desired to do evil but decided not to embarrass the minister. He seemed to be having such a big moment. "The Lord God asks us to be cleansed in three ways, just as He is the three spirits in one God. We cleanse with prayer." He made the sign of the cross over Patrick's head and mumbled a quiet prayer. When he was done, he placed his hand once again on Patrick's head. "We cleanse with water." He motioned to one of his two assistants. The young man stepped forward and handed him a halved geode full of water. The preacher poured the water on Patrick's head and let it spill down his face and neck. Patrick cried out in shock from the cold, but the assistant knew to expect this. He took Patrick's hand and squeezed it in support. Maccabee handed the cup to the second assistant, who went to refill it for Ben's salvation. The reverend turned back to Patrick. "And we cleanse by sacrifice." He nodded to the assistant. The young man pulled Patrick's hand up and back behind him, securing it, palm out, against the trunk of the large tree next to the platform. Maccabee reached into his robes and pulled out a hammer and a thick, iron spike. "What--wait, what are you doing?" Patrick asked, suddenly alarmed. He squirmed and struggled to break free, but the assistant held his hand firmly in place. Maccabee put the point of the spike to Patrick's palm and, with one strong, smooth stroke, drove it right through his flesh and into the tree.

Patrick's scream filled the entire forest. Ben gaped in sheer terror. "Jesus fuck!" he yelled. He ran forward and drove a shoulder into the assistant's chest, knocking him off the platform. The reverend looked at him with surprise that quickly turned to anger. He swung the hammer at Ben's head, but Ben ducked just in time. The force of the swing carried the preacher off balance for a split second. It was just long enough for Ben to grip the spike protruding from Patrick's bloody hand. "I'm really sorry, Pat; I think this is gonna hurt like a bitch," he said quickly. He hauled at the spike with a loud grunt and pulled it out of the tree, back through the hole in Patrick's palm. Patrick screamed again and doubled over, clutching his injured hand against his chest. Ben hefted the spike and turned just in time to see the hammer swinging back down toward his face. He dodged to the side just as the hammer caught his chin. A red explosion of pain clouded his vision for a second. He blinked hard and shook his head. The preacher took the hammer in both hands, raised it high over his head, and growled as he swung down again, hard. Ben sidestepped the third blow and jammed the iron spike up into the preacher's ribcage. He could actually *feel* a lung pop against the metal point. Maccabee's eyes grew wide. He dropped the hammer and clutched at his wound. Ben yanked the spike back out. A steaming line of blood spurted out from the hole. The preacher fell to the platform, gasping for air, his own blood pooling around him. His fingers scrabbled in the sticky red puddle, but his eyes grew heavy, and his irises rolled up into his head. His feet gave one last fluttering kick, and he passed on to the other side.

Ben looked down at the congregation. They stared back up at him in shock. No one spoke. From somewhere in the night, Ben literally heard a cricket chirp. "Patrick," he muttered out of the side of his mouth. "Can you run?"

Patrick was whimpering against the tree. He looked up at Ben, tears of pain and frustration pouring down his face, and nodded.

"Okay. 'Cause we're gonna do that. Right now."

"What about our stuff?"

"Shit. Right. Okay, I'll meet you in the woods." Patrick opened his mouth to say something, but Ben leapt from the platform and sprinted over to the tent. The congregation exploded in cries of outrage. They ran after him, the entire mob crashing through the maze of tents. Ben looked back over his shoulder just long enough to see Patrick hobbling down off the platform and heading out into the forest.

Ben dove into the tent and slung his pack over his shoulders. He hefted Patrick's bag and machete in one hand. *I hope you packed everything before bed*, he thought miserably. One of the young men from the mob pushed through the flap into the tent. Ben whirled around and smashed him in the face with the side of the iron spike. The man stumbled back out through the opening, knocking over the line of angry zealots behind him. Ben threw the spike through the opening as hard as he could and heard it clang off someone's head. He grabbed his bat, did a quick spot check, and found the tent otherwise empty. Then he dove out the rear flaps just as a middle-aged woman came around the corner of the tent swinging a tree branch. He jabbed the bat in her stomach. She doubled over, and the woman running behind her tripped over her collapsed form and splayed onto the dead earth. Ben took off into the woods and disappeared into the darkness.

When he was sure they'd stopped chasing him, he slowed and circled back, giving the campfire a wide berth. After a few minutes of cautious stalking, he heard a loud hiss off to his right. He turned to find Patrick waving at him from behind a tree. Ben jogged over, helped Patrick to his feet, and together they plunged back through the woods to the highway.

8.

"I need to be honest, here, Pat. I did *not* see that coming."

Patrick held his hand up to the sky. He could see the yellow disc of the sun perfectly through the hole in his palm. "It looks worse in daylight," he winced.

"Come here, let's clean it again."

Patrick got up and crossed to the hood of the Mazda where Ben sat with the supplies. Ben twisted the cap off a fresh bottle of water and handed it to Patrick, who took in a sharp breath as he poured a little stream over and through the wound in his hand.

"If you'd just use the dirty creek water like a real man, we could save on the drinking water," Ben pointed out.

"Stop trying to give me sepsis," Patrick said through gritted teeth. He'd somehow gotten a blade of grass stuck to the hole in his hand, and he plucked it out with a little whimper of pain.

"Clean?" Ben asked.

"Cleanish."

"Disinfectant time!"

"You don't have to sound so cheerful about it," Patrick glowered.

"This is an awful waste of good whiskey."

Ben looked at the bottle of Canadian Mist they'd gotten from Horace. "This is a good waste of awful whiskey," he said. "Really, we should be grateful Reverend Crazyass gave you a wound to dump it on." He took Patrick's injured hand and held it firmly in place. "You ready?"

"No."

"You want a drink?"

"No." But he grabbed the bottle and took a quick shot anyway. It burned like kerosene on his tongue. He struggled to swallow it. "*Blugh.* It tastes like scorpion venom and swamp water."

"And only $11.99 a bottle." Ben took a slug himself, made an appropriately pained face, then dumped a few ounces on Patrick's open wound.

By the time he was done screaming, Patrick's throat was raw.

Ben ripped off a fresh, cleanish strip of blanket and wrapped it around the hand. Patrick whimpered as he pulled it tight and tied it off. "Next time the world ends, let's make sure we're stocked up on peroxide and bandages," Ben said.

Patrick glowered at the first aid kit, which lay open on the hood. Its contents included, and were extremely limited to, six Band-Aids, four cotton swabs, a bottle of Tylenol, some nail polish remover, a packet of Midol, a travel box of Clorox Handi Wipes, and a roll of Tums. "Who packed that thing?" Ben asked. "Pee Wee Herman?"

"The really scary part is, that's the kit we had in a house with a five-year-old. Criminy. We're lucky 20 fold-up accordion snakes didn't pop out when we opened the lid." He picked up the Tylenol with his good hand and struggled with the lid for a while before turning it over to Ben. "Help. It's childproof."

He couldn't tell if he really had a fever, or it if was a phantom sickness, but he wasn't taking any chances. The most benign injury could turn fatal without basic medical supplies. And a half-inch hole through the hand was not a benign injury. If the alcohol didn't kill the infection, he'd lose his hand. That's a surgery he didn't want to think about undergoing with full sedation, much less in the backwoods of Mississippi while buzzed on a bottle of Canadian Mist with Ben as his surgeon. He checked the bandage and made sure it was tight. The wound seemed to have stopped bleeding, at least, though he seemed to have lost feeling in his three middle fingers. He didn't take that for a good sign. "We need real medical supplies," he said. "Because I am not letting you cut off my hand."

"What's the point of even *having* a machete if we're not gonna use it?" Ben complained.

They rooted through the abandoned vehicles on their stretch of highway in search of an emergency kit. After fourteen cars, all they'd come up with was a box of Kleenex and three road flares. *Man*, Ben thought, *people were so unprepared for the apocalypse.*

"Did you ever watch The Walking Dead?" Patrick asked, popping open the glove compartment of a Ford Ranger.

"Uh, I don't know, was it about zombies?"

"Yeah."

"Then, yeah, obviously I watched it, idiot. What about it?"

"There was this one episode, I think it was season 2, when they needed medical supplies, so they dug through all the abandoned cars on the highway. Just like we're doing. Except you know what they found?"

"Zombies."

"Well. Yes. But you know what else they found? *Everything.* They found everything they needed. Pain pills, food, guns, one guy even picked up a *completely customized* bladed tool kit. It was like a box o' weapons made specifically to fight zombies that this dead guy just happened to have had made sometime *before* the zombie apocalypse. They got *everything.* And me? I got this bag of plastic toothpicks," he said, holding it up.

Ben shrugged. "Fiction is bullshit. What can you do?"

"My addiction to movies and television has left me entirely unprepared for the harsh realities of post-apocalyptic life."

"Which is strange, considering just how many popular stories took place in post-apocalyptic times."

"Yeah. You'd think somebody would've gotten it right."

They made a decision to stay on the highway in an effort to mitigate run-ins with "backwoods crazyasses," as Ben put it. It was a decision that served them well all morning and into the afternoon, as they trudged deeper into Mississippi along Highway 78. The plan took a turn, though, when they found themselves on the far side of a town called Holly Springs.

"Umm...what happened to the road?" Patrick asked, peering down over the jagged edge of an overpass.

"There's some down there," Ben said, pointing to a pile of asphalt and metal rods on the surface road below. "And some more over there, and some there. Man. What is it with idiots blowing up bridges?"

"Looks like this one died of natural causes," Patrick said, inspecting the edge. The overpass showed no signs of being blown to bits; it had just collapsed.

"Your tax dollars at work," Ben said.

They could just barely see the far end of the overpass through the yellow cloud. It seemed to be intact. They slid down the embankment and crossed over to the lower highway to the other side. They climbed up the hill and once again stopped dead in their tracks. "Okay, now *this...this* is the work of explosives." The entire stretch of 78, as far as the eye could see, was pitted with massive craters in both lanes. Each crater had to have been between 50 and 100 feet in diameter, with a new crater starting every 10 or 20 feet. Dark shadows through the fog indicated similar holes stretching to the horizon.

"Now, what's the point of that? Seriously. Who would do that?"

"Crazy Harry," Patrick suggested.

Ben sighed. "All right, I'll bite. Who's Crazy Harry?"

"You know. That wild-eyed Muppet with crazy hair that goes around blowing everything to kingdom come."

"How do you know that?"

"You'd be amazed at what I know about Muppets. *Amazed.*"

"What do we do now?"

Patrick sighed. The highway cut through what looked like a national park or a forest reserve. The destroyed road was flanked on both sides by dense forest. He pulled the baton from his pocket and flicked it open. "Now we go back into the woods."

Despite the explosions on the highway, the forest here seemed largely untouched. Only a very few leaves clung to the branches, but the trunks stood tall and strong, and, more importantly, they were free of broken bodies. They walked parallel to the highway, or at least as close to parallel as the rough underbrush would allow.

"So, do you want to talk about what happened last night?" Patrick asked tentatively.

Ben shot him a sideways glance. "Do *you?*"

"I just mean that...well, you know...you kind of...killed a guy. Having

154

never killed a person myself, I just don't know if it's the kind of thing one needs to talk about or not."

Ben thought for a few moments. It sounded stupid, but he hadn't really considered it murder. "That guy straight up murdered, like, 300 people. And he got a third of the way to killing you. He was probably the textbook definition of a homicidal maniac. I'm pretty sure that rates him in the 'monster' category, not the 'real human being' category."

"Hey, you'll get no arguments from me," Patrick said, raising his hands defensively. "It was easily the most intense thing anyone's ever done for me. And I say that knowing that my mother was in labor for 23 hours. I just want you to know that if you feel the need to talk about it, you know, we can talk about it. That's all."

"Well, thank you, Maury, I'll keep that in mind."

"Also, I want to make sure you're not addicted to murder now."

"Yes, Patrick, I have the bloodlust."

"Well!" Patrick exclaimed. "I don't know how it works! You get the taste for blood, who knows what you're liable to do?"

"Are you being serious right now?" Ben asked.

"It happens in the movies," Patrick pointed out.

"I am not addicted to murder," Ben insisted.

"You know who else didn't think he was addicted to murder? You know who? Jeffrey Dahmer. You could be the next Jeffrey Dahmer."

"You know, now that you mention it, I *do* sort of feel like committing a murder." He slugged Patrick on the arm with the bat.

"I knew it! Bloodlust!" he cried, spinning away from the bat. "There's only one way to cure you. You'll need to rub poison oak on your neth- ers and put a live bumblebee in your mouth. That's the only cure for the bloodlust. My imagination has made it so. I'll be happy to find you some poison oak, but I'm not applying it."

But Ben wasn't listening. He had stopped short and was now looking around the forest in alarm. "Shh," he whispered. Patrick grew still, and the two men listened. "Do you hear that?"

Patrick listened harder. He heard only the occasional rustle of leaves above. "I don't hear anything," he said, shaking his head. "What do you--" But then he *did* hear something. The rustling wasn't coming from above, it was coming from somewhere behind them. "What is that?" he asked.

"It sounds like footsteps. Someone running." Someone, or *something*.

Whatever it was, it was sprinting through the woods, coming in fast.

"Do you see anything?" Patrick asked, craning his neck to see around the trees.

Ben squinted into the mist. "I can't see a damn thing in this fog."

"It's definitely coming this way." Patrick tightened his grip on the baton. Ben did the same with the bat.

"Get out the machete," he hissed. "Just in case."

Patrick shook his head. "I can't swing it well one-handed, especially not left-handed. I can control my left hand about as well as I can control a Slinky. I'm less likely to put more holes in myself with the baton."

They stood there, facing west, listening to the rapid crunching grow louder and louder. And then they could hear another sound, the wet, gasping snarl of a feral animal. *Cripes, it's a wolf*, thought Patrick, and he severely wished he had a gun. He didn't generally go in for firearms, as a rule, but he heard they did wonders against wild animals. He and Ben both started backing away instinctively, not lifting their eyes from the western horizon for an instant. The sounds grew louder, echoing all around them in the fog. And then, suddenly, there it was.

It was no more than a shadow at first, a dark silhouette against the curtain of yellow mist. It materialized as if the fog itself had formed it; one second it was a shadow, the very next, it was a wild-eyed man, bursting from the yellow mist and running at a full sprint. He was skinny, *incredibly* skinny, even compared to Patrick. His denim overalls hung loosely from his gaunt frame. A long, shaggy bird's nest of hair flowed behind him as he ran, teeth bared, a string of saliva dripping from his lips.

He was running directly at them.

"What's he running from?" Ben asked, panicked.

"What's he running *to*?" Patrick countered. Then he gasped. "The running man." And then, faster than they could believe, the rabid man was on them. He leapt through the air and slammed headfirst into Ben's chest. The bat fell from his hands, and they hit the dirt and rolled, the man snarling and snapping his teeth. Ben punched and kicked wildly. He landed a blow to the man's face, but the attacker didn't flinch. He wrestled Ben's arms to the ground with surprising strength. He opened his mouth and lurched in to bite, but Ben got his feet planted firmly on the man's chest and pushed off with all his power. The man stumbled backward.

Ben threw a kick at his face. The man caught Ben's shoe and attacked it with his teeth, tearing frantically into the leather.

Patrick ran up behind him and swung the baton as hard as his left arm would allow. It glanced off the running man's shoulder blade. "Dammit!" Patrick spat. "Stupid left hand!" Ben tried to kick free, but the man had a firm grasp on his shoe and was ripping through the sole. Patrick tossed the baton away and picked up Ben's bat. He took the bat in both hands, ignoring the screaming pain in his right palm, took a running leap, and swung the bat directly into the back of the man's head. It connected with a sickening *CRACK!* The bat snapped in two, and the man dropped Ben's shoe and stumbled forward, falling face first into a tree trunk. He tottered on his knees, stunned for a second, long enough for Ben to reach into his knapsack and pull out the wrench. He brought it down hard on the crown of the man's head, again and again, but the man didn't fall. Instead, he pushed off the tree and dove at Patrick, who ducked and rolled just in the nick of time.

"Holy shit!" Ben said. "Who *is* this guy?"

The running man screamed savagely. He lunged again. Patrick pulled out his hammer and slammed it against the man's kneecap as they toppled to the ground. He might as well have been swinging a feather. The man clawed at Patrick's face, teeth gnashing. Ben surged forward and drove his shoulder into the man, sending him flailing to his back. Ben cried out in pain. "I think I just broke my shoulder," he said, bewildered.

"You don't need your shoulder to run!" Patrick cried. He picked up the baton, humped his backpack higher up on his shoulders, and took off through the woods, sprinting blindly through the fog. Ben scrambled after him. They could hear the footfalls of the madman just behind them.

They ran down a hill covered in dead leaves. Patrick almost lost his footing, and they heard the man take a tumble behind them. Ben looked back to see him sprawling forward down the hill toward them. He clawed the earth, scrambling to get back to his feet, his face red with fury.

Patrick led them across a small creek and up a hill on the other side. They hurdled piles of brush as they ran. The man chasing them just crashed straight through them. The branches tangled around his feet, and now and then he would go down, screaming and spitting, but he always scrabbled to his feet.

Patrick spun around frantically, searching for something, *anything,* to offer shelter. "There!" he cried as they broke into a clearing in the woods. Across the open field, shrouded in fog, sat a long, low cabin. They bolted across the clearing, the madman tearing close behind. Ben reached the cabin first. He was moving too fast to stop and slammed into the screen door. The screen ripped and caught his flailing arms in its net. He disentangled himself just as Patrick ran up behind him, threw open the screen door, and, to his amazement, turned the main door knob to find it unlocked. They dove into the cabin and slammed the door shut just as the man plowed into it, full force, pushing it back open. They were both knocked to the floor. Ben scrambled back up and threw his good shoulder into the door, avoiding the swiping claw reaching around from the other side. He slammed the door back into the jamb. The man snarled and drew his arm back to push with both hands. Ben took the chance and heaved the door closed. He threw the deadbolt and turned the knob lock, then sank back against the door, wheezing.

Patrick lay on his back, propped at an awkward angle by his backpack. His chest heaved with labored breaths. "I haven't run that much since ever." He grabbed at his chest. His heart hammered away like a sledge. "I think I'm having a heart attack. Oh my God! I'm having a heart attack!"

The man was beating and clawing at the door. They could hear him scraping the wood with his fingernails. The sound raised goosebumps on the back of Ben's neck. "See? This is why you need a secret knock. To keep out the rabid hill people."

They took stock of the cabin and found it to be an abandoned ranger station. A poster tacked to a cork board on the opposite wall welcomed them to Holly Springs National Forest. Beneath it, a large map showed the cabin's position on the western edge with a gold star, along with the locations of several other stations. Three display tables formed a long U along the edges of the cabin, their protective glass tops smashed in. Most of whatever had been inside had been taken, leaving only historic photos and newspaper clippings, old hiking guides, and a handful of rock samples. A wooden, bear-shaped placard behind the middle counter informed them that only they could prevent forest fires. A podium stood against the opposite wall, facing three small benches. The door to the ranger's office hung broken off at one hinge. Inside, the floor and desk were strewn with papers and file folders. The cabin's windows had been boarded up, and the only real light filtered down through a trio of sky-lights in the ceiling.

They heaved one of the heavy display tables over to the door as a barricade. The locks were holding strong against the man's fervent hammering, but there was no use taking chances. Ben pulled off his shoe and held it up to the light. "Holy hell. Look at this thing!" The man outside had ripped right through the sole with his teeth. It hung down freely in the front. Ben shook the shoe so it flopped around like a tongue. "He tried to eat my foot!"

"Not the body part I'd go for," Patrick admitted. "Give me a good cut of cheek any day."

The pounding at the front door ceased. They heard the man's footsteps moving around the perimeter. They moved their eyes along the walls, following the sound from the inside, until the creature stopped beneath one of the boarded windows. The slats there had been nailed haphazardly into place, and a two-inch slit ran between them. The man stuck his eye into the space and screamed. He pounded at the boards in a rage, snarling and huffing with frustration. He clawed at the wood until his fingernails peeled off. His blood flecked against the wood and through the hole. "Oh, gross," Ben said, squinting at the droplets hitting the floor. "Is he bleeding *yellow*?"

Patrick slipped the hammer from his belt loop and cautiously approached the window. The man tried to squeeze his hand into the opening, but it was too small. He howled with his fury. Patrick swung the hammer through the opening and brought it crashing against the bridge of his nose. The man stumbled back a half step, but dove right back against the window, scrabbling and screaming, completely unaffected. Patrick turned to Ben and shrugged. "That's it. I'm out of ideas. Oh, but yes, he's definitely bleeding yellow."

"What the hell is it?" Ben asked, disgusted.

"Let's look at what we know. He's human, or humanish. He bleeds yellow. He's skeleton-thin. He has an insatiable hunger for feet. He's an awfully determined runner. He seems more or less impervious to pain. Anything else?"

"Yeah, he's got skin made of cast iron," Ben said, rubbing his shoulder.

"Talk about body armor," Patrick said, stifling a laugh. "Get it? Do you get it? Skin of iron? Body armor?" He nudged Ben in the ribs. Ben rolled his eyes. Patrick slid into his serious face. "Okay, so, a super-thin human with irregularly colored blood insanely determined to consume human flesh. I think we have to face facts, as weird as it sounds. It can only be one thing."

"A zombie," Ben breathed.

"Huh? No, I was gonna say a politician. Wait, what about that makes you say zombie?"

"What about it *doesn't*? A mindlessly angry man-creature bent on devouring human flesh? Pat, that's a freakin' zombie."

"That is not a zombie, and I'll tell you why. Because zombies don't exist."

"That's what zombies want you to think," Ben said.

"Even if they did exist, they wouldn't have strong, healthy skin. They would be decomposing. That guy out there? Not decomposing. He's doing the opposite of decomposing. He's becoming some weird, thick-skinned evolutionary freak. Definitely a politician."

Ben glowered. "Whatever it is, how do we kill it?"

Patrick gasped. "See? Bloodlust."

"Oh, for God's sake--"

"Wait." Patrick held up a finger for silence. "Do you hear that?" Something was scratching at a window on the other side of the building.

The blood drained from Ben's face. "Oh God." he whispered. "Do you think it's--?"

Patrick nodded gravely. "Frankenstein. Maybe Count Chocula."

"Will you knock it off?" Ben crept across the room to the back window. The slit between the boards here was thinner. He leaned in close and peered through the space. Another man, angry and slobbering like the first, was scratching at the boards. "Shit, it's another one!" he hissed.

"In the interest of total honesty, I want to say that I think we're in serious trouble," Patrick said.

"What do we do?"

"See if we can hurt this one." He pulled out the machete and approached the second window. The man was right up against the boards, clawing and gnawing on the wood. Patrick set the blade of the machete on the top edge of the bottom board and gripped the handle tightly with his left hand. He jabbed the blade through the boards and pushed it into the man's chest as hard as he could. It didn't even break skin. The man stared down at the blade, eyes furious, and grabbed it with his bare hands. He tried to wrestle it through the boards. Patrick let go in surprise, and the thing outside pulled the blade until the handle stuck between the boards. It jerked on the machete, trying desperately to pull it through. It screamed in frustration and began attacking the metal with its teeth. "Okay," Patrick said, bobbing his head nervously, "it's official. This is a problem."

"What do we do?" Ben said again. "Do you think they'll go away?"

"Politicians never go away. They keep coming back 'til they've bled you dry."

"Will you cut that shit out? I'm serious! We're in serious fucking trouble."

"Yes, Ben, I realize that. Excuse me for trying to maintain a sense of levity about our current terrifying goddamn situation!" He stormed off across the cabin. He ducked into the main office, kicking stacks of paper out of the way. There was a metal storage cabinet in the corner, across from the desk. He opened the doors and nearly squealed with delight.

"What?" Ben said, running around the corner. "Grenades?"

"Better!" He held up a large, white plastic box with the words FIRST AID stamped across the front.

They ignored the pressing issue of the creatures outside for a few minutes while they cleaned and re-bandaged Patrick's hand. The wound looked pretty awful. A wide pink halo had spread around the hole, but there was enough antibiotic cream in the kit to last them a few weeks, barring any other serious injuries, and, despite the excruciating pain of applying the ointment directly to the insides of his palm, Patrick's spirits were somewhat lifted. He might be able to keep his hand after all.

"It's too bad napalm isn't included in first aid kits," Ben remarked. "We could really use some of that right now."

"Why don't we dump the rest of that Canadian Mist on their heads? It's basically the same thing." Ben stroked his chin and made a show of considering this option. Patrick smiled and smacked him on the arm. "Come on. I have a thought."

They moved back into the main room. The creature in the front had returned to the door and was beating on it with his fists and his feet. The one in the back was still wrestling with the machete. Patrick examined the room. Finally, he said, "Help me push that table over here."

In a few minutes, they'd made an amazingly unstable elevated platform out of the table, the podium, and the rolling office chair. Patrick did his best to hold the thing steady with one hand as Ben climbed to the top. He balanced himself precariously on the rolling chair, directly beneath the center skylight. He thumped it with his fist. "Feels like Plexiglas."

"See if you can break it with this." Patrick tossed him the baton. Ben almost fell off the chair reaching for it. He flicked it open and hammered it against the window. It gave a little, but remained intact. Ben looked down and shrugged.

"How about your feet? Lay on your back and kick through it. Chuck Norris-style."

"Are you kidding me?" Ben sighed, tossed the baton to the floor, and carefully adjusted his position. The chair rolled back and forth precariously, but he managed to steady it. With a loud grunt, he hauled back and kicked his feet through the hole in the ceiling. The Plexiglas popped off and went skittering across the roof.

"Good thing that guy didn't eat your feet. We need those feet," Patrick observed.

"Har, har. Now what?"

"Now we take a look at our surroundings." Patrick gripped the table and began his perilous, one-handed ascent. "You know the old saying. If you can't beat 'em, run the hell away."

"Run? Run where?"

"Exactly, Ben. Exactly." They hoisted themselves up to the roof and peered over the edge. The sight of the forest floor caused their jaws to drop in almost perfect unison. Dark silhouettes were emerging from the fog on all sides, dozens of them, most of them running, some of them apparently injured and staggering, arms thrown out for balance. The first line of them was just approaching the cabin. None had yet noticed the two men standing on the roof. There had to have been fifty or sixty of them in all, men, women, and even a few who looked scarcely old enough to drive. Every last one of them was emaciated, with fiery, furious eyes. They growled like wild animals, some of them literally diving into the cabin, mindlessly trying to break through its thick wooden walls with their hard, bony skulls. Some still wore clothes, others were naked or close to it, with scraps of torn fabric ringing their necks or waists. More monsters sprinted in from the darkening fog, and in less than a minute, the entire cabin was swarmed on all four sides, the wall of rabid human creatures extending three or four bodies deep in some places. Those in the back rows ripped and clawed at the ones in front of them, trying to tear through to the warm human bodies they thought were inside.

Ben let loose a string of curse words, each one filthier than the last. Patrick shushed him, but one of the maniacs below had heard him. She looked up at them with her sunken, bloodshot eyes. She raised a stick-thin arm and pointed a clawed finger at Ben. She shrieked, loud and long, and soon all the creatures were screaming and pawing at the walls of the house, trying to climb up now instead of in.

"Shit. Shit, shit, shit," Ben spat. "What do we do?"

Patrick looked down helplessly at the hissing, clamoring crowd below. "I guess we watch and wait," he shrugged. "I'm getting something to eat."

They ate their dinner of canned tuna and peaches on the roof. Neither spoke through the meal, but both cast regular, gloomy looks at the ground below. More of the creatures seemed to arrive every ten or fifteen minutes. Some of them had come within a few feet of reaching the roof by climbing on the backs of others, but the flesh eating maniacs didn't seem to work well as a team; as soon as one leapt onto another's back, she was slammed back to the ground and trampled by the others. The weakly filtered moonlight made them look ghoulish and even more grotesque.

Ben finished his tuna and hurled the can at the throng below. It glanced off the forehead of one of the assailants, who didn't seem to notice. "I don't think I'm gonna sleep tonight," he sighed.

"We should try. We'll have to keep watch in rotating shifts."

"I'll take the first shift, and probably all the other ones, too."

Patrick lay down on his back and stared up at the dark fog above. "I remember a time when a man could go to Disney World without fear of being eaten by savages."

"You obviously never flew American," Ben said. "How's your hand?"

"Eh. It's okay. Hurts like the dickens, but I think it's getting better."

"You think they can smell the gash?" he asked, nodding toward the screeching crowd below.

"That is the most disgusting sounding sentence I've ever heard," said Patrick, wincing.

"You always were a prude," Ben said. He hopped up and walked around the perimeter. "I don't know how you and Annie ever—" He broke off.

"Ever what?" Patrick asked, still staring up into the mist. His friend was silent. "Ben? You fall off the roof?" He rolled over and saw Ben crouching near the corner of the building. "What's going on?"

"Come here," Ben whispered, beckoning him with his hand. Patrick stood and looked over the side. A family of deer had just walked into the edge of the clearing, a doe and three fawns. They sniffed cautiously at the grass, their eyes alert, tails pointing straight up in the air. One of the monsters below, one of the injured ones, noticed them first. He spun around and staggered toward the deer on unsteady legs. More of the creatures looked over and saw the deer. They began to turn, one by one, and soon the entire horde was swarming the animals, the limping gimps falling well behind the sprinters. The deer fled into the woods, and the mass of creatures flooded through the clearing like a tidal wave, draining *en masse* into the trees.

"Let's go!" Patrick cried. He ran to the skylight and dropped through the hole with such awkward force that he slipped right off the chair and crashed to the table below. He rolled off to the floor with a groan and hobbled over to the bags. Ben wasn't far behind; he hopped down more gracefully and unbolted the front door. Patrick tossed him the knapsack and shouldered his own bag.

"Which way?" Ben asked, frantic.

"The opposite way."

They cracked the door and peered out, making sure the coast was clear. The last unsteady walker was just plunging into the forest on the far side of the clearing. Ben threw open the door and ran out in the other direction, Patrick close on his heels.

They dove into the trees, and the world became black as tar. They forged onward blindly, taking branches to the face every few steps, but not slowing. After a few hundred yards, they ducked behind a massive, gnarled tree trunk. They listened closely, but there wasn't a sound to be heard.

"Do you think we're safe?" Ben asked hopefully.

"I think the second you ask a question like that, we're doomed," said Patrick. To accentuate the point, a soft scuffle of feet rose somewhere nearby, off to their left. "Goddammit, Ben."

They picked themselves up and sprinted on, already breathing heavily under the weight of their packs. "I changed my mind," Ben gasped as they leapt over a shallow gully. "I don't want to go to Disney World. I want to stay in Chicago."

"Okay. You go back. I'm going this way."

They pushed on blindly through the darkness for several miles, stopping every few minutes to listen for footsteps; sometimes they heard them, sometimes they didn't. Whatever the auditory outcome, they plunged deeper and deeper into the woods.

Almost a full hour after they'd fled the ranger station, they broke into another clearing. Right in the middle of it stood a house, a single story Ranch with candlelight flickering in the space between the window boards. They stopped at the edge of the clearing, wheezing and sweating.

"One, solitary house in a clearing in the middle of the zombie-infested woods? How can *this* go badly?" Ben asked between breaths.

"I think it's better than the alternative," Patrick said.

"Better than running until we find a military base where we'll be protected by overbearing men with crewcuts and AK-47s?"

"Better than running the four more feet until my heart explodes, then getting ripped apart by Tokka and Rahzar," Pat said, nodding at a couple of injured man-creatures clawing their way out through the woods. Ben sighed. So it was settled, then. They huffed their way to the front door and knocked.

"Who is it?" sang a sweet female voice from the other side.

"Please, we need help!" Ben cried. A small group of remarkably uninjured runners burst into the clearing just then and sprinted toward the house. Ben pushed forward and pounded on the door. "Please! Let us inside!"

The voice behind the door mumbled something they couldn't understand. The slathering savages were closing in, quickly. Patrick pulled Ben away from the door. "Amateur," he muttered, shaking his head. He cleared his throat and pressed his palms together. "Ma'am? We hate to disturb you, but it's rather urgent."

They heard a lock slide back, and the door cracked open. "Yes?" asked the woman on the other side, pressing her eye to the slit.

"Let us in, let us in, let us in!" Ben cried, absolutely frantic. He moved to enter, but she held the door in place.

"I don't know you, do I?"

"No! Lady, look! There are man-eating zombies right behind us, for the love of God, please let us in!"

The woman peeked over their shoulders and saw the wild humans sprinting toward them. "Your friends certainly seem rambunctious," she said cautiously.

"Rambunc--? Lady, *they're trying to eat us!*" Ben screamed.

"Mary, who is it?" asked a man's voice from somewhere inside.

"Two boys who want to come in," she said.

"Do we know them?"

"No, dear, they're strangers."

"Did they say what they want?"

Ben slapped the door with his palms. "Lady, please!"

"No, they just said they want to come in," she said, unperturbed.

"They're probably just Jehovah's Witnesses, dear. Go on, let them in."

"They're not Jehovah's Witnesses, darling, they're dirty."

"For crying out loud!" Ben screamed. "I did not come all this way to die on a porch!" He lowered his shoulder with the aim of driving it through the door, but suddenly, the lead runner was on them. The madman dove forward, knocking into Patrick, who collided with Ben, who fell into the door, which flew open under the combined weight. "Oh!" the woman cried, pinwheeling back into the foyer. The three men went down in a heap in the entryway, Patrick scrabbling for the runner's throat to hold his teeth at bay, Ben floundering under their weight. Patrick managed to get his feet planted on the runner's chest, and with a strength he'd never known he had, he pushed off and launched the creature back through the doorway. It crashed into two others just jumping onto the porch, and the three of them went down like bowling pins, screaming and snarling. Patrick scrambled for the door, slammed it shut, and threw the locks just as the monsters outside came smashing up against it.

"What is the meaning of this?" the woman demanded, stamping her foot. They could see her easily despite the night's darkness; candles burned everywhere, on every tabletop, in converted wall sconces, even in the stately chandeliers above. The entire house was as bright as dawn. The woman herself practically glimmered. She was a little shorter than medium height, and slim, wearing a sleeveless blue-and-white polka dotted dress cinched at the waist and poofed out in a wide skirt. Her yellow hair framed her thin, pretty face perfectly, with well-coiffed ringlets pinned back over her ears. Her dark blue eyes, her full, red lips, and her small, pointed nose completed the package of a 1950s middle class housewife to a T. She had her fists planted firmly on her hips, scowling down at the two men on the floor. Even looking angry, she was uncommonly attractive. And exceptionally clean.

"Well?" she said, tapping her heeled shoe on the hardwood floor.

They struggled to their feet. "Those things, they were—"

"Miscreants, from the look of them," she finished sharply. "Barging into my house like animals. I should have you arrested! In fact, I think I'll do just that. Warren, ring the sheriff!" she called over her shoulder.

A man in an argyle cardigan appeared behind her. He wore dark slacks with a sharp crease and a crisp white shirt under the sweater. His black hair was perfectly parted over his left eyebrow, rising in a slight wave in front. "Now, now, Mary," he said, patting his wife on the shoulders, "let's not be so rash. Look at them, can't you see how scared they are? Something's got them in a tizzy. Nothing a good meal couldn't fix, am I right?" He leaned in conspiratorially. "Or if not that, a stiff sip from the bar," he said with a wink.

"Not until the children are in bed," Mary said hotly. "Please excuse me while I have a word with my husband." She took him by the elbow and led him back down the hall. They spoke in hushed tones, hers frantic and punctuated by quick, sweeping hand gestures, his calm and, they hoped, soothing.

"This place gives me the creeps," Ben whispered. The entire house was spotless; the floors were scrubbed and polished, the furniture was dusted, the stairs were vacuumed, pictures still hung evenly on recently painted walls, little knickknacks were organized perfectly on their shelves. Aside from a few necessary post-M-Day renovations, like boarded windows and padlocks on some of the doors, the house looked like it was ready to be photographed for a pre-apocalyptic issue of *Home and Garden*. It was eerie as shit. Ben said as much. "And what's with Betty Draper and Astronaut Darrin? Did we just walk onto the set of *Leave it to Beaver*?"

"Stop mixing your references," Patrick said. "It's confusing."

Their hosts finished their discussion. Mary marched off in a huff. Warren walked back to the entryway, giving the two men a broad, easy smile. "I apologize for my wife. She can be a little...high strung sometimes."

"No, no, no, it's completely fine," Patrick said, waving his hands in the air. "We barged into your house; she has every right to be upset."

"It's just that we were about to be savagely eaten by mutants," Ben added helpfully.

Warren laughed. "We'd be happy if you boys would be our guests tonight. We're just finishing up dinner, but there's some soup leftover, if you're hungry. We'll keep it warm for you, why don't you go clean up? The guest bathroom's just down the hall there. You'll find plenty of water. We draw it from our own well," he said with a proud wink. "When you're all cleaned up, join us in the dining room, right back down this way, the last room on the left, right back there. All right, now? Welcome to our home."

•

The soup was easily the best thing Ben had ever tasted; carrots, celery, onions, kale, white beans, basil, and thyme, seasoned with healthy amounts of pepper and unhealthy amounts of salt. The flavors danced together in a symphony of flavor unlike anything he'd tasted in the last three years. Even the fresh venison of the night before couldn't compare (especially not in hindsight). Paired with the fact that he'd just had his first hot bath in over three years, thanks to his hosts' well and well-stoked fires, he now felt perpetually on the verge of grateful tears. "The soup is amazing," he managed to say between spoonfuls. Warren grinned.

"The vegetables and herbs are grown right here in our own little garden. Mary's got a heck of a green thumb, a *heck* of a green thumb!"

"Oh, stop it," she said, blushing.

"It's true! Isn't it true, kids?"

Two young children, one boy and one girl, sat across from Patrick and Ben. The boy was older, maybe by a year or two, and was dressed like his father, in a red cardigan over a white turtleneck. His hair was parted the same way, too, left to right with a gelled wave in front. The girl wore a pleated jumper over a light blue blouse. Her dark hair was pulled back and tied with matching ribbons that streamed down her back.

"Your father asked you a question," Mary said sharply.

"Yes, father," they answered in unison. The boy rested his head on one hand and drew imaginary pictures on the tablecloth with the end of his spoon. The girl wriggled uncomfortably in her seat, which had been boosted up with dictionaries so she could reach the table. "May we be a'scused?" she asked.

"You may not be," their mother said. "It's not polite to leave the table while others are eating."

"Oh, no, please, we don't mind," Patrick said through a mouthful of kale.

"It's not polite," she repeated firmly. "Nor is it polite to speak with your mouth full."

"Mary," Warren said, "these men are our guests."

She frowned. "I'm glad you're enjoying the soup," she said.

Ben stole a questioning glance at Patrick, but his companion was taking a passive approach to their host's tone by ignoring it completely and hurrying up with his dinner. Ben did the same.

"Now you may be excused," Mary said when Ben had finished slurping the dregs from his bowl. The children beamed and exploded out of their chairs. They scampered out of the dining room with squeals of delight.

"Help your mother clear the table!" Warren shouted after them, but they were already bounding up the stairs. He shook his head and chuckled. "Kids these days, eh?" He stood and began clearing the dishes from the table. Patrick and Ben moved to help, but he shooed them away.

"It's impossible to teach them any sort of decent value in today's television culture," Mary said, shaking her head. Warren agreed.

Television culture? Ben mouthed to Patrick. Even televisions run on generators were useless; the stations had almost all stopped broadcasting. The only active channels they knew of were the ones set to blast pre-recorded emergency information on loop. The information was completely useless, advising people to take shelter in their basements, as if those vulnerable to the Monkey dust could have survived by hunkering down in a cellar. And even those emergency broadcasts were probably dead by now. It was hard to imagine someone keeping them powered this long. There sure as hell wasn't any "television culture" infecting the youth. That was an extinct concern. Patrick just shrugged.

Warren reappeared in the dining room. "I hope you don't mind, I moved your bags and things over to the guest room. That's, uh...that's quite a little arsenal you boys have," he said, more with curiosity than concern. "I suppose you must be...what, some sort of bounty hunters?"

"Uhm...not exactly," Ben said.

"What an exciting life that must be!" Warren continued, his eyes growing glassy with imagination. "Dedicating yourself to tracking down all manner of miscreants and ne'er-do-wells. Sleeping under the stars, traveling to exotic locales, all that excitement and adventure, bringing criminals to justice. I do envy you boys."

"Well, it's not all it's cracked up to be," Patrick said, his voice dropping a whole octave. "It can get pretty dangerous out there, but we like to think we do some good." Ben rubbed at his temples.

Warren shook his head and smiled. "Mm. I do envy you," he said again. "Come on, why don't we head down to the study?"

He led them to a small, comfortable room at the corner of the house. The dark leather of two overstuffed couches matched the stained oak bookshelves that lined the walls. About half of the shelves were full of books; the other half held family portraits, various plaques and awards, and polished woodcarvings of horses, sports cars, and contemplative Native Americans. "Have a seat," he said, gesturing to the couches. They plopped down and sank into the cushions.

"Oooooo!" Patrick said, bouncing a little. "Very nice."

Warren lit a fire in the hearth. Its light still paled in comparison to that given off by the plethora of candles spaced around and above the room, but the warmth was nice. He crossed over to a bar cabinet against the far wall. He pulled three glasses and a bottle of Four Roses small batch from inside. "I'm afraid our ice maker's on the fritz just now. Do you fellows mind taking it neat?"

They toasted to good fortune and sipped their drinks quietly in front of the fire. Warren seemed deeply lost in his own thoughts as he swirled the drink in his glass. "This is a pretty classy man cave," Ben said, breaking the silence. "Put in a pool table and you'd never have to leave."

"Is billiards your game?" Warren asked. "I've never been much for it myself. Too mathematical, billiards. All angles and speed. I'm more of a links man, myself. Do you boys play golf?"

"I hit a guy with a putter once," Ben said. "Remember that, Pat?"

"Yeah. I do. 'Cause that guy was me, you jackass."

Ben smiled at the memory. "It sure was."

"I used to play," Patrick volunteered. "You know, before everything happened."

Warren gave him a queer look. "Before what happened?"

"You know. Everything. M-Day, the Flying Monkeys, and all that. The end of the world."

Warren grimaced and shook his head. "I'm afraid I'm not much for politics," he said by way of apology. "I've always been of the mind that a man should do his duty to his family, provide for them by earning an honest paycheck, and let the rest of the world sort itself out. I don't even bother watching the news anymore. It's gotten so I don't need to listen to a couple of talking heads to know how far the country's fallen. Why, take a look around you. I'm sure you've noticed the board on our windows. The neighborhood kids have broken them so often, with their bats and their stones, heck, some of them just drive their fists right through the glass. I got tired of replacing them and just up and said, 'Enough!' Young hooligans running around screaming and destroying things like that, with complete disregard to a man's private property...well, I ask you, what kind of world is that? Where's the humanity? It's gotten so we don't feel safe sending the children to school anymore. Just last month, I walked the children to the schoolhouse myself. I wanted to discuss their progress with their teachers. William's in third grade now, he has the sour-faced old woman, Mrs. Whatshername, Leidwenger? I tried to have a conversation with her about William's lessons, just casual conversation, you understand, but she just sat there at her desk, ignored me completely, ignored the entire room! It's no wonder the other parents have stopped sending their children to school. Even the teachers have given up on the youth. Of course, that's why they're all vandals and hoodlums. They're not held accountable. There's no discipline anymore. Mary handles the children's education now, and I think she does a fine job, a *fine* job! We don't leave the house much because of it, either. Well, they don't, anyway. A man has to work, of course, but there's not much cause for a woman and children to go wandering about the neighborhood, not with such reckless violence happening everywhere. Having two calm, rational boys like yourselves in the house is a comfort to me, a real comfort. Mary refuses to accept that the neighborhood teenagers have gone feral, some sort of motherly defense, I guess, but they have, oh ho, mark my words, they have. They're the ones who were chasing you, and I knew you two were on the up-and-up. The ferals don't chase each other. It's dangerous times out there, I tell you. I don't know what's gone on with the world."

Patrick and Ben sat wide-eyed as Warren finished his speech and sipped thoughtfully from his glass. Patrick elbowed Ben. Ben elbowed him back. The unspoken message was clear: *Holy shit.*

Warren finished his whiskey and smacked his lips, savoring the flavor. "Would you boys excuse me? It's about time to put the children to bed. Make yourselves at home. Pour another drink, if you'd like. I'll be back shortly." He left the room and closed the door behind him.

Ben jumped to his feet as soon as the door clicked. "What the fuck is he talking about?" he whispered hoarsely. "Neighborhood vandals? Watching the news? Dear God, he sent the kids to school up until last *month*? That teacher was fucking *dead*, probably rotted to a skeleton! These people are out of their minds!"

"Yeah, but they have excellent refreshments," Patrick pointed out, sipping his drink.

"Are *you* out of *your* mind? We have to go!"

"Go where? Back out into the woods? At night? With those man-eating psychopathic politicians running around? No, I don't think so. You go right ahead. I'm gonna sit here by the fire and drink more whiskey." He proved this by remaining by the fire and by drinking more whiskey.

Ben shifted nervously from one foot to the other, wracked with indecision. Patrick was right; if those emaciated man-things were still out there, there was practically no way they'd survive the night. But being inside this house was just as unsettling. "Will you sit down?" Patrick asked. "You look like you have to pee, and that makes me have to pee. And I don't want to go pee because this couch is *really* comfortable."

"Are you sure 'cardigan wearer' wasn't one of the old lady's warnings?"

"No, she never said anything about being attacked by Mr. Rogers."

Ben sighed helplessly. "Okay. We stay here tonight, but one of us should keep watch at all times. Seriously. We can take turns sleeping."

Once they'd said their goodnights and headed up to the guest room, they decided to rotate the watch every three hours that night, with Ben taking the first watch. The plan was successful for exactly three hours and twelve minutes, at which point Patrick lost a poorly fought battle with exhaustion and fell into something just bordering on a coma on the floor. He awoke to a not-so-soft nudge in his ribs. "Mrrwpft?" he said, bolting upright.

The little girl jumped back, startled. She wore a different colored jumper this morning, but the blouse and the ribbons were the same. "Mommy says breakfast is ready," she whispered shyly. Then she turned and ran out of the room.

Patrick yawned and shook his head clear of its cobwebs. He reached up onto the bed and poked Ben in the forehead. "Wake up."

Ben slowly came to, mumbling something about fig trees and pop-injays. He opened his eyes and looked bewilderedly around the room. "What time is it?" he asked. The room was still dark, illuminated only by three candles on the dresser that someone had apparently lit while they were still sleeping.

"A little after six," Pat said, checking his princess watch. "Time for some b-fast."

"Did you keep watch all night?" Ben yawned.

"Yeah. Obviously," Patrick lied. "You looked so peaceful, I figured I'd just let you sleep."

"Huh. Thanks."

Breakfast consisted of mixed Dole fruit, homemade bread, and sweet potato hash. *These nutjobs set a fine table,* Patrick thought.

"Think you fellas'll stick around another night or two?" Warren asked, wiping his mouth with a neatly pressed cloth napkin. Mary shot him a look of alarm from across the table, but he gave her a reassuring wink.

"We hadn't really thought about it," Patrick admitted.

"We probably won't," Ben said. "Lots of ground to cover, and all."

"Nonsense! Mary, what's for dinner tonight?"

She gave him an annoyed glower, but answered, "Lentil and spinach pie."

"Lentil and spinach pie," Warren said, as if that settled the matter. "You don't want to miss that. Plus, you're in no condition to hunt your bounty right now, Patrick. Let Mary take a look at that hand of yours this morning." He wiped his mouth and pushed his chair back from the table. "Well! I'm headed to the office." He stood and kissed Mary on the cheek, and the children on the tops of their heads. "You two troublemakers be good for our guests now, you hear? Don't give your mother any problems. What're you working on today?"

"Multiplication," William said miserably.

"States!" the girl cried.

"That's the spirit, Lucy." He smiled and tousled her hair, shaking a few strands free of their ribbon restraints.

"It took me twenty minutes to get her hair just so. You stop that and go to work," Mary scowled, swatting at Warren. He grinned and danced away from her reach.

Patrick and Ben cleared their plates from the table and dumped them in the sink. "I don't want to stay here," Ben whispered.

"I know, Baby Ben, I know," Patrick cooed, patting the shorter man's head. Ben slapped his hand away.

"You two make yourselves at home today," Warren said, placing his own dishes in the sink and straightening his thin tie. "Don't let Mary talk you into sweeping the floors, now, you're our guests." He headed out into the front hall and grabbed a smart leather briefcase from beneath the entryway table. He beckoned Patrick closer. "The little lady gets a bit disquieted about strangers in the house. You two feel free to hide out in the study if things get a little uncomfortable for you," he said.

"Sure. No problem." They shook hands awkwardly (Patrick grabbing Warren's right with his own left), and the master of the house unlocked the door.

"Should you really go out there?" Ben blurted.

"A man's got to do his duty, hasn't he?" Warren smiled, jangling his keys. "The bread doesn't put itself on the table! Besides, it'll be a long day in winter before a few neighborhood bullies get the best of Warren Tinder." He gave them another wink, then pulled open the door and walked out, calling a final goodbye to the family.

Patrick held the door open behind him. "Where do you think he goes?"

Ben shrugged, but they didn't have to wait long to find out. Warren turned off of the brick walk, in the opposite direction of the driveway. Instead of heading to the garage, he rounded the far corner of the house. Ben and Patrick exchanged confused looks, then followed him out into the yard. They peeked around the corner just as Warren disappeared down a set of steps into the house's cellar, pulling the storm doors closed behind him.

"I don't like this," Ben said. "I want to leave. Today."

Patrick admitted he might be on to something there. "Maybe that'd be best."

Mary was waiting for them in the foyer when they returned to the house, her arms tightly crossed. "You should know the sheriff lives next door. Any sign of trouble, and he'll come running."

"There's no trouble," Patrick said. "We're not trouble. Do you feel troubled?"

"Let's just lay our cards on the table. I'm a woman with two children, left alone in a house with two strange, armed men. My husband seems to think there's nothing wrong with that, God knows why. I want to make it perfectly clear that if you try to assault me or my family in any way, you'll be in handcuffs before I finish screaming for help."

"Well...not to split hairs here, but you're not exactly *alone* in the house with us," Patrick pointed out.

"What is that supposed to mean?" she demanded.

"Your husband," Ben said, confused. "He's downstairs."

"Downstairs?"

"Right?" Patrick asked. "In the cellar?"

"We don't have a cellar," Mary said quickly. "Now, if you're going to stay, you might as well be useful. You can bring in some firewood from the pile out back. Follow me." She led them down the hall and around a corner, past a door secured with a padlock. Cold air drafted from beneath as they walked past. Patrick turned to Ben and mouthed, *Cellar?* Ben nodded.

What the hell was going on here?

They brought a few loads of firewood into the house (after cautiously inspecting the grounds for runners), then politely requested to retire to the guest room to put their things in order. Mary consented, suspiciously, and they hustled back to the room and closed the door.

Ben set right to work stuffing his blanket into his knapsack, but Patrick stood thoughtfully by the door, tapping his cheek and staring blankly into space. "What do you think he's doing down there?" he asked.

"If Hollywood has taught me anything, it's that Warren is creating an army of self-sustaining, man-eating vampire/plant hybrids in that basement. We should get the hell out."

"Maybe he's conducting experiments on sedated politicians," Patrick mused. "Or working on some sort of organic madman antidote, with beakers full of bubbling green potions." He inhaled sharply. "Ooo! Maybe he has a Tesla coil down there!" he said excitedly.

"I don't care if he has a petting zoo down there. I'd rather take my chances with the runners." Ben zipped up his knapsack and slipped the wrench and the knife into his pockets. "Get your stuff together. Let's go." But Patrick barely heard him. He was getting that warm, tingling feeling that he always got when he was about to make an exciting decision.

"Let's go see what's in that basement," he said.

Ben threw his knapsack on the ground. "You know what I hate about you the most?"

"My naturally trim physique?"

"The fact that you're so predictably maddening."

"So you *do* want to go see what's in the cellar?"

"No, I want to leave. I want to go back into the woods because I think we're safer with the freaking zombies than we are with these whackos. They give me the fucking creeps. I just want to go to Disney World and get done with this stupid trip and not end up being cut into pieces by Ward Cleaver."

Patrick pressed a hand to his chest. "You think this trip is stupid?"

"Well. No. It's actually been pretty exciting," Ben admitted. "And I like the fact that I'm not the one with a hole in his hand. So it could be worse. But I really want to get the hell out of Stepford."

"We will, Benny Boy, we will" Pat promised, chuffing him on the chin. "Just as soon as I find out what's in that basement."

•

The plan was simple; Ben would distract Mary while Patrick slipped out and tried the storm doors. If Ben was good for anything, it was a distraction, "But no fire this time," Patrick warned.

Mary and the children were in the living room down the hall. They could hear the little girl babbling happily as the boy struggled with his numbers. "As long as they stay in the room, we're fine," Patrick said. "But if they come out, you go into action."

"What sort of action?"

"Distraction action!"

"What should I do?"

"Be a master of disaster!"

"What kind of disaster?"

"The kind that stops wops!"

"They're not Italian."

"I know, but I had a good rhyme scheme going."

"It was racially insensitive."

"We live in an insensitive world," Patrick said sadly. "Do whatever you need to do, just keep her in the house and not looking for me in it." He strapped on the machete and gave Ben a little salute. "I go to discover the truth."

"You go to discover your arm severed from your shoulder. If you're not back in ten minutes, I swear to God, I'm leaving without you."

"Better make it twenty. If there's some sick science experiment happening down there, I'm liable to get engrossed in it."

"You're likely to become part of it."

Patrick thrust a finger into the air. "Then I go for science!"

•

Ben winced as Patrick closed the front door. He was sure Mary heard the click. But the lessons continued in the room down the hall, and after counting to ten, he let himself breathe again. He looked around to make sure no one was looking, then he slipped into Warren's study. Why he thought there might be anyone around to catch him, or why anyone might care, he couldn't say. He just felt jittery. The Tinder family was batty, even the kids. He could've sworn that he'd woken up in the middle of the night to find the girl staring at them from the doorway. It had freaked him right the hell out. When he rubbed his eyes and looked again, she was gone, and it could've been a dream, but still. These people weren't right.

He opened the liquor cabinet and perused the bottles. Warren might be batshit, but he had good taste in booze. He pulled out a bottle of Grey Goose and a bottle of Kahlua and set them on the bar. He poked around the lower shelves and was delighted to find a container of Coffeemate. He set to work mixing himself a White Russian. It wasn't quite the same without ice (*Definitely not a White Siberian*, he cracked to himself), but, lordy, did it do the trick. He was generous with the alcohol, sure, but the real high was in the familiar comfort of the creamy drink.

He tossed it down, the whole glassful, and mixed up a second. Then he stashed the bottles back in the bar and closed it up. He wandered around the study, drink in hand, examining the carvings on the shelves. Why on Earth someone would collect so many sad-looking Indians for a personal collection was beyond him. It was like the Trail of Tears ended in Colonel Mustard's library.

He inspected the books lining the walls, looking for some concrete evidence of mental instability, something like *American Psycho*, or *Mein Kampf*, or anything by the Marquis de Sade. He was surprised to find a host of classics, peppered with a little science fiction and a smattering of humorous essay collections, mostly from Sedaris and Burroughs. *The real sick shit must be in the basement*, he decided. Warren probably kept *The Necronomicon* down there, or the "Blood Qur'an," or maybe both. Patrick was probably being literally eaten alive by books written in blood.

Speaking of Patrick, where the hell was he? Ben didn't have a watch, so the twenty-minute deadline was pretty meaningless, but it had to be getting close by now. He knelt down and pressed his ear to the floor, but he couldn't hear a single sound coming from the basement. That could be good or bad. He took another sip of his drink. As much as he wanted to get the hell out of Dodge, and as much as he would love to just grab his bag and run, he wasn't about to leave Patrick behind. *And Pat knows that, dammit.* So the twenty-minute deadline was even less than meaningless.

He decided to calm his mind by doing a lap of the house. He needed to check in on the classroom anyway. He and his drink meandered out into the hall. He turned the corner and froze dead in his tracks. Mary stood just outside of the living room, her back to him. The kids were scurrying around the corner toward the kitchen. Snack time? Lunchtime?

Dammit.

He was frozen with indecision. Should he back away and slip upstairs into the guest room and hope she would just not think to bother them? Or should he take the initiative and create a diversion right now? If he did the latter, what would he say or do? His brain wasn't working properly. It couldn't tell him to move forward or backward, so he just stood in place. For a moment he thought maybe Mary would follow the kids and make the decision for him, but, instead, she turned around and caught him standing in awkward mid-crouch, breakfast alcohol in hand.

She gave a little gasp of surprise, then her face quickly fell to annoyance. "Do you need something?" she asked icily.

Make a diversion. Make a diversion, he thought.

He held up the White Russian. "I found this in the kids' bedroom."

•

Patrick crept along the front of the house, instinctively ducking as he moved past the windows, which was stupid, because they were all boarded up from the inside. He slid around the corner and approached the storm doors. He carefully reached down and pulled at one of the handles. The door raised freely an inch or two; it wasn't locked from the inside. He set the door back down noiselessly and looked around. He was alone: no kids, no angry wife, no flesh-eating politicians. He blew in his hands to warm them. The air was cold, colder than usual, and he needed to be warm and springy in case evasive bodily maneuvering became necessary. The fingers on his right hand still felt numb, and the whole injury put him at a serious defensive disadvantage. He hopped from one foot to the other and shook out his arms. Somewhere in the back of his mind, a voice that sounded suspiciously like his late wife's whispered something about going back inside the house and forgetting about the cellar. But that voice had a way of steering him away from the more exciting things in life, so instead of heeding it, he gripped the metal handle and pulled open the door. It was dark as night in the stairwell. Patrick squatted and peered down into the cellar gloom. Dim candlelight flickered around the walls. He stepped down onto the stairs and pulled the storm door closed behind him.

He sat on the third step for almost two whole minutes, waiting for his eyes to adjust to the darkness. When they did, he could see that the stairs led to a shallow hallway, which opened up into the main basement room. The walls were heavy stones held together by cement that was beginning to flake away, but the structure seemed sturdy on the whole. The candles were hidden from view, tucked back behind either side of the entry tunnel, but their glow flickered across the hard earthen floor. Patrick could hear Warren humming from somewhere in the darkness. He eased his way down the stairs and crept slowly along the tunnel.

He stopped at the mouth and held his breath, listening. Warren's humming seemed to be coming from somewhere behind him, on the other side of the concrete. He crossed the tunnel and ducked around the opposite wall. He could just barely see the outline of the staircase ascending to the padlocked door in the hallway above. Why bother locking that door when the storm doors were completely unguarded? The obvious answer sent a chill through Patrick. Tinder wasn't trying to keep people in the house out of the basement; he was trying to keep something in the basement out of the house.

The staircase bisected this half of the room. Flanking it on either side were U-shaped series of metal file cabinets. There were enough drawers to hold all the paperwork for an entire law firm, and then some. A tall candle holder stood in the middle of each section, both of them mounted with thick, squat candles that sat at eye level. He tiptoed toward the file drawers directly ahead and inspected the first tower. The labels were meaningless to him; *Case #115AT Abbot – Paulson, Case #1444PO McKenney – Avondale, Case #13BSP Belmont – Luna.* Carefully, quietly, he slid the button on the top drawer and pulled it open. Metal squeaked against metal. He stopped and listened. Warren still hummed, hidden, from the other side of the cellar. Patrick plucked a file from the drawer and opened it near the candle. The top piece of paper contained a poem written in hasty script:

MY BOLOGNA HAS A FIRST NAME, IT'S O-S-C-A-R
MY BOLOGNA HAS A SECOND NAMEM, IT'S M-A-Y-E-R
I LOVE TO EAT IT EVERY DAY
AND IF YOU ASK ME WHY I'LL SAY
'CAUSE OSCAR MAYER HAS A WAY
WITH B-O-L-O-G-N-A

He turned the page. The second paper in the stack was a piece of withering loose leaf, yellowed at the edges and delicate to the touch. The words on this sheet were written in careful block letters, crisp and precise, placed exactly in the center of the page:

I WAS DRUNK LAST NIGHT, DEAR MOTHER

I WAS DRUNK THE NIGHT BEFORE
BUT IF YOU'LL FORGIVE ME, MOTHER
I'LL NEVER GET DRUNK ANYMORE

"What in the name of Grayskull...?" Patrick mumbled aloud. Then he heard a chair scrape against the dirt floor. He nearly knocked the candle over in surprise. Footsteps echoed toward him. He flipped the folder shut and stuffed it into the drawer, then dove into the corner, where the tunnel wall met the outer wall, and huddled into the darkness. Warren came around the edge of the tunnel carrying a piece of paper and humming his ditty. He strode purposefully to a file cabinet somewhere along the stairwell, popped it open, and thumbed through the contents. He found the folder he was looking for and slipped the paper inside. He slammed the door shut with a quick flick of his wrist and started back toward the other side of the cellar. On his way back, he noticed the open file drawer and cocked his head at it, frowning. The humming stopped. He approached the drawer and inspected it. He looked around the room, but saw nothing in the gloom. Then he shrugged, closed the drawer, and hummed his way back to the chair.

Patrick wiped a line of sweat from his brow. He stood and crept softly to the drawer Warren had just visited. It was labeled *Case #5589DM Abernathy – Pickle*. He pulled it open quietly and picked a random paper from the bunch of folders.

I WANT YOUR DRAMA, THE TOUCH OF YOUR HAND
I WANT YOUR LEATHER STUDDED KISS IN THE SAND
I WANT YOUR LOVE
LOVE, LOVE, LOVE, I WANT YOUR LOVE

He slid the paper back into its place and closed the drawer. Warren said something from the other side of the room, causing Patrick to jump again. "You finish that Drake report yet, Tomlinson? Let me see it." Then footsteps, the rustling of paper, a long pause, and more paper rustling. "Good start. Don't forget the bit about waking up being the best part, et cetera. How about you, Davis? How's that invoice coming along?" More footsteps, more paper rustling. "Hm. Let's reword this fourth line item. Use 'diamond' instead of 'sparkler.' 'Like a diamond in the sky.' That's much better, they can't dispute that charge, no sir. Good work, Davis." Warren walked back to his desk and squeaked into his chair.

Patrick made his way slowly back to the tunnel and peeked his head around the wall. What he saw made him gasp, audibly. He clamped his hand over his mouth and spun back behind the tunnel wall. Warren's chair squeaked once, then was silent. He went back to shuffling his papers.

Patrick peered around the corner again, trying not to lock eyes on the decomposing body sitting at the desk directly to his left. The corpse had been dead for a while and was more skeleton than flesh. Warren sat at his own desk against the far wall, and a third desk was positioned just to Patrick's right, back in the corner, barely visible by candlelight. It, too, was manned by a rotting corpse. Warren hummed happily, making notes and checking his papers against each other. "Twenty more minutes 'til lunch, fellas. Let's try to get this Marcus case knocked off before noon," he said. The dead men stared hollowly through their empty sockets and did not reply.

Warren was officially insane, but it wasn't fear that gripped Patrick; it was pity. He watched the scene for another ten minutes. Warren hummed away at his work, stopping only occasionally to check in on his colleagues. When Patrick had seen enough, he crept back out through the storm doors.

9.

"I can't believe you talked me into staying three nights with Norman Bates and family," Ben whined once the door was closed behind them.

"They weren't dangerous," Patrick insisted. "Here we are, in one piece, or rather, two separate whole pieces, and they sent us on our way loaded down with vegetables and water. How can you not be grateful?"

"Easy for you to say. The wife didn't verbally assault you every time she opened her mouth."

"You *did* try to convince her that her 7 year old had a drinking problem."

"I panicked!"

"Be that as it may. You don't come across so well."

"You've got Jim Anderson copying down song lyrics for eight hours a day in his cellar full of rotting corpses, and *I* don't come across well?"

"Who's Jim Anderson?"

"*Father Knows Best.*"

"Wow. You really know your 50s TV," Patrick said admirably. "Warren's not a homicidal psychopath. He's just...taking a break from reality."

"He's having a permanent severance from reality," Ben grumbled.

"I feel bad for him. That little girl had to be, what, two or three on M-Day? Can you imagine? Dedicating your whole life to keeping your family safe and provided for, having these two kids, just full of all this incredible potential, and your whole family has this entire life to look forward to, and there's all that excitement about getting to watch your kids grow and change and become these amazing, actual people, then you wake up one day and realize the world is tearing itself apart? You've failed completely, and everyone you love is in serious mortal danger. I mean, I don't know *what* I would've done if Izzy had survived. Do you explain to your five-year-old that the world is over, or do you try to carry on like always so her little head doesn't implode? The mental weight of it all. Christ. They broke their minds so they wouldn't have to live with it. It's cripplingly heartbreaking."

They walked a few more yards in silence before Ben piped up. "You know what else is cripplingly heartbreaking?"

"Hm?"

"That I didn't swipe the whiskey before we left."

Patrick sighed and patted his friend on the shoulder. "I can always count on you to ruin a beautiful thing."

•

Calico pressed his knife against the old woman's throat. "If you won't talk to me, you won't talk to anyone," he warned. Her lip trembled, but she remained resolute. Calico snarled and nodded toward a man in a red cap across the room. The Red Cap looped his chain around the tall, thin man's neck and cinched it hard. The man gurgled in pain, his eyes bulging from their sockets, his hands struggling uselessly behind his back against their bonds. Blood seeped out from under the metal links as the Red Cap pulled harder. The man's face flushed dark purple. His choking was heavy and wet. Beads of sweat popped from his forehead, and his legs kicked out wildly until his inflated eyes rolled up into his skull. The Red Cap let the chain go with a satisfied gasp. The thin man fell to the floor. Calico smiled and turned back to the old woman. "You're runnin' low on friends. There's only so many times I can ask." He dug the point of the knife into her throat. It punctured her skin and started a trickle of blood flowing down her chest. She squeezed her white eyes shut and turned away. "Aw, come on, Mama Siquo. Why don't you play nice? Just tell us which way them boys headed out."

.

"Holy shit, we made it to Tupelo! Let's go find Elvis!" Ben cried.

"Will you stop talking about Elvis? Screw Elvis! You know what's better than the King of Rock 'n' Roll? The King of the Mothafuckin' Jungle!"

"There's a joke in there somewhere about the Jungle Room," said Ben, putting a finger to his lips. "Give me a minute, I'll think of it."

"You think. I'm gonna go feed the bears." Pat dashed across the road toward the low, green-shingled building behind the faded wooden sign that read Tupelo Buffalo Park and Zoo. Ben followed at a slower pace, lost in thought. "Elvis was a lion in the Jungle Room? No...King *of* the Jungle Room? With his pale scepter? No. Pale scepter's pretty good though. Heh. Pale scepter. Hmm..."

Meanwhile, Patrick was in and back out of the building before Ben was halfway across the parking lot. "Don't go in there," he said. "Everyone's liquefied. It's depressing. Let's go find the monkeys."

"You do realize that the monkeys are also dead, right? And the bears, and the lions, and the zebras, and the--ooo, they had wallabies?" he said, noticing a dusty, crumpled pamphlet lying open on the ground.

"Wallabies are fucking awesome."

"Not anymore, they're not. They're dead. Everything's dead. Caged animals don't not die after being trapped without food for three years."

"No." Patrick turned and squinted into the bright yellow cloud that hung over the property. "There's life in that zoo. I can feel it. I'm going in." He took a running leap over the low wooden fence separating the zoo from the parking lot. His back foot got caught up on the top beam, and he went tumbling to the ground. He threw out his hands on instinct and screamed bloody murder when he came down hard on his wounded right palm. Ben shook his head with a sigh and climbed casually over the rails. "This is why the machete has a sheath," Patrick spat through the dirt.

"As an engineer, shouldn't you be able to estimate the necessary velocity required to propel yourself over embarrassingly low obstacles?"

"The counter weight of my bag is throwing me off. And now it's pinning me to the dirt. Help me up, please."

Apocalypse or no apocalypse, the Tupelo Buffalo Park and Zoo was the most depressing damn menagerie either of them had ever seen. True, they had high standards, having grown up in St. Louis, a city with one of the top-ranking zoos in the country, but even by Chicago's depressing Lincoln Park Zoo standards, or hell, even compared to Wisconsin's Henry Vilas Zoo (which Patrick had visited once on a drunken Halloween college bender in Madison and which had been the genesis of a certain long-running [if tasteless] joke about Henry Vilas Zoo penguins with slit wrists being black and white and red all over), even by *those* godawful standards, the Tupelo Buffalo Park and Zoo was a horrible wildlife park. The earth was hard and gray, the paths were made of hard-packed dirt instead of decent synthetic rubber, there were no abandoned snack stands, no fake rocks or plastic palm trees to give the appearance of some specific natural habitat or other, no tram lines or train tracks...just flat, gray, bland earth as far as the bored eye could see.

It was like visiting a zoo in Chernobyl, circa 1989.

Patrick bemoaned the animal skeletons they passed along the way, or at least the ones that looked like they might have once belonged to the more impressive animals. He sighed sadly at the neck bones of a giraffe and said a quick prayer over a skull that had been either a zebra or a llama. Or maybe a camel. He didn't really know imported animals. But he blustered right past a cracked tortoise shell, because come on, a turtle? He would spare no tears for a turtle.

At the far end of the property, they finally came upon a deep concrete crater with smooth, angled sides that still seemed mysteriously scalable from the bottom of the pit. Resting in the center of the crater were the remains of either a lion or a donkey. Probably a lion, since it was kept in a giant concrete hole. Patrick saluted the poor, demised creature. Then, having traversed the entire property without encountering a single living creature, they turned and headed out of the zoo.

"I know this is getting to be such a common theme for this trip that I probably don't need to even say it anymore," Ben said with no small amount of glee. "But I told you so."

Patrick frowned. "I guess I knew in my heart that they were all dead. I just *wanted* it, Ben. I wanted it so much."

Ben inspected his friend carefully. "You're using your 'more dramatic than usual' voice, and you look clammy. Maybe we should eat something."

Patrick agreed. "Let's get out of the zoo first, though. It seems wrong to flaunt our food in the presence of those who starved."

They headed southeast across a dirt road lined with trees and came out the other side face-to-face with a small, soggy hedge of decomposing hay bales. Judging by their deflated shapes, they had once been the large and cylindrical breed of bale, at least six feet tall, maybe more. Now the piles of damp straw barely came up to their knees. It was all rotted and putrid, stained vivid yellowish-green from the ever-present fog, and in terms of aesthetics, the decomposing straw was not, in itself, terribly exciting. The fact that the lines of bales stretched and zig-zagged their way through the field to form a one-acre hay maze wasn't all that exciting either (though to be fair, in its prime, it was probably one heck of a labyrinth). No, the exciting thing about the rotting piles of hay was that standing in the center of it all, like a devolved Minotaur, stood a shaggy, dew-eyed buffalo, chewing lazily on its cud.

"*Huuuuuuwwwaaaaahhh!*" Patrick hollered, jumping up and down in place. "I knew it! There *is* an animal! The Spirit of the Illinois has led us to this place!"

"I don't think the Spirit of the Illinois spends much time in Tupelo."

"Her benevolence is far-reaching." Patrick slipped out of his backpack and threw the machete to the ground. He loosed the hammer and baton from his belt loops and tossed them down, too. He held his hands out at his sides in a show of peaceable intentions. He took a step toward the buffalo.

Ben grabbed him by the arm. "I'm pretty sure I'm not gonna like the answer to this question. But what the hell are you doing?"

"Ben. Do you remember Kearney, from college?"

A quick, explosive breath burst through Ben's lips. "Do I remember Kearney? Are you serious? Do I *remember* her? Dude, I was in *love* with Kearney. I wanted to *marry* her. I wrote three novels about Kearney Cant. I dug her name into my thigh with a straightened paper clip. She threatened me with a *restraining* order. And then took out a *restraining* order. Do I *remember* her? Seriously?"

"She once told me that the buffalo was my spirit animal." Patrick ambled over the first row of hay. "Ben. This animal is in my soul."

Ben buried his face in his hands. "And so I ask again," he said, his voice muffled by his palms. "What the hell are you doing?"

"Earning her trust." He walked slowly toward the massive prairie animal, stepping gingerly over the soggy rows of hay. The buffalo simply stood and watched him approach. When he was just two hay rows away, Patrick gently raised his left arm, fingers outstretched. He locked eyes with the buffalo. He saw acceptance in those eyes, and, he thought, maybe love. He moved almost imperceptibly, so slow and careful were his motions. He crept over the last two rows, and then he was standing face-to-face with the creature. He reached out and pressed his palm to the buffalo's shaggy nose. The buffalo gave a quick bob of her head, as if nodding her approval. Patrick patted the beast, rifling his fingers through her coarse, matted fur. "Ben," he whispered over his shoulder, "bring me the rope."

"Why? So you can lash yourself to the stupid thing and be bonded forever?"

"No. But that's a good idea. But no. I need to make a harness. I shall ride this buffalo to Disney World."

•

The lunch that Ben physically forced into Patrick's mouth was small, but it seemed to do some good. The canned pineapple slices brought his blood sugar back up to a reasonable level, and he no longer demanded to ride the buffalo. But he still refused to leave it behind. "Fate has brought us together. I know it. This gentle beast is meant to join us on our journey."

By this time, the argument had been going on in one form or another for almost a full hour, and Ben finally had enough. "For the love of God, Patrick. Fine. If you can get the stupid thing to budge and miraculously follow us, she can come." Patrick pumped his good fist into the air in silent triumph.

As it turned out, leading a one-ton buffalo was really quite simple. Neither of the men knew a single thing about buffalo aside from what they'd learned from *Dances With Wolves*, so it was impossible for them to tell if this buffalo was acting rationally or not by standing still and letting Patrick paw all over her face. When it came time to pack up the utensils and move on, Pat merely took the creature's muzzle in both hands, stared deeply into one eye, and said, "Come now, Ponch," giving her a little pull in the proper direction. That's all it took to get his new pet moving; Ponch began hoofing slowly behind them.

"Ponch?" Ben asked.

Patrick nodded. "The Spirit of the Illinois told me her name."

Ben shook his head in bewilderment as they walked. "Look. I'm not going to say this is the single dumbest idea you've had on this trip because I think we both know that's not true. But it's definitely up there."

"How is it up there?" Patrick asked, tearing a clump of grass from the earth and feeding it to the placid bison. "Look at her. She's harmless."

"She weighs as much as a Chevy Malibu. That's instant potential for harm. What if she stampedes?"

"She absolutely will not stampede, 100% guaranteed."

"How do you know that?"

"Because one animal cannot stampede. You need a whole herd. Ponch here is a gal without a tribe."

"Whatever, you know what I mean. She can still run. Over people."

"Look, if she starts acting up, we'll put her down with the machete."

"You can't kill a buffalo with a machete."

"Are you nuts? The Indians killed them with pointy rocks. I think they can be put down with a machete."

"No, I know they *can* be killed with a machete. I just don't think *you* could do it with a machete."

"Because of my attachment to her?" Patrick asked, rubbing Ponch's nose affectionately.

"Because of your general physical ineptitude."

"*Pbbbbbft!*" Patrick said, shooting streams of spit from his lips. "I've seen *Apocalypse Now*, Ben. I think I know how to kill a giant mammal with a machete. Then we'll have meat and fancy new buffalo coats, and we'll eat the heart and gain the strength and wisdom of the bison."

"Ten of your worthless American dollars says she eats you first."

"You're on."

They plodded along, the three of them, moving in a generally southeastern direction. Ponch slowed their pace a bit, stopping here and there to munch on grass or low brush, but, as Patrick pointed out, they were in no real hurry. Disney World would be just as wrecked in a month as it would be tomorrow.

Complain as he might, Ben eventually conceded to a better mood. The fog was thin, the sun was particularly bright, the day was unusually warm, and the northwestern Mississippi woods had given way to mostly open fields. For the first time in a long time, they could see for over a mile in each direction. Which made it especially surprising when they finally realized they were practically surrounded by runners.

There were four of them, three moving up swiftly from the south, one jogging toward them from the northeast. Ben was the first to notice them on the peripheral. He raised a panicked alarm and drew the wrench from his pocket.

"Ooooooooh, this is not good," Patrick said.

"They're moving more slowly than the other ones," Ben noted. They were quick, but none of them were sprinting like the first runners they'd encountered. Maybe it was the sight of the buffalo that made them approach more slowly, maybe it was the clash of two mini tribes, but for whatever reason, they looked almost cautious. "Maybe they're a different breed."

"Right. Maybe they *don't* try to eat shoe leather and human flesh. You go say hi and see if it's true." Patrick drew the machete. It felt clumsy in his left hand. Ponch pawed at the ground with her great hooves, as if she sensed trouble brewing. "Maybe Ponch will save us," Patrick said, his voice quivering with the fear he tried to shove back down into his stomach.

"Sure. Maybe she's one of those military tactical buffaloes. I'm sure she'll come through."

They didn't have to wait long to learn how Ponch handled herself in a fight. The runners, tired of circling the prey, finally made a collective mad dash for the trio. They acted at the same time, all four of them, like an organized flock, despite their apparent partisanship. Ben let loose a gasp of fright and gripped the wrench in both hands. Patrick raised the machete. The madmen flew into a furious attack. And Ponch snapped into action.

She reared back on her hind legs and crushed the first runner in the face with a massive, cloven hoof. The force of the kick nearly exploded the runner's head, spraying yellow blood and gore into the air in a fine mist. Ponch stamped forward and shouldered through the next two runners, knocking them to the ground, then turned and charged at the fourth, coming in from the north. The runner screamed in anger and leapt at the buffalo. Ponch jerked her head and thrust a long, curved horn straight through the runner's right eye. It lodged in the subhuman creature's brain, killing it instantly. The runner hung limp from the horn as Ponch turned to the other two runners, who were just clambering to their feet. She charged and trampled them underfoot, the gouged runner flying from her horn like a windsock. Ponch crushed right through one runner's leg bones and stamped on the other's skull, flattening it in an explosion of yellow goo. The one with the broken leg hissed in fury and clawed his way toward the buffalo. Ponch shook her head, dislodging the hanging runner, and pawed at the ground. She trotted over to the remaining runner, which was now a crawler, and plopped its entire body weight on the thing's head with a sickening *crunch*.

The entire fight was over in 17 seconds. Ben and Patrick stood speechless for at least three times as long.

"Okay," Ben finally said. "We can keep her."

10.

Leanne stuck the knife into the deer's carcass just under the tail and sawed up through its pale belly to the chin. She yanked back the skin and held the flaps open against the ribcage with a pair of stones. She grabbed the hatchet and straddled the prostrate animal. With one quick, strong swing, she cracked through the breastbone. She flung the hatchet into the ground, grabbed the deer's front legs, one in each hand, and pulled them apart, separating the halved plate and opening the chest cavity. Using her knees to hold the cavity open, she picked up the knife and severed the windpipe just below the jaw. She tossed it and the torn gullet into the open chest cavity and moved on to the ribcage. She pried it up and slipped the knife through the abdomen muscles quickly and delicately, exposing the stomach and intestines, taking care not to nick them. She cut down to the pelvic bone, then switched out the knife for the hatchet once again and cracked right through it. She nearly sliced into the urinary tract and cursed herself for being careless. For the next ten minutes, she sawed at the deer's diaphragm, changing position every so often to push different wet, sticky organs out of the way of the knife.

She was about to cut the intestine free from the pelvic area when a twig snapped somewhere in the woods. She froze immediately, squatting perfectly still over the mutilated carcass. Her eyes darted quickly and efficiently through the tree line with the skill of a practiced hunter. When she was finally satisfied there was no movement in the brush, she turned back to the deer and sawed at the large intestine.

When she was done dressing the deer, she trimmed the edible meat from the muscle and bone and dropped it into a nylon sack. She tied it off with baling twine and dropped the little sack into a larger nylon bag and tied it off, too, leaving the twine long. She hefted the bag over to the creek, tied the excess length of twine to a tree root curling out from the bank, and dropped the whole package into the cold, yellow water. The surface disturbance caused ripples of fine yellow Monkey dust to pile up on each other, creating a thick, wet crust that eddied and swirled down the rapids. She clenched her jaw and watched the crust slip away with hollow eyes. Once it flowed out of sight, she plunged her hands into the water and washed them clean of the blood and gristle.

Back inside the house, everything was quiet. She pricked up her ears suspiciously. Not a sound. The pantry door was padlocked securely, the tripwire at the base of the front door was undisturbed. Nothing was amiss.

She returned to the backyard and dumped a load of firewood into the pit. In a matter of minutes, she had flames flaring up through the kindling and licking at the heavy logs. She tossed the deer's stomach and intestines onto the fire and backed away from the stench. When they'd burned down to cinder flakes, she threw in the other organs. She watched with a wicked grin as the blood still inside the heart started to sizzle and boil. It came spurting out the valves in hot, steaming jets, spraying the ground around the pit crimson.

She stalked over to the back door and grabbed the stewpot. She dunked it into the river, upstream of the deer meat, just in case. She lifted it out, full of gray-green water, and hauled it back over to the fire. Once she'd kicked the logs flat with her heavy combat boots, she set the stewpot down in the center of the fire. By the time the water started to boil, it was raining. The storm came on quickly, and soon it was falling in sheets. Leanne spat curses at the sky as she grabbed the tarpaulins and erected two makeshift tents, one over the fire, the other over the wood stack. She was just tying off the second tarp when she heard another loud *crack* from the woods. It rang clearly in the air, even through the gentle roar of the rain. She flicked her head around like an owl. Between the rain and the fog, visibility was low, extremely low, but another *crack* shot through the mist, and then another, and she knew for certain something was out there. She hurried with the tarp, latched it into place, took three long strides to the house's rear overhang, and grabbed the shotgun leaning against the wall. The rustling from the woods grew louder and closer. She raised the gun to her shoulder just as two men broke through the fog twenty yards to the west. Two men and...sweet Martha's tits, was that a *buffalo*?

"Y'all hold it right there," she called out, leveling the gun at the one with a head the size of a pumpkin. The two figures stopped immediately. "Recite the Pledge of Allegiance." The two figures turned to each other. One of them shrugged. They turned back toward her and, in unbalanced unison, began the pledge.

"I pledge allegiance to the flag of the U—"

Leanne lowered the gun. "That's enough. Y'all kin come in, get yer-selves out of the rain." She turned back toward the house, then stopped. "The buffalo stays outside."

Patrick prodded Ben forward toward the house. "You go first."

Ben shook his head. "You're taller. I can use you as a shield. You go." He practically had to shout to be heard over the rain.

Patrick frowned thoughtfully. "Maybe we should stay with Ponch."

"And drown? Good plan."

"Fine. We'll go together." Patrick patted Ponch on the nose and whispered some heartfelt words of parting.

"It's harder for her to shoot us if we're zig-zagging. We should zig-zag." Patrick conceded that this was a fine idea, so the two of them plunged through the woods, running and hopping at jerky, awkward angles, colliding with each other and with trees as they went. It seemed to work; they made it all the way to the fire without getting shot. "What the hell're you creeps doin'?" the girl demanded from the patio. "Getcher asses in or keep yer asses out." They hustled onto the patio, and she shooed them inside.

Ben grimaced as he inspected the house. "I think I'll go back out and drown," he muttered. The whole house was dark, with no candles lighting the space despite the growing dark of the storm outside. It was a small structure, just a handful of rickety rooms making up a building not much larger than a doublewide trailer. They stood in what Patrick assumed was the living room, mostly through process of elimination. It definitely wasn't a kitchen, and he was almost positive it wasn't a bathroom. Warped wooden boards underfoot slanted down toward the center of the house. An oily bath towel provided the only comfortable space in the room, if the word "comfortable" could be defined so loosely. The room opened up to the kitchen, which was little more than a dry sink, an oven topped with a stove, a rickety pre-fab shelving unit, and a small, circular picnic table covered with a stained, formerly white bed sheet. The oven door was open, and through the gloom they could see an outline of logs. Next to the shelving unit was a padlocked door, presumably a pantry. A hallway led off the living room in the other direction, where there couldn't be more than two more rooms. The whole house smelled like wood smoke and urine. But the house itself wasn't what prompted Ben's concern. No, the catalyst for that was the copious number of sharp metal objects that hung from the ceiling like hog legs in a butcher shop. Suspended from little hooks above them hung a few machetes, two hatchets, a full-size axe, a pitchfork, an entire arsenal of hunting knives, spades, shovels, trowels, and a wide, hard metal garden rake. A scythe was mounted to the far wall. A chainsaw lay in the corner. The kitchen was relatively clear; it supported only a set of butcher knives and a pair of hedge clippers. A rifle lay across the table. Another axe lay buried in a short stack of wood near the kitchen window.

The glass door slid shut behind them with a *choonk*.

"Who are you?" the girl demanded. Patrick whirled to find her standing with her feet set and a hunting knife splotched with red stains clutched tightly by her side.

"Nobody. Really. Um. I'm Patrick. This is Ben."

Ben gave a weak little wave. "We're going to Disney World," he said helpfully.

The girl squinted at them, sizing them up. Then she noticed Patrick's bandaged hand. Her grip on the knife seemed to tighten. "Name's Leanne. What happened to yer hand? You bit?"

"Yeah, by a railroad spike," Patrick said, rubbing his injured hand gently. It only hurt now when he was conscious of the wound, which was basically all the time. "We had a run-in with a crucifixion-happy preacher a few days ago. I think it's getting better though, it--"

"What about you?" she asked Ben, cutting Patrick off completely. "You bit?"

Ben tilted his head. "No. Why? By what?"

"By a duster," she said irritably, as if it were the most obvious thing in the world. Patrick and Ben looked on blankly.

"Like...a crop duster? Or...?" Patrick asked.

"A dust freak!" the girl snapped. "Skinny ass hungry little fuckers? Dusters? Jesus, ain't you two dumber 'n a bucket fulla shit."

Patrick brightened with enlightenment. "Oh, you mean the politicians!"

"I ain't talkin' 'bout no grass-snakin' politicians. I'm talkin' 'bout rabid goddamn dust freaks."

"Runners. Yeah, no, we came across some, but we weren't bitten," Ben said.

She stuck the knife into a leather sheath at her belt, apparently satisfied. "Come on, y'all might as well make yerselves helpful while yer here. Why don't you light a fire in the oven? Logs is there, I'll git some kindling." She opened the door and disappeared out into the storm.

Patrick ran his fingers through his increasingly wild hair. His hand bumped against a trowel blade. "Is everyone besides us a complete psychopath?" he mumbled. He made his way to the kitchen, ducking the sharp, swaying metal above, and began to load up the oven. Ben lingered in the living room, testing the various implements for sharpness.

"Damn, son, she's not screwing around," he said, drawing his thumb across a shovel blade. "This shit is *lethal.*"

The girl reappeared with an armful of kindling, her wild brown hair tangled in a wet rat's nest on her head. She had ruddy cheeks flanking a face full of sharp features. Her jeans and olive green army coat were baggy and bloodstained. She must have caught Ben staring at the red splotches as she pushed past him. "Deer blood," she muttered. "Y'all're safe enough, long as ya mind yerselves."

In another minute, there was a fire crackling in the modified oven. The kitchen brightened into a warm, orange glow that threw long, swaying shadow daggers against the far living room wall. The girl hopped up on the table and pulled her feet up, Indian-style. She picked up the rifle and set it across her lap. "Why don't y'all tell me how you ended up in these woods," she said. "'Specially un-bit and all."

Patrick relayed the story of their trip, hitting the highlights in a quick summary, with Ben offering color commentary along the way. She listened without much expression, though her eyebrows crept up a notch when he got to the bit about Ponch's massacre. The parts about the preacher and poor, insane Mr. Tinder didn't seem to faze her. She even seemed to take a bit of delight in the specifics about how Patrick had gotten the hole in his hand.

"Y'all been lucky with them dusters," she said when he'd finished. "Real lucky."

"You have a lot of experience with them?" Ben asked. The girl nodded. "Are they made of metal? We broke a bat over one of 'em, and he hardly flinched."

"'Course he didn't," she said with a snort. "I swear to hell, you yankees is so fuckin' stupid."

"You yankees *are* so fuckin' stupid," Ben corrected her. Patrick elbowed him hard.

"What are they?" Patrick asked. "We have a bet going. Ben thinks they're zombies, but I say they're just incredibly ambitious politicians."

"Zombies is about right," she shrugged. "Else they're near enough as makes no difference."

"I knew it!" Ben said in triumph. "When hell is full, the dead will rise!"

"I didn't say they *was* zombies, I said they's *about* zombies," she said sharply. "Come see for yerself, if ya want." She hopped off the table and walked out the patio door.

"See for ourselves?" Patrick asked uncertainly.

"Don't go out there," Ben hissed, grabbing Patrick's arm. "Let's just run away instead."

Patrick shrugged out of Ben's grasp and headed after the girl. "You're like a broken record, you know that? Run away, run away! We'd have no fun at all on this trip if you had your way. Besides, whatever she's got out there can't be *nearly* as dangerous as leaving us alone in a room full of slicey things." He ducked through the living room and out the door, dodging the cutlery above. Ben cursed under his breath. Hell, Patrick was right. If he so much as sneezed in here, he'd cut his own head off. He hurried out after them.

The girl hustled across the yard to the shed on the edge of the little river. She fished a key from inside her army coat and unlocked the padlock on the door. There were no windows in the shed, and inside was complete darkness. She disappeared into the inky black. Ben and Patrick looked at each other doubtfully. "I'm not going in there," Ben said. "No way."

"I'm sure it's safe," Patrick lied. "All the shed weapons are in the living room."

"You go on, then. Let me know how it feels to die." But just then a match flared in the darkness, and the girl lit a kerosene lantern hanging on the wall near the door. She made a circuit of the shed and lit six lamps in all, one on each wall and two on the makeshift table in the center of the space, a huge piece of plywood supported by three sawhorses. A lantern sat on each end, and lying long ways in the center was a human body, on its back, the skin of its chest and arms flayed and held open with small rocks. Patrick put a hand to his mouth. Ben ran out to vomit in the rain.

"Don't cry for him none," the girl said, blowing out her last match and nodding to the dead man on the table. "He weren't human no more when he ripped my sister 'part with his own teeth, leastways not human enough to cry for."

"You have a sister?" Patrick asked. Upon immediate reflection, he decided perhaps he had worded that question indelicately.

"Ain't you got no fuckin' ears?" she snapped. "I *had* a sister. Now git yer asses over here if ya wanna learn somethin'." Ben crept back into the shed, wiping his mouth, and together they approached the desecrated corpse. Now that his eyes were adjusting to the dark, Patrick noticed a few more implements of mortal destruction scattered around the shed. Most of the standard tools had indeed been moved inside the house, but there were still plenty of dangerous items to spare. A rubber mallet and chisel lay on the table, near the creature's ruined head (the apparent cause of death had been a shotgun blast to the face), as did another hunting knife. A fireplace poker rested against the sawhorse beneath the thing's legs, and on the corner of the plywood table sat an oily old chainsaw. Its blade and guard were thick with dried, yellowish blood. Lumps of the same hard stuff had splattered across the table and onto the floor.

"You cut him open with a chainsaw?" Patrick asked, equal parts impressed and horrified.

The girl nodded. "You gotta. Ain't hardly no other way to break through. Broke the teeth off two chains cuttin' this'n open." She picked up a lantern and swung it over close to the dead man's sternum. She beckoned them over with her free hand. They slunk over reluctantly, shielding their eyes from the crater that used to be the creature's head, and peered cautiously down into the crusty maw of his opened chest. She pointed to a section just below the shoulder where a thick layer of skin had been pulled back, revealing rotting muscle and sinews. She took the chisel and pushed some of the muscle aside. "See right there? Them little yellow tubes? Them's the arteries."

"They're yellow," Patrick said, confused.

"That's what I jes said, genius. So's they blood. Take a crack at it." She held the chisel out toward Patrick. He looked at it uncomfortably. "Go on, take it." He did, but he only frowned down at the cadaver.

"You want me to cut into it?"

"If ya can," she leered. Her teeth were broken and a little yellow in the lantern light. Patrick sighed. He reached down and prodded one little yellow tube, expecting it to give like a gelatinous straw. Instead, it held firm. The point of the chisel knocked against it with a soft *chink*. The artery didn't budge. He pressed harder. Still, it didn't give. He hauled back and chipped at the artery with considerable force. He might as well have been chiseling at a mountain. "Hard as diamond. Every one've his blood vessels is harder to break 'n a steel rod. That's how come yer bat broke in half when you hit it on the head. Lots of blood vessels in the head."

"How does it happen?" Patrick asked, his natural curiosity eclipsing his horror.

"The evolutionary goddamn zombie virus," said Ben, whose natural terror refused to be eclipsed by anything.

"I told you, they ain't no zombies. It's the dust that does it."

"What dust?"

"What dust? Fer fuck's sake, *what dust*? Open that door," she demanded. The shed door had swung shut. Ben pushed it open, revealing the soggy yellow mist outside. "*That* dust, shit brains."

"How is that possible? I don't understand," said Patrick, his mouth screwed up in confusion. "The Monkey chemical causes the exact *opposite* reaction of hardening. People melt out of their own skin. Plus, we all inhale the vapors, and we're not rock solid." He slapped Ben's arm for reference. Ben yelped in pain. "See? Soft as a baby."

"Jesus, you two really are a coupla fuckin' yankees, ain'tcha? Wait here." She grabbed an old coffee mug from a shelf along the wall and ran out into the rain. A few minutes later she was back, the mug full of murky, brown river water. Yellow Monkey fog particles floated on the surface. She picked up a rag from the floor (it looked like it might have once been the dead man's flannel shirt), spread it on the table, and dumped the cup onto it. The water seeped through the cotton and dribbled across the plywood and onto the floor. She picked up the shirt by the edges and shook the wet, yellow dust down into the center. Then she poured out the little yellow clumps onto the table, broke them up with her fingers, and arranged the fine powder into a long, thin line.

"You're kidding me!" Patrick breathed. "They *snorted* it?"

"This here's the South, Mr. Lincoln. If it can be snorted, smoked, or shot, it has been."

"So the concentrated dust hardens the blood vessels over time. Basically giving them an exoskeleton, protecting their vital organs. But you'd think those would shut down. If your arteries turn to stone, your heart must do the same, and every other organ inside. If the heart turns to stone, it can't possibly pump." He picked up the girl's chisel and poked around in the dead thing's chest. Sure enough, the heart had turned hard and yellow. He slammed the chisel into it like a wooden stake into a vampire heart, but it just flaked off a bit of the outer layer.

The girl shrugged. "I just know what I seen," she said, nodding at the body. "They's hard as iron, and when they do bleed, it's with yellow blood."

"Maybe they operate at shockingly low blood pressures," Patrick continued, millions of theories beginning to spin themselves into existence somewhere in his frontal lobe. "It's fascinating."

"It's terrifying," Ben corrected him. "Invulnerable drug addicts starved for human flesh? How is that *not* the most horrific thing in the world? And why in God's name are they starved for human flesh?"

"Ain't invulnerable," the girl said. "Can't git th' organs, but you sure as shit kin git the brain." She pointed at the dead man's eye socket, which was only barely visible amid the ruin of the creature's face. "It's near 'nough the only way to kill 'em. Skull's hard as shit, and the blood vessels don't make it no easier, so the best way is to shoot 'em through the eye.

Yep. Gotta go fer the brain."

Ben smacked Patrick's arm. "I told you. Zombies."

"I seen some duster fuckers stagger 'round on their legs like they ain't never used 'em before," the girl said, prodding the eye socket with her finger.

"We saw a few of those," Patrick said, remembering the horde at the ranger station.

"Near as I kin tell, they somehow got their legs broke, bones snapped right in half, but the blood vessels, yer 'ex-skelton,' or whatever, it keeps 'em walkin' upright, broken bones and all."

"Jesus," Patrick and Ben muttered in unison. "A hard enough blow to the leg could shatter the bone," Patrick nodded. "The sheer force would send a literally bone-shattering shockwave through the leg."

The girl just shrugged. "Least ways, they're easy to tell from real people. Stick out like a handfulla sore thumbs. Can't speak or nothin'. All they can do is run and bite. You boys see a stranger on the road, y'all make him recite the Pledge of Allegiance, and if he can't do nothin' but moan, you shoot him right through the eye."

"Or trample him with your buffalo," Patrick said.

Leanne locked up the shed, and they dashed back into the house, ducking low to avoid the swinging cutlery. She headed for the kitchen and stirred the fire in the oven. Patrick remembered something their host asked earlier that didn't sit well. "Why did you ask if we were bitten?"

"Whatever sickness the dust causes, it can catch, if it's bad enough. Gets in yer bloodstream, and a few hours later, yer a duster yerself, without never snortin' no dust."

Ben threw up his hands in frustration, narrowly avoiding an axe blade. "For crying out loud, can they be any *more* zombie-like? Can we all just take a few seconds to acknowledge the fact that I was right? Especially you," he said, leveling a finger at Patrick.

"They ain't zombies!" Leanne snapped. "They ain't dead. They's still alive. That's a big diff'rence."

"For all practical purposes, there's absolutely no difference at all."

"If they ain't dead, they kin be cured."

Patrick nodded thoughtfully. Was this girl was working on a cure herself, some medicine or salve she kept samples of locked up in the pantry? Not that he expected her to carry a degree in pharmacology, or to be able to *spell* the word "pharmacology," but she did show some sort of natural scientific instinct, the way she dissected the runner in the shed. Maybe she was smarter than she looked.

Later that evening, after a meal of charred venison, Leanne asked them about their destination. "Y'all said Disney World, right?"

"That's correct," Patrick nodded, wrapping a new dressing around his wound. He winced as he pulled the rag tight.

"Wait here, I think I got somethin' for ya." She stood up and disappeared into the back hall. When she returned she was holding a stack of pamphlets. She handed them to Patrick. "I knowed these was somewheres. Found 'em under my bed. Them's the maps to Disney World, most of 'em, anyways. Couldn't find the Magic Kingdom map, but the rest're there."

"Oh, goodness. Thank you. That's really very nice."

Leanne shrugged. "I ain't got no use for 'em no more. Might as well, right? 'Course, I can't imagine what sorta use you might have for 'em either. Disney World's a stupid ass place to go." She crossed into the kitchen and stoked the fire one last time. "Y'all gonna be okay in here?"

"Sure. Sleeping under a canopoy of knives, what could go wrong?" Ben muttered.

"We're fine," Patrick said.

"All right, then. I'll lock the door behind me, so's you know I ain't gonna murder y'all in your sleep."

"Why would you say that?" Ben said, alarmed. "Why would you say you weren't going to murder us in our sleep unless you were going to murder us in our sleep? Why would you say that? Patrick, why would she say that?" But Leanne just gave him a wink and closed the door.

"Well, isn't she a peach!" Patrick declared, spreading his blanket on the floor. "What a nice young lady she turned out to be."

"Nice young psychopath," Ben said in a low tone. "Who cuts up a zombie, then leaves the fucking thing on display? We're staying in the house of Dr. Moreau!"

"Oh, please. She hunts. She's a hunter. Huntress. Whatever. She catches deer. And butchers them. It's natural."

"No. What's natural is keeping your body in one unflayed piece. *That's* natural."

"If it'll help ease your little baby mind, I'll stay up and keep watch for a while," Patrick said, stuffing the Disney World maps into his backpack. "Would that make you feel better?"

"Yes, it would," Ben said indignantly. "Thank you." He burrowed under his blanket and stamped his head down on his knapsack. As soon as he was out, Patrick laid down on his own pillow and gave in to exhaustion.

•

Ben woke to the sound of a rattling chain. At first he thought it was just part of his weird, Dickensian dream, wherein he was being chased down the streets of Industrial Revolution London by the ghost of a transvestite Jacob Marley. His eyes shot open just as Marley wrapped his fishnet stockinged legs around Ben's waist, but even awake, now, he could hear the chains. He sat up and peered into the darkness. The fire in the oven had burned down to embers, and the living room was exceptionally dark. The sound was coming from the kitchen. Someone was doing some mighty fierce chain rattling in there. There was another sound too, a snarling, slurping sort of sound. It sounded like a starving wolf tearing at some sort of prey.

All in all, they were sounds that should not be coming from a kitchen in the middle of the night. Ben decided to panic.

He shook his sleeping companion. When Pat gave a confused blurb of sleepy grunts, Ben slapped him in the face to wake him up. It did the trick. "What the hell do you want?" Patrick cried. The rattling stopped, and Ben would be damned if he didn't hear the sound of something sniffing the air.

"There's something in here," he whispered.

Patrick scratched his head. "Say what, now?" But before Ben could respond, the thing in the kitchen, whatever it was, sprang into action. The chains rattled across the floor and into the living room, and the creature's snarling grew louder. Ben screamed and leapt to his feet, bringing his head right up into the points of a pitchfork. He howled in pain and reached up, yanking the fork down from its moorings. The chains clinked louder, and the creature's snarling filled the room. Ben could see it now, a figure in the darkness, a thin, bony animal scraping toward them on all fours. He grabbed the pitchfork and struggled with its ceiling hook. With a cry of desperation, he ripped the whole thing down from the ceiling, fork and hook alike, and stabbed the sharp tines down toward the shape of the thing's head. There was a soft *gloosh* sound, and the creature screamed in agony. Then, suddenly, everything fell quiet, and the animal dropped to the floor, dead.

"Wuzzat?" Patrick yawned, his hair sticking up at weird angles.

Ben slumped to the floor and tried to catch his breath. "Where's that lighter?" he asked. Patrick motioned toward his backpack. Ben dug through it and pulled out the little plastic Bic. He held it gingerly out toward the dead creature and flicked it to life.

"Jesus Christ!" Patrick cried, scrabbling away from the heap of flesh on the floor. It was a man, a rail thin, sharply boned man with a thick iron collar around his neck attached to a heavy chain that ran back into the kitchen. The man wore a pair of denim coveralls that hung loosely on his gaunt frame. The second tine on the pitchfork had stabbed right through his eye and deep into the brain.

"It's a fucking zombie!" Ben cried.

"Why is it on a leash?" Patrick asked, trying to shake the sleep webs from his head.

Just then, the chain pulled taut. Someone had picked it up on the other end. The chain hauled back toward the kitchen, pulling the dead man's head back up and over his body, twisting his neck grotesquely back over his waist. The person on the other end yanked hard, and the thing's head and shoulders flew back over its legs so it was dragged backward, belly up, the pitchfork still lodged in its eye socket. Patrick and Ben watched in dumbfounded amazement as the body of the runner disappeared back into the darkness. They stood up and followed it cautiously. They arrived in the kitchen just in time to see the thing's feet disappear around the corner, into the pantry. They were still standing in front of the oven, baffled, when the sliding door opened from the outside. Ben grabbed Patrick and pulled him to the ground, where they were hidden from the living room by the kitchen counter. They heard the door slide shut again, then the sound of soft footfalls moving through the living room and into the kitchen. Ben pressed flat against the counters, praying the darkness would hide them from the intruder just three feet away, when suddenly the person stepped into the red glow of the oven embers.

Ben leapt to his feet.

"What the hell are you doing?!"

If there were hatchets hanging down from the ceiling in front of the stove, Leanne would have sliced her scalp in half when she jumped and screeched. She punched blindly in the air, connecting with Ben's shoulder and his ribcage. He swatted her hands away. She scrabbled in the darkness, grabbing for the hunting knife in her belt. She pulled it out and stabbed it forward just as Patrick cracked her on the back of the head with the stock of the shotgun he'd picked up from the table. She crumpled to the ground with a whimper.

"I got to pistol whip someone!" he cried excitedly.

"That's not a pistol, moron."

"The principle is the same," Pat insisted.

"What the hell was she doing?" Ben asked. He toed at her forehead to make sure she was really unconscious.

"Dragging rabid politicians around the house, apparently. *Bemme lighter.*" Ben handed it over. Patrick flicked it on and cautiously poked his head into the pantry. "Yep. Take a look." Ben craned his head around Patrick's thin shoulders and peered into the small room. It was completely empty, except for the dead man on the floor. What food had once been stored inside had long since been removed, leaving all the shelves absolutely bare. The chain attached to the dead man snaked out through a hole in the wall, about two feet off the floor.

"Where does it go?"

"Outside, obviously. Probably secured around a tree stump, or an A/C unit, or something. So she could let it out for exercise without being in the house. Pretty smart."

"Uhh...okay, but...why?"

"To feed, obviously."

Ben raised an eyebrow. "Hey. I think I found a use for that rope."

11.

The rain had more or less stopped by the time they finished tying Leanne to the tree. Patrick tugged at the loop around her neck. "Think she can breathe okay?"

Ben shrugged. "She's not dead yet."

"Fair enough. I knew this rope was gonna come in handy," Patrick said proudly, wiping his hands on his jeans.

"Think she'll be able to get free?"

"Probably. But not before we're halfway to Florida."

"Aren't we already more than halfway to Florida?"

"I mean from here."

"Oh."

Patrick reached down and gently tapped the girl on the forehead. She stirred and raised her head groggily. She tried pulling away from the tree, but the rope held taut against her throat. She gagged and spat into the mud. Patrick smiled down at her. "Hi. Sorry to wake you. We're gonna head out. We just wanted to say thanks for the hospitality."

"What'd ya do to 'im?" she said, her speech slightly slurred.

"To who? To the human flesh-starved maniac on a chain? We killed him. Were we not supposed to?"

"You sonsabitches!" The girl lashed out with her foot and brought it up, hard, into Patrick's crotch. He let out a squeal of pain and fell backward onto the ground.

"He did it!" Patrick groaned, pointing at Ben. The girl kicked out at him, too, but he was well out of foot range. "You killed my daddy, you murderin' sacks o' shit!" She burst into tears.

Ben screwed up his face at her. "Okay, I'm going to need clarification on two points, here. He *was* a zombie, right? Not just a really hangry hillbilly? I mean, you had him locked in a closet on a chain. Also, you dissected one in your shed. I usually try not to use idioms, but I feel like you're kinda calling the kettle black right now."

"That one killed my sister," she snarled, her voice thick with rage, "I didn't have no choice. I cut him open so's I could figger out what was wrong with 'im so's I could find a cure!" She spat a thick glob of mucus at Ben's head. It splattered against his neck.

"Classy." He wiped the wet, green ball away with his sleeve. "Look, I'm sorry about your dad and all, but first off, he's not your dad anymore, he's a zombie, and you can't cure zombie. And, second, he was going to eat us, so really, I guess I'm not sorry. At all." Leanne screamed again and strained against the rope, scrabbling at it with her short, dirty fingernails, but the trunk was too large for her to reach the knot with her back to the tree. Ben nudged Patrick with his shoe. "Pat? Can we go? She looks really pissed. I want to grab a couple knives and go before she Hulks through the rope."

"Right behind you," Patrick groaned, rolling slowly to his feet. He grabbed his bag and pulled out the folded Disney maps. "I'm keeping these," he said indignantly. "Oh. Yeah. That's right. They're *mine* now." He shoved them back inside, threw the pack over his shoulder, picked up his machete, secured his hammer, and thumbed his nose at the angry girl tied to the tree before wandering off to collect his buffalo.

•

Ponch turned out to be an incredible duster duster. She wiped out two more drug-addled lunatics that evening, and no less than 23 more over the next five days. Whenever they came to a creek or a river, Patrick spent at least half an hour washing the caked yellow goo out of her fur, but if there was no water nearby, Ponch didn't seem to mind. She walked with her giant head held tall, wearing the duster blood like a coat of sticky arms. It was her badge of honor for saving their lives on a daily, and sometimes hourly, basis.

Between the bond Patrick felt with her and the wondrous benevolence with which she saved them from the runners, it was with considerable and heartfelt horror that the two men watched her fall horns-first into a giant sinkhole in the middle of Nowhere, Alabama.

"*PONCH!*" Patrick screamed. He dove onto the edge of the sinkhole just as the bellowing buffalo splashed into a pool of water hidden deep inside the Earth. "PONCH, PONCH, PONCH!" The chamber below was dark, but the sun provided enough light to see the buffalo splashing around in slow, confused circles down below. "Ben! We have to go after her!" he cried.

"Yeah, let's just drop into a dark cave and *lift a buffalo out of it.*"

"Good. We're agreed." Patrick shrugged out of his backpack, unzipped it, and pulled out a sweater. "Here, put this on. That water's gonna be cold."

"What're you, nuts? We're not jumping down there."

"We have to do *something!*"

"Fine. I'll say a few words. I'm an Internet-registered clergyman."

"She's not dead!" Patrick roared. "Don't you dare give her last rites. *Don't you dare!* We're coming, Ponch!"

"Pat, she's a thirty-ton animal trapped down a narrow hole. We'd need a super-winch to get her out of there."

Patrick looked up with thoughtful, glassy eyes. "I could build a super-winch," he decided. Ben rolled his eyes. "No, I could! We need to find a scrap yard. Quick! Pull out your iPhone!"

"You keep saying that. You know I never even *had* an iPhone, right?"

"Ah yes. You communicated by carrier donkey, if I recall."

"I don't like technology," Ben huffed.

"When you write my biography, don't take unfair jabs at me for being a technophile."

"When I write your biography, I'm telling everyone you were a hermaphroditic hair dresser who had a love affair with a wild buffalo."

"It *is* bordering on love, isn't it?" Patrick asked with a frown. "Come on, Ben. We have to at least try to get her out of there. How many times has she saved our lives?"

"I don't know. About a hundred."

"That's right. 100 times exactly. And we've only known her a week! I've known you for seventeen years, and you've only saved my life once."

Ben swore he could actually feel his spirit crumpling in on itself. "Fine," he grumbled. "But we can't just fall in after her. Let's look for another way in."

They set off in opposite directions, plunging through the undergrowth, pushing aside brush piles and saplings in search of a second entrance to the cave. They tramped a wide circle around Ponch's hole, never going far enough from the center to be out of each other's sight. "Hey. Remember that scene in *Batman Begins* where little boy Bruce falls into the bat cave for the first time?" Patrick asked, digging through a pile of branches on the forest floor.

"Yeah?"

"Ponch is like Batman," he said. "She's the buffalo Gotham deserves, but not the buffalo it needs right now."

"She would never fit into a batsuit."

"She'd look *great* in a batsuit. Schumacher's batsuit, obviously. With built-in buffalo nipples."

"Don't ever talk about buffalo nipples again."

"Oddly, this is not the first conversation I've ever had about buffalo nipples."

"Stop talking about buffalo nipples!"

They were still searching for another way into the cave when they heard chanting in the distance. Patrick held up a hand to signal for quiet, which Ben misinterpreted as a call for a high five. "Knock it off," Patrick said, swatting Ben's hand away. "Listen. Do you hear that?" Ben pricked up his ears. The chants were growing louder now. Whatever voices were undulating were doing it in their direction.

"*Ooh-ye, blah-deh, domin-eh*," hymned a male tenor.

"*So-mah dee-bah doo-ba day*," intoned a host of male basses.

"*Dus-oh foam-oh scardin-eh.*"

"*Vos-to oo-ve martin-ay.*"

Patrick and Ben exchanged confused glances. "I might be wrong here, Benny Boy, but I think we're about to get into a street fight with St.

Francis."

The chanting grew louder, and soon the strangers were upon them, cresting the wooded hill. And they did look something like monks; they wore coarse, blue, hooded robes, cinched at the waist with shiny silver ropes. Their hoods were deep and floppy, like giant manta rays that had attached themselves to the back of each brother's head.

"*Tone-day la-fay ari-dos.*"

"*Sacro sancto formidos.*"

The brothers were split into two columns, with a solo tenor leading the pack. Because their hoods were too big for their heads, the front hems hung down to their noses, obstructing their collective view. As they chanted, the leader walked witlessly into tree after tree after tree. "*Ooh-ley mal-tay domi--*" Smack! "*Kee-ree may-oh weer-ee--*" Smack! But he plodded on, bravely weathering each blow to the face.

Eventually, the monks meandered toward the sinkhole and passed blindly within two feet of Patrick. He reached out and tapped the leader on the shoulder. The brother screamed and flailed his hands in the air. His brethren, uncertain about this new ululation, but loyal nonetheless, shrugged and followed suit, screaming in a chorus of high-pitched shrieks and wiggling their hands to the heavens.

"Goodness me!" the leader cried, yanking back his hood. His wiry brown hair exploded outward in a ring around a gleaming, bald pate. "Strangers in the woods!"

"Strangers in the woods," the two columns of friars whispered to each other, "strangers in the woods, hm." Yet not a single one of them removed his own hood, so they could not actually see these strangers in the woods.

"Sorry, didn't mean to startle you, but we're having a bit of a problem. Maybe you can help us. You seem to wind your way around these woods pre-tty well," Patrick lied.

"These woods are the corn upon which we thrive," the leader said with a curt, but not unpleasant nod, "and we, naught but pilgrims upon which nibbling knowledge does tread."

"What is he saying?" Patrick hissed to Ben over his shoulder.

"I think he's agreeing," Ben whispered.

He turned back to the leader and thrust out his hand. "I'm Patrick Deen, this is my comrade-in-arms Ben Fogelvee, and the furry one stuck in the cistern over there is Ponch, our stalwart companion, whose afore-mentioned imprisonment in aforementioned cistern is the source of our aforementioned problem."

The unhooded brother shook his head. He seemed physically pained. "I'm sorry, I have a hard time understanding you. We're not used to such expressive epithets of the common tongue," he explained.

"The common tongue?" Ben asked, raising an eyebrow.

"Yes. 'English,' you probably still call it. We in the Post-Alignment Brotherhood find solace in the communicative power of Latsish."

It was Patrick's turn to send his eyebrows skyward. "Latsish?"

"Mm, yes. The lost language of the ancient Muroos, bequeathed to us in the chaos of the Alignment."

"Thuukos, Muroos," the brothers murmured.

"Your English sounds fine to me," Ben said.

The monk bowed. "Thank you for your kind, if counterfeit, words. I am Brother Triedit, Holy Father of our order. It is a true pleasure to make your acquaintances, Brother Patrick and Brother Ben, and we shall assist you with Brother Porch if we are able."

"Ponch," Patrick corrected him. "And she's a sister. Of the Order Patri-Benicus."

"A member of an order! A fellow true believer?" the monk asked, his eyes wide. He rubbed his hands together. "Then let us not delay! Take me to Sister Porch!"

"Ponch."

Patrick escorted Brother Triedit to the edge of the sinkhole and pointed down at Ponch's calm, quiet figure. "That is Sister Ponch. We require her replacement onto the Earth's upper crust."

Brother Triedit frowned. "She is a buffalo."

"She is the buffalo to end all buffaloes," Patrick said. "Is that right? Buffaloes? Or is it buffalo?"

"Buffaloes," Ben said.

"Buffaloes. Buff-a-loes. Huh. Sounds weird."

"It does sound weird," Brother Triedit agreed. "Are you sure?"

"I'm sure."

Patrick shrugged. "He's sure."

"Wait, now I'm not sure," Ben decided. "Buffaloes? Buffalo? Buffa-loes?"

"Buffali?" Patrick guessed.

"Hm. Buffali."

"We'll take it under advisement," Brother Triedit said. "But regardless, that, down there, is a singular buffalo."

"It is."

"Hm." Brother Triedit nodded slowly. "Yes, I think we can take care of this for you. Brother Mayham!" he called to the group of monks huddled off to the side. One of the friars from the front of the line hurried over to the sinkhole. "Brother Mayham, please take care of this beast of burden."

"She is not a burden!" Patrick gasped.

"Yes, Brother Triedit, of course," Brother Mayham said, bowing respectfully and ignoring Patrick completely. He hurried off and began speaking to his brethren in hushed tones. Meanwhile, Brother Triedit placed his hand firmly on Patrick's shoulder and squeezed. "The Post-Alignment Brotherhood will take care of your buffalo. But let us retire to the friary. You gentlemen must be hungry."

12.

The "friary" turned out to be a system of shoddy tree houses connected by a poorly designed series of rope bridges. As far as Patrick could tell, Brother Triedit's tree house was the only one with a full roof overhead. "Settle yourselves in here and meet us down in the dining pit for dinner," he said, pointing at a picnic table set into a dip in the earth below. Then he disappeared across a bridge and into the chapel, an especially rickety tree house with a poorly angled cross nailed to a branch near the door.

"Go on," Patrick said as they hefted their bags onto the crude wooden floor. "Give me a six-hour rant about how this is dangerous, and how we shouldn't stay here."

"Are you kidding me? It's a society built around tree houses! *Tree houses!* Throw in a ball pit and a grilled cheese castle, and we're pretty much staying in my childhood fantasy town."

"What's a grilled cheese castle?" Patrick asked. But Ben was already out the door and on his way down the flimsy rope ladder.

Brother Mayham and his fellow rescue monks were just returning by the time Patrick and Ben sidled up to the dining pit. "*Dommy novus somi-naaaaay,*" they chanted. Patrick was dismayed to see they had returned sans-buffalo. He approached one of the brothers and tapped him on the shoulder. The brother jumped in surprise. "How'd things go with Ponch?" he asked.

"Oh, very well," the friar said, "very well indeed. We managed to salvage your buffalo."

"Salvage?" Patrick said.

"Yes, salvage. Isn't that right? I'm sorry, we have such a difficult time with your English. What might be a better word to use?"

"Saved?"

"Ah. Saved, then."

"Can we go see her?"

"Oh, no," said Brother Mayham. "She's being prepared!"

"Prepared?" Patrick asked doubtfully.

"Prepared. Yes? She is being made presentable? Is that the word?"

"Presentable for what?"

"For her introduction into our camp!"

Patrick frowned. "I don't know. I'd feel much better if I could see her." But Brother Mayham just laughed.

"Animals may not enter here without proper preparation," he said. He patted Patrick on the shoulder and disappeared up into the trees.

"Must be some sort of religious purification thing," he said to no one in particular. Ben shrugged.

"I'm sure she's fine. She killed a whole football team's worth of zombies, I'm sure she can handle some Gregorian weirdoes."

They feasted early on beefsteak that evening, and by the time the last rays of sunshine drained from the foggy yellow air, the plates had been cleared and Brother Triedit had retrieved a giant bladder flask from his tree house. He squeezed a stream of light purple juice into his mouth, swallowed happily, and passed the flask to his right. He smiled at his guests from across the fire. "Centerwine," he explained. "Our own concoction. Please, help yourselves." The flask passed from brother to brother, each man taking a gulp of the wine before passing it on. Patrick took the bladder gingerly and inspected it in the firelight.

"What is it?" he asked.

Brother Triedit frowned. "Centerfruit, and other various fermentations."

Ben nudged him gently. "Don't piss them off, they wield the God-force," he whispered.

"I don't think you know how religion works," Patrick whispered back. But he nodded his thanks to the Holy Father and squeezed a jet of wine into his mouth. He gagged instantly and spat the whole mouthful onto the table.

"What's it taste like?" Ben asked nervously. "Good?"

Patrick's face soured as he forced himself to swallow a second swig. "Moldy Windex and braunschweiger," he decided. He handed the flask to Ben, who held it like he would a rotting skunk carcass. He pinched his nostrils shut and squirted a quick spray into his mouth. He swallowed with a grimace, his face shading a deep purple.

"My God!" he gasped, shaking his head. "What *is* that shit?" He handed the bladder to the brother on his left, who grinned a broken-tooth grin and squirted a gulp happily into his gullet. Brother Triedit smiled too.

"Centerwine stimulates mammarian development," he said.

Patrick tipped his head to the side. "Beg pardon?"

The one called Brother Mayham cupped his hands in front of his chest. "It augments the boobular region," he explained. "Bazoombas."

Patrick and Ben both groaned. "That's very thoughtful," Patrick said, wiping pale pink spittle from his mouth, "given the importance of a healthy bust and all, but we don't have boobulars. Bazoombas. We have testiculars. Generally housed in this area." He swirled a hand near his genitals.

"It is customary for Brothers of the Post-Alignment Order to consume the centerwine in the hopes of achieving gender transmutation," Brother Triedit explained.

"Gender transmutation?" Ben asked, concerned. The friary suddenly didn't seem quite so much like his fantasy kingdom anymore.

Brother Triedit crossed his legs under himself and leaned forward, almost excitedly. "We are a strictly male sect, as you can see," he said, gesturing to the brothers around the fire. "But we wish to actively encourage the survival of the Order, a pursuit that seems more and more unlikely as we continue to fail to discover worthy acolytes. The Great Alignment, it seems, has claimed the majority of our planet's males in an effort to right the natural injustice of humanity."

"The Great Alignment?" Patrick asked. "You mean M-Day."

"Ah, 'Monkey Day,' yes. Give it what sinful secular title you will, it was a day of great salvation and alignment for the human faithful, but our Order was left without women to assist in procreation. Therefore, with the guidance of the Prayers of the Aligned, we strive to transmute our own selves into the femalular sex so that we might procreate and spread the Word of the Aligned into future generations."

"Lemme get this straight," Ben said, shifting uncomfortably in his seat. "You're all trying to turn yourselves...into women?" The brothers nodded. "So that you can have sex with each other?" More emphatic nodding.

Patrick jumped in with both hands. "And you're hoping that this questionably alcoholic beverage will do that."

"We do not hope. We *believe*," said Brother Triedit.

"Why on earth would you believe that?"

Now it was Brother Waywerd's turn to speak. He was a bookish man with horn-rimmed glasses and a boyish face. "Are you familiar with the scientific fact that some West African frogs are known to spontaneously switch genders, without any warning at all?"

"Why, yes, I *did* see *Jurassic Park*," Patrick answered.

"Oh Jesus," Ben said, his face flushing light green. "If you tell me I just drank frog sperm, I'm throwing up on every single one of you."

"Goodness, no!" Brother Waywerd exclaimed. "No, no. Not sperm. Just blood extraction."

"Centerwine is frog blood?" Ben asked, clapping a hand over his mouth.

"Among other things, yes. That's the main ingredient."

"We also use wild boysenberry, for flavor," explained Brother Triedit.

"You know, I *thought* I tasted boysenberry," Patrick said, wagging a finger at the Holy Father. Ben looked as if he might actually be sick, at least on himself if not on everyone else. Patrick, however, was more scientifically intrigued than physically ill. "Has this screwball plan shown any signs of success?" he asked the hooded scientist.

"Well, not yet," Brother Waywerd admitted sadly, "but as we all know, life finds a way."

"Of course it does. You know, human physiology is a *bit* more complex than amphibian physiology. Does that concern you at all? Make you think, 'Hey, maybe this, I don't know, won't work'?"

"If the Order is fated to succeed, this is the manner in which it will achieve future greatness," Brother Waywerd said simply. "If it *does* not work, then it *should* not work."

"Interesting," Patrick said, tapping a finger to his lips. "Religious zealousy with a strong fatalistic bent. My Aunt Margie would've loved you guys. How long have you been drinking this centerwine?"

"About two years now," Brother Mayham said.

"And tell me, how do you feel?"

"Me? Well, I must admit, personally, I don't feel much different," Brother Mayham said.

"Oh, that's nonsense!" cried Brother Haffstaff from across the fire. "If you ask me, you're much more sensitive now than you used to be."

"Was I not sensitive before?" Brother Mayham frowned.

"You were always a bit of a human tinder box," Brother Haffstaff admitted. "But you're much more empathetic these days."

"I'd say the same for most of us," piped up Brother Wildgardyn. "We're *all* much more sensitive!"

Brother Bickdraft snorted. "*Too* sensitive, if you ask me. It gets worse every week."

"There's no such thing as too sensitive; there is only complete and utter *in*sensitivity!" Brother Haffstaff cried.

"You see? This is exactly what I'm talking about," Brother Bickdraft grumbled.

"How dare you insinuate!" Brother Wildgardyn exclaimed.

"Brothers, brothers, please!" Brother Triedit lifted his hands and waved them gently at the assembly. "Be centered! *Kyrie-eh-so domin-oos,*" he intoned.

On cue, the other brothers immediately relaxed and chanted their answer in unison: "*Dom-ah doos-uh eff-ree-ay.*"

"That's beautiful," Patrick said with a short round of applause. "What's it mean?"

"In each one, we find the center, and in the center, we find all," said Brother Triedit.

"Wonderful. Better even than Pig Latin. Just wonderful."

Brother Wildgardyn raised his hand. Brother Triedit called on him. "I thought it meant, 'Whensoever the sun doth rise, therefore too are the children of the wicket crickets.'"

"That is a wildly blasphemous translation, Brother Wildgardyn!" Brother Bickdraft screamed. "I command you to the Centrification Chamber!" The other brothers nodded their emphatic agreement. It was unanimous; Brother Wildgardyn's blasphemy must be punished. The friar snuffled, collected the folds of his robe in his hands, and walked primly to the edge of camp, where he reached down and pulled up a hidden trapdoor, covered with sticks and brush. He held his breath and jumped into the hole with a loud *SPLASH!* Then the trapdoor fell shut, and the brothers turned back to the fire, each of them brooding on Brother Wildgardyn's failure. Ben broke the silence by clearing his throat.

"So. What else do you guys do? Besides hope for spontaneous sex changes?" he asked. Brother Haffstaff opened his mouth to respond, but Patrick cut in, his voice high-pitched with incredulity.

"Wait, where on Earth did you find West African frogs?" he demanded.

Brother Triedit and Brother Haffstaff exchanged looks. "Well, ahm... we haven't actually managed to locate West African frogs as such," Brother Haffstaff said slowly, tenting his fingers in front of his robe. "Yet!" he added.

"But our frogs are just as good," Brother Bickdraft insisted.

Patrick leaned forward, clasping his hands under his chin. "Let me get this straight. You're hoping for a widespread, irrational sex change from taking a few shots of blood from a species of frog that is *not* the one known for getting surprise gender reassignment surgery?"

"If the Great Centralizer hears our prayer, anything is possible."

"Swell!" Patrick cried gleefully. "That is excellent! Cracker Jack of a plan you got here." He gave thumbs up all around. The flask had made its way back around the circle. He took it happily and squirted another shot into his mouth. "Mm. You know, you're right, you can really taste the ovaries. What do you think, Ben? Ovaries?" he asked, handing him the centerwine. Ben pushed it away in disgust.

Brother Triedit stood and stretched his hands out over the table. "Brothers!" he boomed. "It is time for the Feats of Adulation."

"*Oh-may for-tay lon-ee-yay*," the brothers chanted.

"Oh my forty lawn yards," Patrick echoed, making a religious sign with his hand.

Ben leaned over and hissed, "What's the matter with you? Are you drunk? Are you becoming a woman?"

"This is easily the single silliest situation I have ever encountered," Patrick whispered back. "I'm drunk on incredulity."

"Let us adjourn to the fire," said Brother Triedit. He led the group to the friary's fire pit, around which the men sat down cross-legged in a large ring. "The first Feat belongs to Brother Toldus and Brother Bickdraft." The two monks stood and bowed to the Holy Father. "*Doo-say port-oh mon-groo sat-ay*," they mumbled in unison. Then they turned to each other and bowed again. Brother Bickdraft motioned for Brother Toldus to go first. The latter folded his hands into his sleeves and cleared his throat loudly.

"Tonight I adulate the Great Centralizer with this cedar twig, which I discovered underfoot upon my morning constitution." He retrieved a small branch from within the folds of his robe that still had a few of what Patrick was fairly certain were oak leaves and not cedar needles. Brother Toldus held the twig over his head in both hands, closed his eyes, rolled his head back on his shoulders, and undulated in a proud and powerful *Xena: Warrior Princess* battle cry. His hands flew into a flurry, maniacally shredding the leaves from the twig. Then he broke the tiny branch into a dozen pieces, spun around, and hurled them into the woods. He turned back to the fire, bowed low to the flames, and said, "In Its Name, I adulate." He sat down to the approving murmurs of his brethren.

Now it was Brother Bickdraft's turn to adulate. He drew his hands into his sleeves, just as Brother Toldus had done, and stood straight and tall before the fire. "Tonight I adulate the Great Centralizer with the gift of my tremendous broadsword, which I carved from the trunk of a mewling mulberry tree." He turned and picked a small wooden sword from the ground behind him and held it aloft before the flames.

Ben leaned in toward Patrick. "I'm not a 'Pop Goes the Weasel' expert," he whispered, "but mulberries grow on bushes, right?"

"Yes. I am completely amazed by these lunatics' ability to be scientifically inaccurate about absolutely everything," Patrick said.

Brother Bickdraft took the small wooden sword in both hands and began to perform a choreographed sword-dance routine that could only be described as mesmerizing, in the way that a hairless, drunken yak stumbling in a hoof-sucking muddy swamp might be mesmerizing. He swung the sword in frantic circles over his head, kicking one knee up and hopping on the other foot. He drew the sword back in a lunge attack position and squatted low, bouncing and rocking on the balls of his feet. He fell to the ground, side-planking his body with one arm and holding the sword straight out from his hip into the sky. He rolled across the dirt, sword clutched in both hands and stretched above his head, like an armored wheel spoke, nearly spinning his way into the fire. He leapt from foot to foot, bobbing a wide circle around the ring of brothers, the sword twirling arrhythmically, accidentally slapping into a hooded pate every six or seven steps. He soft-skidded through a pile of dead leaves, swinging the sword from his hips like a clumsy codpiece. He flipped the sword into the air, end over end, clapped his hands three times, then yelped in pain as it smacked against his poorly timed fingers and fell to the ground. He picked it up and stabbed the air three times, let out a squeaky cry of what Patrick pegged as constipated irritation, then bowed to the fire and said, "In Its Name, I adulate." The brethren nodded and murmured approvingly among themselves.

Brother Triedit stood and quieted the brothers with his outstretched palms. "The Champion of the first Feat is Brother Bickdraft." Brother Bickdraft raised his sad little sword in triumph. The brethren nodded their support. "Brother Toldus, step forth and receive the Agony of Defeat." Brother Toldus stood and humbly approached Brother Triedit at the head of the fire. Brother Triedit ceremoniously removed Brother Toldus's hood. Then he reached into the folds of his own robes, retrieved what appeared to be a rotten peach, and crushed it down upon Brother Toldus's head. Dark brown juice and bits of blackish pulp trickled down the friar's face and neck. He bowed low and said, "Thank you, Holy Father."

"*Doh-mus ar-lay fonto-roh*," Brother Triedit said, nodding.

"*Ee-gree eff-no holly-mus*," Brother Toldus replied. He returned to his seat, rotted fruit flesh drying into his beard.

"The second Feat of Adulation belongs to Brother Mayham and Brother Spyndthrift," Brother Triedit announced. Brothers Mayham and Spyndthrift stood and bowed to the Holy Father. "*Doo-say port-oh mongroo sat-ay*," they said. It was decided that Brother Mayham would adulate first.

"Tonight I adulate the Great Centralizer with a wholly accurate moose call, which I perfected just this afternoon." He spread his feet and squatted down a bit, then brought his fists to his mouth to form a hand trumpet. He took a deep breath, then, with all his might, blew a long, low groan into the tunnel of his fists. "*Mrrooooooooooooooooooooggh-qwwuffffffawhh.*" He turned and bowed to Brother Triedit. The monks all acknowledged the astonishing accuracy of his call, and some even applauded lightly, though the squealing moan sounded more to Patrick like a gagged hyena than a moose. He clapped politely anyway. Ben did not.

Brother Mayham's moose call was so well received that Brother Spyndthrift was visibly nervous as he buried his hands into his sleeves and addressed the group. "Tonight I, uh, I adulate the Great Centralizer with a, ahm, with a poem that I wrote before lunch." A few of the brothers audibly groaned. Waxing poetic was not a new hobby for poor Brother Spyndthrift. He ignored their premature criticism and began his recital:

"The woods of yore, yon sickly saps, the braided heartache bring,

A-shoomer, a-shonner, the dead leaves whisper in my ear.

Thy trees of habit grow stagnant in oily pools of befuddled wisdom.

'Were they ever? Were they ever?' sad Atlas asks.

Wisdom is slow, and viscous as sap,

It freezes and pleases nobody but none,

The owls lament the fruit of their lives.

Were they ever? Were they ever? I ask, were they ever?"

Brother Spyndthrift concluded to complete silence. He turned and bowed low to the Holy Father. He returned to his seat and waited nervously for Brother Triedit's judgment.

"Boooooo!" Brother Haffstaff cried. "Booooooooooo!"

"Booooooooooo!" agreed the monks of the Post-Alignment Brotherhood. "Booooooooo!" Someone threw a rock across the fire. Brother Spyndthrift ducked with practiced ease. His poetry had fallen flat before.

Brother Triedit stood and calmed the dissenting clan. "The Champion of the second Feat is obviously Brother Mayham." Whoops and cheers went up around the fire from all but Brother Spyndthrift, who looked not particularly surprised. He stood and met Brother Triedit's rotten peach punishment with as much dignity as a tortured poet could muster. "And for the third and final Feat of Adulation, we call upon Brother Haffstaff and Brother Bicon." The two monks rose, and the others leaned forward in tense anticipation. Brother Triedit acknowledged their excitement and nodded. He reached behind his seat and pulled up a hollow gourd. "The third Feat of Adulation is the Great Test, and tonight's Test shall be..."

He reached into the gourd, trudged around with his hand, and pulled a piece of bark from within. Something must have been written on it, for he glanced at the bark, nodded again, and said, "...a Feat of Rhyme!"

Wild cheers went up around the fire. Despite their collective distaste for Brother Spyndthrift's particular brand of poetry, the Feat of Rhyme was a popular choice among the men. Brother Haffstaff shook out his hands while Brother Bicon rolled his head around on his neck. Brother Triedit gave them thirty seconds to loosen up, then called their Feat to order. The two men faced each other across the fire and shook hands over the flames.

"This looks pretty serious," Patrick whispered to Brother Bickdraft.

"Oh, it is," Brother Bickdraft assured him. "He who fails to adequately adulate in the Great Test is thoroughly punished."

Brother Triedit cleared his throat. It was time to begin. "Yesterday, I packed my van." He motioned to Brother Haffstaff to go first.

"It was driven by a rather merry man," he said.

"He was the leader of the caravan," Brother Bicon shot back.

"His name, I soon learned, was Dan," said Brother Haffstaff.

"He had the most luxurious tan," replied Brother Bicon.

"He received it in the Caribbean." There were murmurs of protest regarding Brother Haffstaff's pronunciation, but Brother Triedit dismissed them with a wave of his hand. He would allow it. And so they continued, back and forth, the rhymes flying faster and faster.

"The man in the van was my biggest fan," said Brother Bicon. Patrick wondered if extra points were rewarded for multiple rhymes, or if he was just showing off.

"He, like I, was born in French Sudan."

"Which reminded me at once of my master plan."

"One I'd concocted playing Settlers of Catan."

"It had to do with the nation of Iran."

"And the wayward policies of the nation's Taliban."

"The man from Sudan with the tan in the van was content to sit and scan."

"While I relayed my plan about Iran on the divan." Both men were growing red in the face. Brother Bicon's hands were clenched in fists of concentration, while Brother Haffstaff's fingers stiffened from his palm like metal rods.

"But now, I saw, the plan was wan," said Brother Bicon.

"So I thought I might as well move to Japan."

"Or better yet, maybe Kazakhstan," Brother Bicon huffed.

"I could live on a farm of the variety pecan," Brother Haffstaff puffed.

"Or spend my days on a catamaran."

"Against hard work, I'd levy a ban." Brother Haffstaff was grasping at straws now, and everyone could see it. Brother Bicon may have been faltering physically, but his mind was still sharp.

"That trip might be over before it even began."

"The natives, I think, I would be better than," said Brother Haffstaff weakly.

"I wonder if you could watch reruns of *Roseanne*."

"I could--I could watch them while making dinner in my pan," Brother Haffstaff wheezed.

"At least you'd be far from the Ku Klux Klan."

Brother Haffstaff's face was chalky white, and damp with sweat. "And I could buy a house near an alluvial fan," he gasped.

"Fault!" cried Brother Triedit. "Repeated use of the word 'fan.' The title of Great Adulator falls to Brother Bicon." The brothers gave him a rousing applause. "Well done, brother! The Great Centralizer is fittingly adulated, and yea, art thou bright in his eyes, *oo-fray dic-tus homy-noo*." Brother Bicon bowed low to the Holy Father and responded in the order's gibberish. Brother Triedit blessed him with the Sign of the Wobbly Circle, then clapped three times. "Brother Mayham, bring forth the Book of Failure and Disgrace." Brother Mayham shimmied up the trunk of a great oak tree and returned with a heavy, leatherbound book the size of a tombstone. He lowered himself to one knee and presented it humbly to the Holy Father. Brother Triedit took the tome and flipped it open to what seemed to be a random page. "As Fortimus did shame his family with the forfeiture of his larger-than-average genitalia in exchange for a piddling sum, so too are we shamed by the catastrophic failure achieved thence by one of our own cloth." He closed the book with a heavy *thud* and beckoned Brother Haffstaff forward. "Step to, Pillar of Embarrassment, and receive the Divine Shaming." Brother Haffstaff fell to his knees before the Holy Father. Brother Triedit cursed him with a Reverse Wobbly Circle, then lifted the book high in the air and brought it crashing down on Brother Haffstaff's shoulder. The Pillar of Embarrassment was knocked to the dirt.

"*Tho-nus don-tus farky-nom,*" he said.

Brother Triedit turned to the other members of the Order. "Come, brothers, and form the Line of Severe and Direct Punishment." The monks stood and shuffled toward the prostrate failure. Patrick and Ben followed, casting each other questioning glances. They squeezed themselves into the line that formed behind Brother Spyndthrift. Brother Triedit handed Spyndthrift the book. He hauled off and whacked Brother Haffstaff in the leg.

"*Tho-nus don-tus farky-nom,*" said Brother Haffstaff.

"Is there anyone left in the world who's not roundly insane?" Ben whispered to Patrick. Brother Bickdraft overheard him and intervened.

"Only one of our number receives the Divine Shaming each night during adulation," he explained quietly. "It's practically an honor."

Patrick watched doubtfully as the other brothers took their turns battering the inadequate rhymer with the heavy book.

Wham!

"*Tho-nus don-tus farky-nom.*"

Whack!

"*Tho-nus don-tus farky-nom.*"

Whomp!

"*Tho-nus don-tus farky-nom.*"

Whuff!

"*Tho-nus don-tus farky-nom.*"

…And so on. Soon it was Ben's turn to bludgeon the poor bastard. Brother Toldus handed him the book. Ben almost fell under its surprising weight. He hefted the thing and cast an uneasy look at Brother Triedit. The Holy Father nodded, urging him forward with his hands. Then Ben looked down at Brother Haffstaff, splayed out awkwardly in the leaves and brush. He, too, nodded up at Ben, and even gave him a thumbs up. Ben shrugged. Then he hauled off and whacked Brother Haffstaff in the head.

"Well done!" Brother Triedit exclaimed. "You Shame as well as any practiced member of our order." The other brothers bobbed their heads in agreement. Ben beamed.

He handed the Book of Failure and Disgrace to Patrick, who nearly dropped it. The damn thing was heavy, and he only had one good hand.

He looked down on poor Brother Haffstaff, who gave him an encouraging smile. Patrick bent down and lightly tapped him on the shoulder. Then he handed the book back to Brother Triedit.

The Holy Father frowned. "Not the strongest Shaming I've seen," he said bluntly.

Patrick shrugged. "I'm not really a shaming kind of guy."

"The road to True Centralization is paved with tiles of Great Shame," Brother Triedit pointed out.

Soon, it was roundly considered late enough to call it a proverbial night. The brothers stood and bid good evening to their guests before ambling up the trees. Ben stood and stretched. "You turning in?" he asked.

Patrick shook his head. "I think I'll keep the fire company a little while longer. You know how lonely fire gets."

"It's the fourth loneliest of all the elements." They high-fived goodnight, and Brother Toldus led Ben off to the guest tree house. Aside from Patrick, only Brother Triedit remained.

"Thank you again for putting us up. Heh, heh." He pointed at the trees. "Get it? Up? That wasn't even on purpose."

"You are most welcome, Friend Patrick. The Great Centralizer has sent you to us, and we heed Its providence."

Patrick flexed the fingers of his injured hand. They still tingled numbly, and they refused to straighten all the way. But the infection didn't seem to be spreading through the hand. That was providence.

"Tell me," continued Brother Triedit, "your friend, Ben, is he a man of steadfast beliefs?"

"He's a man of much steadfastness," Patrick admitted. "Though it's generally more accurate to say I have a steadfast belief in him."

"Yes," Brother Triedit said, stroking his chin. "Hmm."

Patrick reached for the abandoned flask of centerwine and squeezed down another gulp. "It's getting better with age," he groaned.

Brother Triedit quickly scanned the area for any lagging monks, then reached into his robes and retrieved an honest-to-goodness metal flask. He screwed off the lid and raised a toast.

"Is that the real deal?" Patrick asked.

Brother Triedit nodded. "It gets no realer." He tipped Patrick a salute. "Heavy is the head that wears the hood," he said before knocking back a swig.

"Could I have some of that? My head's naturally heavy." Brother Triedit handed him the flask. Patrick glugged from its tinny depths. "*Gaaaaah*," he hissed as the drink burned its way down, and possibly through, his esophagus. "That is *not* the real deal," he gagged, handing the flask back to Brother Triedit.

The monk frowned as he took the little metal container from his guest. "I made this fermentation with my own hands," he said, his feelings obviously hurt. "How could it possibly be more real?"

"That's true," Patrick conceded, scrubbing the tears from his eyes. "The only way it could get more real is if Bruce Lee jumped out of the bottle and roundhoused you in the face." He shook his head, cleared his throat, and took a deep, cleansing breath. The red in his cheeks slowly started to fade. "Say, lemme ask you something. Where are you guys from?"

"Oh, here and there. I'm from southern Wisconsin myself. Brother Haffstaff and Brother Spyndthrift are from Illinois. Brother Toldus is from Mississippi, I think. Or Louisiana? Brother Mayham hails from Arkansas. We're a motley group."

"Midwesterners, all," Patrick said. "Hm."

"And you?"

"St. Louis, originally."

"A place of heathens," Brother Triedit said, with no further explanation. "What brings you men to Alabama? Ben mentioned something of a quest, I think?"

"You could call it that," Patrick said, nodding. "In some ways, I suppose it's the ultimate quest. A quest to reclaim a misspent childhood. A quest to scrape through the rust of apocalyptic ruin and let pre-M-Day chrome glimmer in the light of hope. A quest to determine if the reasonable shelf life of an overcooked concession stand hot dog could possibly be more than three years. Brother Triedit, we quest for Disney World."

"Truthfully?"

"Fully of truth."

"May I ask why?"

"You may."

Brother Triedit looked expectantly at Patrick. Patrick looked expectantly at Brother Triedit.

"Why?" the monk finally said.

"Glad you asked!" He reached around and pulled the worn paper from his pocket. Maybe it was the hooch, maybe it was the centerwine, maybe it was the gender transmutation starting to take effect, but Patrick realized he wanted to share it with someone. Not with Ben...not yet. But Brother Triedit was a loon, and there's a sort of protective comfort in lunacy. He handed the paper to the monk.

"I see," Brother Triedit said when he had read the faded words. He handed the paper back to Patrick. "You must feel extremely..." He searched for the right word. "...Misaligned."

Patrick nodded slowly. *Misaligned.* "That actually sums it up pretty well," he said.

Brother Triedit crossed his arms and leaned toward the fire. "The M-Day, as you call it, as the entire wasteland calls it, I suppose, wasn't a day of destruction, Friend Patrick. It was a day of centrification. Before the Great Event, I was a pre-owned vehicle salesperson. Brother Bickdraft was a high school gym teacher, Brother Spyndthrift was a traffic attorney, and Brother Haffstaff was a night clerk at Dunkin Donuts. All of us, so far in our former lives from the beings we have realigned into, and so different from each other. Yet we had one thing in common; we felt *displaced.* Do you ever feel displaced, Friend Patrick?"

"Only when Ben puts me away in the wrong toy chest."

"I can see that you do. We all did as well. We all knew there was *something else* we were meant to be. We'd lost our way, both as individuals and, I believe, as a species, and the Alignment brought us back to ourselves. It started with the Mesopotamians, of course, and their modern notions of civilization. Ridiculous! Man wasn't meant to live in collective housing and certainly not in encampments made of stone and mortar. We were made to live in the trees, just as our winged ancestors did before the evil magician Toomralan cursed us with arms of flesh and unfeathered skin. We didn't know this truth before the Great Alignment. How could we have? We were born into Maladjustment. But the Alignment... ah, the Alignment. The Great Centralizer brought us back to ourselves. It reminded us of the true Latvish tongue, and, again, I do apologize for my horrendous English. I'm sure you don't understand half of what I'm saying. But the Great Centralizer revealed to me the truth of our existence, Friend Patrick, and in the dozenth year of the Post-Alignment

Calendar, I have seen that we shall all break free of these human shackles and return once more to our proper sparrow state. I only pray we're able to transmutate enough of our men into women in order for my blood-line to live long enough to experience this Tremendous Centralization of Being."

A gulf of silence passed between the men. It became obvious that Brother Triedit was anticipating a response. He kept jiggling his eyebrows up and down like hairy jump ropes. Finally, Patrick just said, "Well, we all have our quests." Then he snatched back the flask, held it high in sa-lute, and drank down its entire contents.

13.

Ben awoke early the next morning to the sounds of shouting and splashing from somewhere below his tree. He rolled blindly out to the rickety wooden balcony and squinted through sleep-crusted eyes at the world below. All was quiet; not a single hooded brother stirred. Yet, the hollering and the splashing continued. Then Ben saw the trapdoor in the forest floor and remembered Brother Wildgardyn's banishment to the Chamber of Secrets, or whatever the hell it was called. Someone else seemed to remember it, too, because just then a wooden slipper was flung from a tree across the clearing and clattered against the cistern's door. "In the name of the Great Centralizer, shut the bloody fuck up!"

Ben rolled back into the tree house and tried to fall back asleep, but it was useless. All that splashing had snapped his bladder to full attention. He looked over at Patrick, who was snoring softly, one arm flung crazily over the sack of rotted leaves that served as a pillow, his head awkwardly propped between the floor and the wall. Ben shuffled out the door, slip-fell his way down the rope ladder, and wandered off into the woods to relieve himself.

When he returned to the clearing, Brother Triedit was up and reenergizing the fire. "Ah! Good morning, Brother Ben," he said, already chipper.

"Ah, hi. Just Ben is, really, is fine." Ben plopped down on one of the logs and held his hands out to the growing flames.

Brother Triedit smiled sweetly at him from across the fire. "Of course, my mistake. Though if I may say, you certainly do have the feel of a Post-Alignment Brother about you."

Ben's face grew hot. *Evangelization. Perfect.* "I'm not religious," he said quickly, dropping his eyes to the ground. He wondered what the best way to slink away from this conversation might be. Clubbing Brother Triedit over the head with a log would be a little obvious. Maybe he should just make a run for it, dash into the woods, catch up with Patrick after breakfast.

"Oh, I wouldn't call what we do 'religion,'" Brother Tried said, still smiling. "No, don't think of it as religion. Think of it as a cult."

Ben blinked. "I'm not--that's also--I don't--just--no. Thank you."

"Do think about it. Promise me that, at least. We were none of us always keen to the idea of Centralization. It is a difficult discernment, but one that often comes with time and reflection. You'd make an excellent female breeder; you're gifted with wonderful birthing hips for a being of your stature. Will you at the very least drink more centerwine, see if it gives you a tingling in your genitals?" he asked hopefully.

Just then, Patrick stumbled out of the tree house. He sifted dry coffee grounds into his mouth from his fist. "Mrrning," he said through a mouthful of grit.

"Good morning!" Brother Triedit called, beaming. "I'm just having a talk with Brother Ben here about our Order. He has some questions, but it looks like you might be continuing your quest on your own." Ben shook his head violently from side to side. Patrick smiled.

"That makes sense. Ben's very religious." Ben's face darkened. "What do you say, Benny Boy?" Patrick clamored his way down the rope ladder. "You wanna stay with the Lost Boys? I'll be fine going on alone," he promised.

Ben was caught between the sheer terror of staying with these nutjobs and the equally sheer terror of pissing them off. They'd stuck one of their own in a well for speaking out of turn; what would they do to a complete stranger who roundly snubbed them? "I don't want to be a woman," he said awkwardly.

"None of us *wants* to be a woman, Ben. But it's not for you. It's for the Order," Patrick said. Brother Triedit nodded in agreement.

Ben wanted to reach out and smack Patrick's giant head. "No. Seriously. No."

Brother Triedit shook his head sadly. "Well, perhaps your personal Alignment is yet to come. The Great Centralizer may return you to us yet, and it would be a great providence." He traced the backs of his fingers down Ben's cheek. Ben froze and pleaded with his eyes for help. Patrick just shrugged. *Supportive as always,* Ben glowered.

The rest of the brothers slowly began to stir. Soon the fire was once again surrounded by disheveled men in heavy blue robes. Ben thought Patrick's eyes would pop out of his head when Brother Toldus noticed him shoveling coffee grounds into his face and suggested he might have better luck with the Order's percolator. "Brother Wildgardyn is in charge of utensil detail," he said. "He'll know where to find it."

Patrick leapt up, sprinted over to the wooden trapdoor, and pounded out a mighty tattoo on it. "Coffee!" he screeched. Through a series of splashes and near-hysterics, Brother Wildgardyn managed to impart the location of the percolator. Patrick dashed off, ignoring Wildgardyn's desperate pleas for mercy and salvation.

After breakfast, the pair decided it was time to be back on their way. "Disney World waits for no man," Patrick said. Ben was too desperate to be rid of these blue-robed yahoos to point out that Disney World had nothing to do *but* wait. "Let us collect our buffalo, and we shall be off," Patrick said, shaking Brother Triedit's hand.

"Of course!" said the Holy Father. "Brother Mayham, please gather the buffalo and bring it hence to our guests." He turned back to Patrick. "Gather? Is that the right word? The English language, it is so confusing to me."

"Sure. Gather works. You could also say, '*Bemme*.'"

"*Bemme*?"

"*Bemme* the buffalo."

"English is indeed a strange tongue," Brother Triedit said, looking troubled.

"Its mysteries are not for us to understand," Patrick mused, patting the monk on the shoulder.

By the time they had gathered their belongings and girded their weapons, Brother Mayham was returning from the forest. He had a burlap sack slung over his shoulder, but Ponch was nowhere to be seen. He sidled up to Patrick and handed him the sack. "Here's the beefsteak left over from last night's dinner," he said. "We smoked it so it'll keep. It should feed the two of you for a few weeks. There was quite a lot left over."

Patrick opened the sack and looked in. "Oh. Thanks," he said, eyebrows furrowed. He closed the sack and tied it to his backpack. "So, where's Ponch?"

And suddenly, Ben understood. "Oh, Christ."

"What?" Patrick asked.

Ben took his friend's head in his hands and held it firmly by the ears. "Look at me. You need to take some deep breaths."

Patrick squirmed in Ben's grip. "Why?"

"Because you're about to lose your shit. Breathe, okay? Like this." Ben demonstrated with an exaggerated expansion of his lungs. Patrick tried to swat his hands away, but Ben held firm. "Stop it! Listen to me! You're gonna figure this out in about six seconds, and you need to stay calm."

"Figure what out?" Patrick asked. "I just want to get Ponch and go."

"I know you do. The weirdo said he was going to get Ponch, and then he came back."

Patrick shook his head as much as Ben's grip would allow. "Yeah, with a sack of meat, not with Ponch." Ben winced. He counted down to complete understanding. *Three...two...one...*

"*AAAAAARRRRRRGHHHHHHHHHH!!!*" Patrick's scream shook the entire world.

"Okay, calm down. Calm down. Patrick, calm down. Listen to me. It's fine."

"It is *not* fine!" he wailed. "They killed Ponch! They killed her! Oh my God, and we ate her! Ben, we fucking *ate Ponch!*" He broke free of Ben's grasp and retched into the leaves. Ben rubbed his back awkwardly. Brother Mayham looked at Ben, bewildered.

"They were close," he explained.

Patrick wiped the spittle from his mouth and wheeled around. "How could you?" he gasped, leveling an accusatory finger at Brother Triedit. "How *could* you?"

Brother Triedit's eyebrows knit themselves into webs of confusion.

"I'm afraid we may be experiencing the complications of our unfortunate language barrier," he said. "I'm not sure what you mean."

"I mean, how could you? How *could* you?" He reached behind him and slid the machete from its case. "*How could you?*"

"Great Demoralizing Centralizer!" Brother Spyndthrift cursed. He turned and fled into the woods, followed closely by Brothers Toldus, Bickdraft, and Bickon. Brother Mayham stumbled backward in surprise, tripped over a log, and crashed into the fire. He screamed and rolled out of the flames, hammering his smoking robes with flat palms. Brother Triedit stood frozen in fear. Brother Haffstaff pulled his hood down low over his eyes and crumpled into a noisy ball on the forest floor.

"What's going on?" Brother Wildgardyn demanded from his soggy hole. "I want to see!"

"Patrick, please don't," Ben sighed, shaking his head.

Pat swung the blade wildly around his head. "I will!" he cried. "*How could you?!*" He smacked the broad side of the machete against the nearest tree. The metallic ring was nowhere near as shrill as Patrick's screams. "How *could* you? How *could you?*" He started hacking at the trunk like a psychopath. Bits of dry wood flew through the air like spittle. "*How could you? How could you? How could you? How could you? How could you?*"

Brother Triedit was no less confused. "I'm sorry...in our culture, when an animal is offered for sacrifice to the Great Centralizer, it is custom to distribute the meat among the Brothers as sustenance after killing the beast in the most embarrassing, painful, and inhumane manner possible. Was Ponch *not* meant for sacrifice? Because you never said that it wasn't."

"*Yeeaaarrhhhh!*" Patrick screamed. He threw the blade aside and lunged at Brother Triedit. The two men went down in a heap of flying fists and feet. Ben looked on with mild interest. A better man might have broken up the fight, but Ben knew that Patrick hit like his fists were made of marshmallows, even when he had two good hands, and Brother Triedit's assaults seemed equally impotent. Plus, live entertainment was hard to come by these days, so he decided to let them go ahead and work out their differences. In the mean time, he picked up the burlap sack and plucked out a few strips of meat. He was still hungry, and damn it all if Ponch wasn't delicious.

14.

Calico shook out the last few drops and zipped up his fly. The steaming urine had left a Pollack trail in the hot ashes. "Find anything?" he hollered over to the group of Red Caps digging through the rubble.

"Something in the basement," one of them said, wiping a sooty forearm against his brow. "Bodies, looks like."

Calico grinned his sharp-toothed grin and began dancing little circles in the ruins. "Not our boys, I hope. Ain't no fun in that." Two Red Caps burst through the charred storm door like resurfacing miners. They heaved two brittle corpses onto the cold ground. The second one popped into pieces when it hit the earth. The head jerked loose and rolled over to a bearded man on the perimeter, who stopped it with his boot and stared down at it with calm, disinterested eyes while Calico examined the torso. "Naw, them ain't our boys," he said with a smile. "Them's too old. One've 'em's a woman. Piker, you wanna let 'er make a man outta you?" The other men laughed. The one called Piker turned dark red. "Go on, boy, take 'er in the woods, we won't watch none." He picked up a splintered piece of lumber, charred with fire and glowing red embers at the tip, and pointed it at the family huddled together in the lawn. "Why you got two dead bodies rottin' in your basement, there, friend?"

"Those are my associates," Warren wept. "You've killed them!"

Calico squinted through his mismatched eyes. "Crazier 'n a shit-house rat," he muttered. The bearded man on the perimeter gave a curt nod. Calico refocused. "Hey. Shit-rat. I'm gettin' tired of askin'. Why don't you tell me where them boys're headed?"

Warren shook his head. "I don't know where they're going, honest. They never said."

"It's true," the woman screamed, "we don't know anything!" She picked up the folds of her dress and dabbed at the blood running down Warren's puffy, purpled face. His once-green sweater vest was now a Rorschach of vile crimson. The two children cowered behind them, whimpering and wiping at their little wounds.

Calico shrugged. "Well, hell. We done burned yer house down 'n' raped yer wife. I reckon you'd'a told us by now if ya did know it. Guess we'll keep goin' the way we're goin'." He danced over to the frightened family, burning stick in hand. He did a little jig, then jammed the wooden poker through Warren's left eye. The heat cauterized the wound instantly, and no fluids drained from the man's seizing brain when Calico yanked the stick back out. He soft-shoed his way over to the little boy and picked him up by the hair. He screamed and scratched at the larger man's hands, but Calico held tight. "Hey Piker, this one's live, 'n' prolly more yer style. Why dontchoo take *him* back in the woods instead?" He flung the boy into the smoldering rubble. "And what about you, girlie? You gonna be any use for us? You got any grass on the field? Plunkett, check 'er out. She got grass, play ball." He tapped her on the head with the gory stick and crossed to the man at the property edge. "Trail says they went southeast. Should be able to track 'em down easily 'nuff."

"Kill the others. I want to move before nightfall. We're losing ground."

"Don't you worry none," Calico said with a grin. "Ain't nothin' ol' Calico cain't track."

•

"Okay, I admit it," Ben said, pulling his new coat tighter around his shoulders. The temperature had been falling steadily since they'd left the Post-Alignment Brotherhood a week earlier, and even with the new layers they'd swiped from a sparsely stocked Dickey Bub, he was still feeling the chill of chemical winter. "I did it. I ate more Ponch."

"Ah *ha*!" Patrick cried, whirling around. "I *knew* it!"

"Well, what do you expect? She's delicious!"

"Someday I'm going to say that to people about you. 'Yes, I ate my best friend, but what do you expect? He was delicious.'"

"I probably *would* be delicious," Ben considered. "And if I met with horrible, horrible death, I'd want you to eat me. For the greater good. I would want to make that sacrifice."

"You might just get your chance," Patrick said through narrowed eyes. "I'm giving you 3-to-1 odds of waking up tomorrow in my belly."

"Shh. Be still now, tauntaun Patrick."

"I'm going to forgive this slight," Pat decided, "because I think Ponch would have wanted you to be the one to eat her. Almost as much as she would have wanted to not be eaten."

"A fair assessment."

Patrick sighed. "What's done is done. Yoda taught me that. Speaking of Yoda, is it just me, or are we smack dab in the middle of a swamp?" he asked, lifting his foot out of a puddle of thick mud with a sucking *THLOOOP!*

"Definitely swamp," Ben agreed.

"Do you think we're in Florida yet?"

"I don't know, Great Navigator Who Gets to Lead the Expedition Because He Knows Lake Michigan Isn't to the South, what does your magnificent internal compass tell you?"

Patrick stuck his tongue through his lips and squinted into the bright green glow of the mid-morning fog. "My magnificent internal compass tells me that yes, yes we are in Florida. I just Ponce de Leoned the hell out of this state."

"I bet we're in Georgia," Ben said, surveying the land around them. "That looks like a peach tree."

"You have no idea what a peach tree looks like."

"Yes I do."

"What does it look like?"

"Like that."

"Yes, well, I suppose I set you up for that one, didn't I?"

"You did."

"You know what I've been thinking?" Patrick mused. "If we had a tall staff of just the right height, and a map of Florida, we could put the map on the ground, sit my hand right on top of the staff, and the sun would just burst right through the hole in my palm and show us exactly where to find Orlando, all *Indiana Jones* style."

Ben furrowed his brow. "Of all the things in the world you could think of, that's what you've been thinking?"

"And you would be Short Round!" Patrick beamed.

"Okay, time to feed you," Ben said warily. He tossed his knapsack on the ground next to the highway and began rummaging through it.

"I can't watch you eat Ponch," Patrick whined, plopping down in the loose gravel of the shoulder. "Every time you take a bite, another piece of my soul will dump a can of gasoline on itself and light a match."

"Cheer up, she's almost gone." Ben pulled out the sack of buffalo meat and tossed it at Patrick's feet. "That's the last of her. Go on, I bequeath it to you."

Patrick frowned. "I'll have beans, thank you."

"No, you'll have Ponch," Ben said. "Beans'll keep. We have no idea how long the meat'll stay fresh, and we're not letting it go to waste."

"They smoked it. It'll keep. It'll keep longer than your heartless, cannibal teeth."

"Yeah, they smoked it all right. You know what else they did? Made each other drink frog blood in the hopes they'd all lose their balls and get knocked up by other dudes. They did that, too. They also told you Ponch was fine, when in reality, they'd hacked her to pieces. And you know what else they did? Had rhyme battles. Like a less painful version of *Eight Mile*. And they think a magician's going to turn them into sparrows. What do you think the odds are that they actually know how to smoke a buffalo?"

"She *does* look a little green," Patrick admitted, inspecting a strip of meat.

"She'll probably make us sick, then you can throw her up in effigy. Now eat." Ben pried open a can of Dole mixed fruit to go along with the last of the bison, and the pair ate their lunch as the yellow mist roiled around them.

"Ponch would want me to be the one to eat her," Patrick said sadly. "I know I said it was you, but I lied. It's me. The great Spirit of the Illinois would like Ponch's buffalo strength to transfer to me rather than anyone else."

"Is it a problem that I already sucked down 98% of her buffalo strength, then?" Ben asked.

"No, I'll just have to eat you next."

Ben was sipping the juices from the bottom of the fruit can when he noticed the road sign across the highway. "Hey, how sure are you that we're in Florida?"

"Surer every second," Patrick said, swallowing the last bit of Ponch. "I was only 89% sure before lunch, but as you know, Ponch had excellent directional capabilities, and now with her navigational prowess augmenting my own, I can say that I am 100% certain that we are, in fact, in Florida."

"Really."

"Yes, really. I'd stake your reputation on it. Why do you ask?"

"Well, I'm just wondering why Florida would have a state highway sign in the shape of Alabama." He pointed to the sign. Patrick turned and examined it.

"So much for your reputation," he grumbled. "Such as it was."

"You truly are a marvel of...what was it? Navigational prowess."

"Shut up. Florida's right over that hill. I can feel it, Ben. And it feels like retirement."

But Florida was not waiting for them over the next hill. What *was* waiting for them over the next hill was a sign that said *Welcome to Mobile, Alabama*. "Weird name for Florida," Ben said.

"Well, I'm sure we're close," Patrick muttered, fumbling with his bag. He turned away from Ben and dug through the backpack. When Ben moved to approach, Patrick quickly shifted his position to keep Ben's prying eyes away. "Hey, what're you doing?" Ben said.

"Nothing, go away."

"I want to see!" Ben complained.

"I'm looking for my underwear," Patrick lied.

"You are not!" Ben grabbed Patrick's shoulder and pulled him off the bag. Patrick turned and swatted with his bad hand, but Ben dodged and dove for the backpack. He snatched it up and peered inside. "An atlas! An atlas?! Where the hell'd you get an atlas?" But the red dots on a few of the maps inside told all. "You stole it from the journalist?!"

"No, I *bought* it from the journalist."

"With what?"

"With my charm."

"Wow. She really came out behind on that deal."

"Well, she didn't *know* I was buying it from her. But that's the price of being charmed."

"I knew you didn't have an internal compass! I *knew* it! You're a phony! And even with a map, you got us lost! Mobile, Alabama instead of Florida. You can't even cheat right!" He flipped to the map of Alabama and scanned the southeast border looking for Mobile, but came up empty. "Is Mobile even *on* this map? His traced his finger along the state until he located it. Then he closed his eyes and dropped the atlas. "You. Fuck."

"What?" Patrick picked up the map and looked for himself.

"You took us at least three days in the wrong direction!"

Patrick spotted Mobile on the map. "Ah. So I did." He cleared his throat as he closed the atlas and stuffed it back into his bag. Then he clapped his hands together. "Well! Listen. Don't think of it as three days in the wrong direction," he insisted. "Think of it as three extra days that two best friends get to spend together on their last great adventure. Besides, this is great material for my biography."

"Oh, I've got *plenty* of material for your biography. *Plenty* of material. And also, I'm not writing your biography."

"Who do you think you're fooling?"

•

Mobile was, to be blunt, a disappointment. "In death as it was in life," Patrick observed.

"You've been here before?" Ben asked.

"No."

The city was boring and colorless, without even much rubble to give the landscape a bit of flavor. Only one building really stood up against the pale yellow skyline, a weird art deco-modernist hybrid that looked a little like a miniature Empire State Building topped with a conceptual metal flame. Most of the other buildings were squat, ugly, rectangular dwarfs edged with brown weeds and trash-strewn city sidewalks. Even the water was depressingly brown beneath its bobbing yellow dust surface.

The relatively warm gulf air whipped the apocalypse fog away from the bay, giving them a wide panoramic of the ocean down below. Yellow Monkey dust crusted the entire Gulf of Mexico, as far as they could see.

"How much of the ocean do you think got Monkeyed?" Ben asked, indicating the yellow, filmy crust.

"Ben, there's a stastically significant chance that the entire *world* got Monkeyed."

"Oh yeah, Nate Silver? How do you figure?"

"Well, when we got bombed, the dust had to have gotten caught in the jet stream, right? Given the average strength and speed of jet stream winds, it should have blown out of the U.S. and into the Atlantic in a matter of weeks. Think back to the second or third week of the apocalypse. Did the fog thin out?"

Ben struggled to remember so far back. "No," he decided. "No, right? It got worse. Didn't it? Wait, did it get worse? Maybe it was better. Wait, trick question! It stayed the same?"

"Your powers of observation rival those of even the greatest stick. No, it got worse. I mean, look around you. It's *constantly* foggy. We actually got more of the chemical compound blowing into the States, which means a new batch originated somewhere in Europe. Or maybe the Balkans. I'm willing to concede that it may have been the Balkans. Those Jamaicans got us good."

"Fucking Jamaicans," Ben grumbled.

"Fucking Jamaicans," Patrick agreed.

"I can't believe my Spring Break '06 dollars went to funding global terrorism."

"My Spring Break '06 dollars went to funding Tijuana donkey farms," Patrick shrugged.

"Six in one hand, half dozen in the other."

They ambled down St. Joachim Street, passing through St. Louis, St. Michael, and St. Francis Streets. "Religious bunch, weren't they?"

"You do realize we're in the Bible Belt, yes?"

"I thought Baptists didn't believe in saints."

"Well, you can't call every street Jesus Street or Mary Street. At some point, you have to make concessions."

"You know what I don't get about the South?"

"I'd wager there's plenty you don't get about the South. Like noodling. And grits."

"Yeah, I don't know what the fuck those words mean," he nodded. "But, also, how can they have a reputation for being both emphatically religious *and* extremely racist? Isn't there a bit of a conflict of interest there?"

Patrick patted Ben on the shoulder. "That, my good sir, depends on which racist preacher you ask."

They continued on St. Joachim, past its New Orleans-style second-story iron porches, across Dauphin Street, where the path became markedly cleaner. On the right stood a tall brick building with a rusty theatre marquee hanging precariously over the sidewalk with the name *SAENGER* painted in flaking, dappled cream against a faded red background. The sidewalk and street in front of the Saenger Theatre were clean for almost the entire block. Not just clear of rubble and trash, but actually *clean*, as if someone had recently swept and mopped the asphalt and polished the low metal pylons guarding the theatre entrance. Patrick let out a low whistle. "This block seem alarmingly tidy to you?"

Ben nodded. "'Alarmingly' is the key word."

"Yep. That settles it," Patrick nodded. "This street spells *adventure*." He unsheathed the machete and sliced it a few times through the air.

"For crying out loud, Pat. Can't we go the boring way just once?"

"Boring?" cried a high-pitched voice from above. A spry little man bounced to life above the theatre's marquee. The entire heavy, metal overhang rocked back and forth with the weight. He grabbed onto the giant *S* adorning the front and dangled over the street. "Did you say boring?" He swung over the edge of the metal roof and spun lightly to the ground. He was small, easily a foot shorter than Ben, with bushy white whiskers and mischievous green eyes. He wore brown pants with purple stripes and a clean white shirt under a purple patchwork vest. On his head, he wore a brown bowler hat with a wide, purple satin ribbon. On the whole, he looked like some sort of homeless leprechaun. "Nothing's boring on *this* block, not if the Saenger Players have anything to do with it!" He danced a quick little jig over to the entry doors and grabbed a black curtain that Ben hadn't noticed before. It hung from a track that ran along the perimeter of the marquee above. The little man ran around the sidewalk, sweeping the curtain shut behind him. "Come," he said, beckoning to the two visitors with his free hand as he ran, "and experience the wonder, the excitement, the grandiose entertainment of the stage!" He whipped the curtains all the way closed with a *schnook*, closing himself inside the overhang.

Ben raised a finger to Patrick before he could open his mouth. "No. Absolutely not."

"Oh, I think it sounds fun!" Patrick said.

Ben shook his head emphatically. "You are such an idiot. Where's the notebook?" Patrick dug it out of his backpack and handed it over. Ben opened to the page of perils. "You know what a mummer is? It's an entertainer, like a jester. Or an actor. Like Willy Wonka in there. We've seen enough peril, okay? I'm sitting this one out."

"Oh, *puh*. I'll have you know that I've been thinking about that list, and I don't think it's even accurate. I think Old Lady White Eyes was full of stuff and nonsense."

"Oh, really?"

"Oh, really." Patrick crossed his arms and *harrumphed*.

"Well!" Ben held the list up and ruffled it dramatically. "Let's just see what we have here! The light bringer."

"I have seen no lights worth noting, nor any bringers of such," Patrick insisted.

"No, just a demonic preacher who drove a stake through your hand."

"He was not made of light," Patrick pointed out.

"But he sure as hell thought he was bringing you into the Light of The Lord. Let's see, what else. The running man. Oh, my. If only we'd come across a running man somewhere along this trip."

"There's no proof that she meant *those* running men," Patrick said. "Lots of men run. Not just drug addicts and politicians."

Ben continued. "The demon's daughter. I seem to recall a feisty little Southern belle with a zombie for a father. The butcher. I think we can all remember a little group of hopeful transsexuals who turned out to be excellent butchers, can't we?"

"Don't you dare bring Ponch's death into this!" Patrick cried, leveling a warning finger at Ben's nose. "Don't. You. Dare."

"The butcher," Ben insisted. "And the fire drinker."

"I have not met a single fire drinker!" Patrick said, stamping his foot. "Of that, I am absolutely certain."

"We met a man whose last name was Tinder and who had a killer bar in his study."

"Oh, come on. A Tinder who drinks is a fire drinker? That's a stretch."

"It's also a match. That leaves the siren, the something Tom/hollow man duo, and the mummer. *That*," he said, pointing toward the curtain, "is a mummer. Please, for the love of God, let's just keep moving." He stowed the notebook and took a few exaggerated, leading steps down the road. "Come on. Let's go. Away from peril."

But Patrick just stood, staring at the black curtain and stroking his paltry whiskers. "If what you say is true, and the batty old disappearing woman was right, then I think we have no choice *but* to go into the mummer's lair."

Ben shook his head violently. "No, no, no. We *do* have a choice. Right now. I'm giving you the choice. Let's go."

Patrick's eyes narrowed, and he bit thoughtfully on his thumb. "You know what I think? I think this is fate."

"It's not fate, it's stupidity."

"I find the two are often interchangeable."

"With you, they often are," Ben sighed miserably.

Patrick grinned. "Hey. Benny Boy."

"What?"

"Remember the first rule of the trip?"

"Oh, please don't."

"I call the shots."

"Then you can go in alone."

"You'd send me in to certain doom alone? No, no, no, I call this one a double barrel shot. We both go. Friends to the end."

"If you drag me in there, our friendship is staying out here."

"Friends to the end!" Patrick insisted.

Ben pulled out the wrench. "I want you to know that I'm doing this under protest, and that if I find a professor's jacket somewhere on this trip, I'm braining you with this wrench in a study." He smiled smugly and pumped a fist into the air. "Clue joke. Nailed it."

"Noted."

They pushed through the heavy black curtain. The little man had been busy while they lingered outside; he'd pulled a large puppet cart out onto the sidewalk from inside the lobby. It was a sturdy wooden cart topped with a high frame made of two-by-fours. A silky blue curtain was draped along the frame. The cart itself was painted a darker blue with small white stars dotting the plywood night sky. The words *SAENGER HARLEQUINS* were painted in the center in huge, block letters. A pair of feet showed beneath the cart. The puppeteer, whoever he was, was already in place. The old mummer stood just off to the side of the cart, his hands clasped proudly behind his back.

"Good evening, gentlemen," he squeaked.

"It's early afternoon, tops," Ben grumbled. The mummer pushed on, undeterred.

"Welcome to the historic Saenger Theatre, where the lights light, the props prop, and the actors do their best to act. Our next performance will begin in just over fifteen minutes. We apologize for the delay, but we do hope you'll enjoy a bit of preliminary entertainment before the show." He gestured grandly to the puppet cart and stepped dramatically away, slipping off to the edge of the sidewalk. The curtains slid open and revealed a standard Punch and Judy set-up.

"Judy? Judy! Where are you?" the little Punch doll demanded.

"I'm right in front of you," said Judy. Punch jumped in surprise.

"Gads! I didn't see you. It's this cursed yellow fog. It's utterly destroyed my eyesight."

"That explains a few things about your bedroom performance last night!" Judy cackled.

"Why, you!" Punch picked up a bat and swung. Judy ducked, and Punch fell over from the momentum. Judy beamed, open-mouthed, into the audience.

Ben heard a light footstep behind him. He turned just in time to see the small mummer swinging his own bat directly at Ben's head. Ben wasn't as quick as Judy; the bat caught him just above his right eye in an explosion of colors and pain. He hit the floor and fell into darkness.

15.

It was Calico who saw the girl first. He gave the signal for the men to halt. He moved in closer, creeping through the Mississippi woods. When he reached the clearing by the little river, a wide grin spread across his face. The girl was tied to the tree, and she was alive. That damn near made her the girl of his dreams.

•

When Ben came to, some hours later, he was alone on the curtained off sidewalk. The puppet cart was gone, along with the puppeteer, Patrick, and the old leprechaun bastard with the bat. Thudding pain crushed through his head. He struggled to his feet and groped blindly for the curtain. His hand closed on the heavy velvet, and he tugged at it until he found the edge. He threw it open, and dim, watery light filled the sidewalk. Even the low glow of the Monkey fog pierced his eyes like tiny pins. He shied away and waited for his eyes to adjust. Dried blood cracked and flaked from his right cheek as he grimaced the pain away. *If Patrick's still alive, I'm gonna kill him.*

He staggered out of the portico and into the street. He peered out into the gloom, and as he watched, the building across the way pulled itself apart like an amoeba, then jellied back together. *Well, that's not right*, he thought. He blinked hard. The building pulled itself back into soft focus. It still wavered, but not quite as badly. He scanned the road, searching for a clue, *any* clue, as to Patrick's fate. He found a very good clue in the shape of two spindly legs kicking out from the top of a round, metal trash can one alley over. Ben shuffle-stumbled his way toward the frantic feet, his own legs behaving oddly. They appeared to be averse to head wounds.

The closer he stumbled to the alley, the louder Patrick's muffled cries became. "Grmmuh orrahir! Ffash tishffel!" he bellowed from inside the can.

Ben approached the alley and reached for the can. He slip-stumbled toward it, the world swimming in and out of focus, and lost his balance. He pitched forward, smashing into the metal can with the crown of his head. The can, its occupant, and the rotten trash inside all tipped over with a mighty *CRASH*. Patrick wriggled out of the felled can and spat something out of his mouth that might have been either a coffee filter or a diaper. Either way, it was used.

"What were you saying?" Ben asked.

Patrick plucked loosely rolled cigarette butts from his hair. "I said, get me out of here, this trash tastes awful. Are you okay? I thought you were dead. There was a lot of blood."

"Yeah, I don't feel so well." He put one hand on the brick wall and the other on his hip, trying to stabilize both his legs and his stomach.

"You probably need a transfusion," Patrick pointed out, wiping some soft, yellow, crumbly paste from his shoulder. He brought a bit to his nose and sniffed. "Wuf."

"You volunteering your inner juices?" Ben asked.

Patrick shook his head. "All my innards are full of garbage. Maybe we'll find a Red Cross tent. They like to pitch those things in disaster areas, don't they?"

"Yeah, usually. They really screwed us on this whole apocalypse thing."

"Abandoned us in our time of greatest need. I never trusted them. They probably blew all my donations on crack and whores. Or maybe that was Toys for Tots...?" he wondered. He dismissed the thought with a wave of his hands. "Bah. Doesn't matter. Either way. Short of finding a hollow tube and two clean needles in this rubbish, you should rest before we move on. Build some of that blood back up. Don't move, okay?" Ben nodded. "Okay. But also, we can't stay here. I don't think it's safe."

"You know what I like about you? Your clear-headed leadership."

"It's one of my many excellent qualities."

"Never taking my advice, that's another great quality you have. I think I'm legitimately sick of saying I told you so." He proved it by retching into the gutter.

"Oh, boy. Don't be alarmed, but I'm pretty sure you have a concussion."

Ben groaned as he pressed the hem of his shirt to his head. It instantly soaked through with blood. "That's because I got smashed in the head with a baseball bat. Why didn't he use *you* for batting practice?"

Patrick shrugged. "Probably out of respect for my sheer awkwardness. It's not nice to kick a man when he's down, cosmically speaking. He hit you, then threatened me, and I, of course, flew into my instinctive and lethal opossum mode."

"You fainted?"

"I woozed."

"And the Smurf was able to stuff your ass in a garbage can?"

"Technically, he stuffed my *head* into a garbage can."

"Great. I get a concussion, and you get a Charlie Chaplin film."

"You have a hole in your head, and I have a hole in my hand! It all works out in the end!" Patrick said cheerily. "Seriously, though, we should get the hell out of here. Think you can make it a few blocks? There's got to be a cozy gutter somewhere a little more out of the way."

"Yeah. I can make it." Ben heaved himself off the wall, faltered a bit, then stood on two uneasy legs. "Can you grab my bag?"

Patrick sucked in a mouthful of air through his teeth. "Baaaaaaaag," he said slowly, inclining his head ever so slightly. "Riiiight. Yes. The bags. Your bag and my bag. Well. See. The thing about the bags is, the King of Munchkin Land took them."

Ben's head lolled back on his shoulders, narrowly missing the brick wall on its way down. He snapped it forward again and wobbled as dark stars beamed in front of his eyes. He wasn't doing so well. "What do you mean he took them? He took who?"

"He took *whom*. And whom he took is the bags. Both bags. Two bags. Your bag, and my bag. And also, the machete."

"What?" Ben blinked.

"And the baton. And the hammer. Also, the knife. And, also, the wrench."

Ben's hand flew to his belt loop. It was empty. "Son of a bitch!" he screamed. His head rushed with helium, and he toppled over against the alley wall. "He took *everything*?"

"No, he didn't take *everything*. He didn't take our lives, and I think we should be grateful for that." Patrick tried for a little hug. Ben slapped him in his forehead.

"Jesus, Patrick, our food? Our supplies? Our weapons, how could you let him do that?!"

"Oh! I'm sorry! I should have consulted with you before I let myself be thrown into a trash can by a midget with remarkable strength, except I couldn't, because you were on the ground, unconscious, and completely useless! As a matter of fact, the way I see it, this is *your* fault!"

"*My* fault!" The little blood Ben had running through his veins was pumping like gasoline. "How in God's name is this *my* fault!"

Patrick, however, remained oddly calm. "Because you let yourself get hit with a bat. And that was the wrong thing to do in that situation." Ben opened his mouth to scream some more, but his strength left him, and he crumpled to the ground. He pitched forward and pressed his cheek to the cold asphalt. Patrick continued. "It's especially surprising after that run-in we had with the first duster. You saw how he used his head to smash that bat to bits. That's what you do when someone swings a bat at you. You use your head to smash it to bits, you don't let him bash your brains out with it. I hope you learned something valuable here today."

And then, for the first time in probably two decades, and completely against his will, Ben began to cry.

Patrick frowned down at him, his hands on his hips. *Oh my God*, he thought. *I broke Ben.* "Come on, Benny Boy," he said, crouching down and patting his friend lightly on the back. "Can I say something? This just makes it more of an adventure! And I think we can both agree, that's a positive thing."

Ben spit a stream of pink, foamy mucus. "Remember when you said,

'Hey, let's go watch this dumbass show, because I'm fucking retarded,' and I said, 'No, you *are* fucking retarded, but we should go and not follow this creepy ass midget into a dark theater'?"

"I don't think those were the words exactly--" Patrick began.

"This is what happens when you make the rules," Ben rasped. "You get a hole in your hand, your buffalo gets slaughtered, you find rotting bodies in a lunatic's basement, we get attacked by drug addicts, I get my skull broken by a midget with a bat, and we lose every bit of food we had in a place where it's very, very difficult to find more food. That's what happens when you make the rules. Do you understand that?"

"Actually, I've been meaning to remark on how shockingly *easy* it's been for us to find food on this trip."

"Yeah. Keep making jokes. You're pretty fucking good at that. You're not very fucking good at keeping your best friend safe, you're not very fucking good at keeping *anybody* safe, with your stupid ass decisions, but, hey, you can deliver a punch line. Congratu-fucking-lations."

Patrick sat down on the freezing asphalt. He picked at the bandage around his hand. After three years, he could still recall the entire conversation he'd had with Annie that last day on the phone, every single word of it. He also remembered the words that had gone unsaid. *Where are you? Why aren't you here? Why didn't you protect me?* And he remembered that he didn't have an answer. Not then, and not now. "Benny, my boy," he said quietly. "Look. All joking aside. You're right. I'm still living like it's five years ago and bad decisions are fun because no matter what sort of trouble you get into, there's always a doctor, or a lawyer, or a policeman, or a wife to get you back out of it. But that's not the world we live in." Ben snorted. Patrick continued. "I don't know how to deal with this. With any of this. I don't know how to do this, to live this life, without them. I'm flying blind, here, and I'm mucking it all up. I'm just...I'm sorry. I am really sorry. It's a serious thing that you got hurt, and a serious thing that I got hurt, and a serious thing that we've lost our supplies. But I want you to know that as soon as we get you back on your feet and not possibly dying of blood loss in a gutter, we're going to find the evil leprechaun who did this, and we're going to get our shit back. Because he has our weapons, and our food, and our bandages. And he has the pudding. You know the trip is pretty much for nothing without the pudding."

Ben sighed. "No. I don't know that. Because honestly, I have no goddamn idea *why* we're on this trip. Except for the fact that it now apparently has something to do with Izzy's pudding."

Patrick bit at his lower lip. Then he nodded, mostly to himself. He slipped the folded piece of paper from his back pocket and held it out. Ben eyed it suspiciously, raising one eyebrow high. "Go on," Patrick said. "Read it."

When Ben was done, he refolded the paper and handed it back to Pat. He shook his head and rubbed solemnly at his temples. "Jesus, Pat," he breathed. He struggled to his knees. "All right," he said. "All right." Patrick grasped his arm and helped him up. Ben steadied himself against the brick wall and turned his crystal blue eyes to his friend. "But from now on, we make decisions together. If we live long enough to make any more. No more of this King of the Road bullshit."

Patrick raised two fingers. "Scout's honor."

"You know I'm going through this hell-fuck-odyssey because of you. And, frankly, that's pretty much as good a reason as any. But I do not want to die for this. 'Cause dying is bullshit."

"Dying *is* bullshit," Patrick agreed. Rule Number 22.

Patrick looped his arm under Ben's and braced him as he tested his strength. Together, they hobbled out of the alley and turned onto Conti Street. The sun must have been near to setting as they walked; the Monkey fog was dappling into its pale pinkish-grayness. They could hear water lapping in the distance. The muffling fog made it difficult to determine from which direction the sound was coming, but they took a right at Royal Street and headed south.

The roads were quiet. Eerily quiet, even for an abandoned city. The air itself hummed with a white noise charge, which somehow made the atmosphere seem even more desolate and bare. Patrick slowed to a stop, his good hand still clutching Ben's arm. "Does this feel strange to you?" he asked.

"What do you mean?"

Suddenly, a torrent of rain crashed down from the sky.

With no warning, they were deluged by a brick wall of water. It battered down on them and drove them to their knees in the street. In just seconds, the gutters were overflowing. The rushing runoff threatened to sweep them away. "We gotta get out of this!" Patrick shouted, but even he couldn't hear his words over the sudden and crashing storm. He looked wildly from side to side. Off to the right, he saw a pair of figures dart down the next street and into the intersection. They ran up to a building on the southwest corner and pounded on a large metal gate. It pushed open from the inside, a weak flame barely illuminating a man who ushered them in. Ben tugged on Patrick's sleeve and pointed toward the building. Patrick nodded, and they darted through the rain. The man with the lantern caught sight of them just as he began to swing the gate closed. He waved them forward.

Sloshing across the street, Ben's eyes began playing tricks on him. From here, the building didn't look like a building at all, but a high stone wall, like a castle wall, with cannon nooks cut into the top every few dozen feet. It was something off the set of *Monty Python and the Holy Grail*. Ben must've lost more blood than he realized. He was hallucinating castles in Mobile, Alabama.

They hustled past the gesturing gatekeeper. The stone wall wasn't terribly wide, and there was barely room for the three men to stand out of the rain under the archway (though technically, none of them was truly *out* of the rain, which seemed to be exploding on all sides like grenades and spattering them with cold, wet shrapnel). The man with the lantern pointed at a building across the castle's courtyard. "See that doorway? With that light? That's where we're going, okay?" he shouted. They both nodded. The man hauled the heavy door closed and latched it shut. Then the three of them bolted back into the rain and across the swampy courtyard. The rain felt unusually heavy, like soft lead balls, and Ben stumbled a few times as he trudged across the yard. He could practically feel the thinness of his own blood as it splashed through his veins. His head was spinning when they finally reached the rectangle of light. He tripped over the doorjamb and splayed out onto the hard, knobby wood floor. It seemed as good a place to black out as any.

16.

"He's fine," Patrick insisted, blowing steam from the hot mug in his hands. "I told him he should eat some cookies after giving so much blood, but the boy just doesn't listen."

"He looks pretty banged up," said the man from the gate. "And you don't look so hot yourself. You guys run up against the Carsons?"

Patrick shrugged and sipped his tea. It tasted earthy, like mud and bark with some flower petals thrown in. He picked a splinter of some dark root from his lips and wiped it on his jeans. "We met old man Mighty Mouse at a theater up the road," he said. "Short guy, dressed like the Joker, not very hospitable."

"Spiver," the whole gang said in unison.

"Bat or knife?" asked a somber-looking girl by the fire. Her eyes were large and sad, pale green against the orange light of the flames. She had delicate, pale skin and dirty blonde hair pried back from her face into a long ponytail. She was rail thin, with knobby elbows wrapped around pointy knees. Her wide eyes gave her a look of perpetual sincerity. A long, white scar ran down the right side of her face from temple to chin. Patrick thought she looked like the saddest girl in the world.

"Bat," he answered. The girl nodded thoughtfully.

The man who had opened the gate clapped his hands together and rubbed them excitedly. His irises were deep brown, but full of light. The corners of his eyes crinkled from years of easy smiles. His brown, curly hair tufted out at all angles, and his beard was splotchy with uneven bristles, but his unkempt appearance somehow served to make him look boyish and playful, despite being maybe 30 years old, by Patrick's estimation. "All right! Introductions. I'm James, and that's my sister, Annie," he said, pointing to a freckled firecracker of a redhead on the other side of the room. She smiled with all of her teeth.

"That's an excellent name!" Patrick said, giving her a small nod.

"Ugh, I hate it," she soured. "It sounds like a West Virginian prostitute's name."

"It was my wife's name," Patrick pointed out. James coughed lightly.

Annie leaned forward. "Was she from West Virginia?"

"And this is Sarah," James hastily interrupted, motioning to the sad looking girl by the fire. Patrick nodded hello, but she only blinked at him. "And this dislikable fellow," James said, clapping the man next to him on the back, "we call Dylan. He won't tell us his real name." Dylan appeared to be the source of a sour, faintly herbal scent in the air. A thin, tightly wrapped joint hung from his lips, its gray smoke twirling toward the ceiling. He was easily the oldest member of the group, his graying hair pulled off his forehead with a wide bandana. His eyes were hidden behind small, dark, circular lenses. He was more or less clean-shaven, with rough stubble coating a small portion of his jaw. He wore loose, faded clothing of indeterminable material. An odd tic claimed his left hand; he clenched his fist, opened it, wiggled his fingers, then clenched again, opened again, wiggled again, over and over, incessantly.

"Dylan, as in Bob?" Patrick guessed.

"Dylan, as in anyone but Thomas," the older man said in a gravelly voice, rough from years of inhaling God knows what. "Welsh fucks, cattle bleeders and sheep stickers," he muttered. He took a long pull on his joint.

"You're not Welsh, are you?" Annie asked with a grin.

"I've never bled a cow in my life," Patrick pledged.

"Our resident Dominican friend Amsalu is around here somewhere," James continued. "Probably out on one of his little getaways. He'll be back. You'll meet him later. And that's it these days! A colony of five."

"Will you stop calling us that?" Annie groaned. "You make it sound like a reality show."

James smiled his easy, lopsided smile. "Sorry for my sister. She's socially retarded." Annie slugged him in the shoulder. "And physically abusive," he added.

"You're more anti-Annie than actual Annie," Patrick decided.

She opened her mouth to defend this accusation, then stopped, considered, and finally nodded. "I can roll with that."

"Well. It's nice to meet you all, up to and including anti-Annie. I'm Patrick, and that poor sod snoring away in the corner is my friend, Ben. Thanks for taking us in. Between the bat beating and the hurricane, we were pretty much ready to call it a life."

"Hurricane? This?" Annie asked, jerking a thumb toward the window. "Ha! This is a spring drizzle."

"You haven't spent much time in the Gulf, huh?" James asked. "These storms pop up pretty much every day. They come in hard and fast, then they're gone thirty minutes later. You'll see. Should be wrapping up any minute, now."

"I'm a St. Louis-Chicago hybrid," Patrick admitted. "I know very few things about the Gulf. You need some lake effect snow information, though, I'm your man. Are you two from the Gulf? You don't have the accent."

"We're from Iowa, originally. But we both went to Tulane. We blew around a bit after Katrina, but found ourselves back here after the Big Bombing."

Annie rolled her eyes. "Leave it to my brother to find us a military fort after the apocalypse."

"Oh, what, you're complaining?" James teased.

"Which part of St. Louis are you from?" Sarah asked, hugging her knees tightly to her chest.

"Jeff County. One of the lucky few who escaped without a mullet."

"I'm from St. Charles," she said quietly, her green eyes clouded with memory. Patrick waited for her to continue, but she had nothing more to say.

"I liked St. Charles," he said, acutely aware of the statement's insufficiency. "What about you, Dylan? What part of the Midwest are you from?"

Dylan sucked on the joint and held the smoke deep in his lungs. "Midwest?" he squeaked, small grey puffs escaping from his mouth. He beat his chest three times with his stable hand and exhaled a long, twisting serpent of smoke. "Do I look like I patch-fuck gun barrels and self-pleasure pie?"

Patrick cocked an ear toward him, thinking maybe he'd misheard. "Sorry?"

"I'm not from the Midwest," he said, shaking his head lazily. He said the word *Midwest* like one might say the word *disgusting* when referring to a particularly perverse and heinous joke. He reached into the cloud of smoke with his twitching left hand and scattered the wisps to the ceiling. "I'm from the Land of Koonoo, man, in the Valley of Pity and Lust."

"His accent is Pittsburghese," Annie said. "Maybe Philly. But I don't know. He's pretty dickish, even for Philly."

"What are you smoking?" Patrick asked, enchanted by the madman's nonsensical responses.

"Ash," he answered, stubbing out the last few centimeters of the joint. He reached into the front pocket of his oversized shirt and pulled out a small, battered tin with a rusty hinge lid and passed it over to Patrick. It appeared to be an old-fashioned tobacco tin, apparently licensed by way of some gross oversight on the part of Jim Henson's marketing team. The familiar white carnival letters of *The Muppet Show* were now yellowed to match the sour orange hue of the logo background. A cartoon Kermit sat in the *O* of *Show*, his little green head propped up on green toothpick arms. If the very existence of a Muppet tobacco tin was surprising, then the racy drawing of a completely nude Miss Piggy with a human woman's body on the underside of the lid was outright troubling. "Peekaboo box," Dylan explained, wiggling his fingers. "Peekaboo."

The drug inside was indeed a grey, flaky ash, cut with wild lavender, grass clippings, and a dark, brittle bark that smelled like mushrooms. Patrick admired the mixture with what he considered to be the appropriate combination of horror and awe. "I didn't know you could smoke ashes."

"With enough flame, will, and puddle-fucks, you can smoke anything you set your mind too," Dylan said, gesturing for Patrick to return the tin. "This isn't a drug, man. This is rollable education. This is the universe and all its parts siphoned through the dusty trumpets of the Tree of Knowledge. This ash, man. This ash is *life*."

Patrick nodded. "I can tell it's very nurturing."

"It's why I have the age of the spirit. I will smoke this on your graves," he said, rolling another joint.

James shook his head and grinned. "So you can see why we like to keep Dylan around," he said, patting the old stoner on the back. "Don't mind him too much. In some of his more lucid moments, he's admitted to being an undertaker in his former life. Says he used to 'do a lot of embalming fluid.' I have no idea how on earth someone might 'do' embalming fluid. But it doesn't seem to have preserved his brain so well."

"Embalming fluid!" Patrick started. He raised his eyebrows at Ben. "That might just explain a thing or two." Ben grimaced.

Just then, James held up a finger and pricked up his ears. "Hey, check it out! The rain stopped." He hopped up and threw open the front door. Sure enough, the air was once again calm. The violent winds had whipped away the Monkey fog, and Patrick could actually see thin gray clouds overhead. Annie bounced to her feet and raced out the door. Sarah remained near the fire, stroking her long hair thoughtfully. James beckoned to Patrick. "Come on, I'll give you a tour of the place." Ben was still snoring away peacefully on the cot, so Patrick shrugged and followed his host.

Now that the world was lighter, Patrick could see that the building in which they had been sitting was just one in a row of low apartments built up against the wall of the fort. "All these buildings were here when we found it," James explained. "I guess that's pretty obvious. Like we're gonna build row houses, right? They're all pretty much the same. We use a few of 'em, mostly storage and stuff. We keep a few empty, in case more people drop by. You guys can have the second from the end there, if you want. I mean, you don't have to, you can do whatever you want, that one's just a really cozy one. Some of them have drafts, you know, but that one's pretty nice."

"Which one has the hot tub?"

"Oh, we just had all those taken out. Low efficiency. If you want, though, the Gulf gets pretty warm in the afternoon. 40 degrees, easy."

"Hm. Got anything less tropical?"

"Sorry. That's the problem with being a post-Doomsday resort. We don't offer anything less than the absolute best."

James took him around the perimeter of the wall and pointed out a few stone foundations of buildings that seemed to be original to the fort. "I don't know if they fell down because of Doomsday, or if they'd been down for a century. We stay away from 'em, though. Out of respect."

Patrick nodded. "Respect for the fallen. Stones."

James shrugged. "Any time a massive structure falls down, I assume someone got killed in the process."

"Safe bet. I'll tell Ben not to desecrate the area."

"Thanks. We actually have a great desecration area right outside the walls there, lots of sticks and shovels for ruining stuff. He'll love it."

"Perfect!"

James clapped Patrick on the shoulder and spun him around to face the center courtyard. "And this," he said proudly, "is the heart and soul of Fort Doom."

"You named this place Fort Doom?"

"It seemed appropriate," James shrugged.

"That is a *fantastic* name."

"Thanks."

"Sorry to interrupt. You were saying? Heart and soul?"

"Yes! Hold on, let's do another take. Get the drama going. Turn back around." They did, and James once again put his hand on Patrick's shoulder and spun him toward the center. "And this," he said proudly, "is the heart and soul of Fort Doom."

Patrick gasped and applauded enthusiastically. Of course, it wasn't as if he hadn't noticed the massive swath of garden as soon as they stepped out of the living quarters. The vegetation accounted for 80% of the space within the fort's walls. It was hard to miss. Cabbages, carrots, potatoes, onions, and a dozen other cold weather vegetables grew evenly spaced in long, neat rows. There was enough food in the ground to keep the little group of gardeners in meals for eight or nine months, with a little conservation. It was the first organized agricultural project Patrick had seen since M-Day, and it was truly an applause-worthy sight.

"It's incredible," he admitted. "How long have you been doing this? I mean, is it safe? What with the poison chemical gas and all?"

"Pfft. Poison chemical gas, schmoison chemical gas," James said with his easy grin. "Actually, we were pretty worried about the first crop. Obviously we didn't die from the airborne gas, but once it got into the soil, who knows how concentrated it got, you know? We actually drew straws to see who'd eat the first carrot to see if it'd have any negative effect when he ate it."

"Who won that lottery?"

"Dylan. He was the first to try it."

"How on earth would you know if it harmed him?"

"Exactly! Ha! He ate it and was just as weird as ever, but shit. So we drew again, a guy that used to be with us, Turk, he tried a potato, and five days later, he was still fine. We've been farmers ever since."

"Put in a few sheep and an outhouse, and you'd never have to leave the fort," Patrick said.

James snapped his fingers. "That's what I forgot! The last room on the end there is the outhouse."

"Ah! Good to know."

"Yeah. You don't want to sleep in that one."

Patrick toed the dirt piled high around the flowering cabbages at his feet. "Not bad dirt, all things considered." It wasn't exactly potting soil, but it was rich enough, and moister than he'd expected. He nodded toward a patch of wilting carrots two rows over. "Any idea why some of these aren't coming in so well?"

"You just saw it. The storms make it hard to grow with any sort of consistency. The rain falls so hard, it washes out a lot of the younger crops, or drowns the bigger ones. We lose probably 60% of what we sow."

Rusty wheels slowly creaked to life in Patrick's brain. He rubbed his chin, staring thoughtfully at the garden. "You know what you need," he said, squinting and wagging a finger in the air. "You need a water distribution system. Something that'll collect the rain and distribute it evenly through the garden over a longer period of time. *That's* what you need."

James nodded. "That sounds useful. Think they have those at Home Depot?"

"Sure, you could pick one up next time you run into town. Or! Or. You could have one custom designed by a wandering, talented, yet unfortunate-looking engineer."

"Aw, damn. We just lost our last wandering, talented, yet unfortunate-looking engineer last week."

"Fear not," Patrick said, clapping James on the shoulder. "For I, too, am a wandering, somewhat talented, yet unfortunate-looking engineer. And believe me when I tell you, I would be thrilled to design a water distribution system for you."

"That sounds good to me," James nodded, smiling out over the garden. "How long do you think it'd take?"

"The design itself wouldn't take long. I could have something drawn up in a day or two. Building it, though, that'll take some time. Maybe two, two and a half weeks, depending on how easy materials are to come by."

"Well, we'd sure appreciate any sort of plans you could come up with, if you don't mind sticking around a day or two."

"I'll do you one better. I'll help you build the whole blessed thing."

James raised an eyebrow. "You don't have anything better to do for the next few weeks than build a glorified watering hose?"

"I have very good things to do," Patrick admitted, "this is true. But James, old boy, fish gotta swim, raptors gotta hunt, and engineers gotta geek out over complex structures."

James' lopsided grin nearly tipped over the side of his face. "Well, we're happy to have you. Like I said, you're welcome to an open cabin, and stay as long as you want."

"I hereby declare that I will not rest until your water distribution system is complete!" Patrick cried, hoisting a determined finger in the air.

"You should probably rest at some point," James said.

"Well, sure, I'll rest. I didn't mean that in the strictest sense. More in the royal sense." Patrick rubbed his hands together. Dozens of designs were already cranking through his brain. He felt an old, familiar flush of excitement. It was no steam-powered locomotive death engine, sure, but it was a *project*. But before he got started on the watering system, first things first. "You said the last one on the end there is the outhouse?"

"Last one on the left," James said. He reached down, plucked a few cabbage leaves, and slapped them into Patrick's hand. "Enjoy."

•

Something inside Ben was burning. Not like acid reflux burning, but like blazing pit of hell burning, as if a pot of coals had caught fire somewhere in his left lung. *Oh shit*, he thought. *Shit, shit, shit, I swallowed a firefly. It broke open in my throat.* Then he saw the rascally little firebug, not with his eyes, of course, but with some internal unseeing, all-seeing vision. The firefly's bioluminescent behind had been swapped with a tiny kerosene lantern, and Ben watched as the lightning bug buzzed around and around his lung sacs, until it spun out of control, heady with vertigo, and smashed into his upper lobe. The lantern broke, the bug's fire exploded into Ben's pleural cavity, and he caught fire from the inside out, like that big poor bastard whale in *Pinocchio*, with plumes of black smoke billowing out of his mouth, his nose, his ears, and his tear ducts.

He coughed his way awake, though it was at first impossible to tell dream from reality, because when he opened his eyes, he did indeed see smoke, a great charcoal pillar of it enveloping his head. And when he spied the round face of a bespectacled stoner pushing through to the surface of the haze, he knew he was in hell, his own personal hell, where hippies would torment him for all eternity. "Breathe it in, man," said the hippie, his voice echoing through the fumes. "Breathe it in, and be free."

Ben was weak, so weak, and his throat was raw with secondhand smoke. He was on the cusp of damnation, but for this one, last moment, his will was still his own. He summoned his last, desperate breath, and rasped, "Don't...tell me...what to do...hippie."

He closed his eyes and fell back onto the pillow, conceding his soul to the fire within. But then gentle fingers touched his cheek, fingers too soft and smooth to be attached to the patchouli-stained hand of the flower child. He cracked open one eye. There was another face next to the hippie face, a smooth, ovular face with large, sad eyes and a long, sad scar running down the cheek. "Get out of here, Dylan," she said, her voice a thin lilt. With a flick of her hand, she fanned the hippie away, and his devil's smoke with him. The air cleared. The fire in his lungs petered out. This woman, this sad angel, had saved his life. In return, he hacked smoky phlegm into her face.

"Oh God," he said, sitting up and wiping his hand across his mouth. "I am so sorry. I am so sorry. That was--" He turned his head and retched out a few more clouds of smoke. The girl bristled noticeably.

"It's all right," she said evenly, her lips thin. "You inhaled a lot of smoke. Are you okay?"

He nodded and hoped his watery eyes wouldn't betray him. "Fine. I'm--*ahem*--I'm fine. Smoke is just--*cough*--it's bad for my lungs." *Yes.*

Perfect. A sparkling conversationalist am I, he thought. Christ.

"That smoke is bad for most people," she said softly.

The hippie wheezed somewhere off to the left. Ben pulled himself all the way up and examined his surroundings. He was in a cabin that was divided into two rooms, a living room and a room that maybe passed for a kitchen. The front door was closed, but windows on either side showed it to be dark out, probably dusk. A low fire crackled in a small stone fireplace against one wall. The old hippie sat before it. He held a thin joint between his lips, and he was leaning in close to the fire, trying to light it with no hands. His salt and pepper bangs flopped forward into the fire and began to smoke. The smell of burnt hair and sweet ash filled the room. Ben thought he might vomit.

"Is there a bathroom?" he asked, burying his chin against his chest. He might have coughed on the sad angel, but by God, he would not throw up on her.

"Out the door, down the row, last cabin on the left," she said.

"Thanks." Ben pulled himself to his feet and took exactly two and one-third steps before his legs turned to jelly and he crashed to the floor. The hippie made a *cluck-cluck-cluck* sound. The girl just stood over him with her arms folded.

"You've inhaled too much ash. Do you need help?"

"Nope. I'm good. It's nice down here." The floor was cool against his cheek, and the nausea passed. *Thank God.*

The girl watched him disinterestedly. Finally she said, "I'm going to find your friend." She left him alone with the hippie, who retrieved a broken piece of chalk from his hip pocket and began to draw the solar system on the wood slats of the floor, using the fire as the sun. He worked his way across the room, drawing spheres and rings in increasing distances from the fiery center. Ben was lying directly on top of where Saturn should go, so the hippie drew a circle with a thick ring right across his cheek. "Thank you," Ben said, closing his eyes.

"Shh. Do not speak, Cronus."

•

"Ben! Benny Boy! You live!" Patrick exclaimed, bursting through the door. "You live!"

"I lie," Ben mumbled from the floor.

"Yes, you lie," he agreed. "Well, to lie is to live, if you live to lie."

Ben groaned. "My head hurts."

Patrick plopped down on the floor next to his fallen and chalk-dusted friend. "The damsel with the serious expression tells me that you, my friend, are as high as a gym teacher's hem."

"The hippie did it," Ben grumbled, pointing at Dylan.

"Hippies never do anything," Patrick said, patting Ben on the head. "You know that."

"He lives!" cried James, stepping into the cabin. "Too bad. We could've used the fertilizer."

"Who's our hilarious new friend?" Ben said, not looking up from the floor.

"This, my good man, is our noble host, James. We are guests in his camp and shall show him all proper respect. You may throw yourself prostrate at his feet." He clapped his hands together. "Perfect. Well done."

James stepped forward and handed Ben a leather flask. "Here, drink this."

He eyed the jug suspiciously. "What is it?"

"Beet juice. Freshly squeezed from our own garden. It'll clear you right up."

Ben took the flask and drank. He turned his head and spat the beet juice into the fire, which in turn had much the same reaction. "Holy God," he coughed, his face pinched in disgust. "I think I'll just let it run its course."

"Nope," Patrick said. "We're the guests of honor at dinner, so you need to be clear. Drink up."

•

As they ate, Patrick regaled the crowd with a spirited retelling of his and Ben's cross-country adventure. Sarah asked about the bandages on his hand, and the answer turned into the full, epic tale of their journey from Chicago to Mobile, flavored here and there with the spice of exaggeration. Ben's shortened message of flame became a sweeping prairie fire. Madame Siquo's restaurant transformed into a dark, dank cave. Reverend Maccabee's eyes became the dark, bottomless pools of inky black hell. The dusters became green skinned, salivating monsters. The Tinder family began speaking only in robotic monotone. Leanne was now a psychotic female Rambo. The Brothers of the Post-Alignment became shabbily-robed nincompoops who beat each other about the head with Nerf bats. Ponch took on folk hero status and spoke directly to Patrick with his soul. Then, of course, Ben got the shit beat out of him, and that's how they ended up at Fort Doom.

"What's the next stop?" asked James.

Patrick slapped his hands together. Fire rang through his injured palm. "Ow! Dammit. Why do I keep forgetting about that?" he wondered aloud. "Anyway. Our next and final destination is Orlando, Florida, and the Wonderful World of Disney."

"You're going to Disney World?" James laughed.

"We are."

Annie snickered. "If you leave now, you can make breakfast with Mickey."

"A capital idea! Ben, add it to the royal itinerary."

"What's at Disney World?" Sarah asked gently, picking at her toes on the other side of the room.

"What *isn't* at Disney World?" Patrick cried.

"Doctors," offered Annie. "I think I need one. My left foot started smelling like cottage cheese today. All on its own. With no discernible catalyst. Definitely not healthy. Thoughts?"

James groaned. "Anyone care to offer a subject change?"

Patrick raised his hand. "Some say love, it is a razor that leaves your soul to bleed. I say love, it is a flower, and you its only seed. Discuss."

"Let's go back to the foot," Ben groaned, eyes rolling.

"The cosmos are one big, great fuck you. Unless you're a worm spore. But that price is hiiiiigh, *hombre*."

Annie guffawed. "Please, Dylan, the grownups are talking."

"Tell us more about the omens," Sarah asked, her dull eyes brightening a bit. "The perils from the oracle. Have you hit them all yet?"

"Ah! An excellent question!" Patrick straightened up into full storyteller posture. "As it happens, we have not. The oracle has foretold of two more challenges that will plague our odyssey--sirens, and Bobcat Tom and the Quiet Man."

"That's three things," Annie pointed out.

"Boy, I take it back. You *are* like the real Annie," Patrick said, shaking his head. "The last two are one. I think they're one. You know, she never actually said that, come to think of it. It was more the *way* she said it that makes me think that. So at least two more challenges, possibly three. Sirens, Bombastic Tom, and the Invisible Man."

"I thought it was the Quiet Man," said Annie.

"And is it Bobcat Tom or Bombastic Tom?" added James.

Patrick frowned. "Did I say--? What did I say? Secretary?" No one spoke. Patrick coughed and looked pointedly at Ben.

"Oh. That's me? I'm the secretary now?" he asked.

Patrick nodded happily. "Yes. Please read it back."

"I'm not your secretary."

"Fine," Patrick huffed. "Give me the script. I'll take it from here."

"There is no script."

"*I mean the notebook*," Patrick hissed in a loud stage whisper. "*Hand me the notebook.*"

"Yes, I know what you mean. We don't have the notebook. It was stolen, along with everything else we own."

"*Used* to own," Annie said happily.

"Well. You're as bad a stage manager as you are a secretary." Patrick frowned. He turned to the rest of the group. "At any rate, the last two are almost certainly a pair, but I seem to have forgotten what they're called."

"But the other one is definitely a siren?"

"Definitely," Patrick nodded. "That one, I know."

"What sort of siren?" Sarah asked.

"Like, ambulance sirens?" Annie asked.

"Maybe," Patrick admitted. "The whole fortune telling thing was cryptic."

"It could also be sirens in the Greek sense," Sarah suggested, tapping her chin thoughtfully. "Women with beautiful voices that drive men to crash on the rocks."

"There are a lot of rocks around here," James nodded. "Right along the coast. If you got into a boat, you could definitely circle back and crash into some."

"How are your voices?" Patrick asked.

Annie laughed out loud. "Mine's about as sweet as a bullfrog's." James nodded his agreement, and one look from Sarah made it clear she did not sing.

"Amsalu plays the guitar," James said, "but he can't sing. And who knows how long he'll be gone this time. Could be months. So I think you're safe."

"Also, we don't have a boat," Patrick pointed out. "We're definitely safe."

"For now," Ben said miserably. "It'll catch up to us eventually."

Patrick agreed. "Sure, it's like the Buddha said: 'Certain brutal death will always seek you out.' But all will be well," he added. "The witch promised a safe arrival at our destination."

"A tender soul with a warrior's arm," said Dylan suddenly. He breathed deeply of his ash and turned to face Patrick. A reflection of firelight gleamed from his glasses. "In the end times, a man will come. A man built to stand the test. He is good, and strong, a leader of men. He is the icon of the apocalypse. The apocalypticon." He blew a line of smoke in Patrick's general direction. Pat coughed and waved the smoke away. They waited for more, but Dylan was finished. He turned back to the fire and relit his joint.

"Anyway," said Patrick, bringing them all back. "We should focus on the here and now. This potato soup, for instance, which is here right now, is terrific." He slurped down the rest of the watery soup.

"Glad you like it," James said.

"Where did you get salt?" Ben asked, draining his own bowl.

"We make our own fish oil. Believe it or not, Annie's actually good for something."

"I catch fish like sorority girls catch the clap," she said proudly.

"You know, there was a time," said Patrick dreamily, "...and I'm speaking of the time before this afternoon...when we had a splendid cache of wine that would pair wonderfully with this soup."

James' eyes grew wide. "You had wine?"

Ben nodded. "And vodka."

"And vodka," Patrick agreed. "And wine."

"And I think some bourbon too. Was there bourbon, Pat?"

Patrick shrugged. "Who can keep track? There was definitely something brown that was intoxicating. It may or may not have been bourbon. As I was saying to Ben earlier, it's been *stunningly* simple to come by luxury victuals in this post-apocalyptic wasteland."

There was a soft, moaning sigh from across the room. It was Annie, whose eyes had gone glassy. A line of drool trickled out from the corner of her mouth. James was similarly affected, and even Sarah couldn't suppress a twitch of longing. In fact, the only one not having some sort of palpable reaction to the idea of liquor was Dylan, who was distracted by a quest to determine which of his arms was longer. After several moments of stunned silence, it was James who snapped to action first. "That settles it, then," he said, slapping his legs in determination. "Tomorrow, we steal back your things. And you'll reward our bravery with wine and whiskey," he said.

"So the food and weapons that might keep us alive don't interest you one little bit, but the hooch gets your bravery fires burning?" Patrick asked.

"Well, sure. You don't need food or weapons. *We* have food and weapons. And what's ours is yours."

"Communism," Ben said sharply. Patrick elbowed him in the ribs.

"Don't piss off the Reds."

"Sorry."

James smiled and continued. "But what we *don't* have is alcohol. And, man, is that something we miss." Annie nodded vigorously and did her little sigh-moan again. She looked like she was about to melt all over the floor.

"I miss my hammer. I wouldn't say no to a morning snatch-and-grab," said Ben.

"I've never said no to a morning snatch-and-grab," Patrick snickered. "High five!" He put his good hand up. Ben did not slap it. "Come on, Ben. I mean, like...sex. Get it?"

Ben sighed.

"Spiver's not the brightest bulb in the box," James continued. "He only has two or three hideouts, and if we go search him out first thing in the morning, he'll either be passed out or hung over."

"On our liquor," Ben said sadly.

"On some of it," James admitted. "But, hey, he's small. And alcohol's hard to come by, his tolerance is probably low as hell. It won't take much. I'm sure there's plenty left over."

"What about the rest of his gang? He was with at least one puppeteer that we know of."

"And then some," Sarah said. But James shook his head.

"The Carsons are a loose pack. It's rare for them to all band together if they're not raiding. And no one raids at 7am. Ol' Spivey might have a friend or two lying around, but we won't see the whole gang. And I think we can take a small, hungover group of theatre dorks."

"I love this plan!" Patrick exclaimed. He clenched his good fist. "My hand feels empty without my machete."

"Your hand *is* empty without your machete," Ben said.

"So it's not just me, then."

"We'll head out right after morning chores," James said, looking to the group for confirmation. They all nodded, except Dylan, who was inspecting the floor for messages from an alien race.

"Chores! We love chores!" Patrick declared. "What can we do to help?"

"Come on," James grinned. "You're our guests. You do nothing. We'll wake you when we're done, we'll go get your bags, and then we'll celebrate on into the night."

"And I can get the plans for the watering system underway. Because let me tell you, if there's one thing I like better than designing complex tools, it's designing complex tools after a few shots."

And so it was settled. They finished their dinner, lounged around the fire for a while, then bid each other good night. As Patrick and Ben left the little cabin to make up a bunk in another, Ben thought he caught Sarah giving him the wryest little smile out of the corner of his eye. He turned toward her, but if there had been a smile, it was gone now, replaced by her typical facial reservation. Still, she *had* smiled. Hadn't she? Maybe? Something down behind his intestines fluttered. Alabama wasn't so bad after all.

17.

"Today feels like a good day for justice," Patrick decided. "What say you, comrade-in-furry-little-arms?"

Ben looked up from his bowl of boiled carrots and dried apples. "I just want my wrench back," he said, his mouth full of food.

"Well spoken," Patrick said. "We should retrieve your wrench or die trying."

"No, not die trying. I don't want to die trying. I refuse to die trying. Let's just get the wrench back. By trying," he added.

"Fear not, Gentle Ben, for the Lady of the Illinois has foretold to us the--"

"Yeah, yeah, yeah," Ben said, waving off his friend. "Your imaginary friend says we live. I got it."

"What you got is *firepower!*" Anti-Annie hollered, kicking her way into the cabin. The door smashed against the far wall and snapped off at the top hinge. "Whoops..."

Ben had started at the sudden burst, and his breakfast now coated his shirt. "Aw, come on..." he mumbled, brushing the lumpy carrots to the floor.

"A decent entrance," Patrick decided. "I give you a seven."

"*You will give me a mothafuckin' ten!*" Annie yelled. She hoisted two large M-16s, one in each hand, and stood in the doorway with her legs spread like a deranged rock star.

"Whooooa," Ben breathed, forgetting about the mess on his shirt. "You guys have assault rifles?!"

"*That's* what we're using against Spiver?" Patrick breathed, horrified.

Annie shrugged. "Nah." She tossed the guns to the floor. They fell like dead weights. "They're just for show. No bullets. Great for an entrance, though, right?"

"Top of the mornin'," James said, shouldering in past his sister. "How'd everyone sleep? Good?"

"I slept the sleep of the sleepy," Patrick said.

"Fine," muttered Ben, who was more than a little disappointed he wouldn't be getting to use a machine gun.

"I see Sarah brought breakfast," James said, nodding to their mostly empty bowls. "Ben, just so you know, for tomorrow morning, the food goes *inside* the mouth."

Patrick shook his head sadly and clucked his tongue. "I still have so much to teach him."

Annie toed at one of the assault rifles. "Think we should bring 'em? For effect?" But James shook his head.

"They look good, but they're heavy as hell, and if we do get into a firefight, they'll learn pretty quick that we don't have any ammo."

Annie sighed. "No fun." She scooped up the guns and bustled them out the door. James turned back to his guests.

"You gentlemen ready for a little early morning justice?"

"I was just ranting about what a perfect day this was for justice!" Patrick beamed. "Wasn't I, Ben?"

Ben shrugged as he scooped the rest of his breakfast into his mouth. "You were ranting about something."

Patrick waved off his friend. "Don't mind him. He's grumpy in the mornings. And afternoons. And most evenings. And probably while he sleeps."

"Well, finish up your breakfast, then meet us outside," James said, flashing his easy grin. "It's time to choose your weapons."

They joined the rest of the commune out in the yard. Their new friends were huddled around a low fire, inspecting various implements of death in the flickering light. "Pick your poison," Annie said happily, gesturing to a large cache of weapons on a blanket near the fire. "We usually draw straws, but we figured since you're the guests, you can pick first."

"The fires of Solomon burn heavy in my eye. The weight of the earth is a feather to the one who sees," whispered Dylan.

Patrick took James by the arm and muttered under his breath, "Is he going on this little mission?"

James grinned. "He's good in a tight spot. You'll see."

Ben leaned in over the blanket and inspected the weapons. "Holy shit, you guys have a *crossbow*?"

James nodded. "Only two bolts, though. And it's hard as hell to load, it's a really old model, and the crank doesn't--" But Ben wasn't listening. He snatched it up and hugged it tightly to his chest.

"Wow. I'm going in with a *crossbow*," he breathed, in total awe of himself.

"Aw, man," Annie frowned. "I wanted the crossbow."

"You've never used the crossbow in your life," Sarah said quietly from the far side of the fire.

Annie shrugged. "Yeah, but now that he has it, I really want it."

"How about you, Pat? What looks good?" James asked.

Patrick rubbed his hands together (carefully) and approached the weapon cache. "It all just looks so good," he said. There were ten different kinds of knives, a length of rusty pipe, two sets of brass knuckles, a sledgehammer, a rubber mallet, three tire irons, a couple of bricks, and even an old fashioned branding iron.

"Washed up on the beach last year," James grinned, following Patrick's stare. "It has a PC brand. And it's pretty handy. If you like the letters PC burned into things."

"I do!" Patrick exclaimed. "I also like playing Jack Bauer in the interrogation room!" He reached for the iron, but another little implement of destruction caught his eye at the last second. "Oh, goodness," he breathed. "I think I'll have that." He reached over and pulled a bullwhip from the pile.

"Apocapop," Dylan said through an exhale of smoke. The gang turned to look at him. He opened his mouth and hissed at them from the back of his throat. The rest of the group shrugged and turned back to the fire.

"Are you sure you want the whip?" James asked. "It can be sort of--"

"*Look out, Short Round!*" Patrick screamed. He whirled the worn, brown handle excitedly around his head and flicked it toward Ben. The thong flailed out madly and sailed across the fire in a shaky arc. The popper brushed lamely against Ben's shoe. He looked up at Patrick, unimpressed.

"Hold on, hold on," Pat said, reeling in the whip, "I can be Indiana Jones. I can do this." He gathered it in again and took a deep breath.

"Maybe you shouldn't--" Sarah began, but he cut her off with a wild war cry.

"*AAAIIIIIII!* Take *this*, Nazis!" He twirled the whip around and around his head, doing his best human helicopter impersonation. The others dove for cover, Annie missing a popper to the eye by just inches. Patrick twisted his wrist and snapped the handle. The thong waved crazily through the air, then snapped back and bit Patrick on the shoulder. "Ow! *Guten morgen!*" he cursed.

Ben held up a cautious hand. "Pat, maybe you should just--"

"No, I can do it. I can do it!" He took a deep breath and gripped the whip as tightly as his injured hand would allow. Then, with all the grace of an elderly moose, he spun around, leapt into the air, and threw his wrist toward the stack of logs near the fire. But the fall of the whip caught around his ankle, and the thong fell lamely against his chest. He shook the whip, trying desperately to dislodge it from his ankle, but the more he struggled, the tighter it cinched around his feet. He flailed against the leather thong like a man caught in a giant spider web. He yanked the handle and gave it a final, hard snap. The whip jerked his own feet out from under his legs, and he landed on the cold earth with a hard *thud*. "Must be my injured hand," he gasped, out of breath, staring up at the sky. "It doesn't whip like it should."

"Must be your injured brain," Ben said. "Take the branding iron."

"No, the whip will be fine. I've got the hang of it now."

"Clearly."

Ben helped Patrick to his feet while the others selected their tools of doom. James grabbed the rubber mallet, and Dylan chose the branding iron. "For reclamations paid out on the devil's corporate culture," he explained.

Annie picked up the iron pipe and hefted it a couple of times in her right hand, testing its weight. "This oughta do," she decided. Then she raised it above her head and ran full speed at Ben. "Give me that crossbow!"

James caught her around the waist and hauled her back. "Easy, kiddo. Play nice with our new friends."

"My pipe wants to play nice with his head," she hissed.

Ben sighed. "Look, if you want the crossbow, you can have the crossbow," he said.

"Really?"

"Hell no!" He raised the weapon and leveled the bolt at her chest. "But you can have the arrow."

"Stop this," said Sarah, her soft voice taking on the slightest edge. Her sad eyes carried an eerie, grave weight. "You're wasting time."

"Sorry," Ben and Annie mumbled in unison. Ben lowered the crossbow, and Annie stuck the pipe in her belt.

It was decided that Sarah would stay behind to guard the fort while the rest of them went in search of duffel bags and vengeance. "Stay close to the gate," James warned. "There's a good chance we'll be coming in fast with the Carson gang on our tail."

Sarah nodded, once. "I know."

"You sure you're gonna be okay here by yourself?" Ben asked.

She squinted at him. "Why wouldn't I be?"

"Uh--I don't--I just--"

"Ben's just a chivalrous sort of creature," Patrick said, throwing his good hand around Ben's shoulder. "He meant no offense, heroine of Fort Doom."

"I just--yeah," Ben sighed. Someday, he was going to talk to a girl like a grown-up.

"I wish Amsalu were here," Annie whined. "Just the *sight* of him, and Spiver wets himself."

James nodded. "He picked a bad time to go rogue. But what we lack in intimidating immigrants, we'll make up for in really hard swings of metal."

"And leather!" Patrick cried, shaking the whip. "Really hard swings of leather."

"Will you please take a weapon you know how to use?" Ben sighed.

"Absolutely not."

"All right, everyone ready?" said James, rubbing his hands together excitedly. "Let's go kick some ass."

•

"*Oo-lay for-tay paw-la-tay.*"

"What did I just say?" Calico asked, hitting the monk in the jaw with an oak branch. "No more bullshit."

"Please, there's no reason for this," said the head brother, wringing his hands nervously. "We're happy to speak with you. I just ask that you have patience until we finish the ceremonious Birth of the Post-Alignment." Calico glanced at the scrawny monk near the fire, who had stripped down to his underpants and was lathering himself with something that looked like egg whites. Another monk was applying the same shiny, slippery gel to an oval-shaped hole they'd hacked through the trunk of a tree.

"Piker, you ever know me to have much in the way of patience?" Calico asked, spitting a long, brown stream through his front teeth onto the head monk's feet.

"I ain't never knowed you to have any decent qualities," Piker admitted.

"Shut the fuck up," Calico said, smacking Piker in the forehead with the branch. The Red Cap fell like a sack of potatoes. "'Course, he's got a point there, Brother Damnhell."

"Brother Triedit," the monk corrected him.

Calico's blue eye twitched. "Don't never correct me."

"Yes, I'm sorry, of course. If we could just finish our ceremony, I'd be happy to--"

"I tell you what," Calico interrupted. He stripped a thin twig from the branch and used it to pick at his teeth. "You stop talkin' right now, or I'll give you a sodomistic experience with this branch." The monk gasped, then clamped his mouth shut. Calico wheeled around to the rest of the hooded assembly. "I need answers, but I'll take smashin' in faces just as quick," he bellowed. "Two men came thisaway not too long back, a big-headed skinny one and a stupid-lookin' small one. I wanna know where they's headed. We'll start with you." He pointed the branch at a dopy looking monk with nervous sweat dripping down his face. "What's your name?"

"B-brother H-haffs-staff," he gasped.

"Who the fuck names you people," Calico muttered under his breath. "All right, Haffstaff. Where they headed?" The monk looked around at his brethren nervously, uncertain whether or not he should speak. Calico helped him make up his mind by hoisting the branch and cocking it like a baseball bat.

"Disney World!" the monk cried, closing his eyes and holding his hands up to block the blow. "They went to Disney World!"

Calico lowered the branch and eyed the monk suspiciously. "What the fuck they goin' to Disney World for?"

"We don't know," piped up one of the monks down the line.

Calico whirled around to face him, a fire blazing in his eyes. "Bullshit."

"Ahh!" The monk fell to the ground, cowering under Calico's seething figure. "It's true! They never said!"

"They didn't, they didn't," agreed the other monks, bobbing their hoods from side to side. Brother Triedit said nothing, but averted his eyes to the ground.

Calico lowered the branch. Truth be told, it didn't much matter if they knew the boys' motives or not. He grinned widely, turning his sharp teeth toward the nodding brothers. "Y'all've been very helpful," he hissed. He bashed them each in the head with the branch anyway, for good measure, then gathered the Red Caps and galloped southeast.

•

It only took them an hour or so to track Spiver down. After they came up empty in the Sanger, Annie led them to a small apartment building on Dauphin Street. "It's one of his flophouses," she said. "I followed him back here after he torched the FBI building that time."

"You followed him?" James asked, eyebrow raised.

"Hell yeah I followed him. He'd just set fire to the *FBI*, you guys. It was, like, the most turned on I've ever been."

James groaned and shook his head. "Please tell me you're joking. Oh God, and *please* tell me you didn't--"

"A lady never tells," she said indignantly. The group fell uncomfortably silent. Ben turned away and tried to look disinterested. Patrick cleared his throat. "*What*?" Annie demanded. "It was before I knew he was such an asshole, he was just some guy who'd turned a federal building to ashes, and you can't tell me that's not hot." More silence from the crew. Annie huffed. "I can't help it," she whined. "Rebellion makes me horny as--"

James held up his hand. "Please stop talking, sister."

They crept into the apartment building through a busted out window on the ground floor. Inside, the dark walls were covered with black mold. The sweet, tangy smell of must and decay perfumed the heavy air. Patrick pulled the collar of his shirt up over his nose as they slipped through the room and mounted a flight of creaky, dilapidated stairs. They moved slowly, each of them wincing every time a wooden stair squeaked underfoot. Halfway up, Annie leaned against the thin metal railing. It groaned under her weight.

"*Shh!*" James hissed.

Annie shrugged. "Sorry."

They tiptoed their way to the second floor, where they found Spiver snoring away in a wreck of a room at the end of the hall. He'd managed to light a dozen or so homemade candles before passing out cold, and a few of them still flickered with the last gasps of life. In the dim light, they could just make out the stolen backpacks behind Spiver's sleeping form. They could also see the outlines of three other men, their chests slowly rising and falling with sleep. James silently beckoned the group out of the room and led them back down the ruined hall.

"Looks like they're pretty well out," he whispered. "If we're quiet, we might be able to grab the gear and slip out unnoticed."

"The unseeing eye sees all," Dylan warned, sucking down a long drag of ash. "It sees you. It sees the traitorous moon. It sees the *lava*."

"Okay, so you stay out here in the hall," Patrick said, patting Dylan's shoulder.

"You *all* stay out here in the hall," Annie whispered. "I'll get the bags." She turned and took a step back to the apartment, but Ben grabbed her shoulder.

"Are you serious? You're like a feral cat in a trash can. I'll go, I'm stealthier."

"It's true," Patrick agreed, "his shaved head makes him built for speed. All he needs to make a clean getaway is a good hand with a whip covering his six." He unfurled the whip and flailed it around the hall. The thong slapped against a rusty sconce holding on by its last screw. The battered piece of metal went clanging to the ground.

There was a low "*Ffffth!*" as every single member of the group drew in a sharp breath. They held it and waited for the sound of stirrings from the apartment down the hall. But there was nothing but silence.

"Maybe you should stay here too," James whispered.

Patrick nodded. "That's probably best."

"Ben, I've got your back." James gripped his mallet and gave it a few practice swings.

Ben gave him a curt nod. "Let's go."

The two men crept lightly down the hall. Spiver's candles glowed dimly in the apartment at the end of the tunnel, guiding them through the darkness. "How dangerous are these guys? Like, when they're awake?" Ben whispered.

"Dangerous enough. Spiver alone's probably got five or six notches in his belt, and he's the tame one."

"And by notches in his belt, you mean...?"

James grinned. "Let's just say, he probably won't leave you alive a second time."

The men were still snoring away when they slipped back into the room. Ben held the crossbow to his shoulder and wished he'd taken a few practice shots out in the street. Preferably at that Annie girl. She was the worst.

James tapped him on the arm and brought his lips close to Ben's ear. "You get the bags. I'll watch out." Ben nodded. He snuck forward, avoiding broken glass and plaster where he could see it through the gloom. He shuffled carefully past the free-standing kitchen island, where he saw a half-empty bottle of his vodka. A low heat burned in his cheeks. It was one thing to bash someone over the head and leave him bleeding on the sidewalk. It was another thing entirely to drink another man's booze. *This aggression will not stand.*

Spiver and company were in the adjoining living room. One man slept on the couch near the window; Spiver and the other two men lay on the floor, forming a low, grumbling wall between Ben and his bags. One of the sleeping men grunted and shifted, rolling over and slapping his palm onto the floor just inches from Ben's foot. Ben looked doubtfully at the crossbow. Upon further reflection, it probably wasn't the world's best close-range weapon. He slipped the bolt out of its groove and set the crossbow on the countertop. He gripped the arrow tightly in his fist, holding it like a knife, pointy end down and ready to stab something.

He tiptoed over the closest man's hand and skirted around the prostrate Spiver. He crunched lightly over the rubble, wincing with every step. The low-burning candles threw wavering shadows across the floor and up the walls, and every time he took a step, Ben was sure someone was stirring. He held his breath and reached for the first backpack. The food shifted inside as he lifted it, and Ben gritted his teeth as the cans *clacked* against each other. The man on the couch snorted and rolled over. He tumbled off the couch and crashed to the floor. He yelped in surprise, punched the ground drowsily with his fist, and mumbled nonsense at it. Then he picked himself up, threw himself back up onto the couch, and settled back into sleep. Ben exhaled. He slid his arms through the nylon straps and pulled the backpack in tight against his shoulders.

He reached for the second bag. It was unzipped, and the weapons inside stuck out of the top like an apocalyptic cornucopia. As he lifted the bag by the nylon loop at the top, the zipper fell open farther, and the pipe wrench tipped out. Ben shot out his other hand, dropped the arrow, and caught the wrench just six inches from the floor. He turned toward James and thrust the wrench into the air. *Did you see that?* he mouthed, even though there was no way James could see his face in the dim light. *I am Bruce fucking Lee.*

James waved him back with his hand. *Hurry up.* Ben tucked the pipe into the bag and picked up the arrow. He grabbed the front flap of the backpack and cinched it closed with his hand. There were a few random supplies lying around the room--some food, a couple bottles of liquor, the machete--but he figured he'd come back for them. Or just leave them there and not risk his life again. Either one.

He turned back and stepped between Spiver and another member of the gang. Spiver shifted in his sleep, and Ben had to change direction mid-step to avoid coming down on the outlaw's ribs. He hopped forward, and his foot came down hard on a discarded shot glass. It shattered under his shoe. Ben gasped as the tinkling of breaking glass echoed off the walls.

Then, all hell broke loose.

A new form, one they hadn't seen in the darkness, leapt up from behind the couch, mumbling and grunting. He pitched forward, toward the front hall, but he slipped on plaster dust and went crashing into the wall, shoulder-first. He let loose a low growl of surprise and pain, wheeled away from the wall, and tripped over the arm of the couch. He went sprawling to the floor, crashing into Spiver. Spiver cried out in pain and flailed out with his hands and legs, scrabbling to push the other man off him. His fist caught Ben in the shin just as he was hurrying past. It was enough to push him off balance and send him stumbling over the man sleeping against the wall. Ben's heel came down on the man's hand. He awoke with a scream and lunged forward, driving his shoulder into Ben's hip and pushing him back over Spiver and the other man wrestling on the floor.

"Get in here!" James screamed over his shoulder. "*Now!*" He ran at the nearest gang member, the one who'd rolled close to the kitchen. He was just sitting up, groggy and confused, when James brought the rubber mallet crashing down on his head. There was a soft *crunch* as a piece of his skull snapped off and caved in. He crumpled back to the floor.

Ben dropped the bag he was holding, and weapons splayed across the floor. He rolled off Spiver, but the man on the couch leapt from the cushions and tackled Ben into the floor, hard. He beat down on the back of Ben's head with huge fists, smashing his face down into the concrete floor with each blow. Ben turned the arrow over in his hand and stabbed wildly back over his head. It caught the man in the shoulder, sinking deep into his flesh. The man howled and backed away, scrabbling furiously at the arrow.

Patrick burst through the doorway, yelling and flailing the whip. He dove into the man with the arrow sticking out of his shoulder, but bounced off him like a raindrop off a windshield. He fell into a heap near the couch, where Spiver and the other man grappled and rolled over on top of him.

The other man, the one whose hand Ben had stepped on, dove forward and grabbed the hammer that had spilled out of the backpack. He swung it at Annie, who had run into the room with her pipe held high. She dodged back, but the hammer caught her right hand, and she cried out in pain as the pipe went clattering to the floor. The man shoved her, hard, and she slammed back into the wall. James darted forward and swung the rubber mallet, but the man turned just in time, and the mallet glanced off his meaty upper arm. The man jabbed the hammer into James' stomach. James doubled over, and the man drove his knee into James' forehead. He went down hard.

Spiver and the man from behind the couch were still grappling on the floor. Spiver planted his feet against the man's chest and launched him backward. He crashed into Patrick, who was just getting back to his feet. Spiver leapt up and drew a knife from his boot. He lunged at Annie, swiping at her with the blade. She danced away from it, whirling just out of reach as Spiver hacked at the air. "I've been waiting for you and your band of misdicks," he snarled.

"What the hell's a misdick?" Annie said. She jogged to the left as Spiver sliced from the right and collided with the man with the arrow in his shoulder. Spiver plunged forward with the knife, and Annie ducked to the floor. Spiver's blade buried itself deep into the chest of the other man.

"Well, shit," the man muttered in surprise, staring down at the blood spurting out of his chest. Then his eyes rolled up into his head, and he fell over dead.

"You *bitch*!" Spiver snarled, yanking the knife out of the man's chest.

"Hey, you're the one who did it," Annie said, scrabbling on the floor for something to hit somebody with. Her hand closed on the pipe wrench, and she whirled around, aiming for Spiver, but hitting Ben instead, who had just pulled himself back to his feet.

The gangster with the crushed hand had wrestled the man from behind the couch off Patrick and was holding him firmly by his hands, which appeared to be tied behind his back. The bound man snarled and spat angrily, but his words were muffled by a dirty piece of cloth that had been tied around his mouth. The man holding him opened his mouth to speak when the prisoner threw his head back, right into his captor's face. The man's nose broke with a wet *snap*. He let go of the prisoner and covered his bleeding face with both hands. "You motherfucker!" he shrieked. James climbed unsteadily to his feet and stumbled over to him. He brought the mallet down against the man's temple. He crashed over onto his side, spitting and cursing. James finished him off with a few hard swings of the mallet.

"Drop your goddamn weapons!" Spiver screamed. Everyone looked up. The little mobster held the prisoner, his knife pressed tightly against the man's neck. "Put 'em down, or I open his throat."

Patrick frowned up at the prisoner. "Who on earth is that?" he asked.

"It's Amsalu," James replied. "He's one of us."

The dark-skinned man struggled against his bonds, and Spiver pulled the blade closer against his throat. "Put 'em down. *Now*," he demanded. James slowly set his mallet on the floor. Annie cursed and tossed down the wrench. Patrick briefly considered using his whip to catch Spiver's wrist and fling the knife away, but decided that move was perhaps a little advanced, given how dark it was in the room and all. So he tossed the whip aside. It landed on the prostrate Ben.

"Hey," Ben said weakly.

"Sorry."

"One step, and I'll slice him open," Spiver snarled.

"No one's stepping anywhere," James said, raising his hands into the air. "Just let him go, Spiver. You let him go, and we'll let you go."

The little man spat laughter back at them. "Sure, sure, sure." He tightened his grip on Amsalu's bonds and pulled him backward, knife still poised to slice at his throat. Amsalu, for his part, seemed weary beyond belief. Heavy, black circles sagged below his eyes, and he wavered on his feet like a punch-drunk boxer. Though he was quite a bit taller than his captor, there was no mistaking who was in charge.

"Just let him go, you asshole!" Annie screamed. She kicked at the rubble on the floor, sending bits of plaster skidding against their feet. Spiver growled and pulled Amsalu back toward the door.

"You wait til the boys hear about this," he snarled. "You've just signed your death warrants, you goddamn meddling sons of bitches." They scooted back into the kitchen. "Your little camp is gonna burn," he spat. "And you're all gonna burn with it! You hear me? You're all gonna burn wi--"

Dylan's branding iron came down hard on the crown of Spiver's head, staving in the skull and squirting blood across the kitchen.

"The cavernous worm leads the stars to water, and all things must go their path," Dylan said softly, puffing on the joint balanced between his lips.

James shook his head and nudged Patrick in the ribs. "See? Told you he was good in a pinch."

Annie unbound Amsalu, who needed help standing. He gave them the Cliff's Notes while bracing himself against the kitchen island. He'd set out for a few days at Bellingrath Gardens, a place where wildflowers still grew, a place he often went to be alone and "calm his mind," often for weeks at a time. But before he'd even made it out of Mobile, the Carsons had jumped him and dragged him back here, to the apartment. He'd been bound and gagged in the corner for almost a week, surviving on the slick dregs of canned beans.

"Looks like they worked you over pretty good," James frowned, inspecting Amsalu's wounds. The man nodded once, angrily.

"Any particular reason? Or are they just that brand of sadist?" Patrick asked.

"They think I am Jamaican," Amsalu replied.

He dug into a packet of crackers they found in the living room while the rest of the gang gathered up the weapons, food, and liquor and stuffed it all back into the knapsacks. Most of it was coated in blood. Ben pulled his arrow out of the man's shoulder and gingerly wiped it against the dead man's shirt. "Sorry, guy," he mumbled. "Insult to injury. But it was your blood in the first place."

Despite the circumstances that led to their death, it didn't seem right to leave the corpses strewn about the apartment, though no one was champing at the bit to dig four graves. So Annie stayed behind and, with the others watching from the sidewalk, happily set the whole apartment building on fire.

As the flames consumed the building, Amsalu mumbled something into the blaze and made the sign of the cross with his hand.

"Last rites?" Patrick asked when he was done.

"Even those who stray are children of God," he replied.

The mourning period didn't last long. Once they were safely back inside the walls of Fort Doom, Annie snatched a bottle of whiskey from Ben's bag and thrust it triumphantly into the air, whooping and laughing like she were already drunk. The rest of the crew joined in, laughing and slapping high-fives and shaking off the general unpleasantness of justified slaughter.

Sarah pulled Ben aside and inspected his head wounds. "These look bad," she frowned, prodding at his bruises.

"Yeah, well, the--ow!--the floor was pretty hard," he said.

"Come with me. I'll help you clean up." She took his hand and led him to one of the cabins. Ben's heart battered against his chest cavity like a caged animal at her touch. He shot Patrick a pleading look over his shoulder and mouthed, *What do I do?* Patrick gave him a thumbs up and mouthed back, *Just don't be yourself.* Ben frowned as he stumbled after her into the cabin.

Patrick slipped off his backpack and set it on the ground in front of him. He closed his eyes and took a deep breath. Then he opened the bag, dug through the cans of beans and vegetables, dug all the way to the bottom, and there, dented but unbroken and unopened, lay the butterscotch pudding cup. He exhaled with a smile and cinched the bag shut.

James stoked the mid-morning fire while Annie cracked open the whiskey. Amsalu went in search of his guitar, and Dylan retrieved a fresh tin of ash. Patrick leaned back against a log and twisted the cap off a bottle of wine. He clinked bottles with Anti-Annie, took a long swallow of the sweet red, and passed it across to James. Eventually Ben and Sarah rejoined them, Ben's head wrapped in dirty bandages. They sat around the fire, drinking whiskey and wine, singing old songs, and swapping stories about the absurdity of the apocalypse. Tomorrow, Patrick would start on the rain-catching system, and Ben would practice talking to a girl. As for the next day, or the next week, or the next month, who knew what awaited them, but for that moment, right then, with Amsalu strumming his guitar, James grinning his lopsided grin, Annie shrieking with laughter, Dylan smoking his ash, and even Sarah cracking a smile, there was no doubt in either of their minds that they were exactly where they were meant to be.

•

Calico crouched low, inspecting the dirt underfoot. He plucked a long blade of browned grass and chewed it thoughtfully.

"What," the man standing over him said.

Calico raised his mismatched eyes and grinned. "Looks like our boys started to drift." He stood and arched his back, popping it along the spine. "Florida's that-a-way," he said, pointing away from the sun. "But they looped their way south."

The other man gritted his teeth. "The monks lied."

But Calico shook his head. "Naw, don't think so. That little piece tied to the tree and those weird-ass monks told the same story. They headin' to Disney World, all right. They just got no clue how to get there."

The other man removed his cap and rubbed at his temples. "Options," he said quietly.

"Well, hell, we could keep on after 'em. I'd say they're up on us by three days, we could prolly make up that ground. But I think we keep on keepin' on to Florida. That's where they headin', that's where they'll end up. Stop goin' after them; let them come to us.

The other man nodded slowly. It was a fine plan.

18.

Patrick yawned and stretched and mumbled a sleepy hello to the morning sun. He pulled on his sweater and crept out into the yard, closing the door gently so he wouldn't wake Ben. He wiped the sleep from his eyes as he crossed to the fire.

"Morning," James said. He picked the percolator from its grill shelf above the flames and poured a cup of steaming coffee into the empty mug at his feet. He set the percolator aside and handed Patrick his mug.

"Mornin," Pat replied with a yawn.

"You looked a little shifty sneaking out of your bunk this morning," James grinned. "Trying not to wake the mice?"

"Trying not to wake Benny Boy. Those mice, they'll sleep through anything. But Ben, he needs his beauty sleep."

"Not likely, with you clomping around like a sick elephant," Ben said, emerging from the cabin. He yawned and stretched and scratched his belly. Then he zipped up his jacket and ambled over to join them.

"I do not *clomp*," Patrick said, hurt. "If anything, I saunter. Some have said that I sashay."

"Whatever you do, you do it loudly, and clumsily."

Patrick sighed. "Not the first time I've heard that."

"Morning," James smiled, pouring Ben his own mug of coffee.

"Morning," he mumbled. He took the mug and blew away the rising steam.

"I think you're beautiful, no matter *how* much sleep you get," James said. Ben snorted grumpily. "So, Pat, how's your paw these days?"

Patrick proudly unraveled the bandage around his palm and held his hand up for all to see. "I do believe it's just about healed!" he said. "No more hole."

"Excellent news!" said James. "Fort Doom: Gangrene-free for almost two full years."

"OSHA would be proud."

James grinned. "So what's on the docket today?"

"Ah! An excellent question! I've got some repairs to make to Gully, then I--"

"Gully?" Ben interrupted. "Who's Gully?"

Patrick gestured to the giant tin-and-tarp structure looming over the garden. "*That* is Gully."

Ben sighed. "You named your water spreader?"

"It's not a water spreader, Ben, it is a high-concept precipitation distribution platform," Patrick insisted. "And it's not an it. It's a she." He turned back to James. "Anyway. Gully needs a little work, and I have to mess with the new alarm system. I tested it out last night, stepping on the panel only gets one of the groups of cans clanging. Need to figure that out. Then I thought I'd try my hand at designing a rapid-launch weapon system to mount above the gate over there."

"Ooo, rapid-launch weapon system? That sounds exciting."

"Well, don't get *too* worked up. It'll likely only launch very small rocks. But if all goes according to plan, it'll launch them very, very quickly."

"I like it!"

"Why don't we just fill a bucket with rocks and dump it on people who attack?" Ben asked, sipping his coffee. "That's pretty rapid delivery."

Patrick frowned. "It's also eighteen times less fun. Stop waging a war on fun, Fogelvee!"

"What about you, Ben? Any plans for the day?"

The door to Sarah's cabin opened, and she stepped out into the yard. The three men turned in unison to look at her. She marched directly over to the outhouse cabin without sparing so much as a glance at any of them. When she closed the door with a quick, curt slam, Ben turned back to the fire. Patrick and James grinned at him like a pair of idiots.

"What?" he asked.

"Perhaps today is the day you finally speak to yon fair-haired angel in a tender and romantic manner?" Patrick teased, jiggling his eyebrows up and down.

"Shut up. And no. I'm going to start patching the southern wall today. Amsalu and I'll bring back a few loads of bricks and start working on the hole."

"Bricks!" Patrick cried. "How resourceful! Where'd you find them?"

Ben squinted at Patrick. "Gee, Pat. I don't know. Where in this apocalyptic wasteland full of building rubble could I possibly find some unused bricks?" He shook his head and sipped down the rest of his coffee.

"Man," said James, slapping his hands against his knees, "an irrigation system, an alarm, a rocklet launcher, a new wall. You guys are spoiling us."

"Just trying to earn our keep," Patrick said.

"Ha! You've done more than the rest of us combined, and we've been here for two years. You guys have only been around for--" He trailed off, frowning in concentration. "How long *have* you been here?" he asked.

"Who knows?" Ben shrugged. "Rule Number 18."

Patrick leaned back on his log and did some quick calculation. "If I had to guess, I'd say...14 weeks? Maybe 16?"

James let out a low whistle. "Four months already?" He shrugged. "I guess time flies." He picked up a stick from the ground and used it to stoke the pale flames. "Remind me where you guys were headed when you got here."

Patrick opened his mouth to speak, but stopped himself. Where *had* they been going? He crossed his arms and bit his lip, struggling to remember. He knew they'd been headed *somewhere*. They didn't just leave Chicago for no reason. Did they? He cast an uneasy glance at his friend. "Ben?"

But Ben was struggling too. He furrowed his brow and scratched his cheek. "Maybe...Neeeeeeeew Orleans...?" he asked uncertainly. "That sounds like a place we'd go. Right? Or no?"

James shook his head. "We talked about it your first night here, I know that. But for the life of me..."

"Huh." Patrick stared quizzically at his shoes. "Where were you taking me, feet?" He wasn't accustomed to memory lapses, and his brain was coming up alarmingly empty on this one. The feeling was...unsettling. "Ah, well," he said, waving away the mystery with a swoop of his hand, "it'll come to us. And besides, wherever it was, it can't be any better than this. Food, water, and friends, am I right?" he said, nudging Ben on the shoulder.

Sarah emerged from the outhouse and walked swiftly back to her cabin. "Yeah," Ben said, following her with his eyes. "It doesn't get much better."

"Huh." James tousled his tangled hair and shrugged. "Well, at any rate, we're glad you stayed," he grinned. "And speaking of things that're on dockets, laundry's the first on my list today. You guys have anything you need washed?"

Ben shook his head. "I just washed my shirts yesterday. And jeans are always clean."

"How 'bout you, Pat?"

Patrick sniffed at his knee. "Oof. Jeans are *not* always clean," he decided, pushing himself up to his feet. "These are due. Let me go find a decent pair of replacement pants, and they're all yours."

•

James ambled down to the water's edge and dropped the bundle of laundry on the ground. He worked open the knot and opened the blanket, letting the dirty clothes tumble out onto the rocky beach. He lifted up a pair of Annie's jeans and inspected a fist-sized bulge in one of the pockets. He reached in and pulled out a whole potato. He sighed. He didn't even want to know.

"Guess I better check 'em all," he muttered.

He searched through the pile of clothing and scavenged a guitar pick from Amsalu's jacket pocket and a straight razor from Dylan's patched pants. He didn't even know Dylan *had* a straight razor. That'd be something to discuss at the next round table.

He set the pick and the blade down on the blanket and moved on to Patrick's jeans. He felt around the pockets and was about to toss the pants aside when he heard a light crinkle. He turned the jeans over, reached into the back pocket, and pulled out a worn, folded piece of paper.

"I shouldn't read that," he said aloud. "Probably none of my business." Unless, of course, it *was* some of his business. What if his new friends were keeping something from him? Something important? Could Patrick and Ben be spies for the Carsons? Or one of the other Mobile gangs? Or, good lord, someone worse. Someone new to town looking to make a hard move into the city. They could be on an embedded recon mission. Was that insane? Of course it was insane. Right? Right. But, then again, there weren't many uses for written notes these days. It had to be communication from *someone*. And how much did he really know about those two? Only what they told him.

James shook his head. It was unlikely. And it was a ridiculous idea. But they themselves had shared with him one of their rules, number 12: Err on the side of crazy.

He unfolded the note. *Better safe than sorry.*

As his eyes moved over the note, his heart sank. The words became blurred, and he realized that he had tears in his eyes. Which was stupid, because he wasn't a cryer, hadn't cried in years. He scrubbed his eyes dry. He refolded the note, sat down on the cold beach, and looked out at the swirling yellow mist roiling above the ocean. For almost a full hour he sat there, note in hand, staring out at the water, thinking. But there really wasn't all that much to think about. Something had to be done. And he had to be the one to do it.

When he returned to the fort, he hung the clean clothes on the drying line, then he sought out the rest of his group. Ben was lugging bricks over to the southern wall, and Patrick was busy tinkering with the alarm system outside the gate, so James gathered the rest of the crew together behind the row of cabins. "Listen," he said uneasily. "We have to talk about something."

19.

The next morning, Patrick awoke with a start. "Something's amiss," he said aloud. He didn't know how he knew it, but he knew it. There was something in the air.

He propped himself up on his elbows and glanced around. Ben was snoring softly in his bunk on the other side of the room. "Ben, wake up," he yawned. "Something's amiss." But Ben was too soundly asleep to answer, so Patrick fell out of bed, stumbled over to the other side of the room, and brought his lips close to Ben's ears. "*I say, something's amiss,*" he cried. Ben bolted upright with a scream, slamming his forehead against Patrick's nose. "Cripes!" Patrick yelled, the front of his face going warm and tingly. His eyes watered. "What's the matter with you?"

"Me?" Ben demanded. "Why're you on my face?! Are you kissing me in my sleep?" He shoved Patrick away, then rolled over and burrowed under his blanket. "And why are you waking me up? Let me sleep, it's Saturday."

"Is it? Really?"

"If I convince you that it is, will you let me go back to sleep?"

"Absolutely not." He lifted Ben's cover and slapped him lightly on the forehead with his palm. "Wake up. Like I said while you were ignoring me in your sleep, something's amiss."

"What's amiss?"

Patrick narrowed his eyes. "*Something.*"

Ben pushed him off the cot. "Okay, well, when you figure out what it is, come wake me. And when you do, bring coffee."

Patrick gasped and snapped his fingers. "*That's* what's amiss!"

"The coffee?"

"The fire! The fire that makes the coffee *coffee*. Listen." He held up his hand for silence. The only sound was the Gulf wind whistling through the hole in the southern wall that Ben hadn't quite finished with yet. "Hear that? No crackling fire."

Ben shrugged. "So go start one."

"But I don't *have* to start one. That's one of the perks of living in Fort Doom. James is always up first, and he always starts the fire. Right?" Ben conceded this was true. In all the weeks they'd been living in Mobile, James had been the first to rise every single day and had, indeed, gotten a good blaze going in the pit. Patrick rubbed at his chin. "Something is definitely amiss."

"Will you stop saying 'amiss'?"

"Why? Is it making you feel amiss?"

"Keep it up, and my a-fist isn't gonna a-miss your face."

"The apocalypse has made you cranky. Come on, let's go investigate."

Ben grumbled his dissent but flung the covers away all the same. They stepped out of the cabin and grimaced against the bright glow of the early morning fog. The yard was completely empty; there wasn't another soul in sight. The charred logs from last night's fire lay dark and cold in the ash of the fire pit.

"Maybe he slept in," Ben offered. "Maybe he thinks it's Saturday, too."

They crossed up to James' cabin, and Patrick knocked gently on the door. There was no response. He knocked a little louder. Still nothing. He pressed his ear to the door. "I don't hear anything," he frowned.

"See if it's unlocked," Ben whispered.

"You want to just barge in? What if he's having, like, a private orgy in there? That would be awkward for everyone."

"With who? His sister?"

"Maybe he picked up some tail at a bar last night in town. And now they're having a private orgy."

"If they were having a private orgy, I think we'd hear it."

"Not if they're really bad at it."

"Just open the door."

Patrick turned the handle. The door fell open with a low creak. A rectangle of light fell into the cabin, illuminating the small space. It was empty. "Huh."

They peeked in on every cabin in the row, but they were all empty. Even the fire that perpetually burned in Dylan's room, the one he even left burning when they left the fort, had gone out. "What's going on here?" Ben asked anxiously.

"I have no idea."

They crossed the yard, searching all the buildings along the way, but there was no sign of anyone. The gardening tools were stowed in the shed, the vegetable baskets were empty and stacked in the corner, and the clean laundry from the day before had been pulled off the line.

Patrick stood in the center of the grounds with his arms folded across his chest. He glanced sharply around the area while Ben paced anxiously along the wall, looking for any sign of...well, anything. "Look at this," Patrick said, sweeping his hand around the yard. "Does this strike you as odd?"

"The fact that no one's here? Yeah it does."

"No. The fact that everything is so...tidy."

Ben stopped. He had a point there. Since when did garden tools get put away? When were the baskets ever stacked? When were there not a few pairs of pants perpetually clinging to the clothesline?

"You're right," Ben said. "Something's wrong."

"I think you mean something's amiss," Patrick said, but there was no mirth in it. They hustled over to the front gate. It was closed, but unlocked. "Benny Boy," he said, "I think we've been abandoned."

Ben started. "Bullshit. We haven't been abandoned. Why would we be abandoned?"

"I have no earthly idea," Patrick admitted with a frown. "But look. The gate only locks from the inside. And it's *never* left unlocked. So the only reason to leave it unlocked is if there's no one left to lock it from inside. Get it?"

Ben shook his head. "So what? They all went for a walk. They went to go take pot shots at the Carsons. They went to do whatever, but they're coming back."

Patrick rubbed his hands down his face and signed. "I don't think so."

"What do you mean you don't think so?" Ben asked, his voice tinged with panic. "Why not?"

"Because it's not just that they're gone. It's that *everything* is gone." He walked back to the row of cabins, Ben following close on his heels. They burst into James' cabin. Patrick made a sweeping gesture around the room. "Look. It's all gone."

It was true. James' floor, usually littered with clothes and books, was completely bare. The water bottles he kept in the corner were gone. Even the blanket from his bunk was missing.

"No," whispered Ben, his eyes growing wide. He dashed out of the room and ran to the next bunk, Annie's. He shouldered his way past the door and came to a screeching halt in the center of the room. It was completely bare. The same was true of Sarah's room, and Dylan's, and Amsalu's. Nothing of any of them remained.

"Someone kidnapped them," he decided, storming back out into the yard. "Those fucking Carsons. We have to go find them." But Patrick merely stood by and tapped his lips with one finger.

"That doesn't make sense. 'Hey, we're kidnapping you, but only you five, not the other two, and hurry up, we'll let you pack your things.' No way. There's no sign of struggle, not even any sign of rush. It's like they planned to go."

"They didn't abandon us!" Ben yelled hoarsely.

Patrick sighed. "I think maybe they did, Ben." He patted Ben on the shoulder. "But come on, we'll take a quick look around town."

Ben started off toward the gate, but Patrick turned and headed back to their cabin. "Where are you going?"

"To change clothes," Patrick said. "I'm not going adventuring in pajama pants. There's such a thing as dignity." The only problem was, he didn't know exactly where to find his jeans. They'd been on the clotheslines with the rest of the laundry. But he had a hunch.

He went inside their cabin and looked around. Sure enough, the jeans were folded neatly on the floor near the door. Someone had delivered a full laundry service in the night while they slept. He sighed and picked up the jeans. When he did, a yellow piece of paper fell out of the folds and onto the ground.

Patrick stared quizzically down at the note. *Where did that come from?* And why did it look so familiar?

He picked it up off the floor. It was old, weathered, practically falling apart. He opened it gingerly, careful not to rip it along the folds. He smoothed the paper on the bunk and read the words written there.

"Holy shit," he breathed.

Ben poked his head into the room. "You ready or what?" Patrick shook his head and beckoned Ben inside. He held out the paper. Ben frowned down at him.

"What's that?"

"Read it," Patrick said quietly.

Ben took the note and skimmed it. Then he read it again, more carefully. Then he read it a third time. Then he read it again.

"What is this?" he said, brow furrowed. "Who wrote this?" And then again, "What is this?"

Patrick sighed and took the note back. He folded it carefully. "It's the reason for this trip," he said, his eyes glazed over with tears. Then, quietly, to himself, he said, "How could I forget about this?"

Ben narrowed his eyes. "*That's* why we're going to Florida?" Patrick nodded solemnly. Ben scoffed. "Well, shit, Pat, why didn't you just tell me that?"

Patrick shrugged. It suddenly seemed to be a great effort for his thin, shaking shoulders. "I don't know. I thought you'd think it was--" He trailed off. "I don't know."

"It's a hell of a lot better than, 'Because I've never been,'" Ben muttered. "But, Pat, how did you forget something like that? I mean, how *could* you?"

Patrick just shook his head. "I don't know," he whispered, his eyes glazed over with tears. "I don't--" But then the oracle's words returned to him, echoing through his cobwebbed brain. And suddenly, he knew how. "Sirens," he breathed.

"What?"

"Sirens. This place, these people. The unlimited number of engineering projects for me, the pretty, enigmatic girl for you, food and shelter and good company. Ben, they're nothing but sirens. Luring us onto the rocks, making us forget."

Ben bit his bottom lip and kicked the doorjamb so hard the whole cabin shook. "That's bullshit," he said, but they both felt the resignation in his voice.

Patrick sighed. "Ben. We have to go."

It didn't take them long to pack. Their liquor stores had been all but depleted, so even with the addition of a spade and a trowel that Patrick pilfered from the shed ("Because you never know when you'll have a digging emergency"), their load was considerably lighter. Patrick spent a good ten minutes scouring the cabin for the pudding cup. He knew he hadn't eaten it, but he couldn't speak for the rest of the group. Like the note, he'd forgotten all about the Snack Pack, and the more he searched for it, the more frantic he became. He tossed their sheets, dumped out their bags, shook out their clothes, becoming more and more panicked, his heart hammering in his chest, a sudden sheen of sweat covering his face. He gripped his bunk and hauled it away from the wall in a burst of desperation, and there, on the floor, still unopened, sat the little cup of butterscotch pudding. "Must've hidden it from myself," he said, exhaling his relief. "Thank you, instincts."

He went out to pull some vegetables from the garden while Ben did a final inspection of the cabins, searching for some sign, *any* sign, that the rest of the group had found it hard to leave. But there was nothing.

Their new family was completely and utterly gone.

"How could they do that?" he asked angrily, joining Patrick outside in the yard. "How could they just...leave?"

Patrick shook his head. "I don't know. But they obviously didn't want to be here when we woke up." He placed his hands on Ben's shoulders and looked him squarely in the eyes. "Listen to me. When we're done with Disney World, we'll come back. If they're not here, we'll go looking for them. We'll spend the rest of our lives looking, if that's what it takes. That'll be our new quest," he promised. "So speaketh the apocalypticon."

•

They watched in silence from the roof of the building across from the fort as the two men passed through the gate and turned down toward the bay.

"Guess they found the note," Sarah said quietly, her arms crossed tightly at her chest. Her cold, dull eyes followed them as he ambled down the street, looking back over his shoulder every few steps, looking, she knew, for her.

"It was the right thing to do," James said. He placed his hand on her shoulder and squeezed, but she shrugged him off.

"Some great friend you turned out to be," Annie told her brother, rolling her eyes.

James frowned. "It's tough love," he said. Then he added, quietly, "Tough for all of us."

"Do not worry," said Amsalu, closing his eyes lifting his face to the mid-morning light. "We will see them again if it is God's will."

Dylan snorted and flicked his spent joint off the roof. "The city of God has a vacancy sign," he said. "Elvis has left the building."

20.

"Rock, paper, scissors!" Patrick threw rock. Ben bounced an extra time, then threw scissors.

"Dammit, Pat!" he cried in frustration. "You said one, two, three, *then* shoot!"

"That was seconds ago, Ben. Literally *seconds*. I can't be expected to remember paltry details for entire seconds. Besides, that gave you the upper hand, you could see what I threw, and you still lost! That means I double win, and we take to the sea. And may God have mercy on your pitiful hand-eye coordination." He headed down the street toward the sound of the Gulf, whistling a merry tune.

"I want to be on record that this is the latest in your string of really stupid trip decisions," Ben grumbled, shuffling down the street after him. He cast a few hopeful glances back over his shoulder, but the streets behind them were empty. "Glad to see we're picking right up where we left off."

"This is not a stupid idea," Patrick insisted. "Some of those earlier ideas, yes, those were stupid ideas. But *this* idea? This idea is an *excellent* idea! I feel the Gulf wind calling us. We will sail ourselves to Florida!"

"Do you know even anything about sailing?" Ben asked sourly, his cheeks flushing red. Patrick got the sense that maybe he was not on board with this exciting new plan.

"Ben, I get the sense that maybe you're not on board with this exciting new plan," he said. "But I don't want you to worry. What's to know? You get a boat, you raise the sail, and you wait for a giant cloud with a face to float down and blow some wind. I've seen cartoons before, I know how this works. Or are you forgetting Rule Number 26?" *When in doubt, defer to entertainment media.*

"That is a stupid rule," Ben declared.

"You came up with it!"

"Because you didn't want me to have a dog!"

"That stupid *I Am Legend* dog didn't exactly save Robert from blowing himself apart with a grenade, now, did he?"

"But he made life bearable!" Ben insisted.

"And your dog pissed on your head when you slept."

"He had a nervous condition."

"He probably got a whole lot more nervous when you threw him out into the Chicago wasteland."

"What, you think I'm gonna sit there and get peed on every night? No, thank you. Who am I, Charlie Sheen?"

This continued into a fierce argument that made Patrick extremely regretful that he'd ever agreed to dispel the First Rule of the Road. He briefly considered invoking Martial Law, but then he remembered that Ben was approximately all the way stronger than him. And, besides, the argument was healthy. It was getting Ben's mind off what they were leaving behind.

"You'll love sailing," Patrick promised as he sauntered down toward the bay. "Fresh air, cool breeze, minimal Monkey fog, calm waters. This will be great and in no way dangerous or life threatening. I promise."

Before long, they reached the water's edge. A little ways down the coast, a handful of empty docks jutted into the Gulf. The only boats in sight were ones that had smashed against the rocks or had run aground on the beach. They were either half sunken in water or splintered on the shore. Any boat retaining its ability to float had long since pushed off from the wharf.

"Okay, Popeye, now what?" Ben asked. "We can't sail without a boat."

Patrick turned and searched the edge of the city. An old, rusty sign declared a particularly skeezy looking building to be the Two Hearts Motel. A broad smile spread across his face. "Benny Boy," he declared proudly, "I have a plan."

•

"You have got to be kidding."

"I never kid about romance," Patrick said.

"There is nothing romantic about this." Ben tried to imagine what the room might have looked like three years ago, before the apocalypse. He gave the motel as many benefits of the doubt as he could mentally muster, but even so, the place had been slimy. He pictured the brown shag carpet, luxurious and new, unsoiled by the mysterious stains that he knew were probably there long before the end of the world. The circular bed had either spun or vibrated (possibly both) when whatever Deep South Don Juan inhabited the room for the night (or, more likely, for the hour) dropped a quarter in a now defunct box on the wall. A dramatic trident-shaped candlestick of tarnished brass held the uneven stubs of three mostly melted candles that had once glowed dimly against the soft pink walls. The ceiling had once been fully mirrored, though now it looked like a reflective checkerboard. A few of the mirror panels lay shattered on the soiled carpet, the lazy brown webs painted on the surface almost a perfect match for the dusty shag. The silk bed sheets were still in reasonably good shape, though in his mind, Ben preferred to picture them without the large ovals of sticky residue that signified that this room had been inhabited at the time of the Jamaican attack. The lovers' clothes were still splayed across the floor, in various stages of decomposition.

But the thing that held Patrick's attention wasn't in the main sleeping area. It was in the oversized bathroom. In fact, it practically *was* the oversized bathroom. "It" was a large, heart-shaped Jacuzzi bathtub, set loosely into a wood paneled dais. It was filthy, covered in dust, dirt, years-old soap scum, and a thin layer of Monkey dust, but the fiberglass appeared to be sturdy and unbroken.

"It *used* to be romantic. In simpler times. And, if you play your cards right," he said, placing a hand gently on Ben's arm, "it might be again."

"Get off me," Ben demanded, squirming out of reach. "What the hell are we supposed to do with this thing?"

"This 'thing,' as you so disdainfully call it, is our ticket to the seven seas!" Patrick rubbed his hands together excitedly.

"It's a bath tub."

"It's a Jacuzzi," Patrick corrected him. "Which means this outer piece is our fiberglass hull. Grab that end." He pointed to the tub's left ventricle. Ben sighed and approached it reluctantly. The lip of the tub had conveniently come away from the wooden support. He wedged his fingers in the crack and tried not to think of the fact that they could be across the Florida state line by now if they'd headed out north from Fort Doom on foot. "All right," Patrick said, grabbing the pointy tip of the heart. "Now, pull!" They both heaved against the dirty red fiberglass. The tub creaked and moaned against its moorings, but age and neglect had weakened the wooden base, and a series of pops indicated success. They groaned with effort as they pried the tub up away from the base. Ben pulled the edge of the tub up one foot, two feet, three feet, until he could comfortably grab the plexiglass with both hands. He wrenched his arms up, deadlift style, and the giant heart broke completely free of its bonds.

"You are so handy," Patrick panted, setting his end back down. "Now. We just need to haul this thing out of here, find a way to seal the jet holes, and we've got ourselves a boat."

It took about twenty more minutes to lug the tub out of the bathroom and through the motel room door. Both doorways were just slightly too narrow for the tub to go through on its side, so the men kicked away the cheap wooden trim and rammed the sturdy tub through the naked doorways. Streaks of broken drywall dust lined both sides of the Jacuzzi as they rolled it to a crashing halt outside the motel.

Ben stopped a minute to catch his breath. Patrick had a few good qualities, but physical strength was not among them. Ben had been doing almost all of the heavy lifting. "How'd you know there'd be a heart tub in here?" he wheezed. "Please tell me you've stayed here before."

"No. But if B horror movies have taught me anything, it's that shady love motels are guaranteed to have Jacuzzis. The heart shape is an unexpected and pleasant surprise."

"It's something, all right," Ben murmured.

"It's naturally aerodynamic," Patrick explained. "This baby'll cut through the water like a knife." He went back into the room and retrieved the stubs of candle wax from the holder by the bed. He searched through three rooms before digging up a half empty book of matches with *Two Hearts Motel* stamped in gold on the cover. He lit one of the candles and used it to melt the other two, dripping the wax over the jet holes on both sides of the tub.

"Will that hold?" Ben asked, a familiar cloud of dread settling over his brain.

"No clue," Patrick admitted. "But we're about to find out." He pointed up at the sky. Ben turned to find a solid wall of thick, black clouds. Almost instantly, lightning cracked against the horizon, and huge pellets of rain began slamming down from above. "Quick!" Patrick cried, lifting the side of the tub. "Everybody under!"

Ben wondered why his default response was always obedience. What he really wanted to do was run back inside the motel room and wait out the storm, but instead he ducked under the tub, and Patrick lowered it down over them.

"Ah! So cozy!" Patrick declared, snuggling up to the grimy sides of the overturned heart. Ben, on the other hand, tried to stay as centered in his ventricle as possible. The smell of the dust and filth made his stomach flop.

Rain deluged the tub. The pounding was deafening. What dim light there was outside filtered through the red fiberglass, casting a grayish-pink glow inside the little red shelter. Ben could see streams of rain running down the outside of the tub, and some little rivulets of water pushed their way under the lip of the Jacuzzi between the fiberglass and the asphalt. But the wax seals held tight, and not a single drop of water seeped in through the closed jet holes. After about fifteen minutes the storm passed, and Patrick flipped the boat over excitedly. "She'll hold!" he cried, literally jumping up and down.

They sloshed their way through the puddles back down to the water's edge, holding the heart boat up over their heads. When they reached the ocean, they heaved the boat down onto the beach and dug it securely into the rocky sand. "Now we need a sail," Patrick said.

After a little scrounging, their best hope was a long vinyl banner, about 15 feet in length and three feet wide. There were words written on one side of the banner, albeit in a language that neither of them recognized. JEBALEM TWOJA MATKA was stamped into the dirty white vinyl in blue letters big enough to read from 100 yards away. "What do you think it says?" Ben asked.

"I believe it says, 'Safe passage.' I feel that in my heart."

As they scavenged for a mast and rope, a few native Mobilians began to stir. They were all silent, haunted folks, most of them gaunt and hungry. Ben eyed them all suspiciously. Most of the locals they'd run into over the last couple of months had been peaceful enough, just as wary of the Fort Doomers as the Fort Doomers were of them. But there were just enough malicious assholes out there to keep a man on his toes. Every time someone came within 50 feet of their boat, Ben pulled out the spade and made violent stabs in their direction. It seemed to get the point across fairly well.

Patrick took a different tact with the quiet natives. After Ben chased them away, he waved happily after them, calling, "*Jabalem twoja matkai!*" This garnered him more than a few strange looks, and even the occasional glare. But before long he'd been able to rig up a mast out of driftwood and a set of discarded bungee cords, and by the time the sun sank over the horizon, they had a homemade sailboat.

They stood back and admired it in the green-tinged sunset. It looked like a kindergartener's art project, set to scale.

"This'll go badly," Ben said, knowing with absolute certainty that it was the truth.

"This'll be *exciting*," Patrick countered. And Ben had to admit that this, also, was true.

•

They took turns guarding the boat that night, and at first light, they pushed it groggily into the Gulf. "Oh good Christ, that is cold!" Patrick screamed as he stumbled clumsily into the water. "It's like ice daggers in my leg souls!"

"Your legs are soulless, just like the rest of you." Ben hopped into the boat from the dry beach and fell into it with a *thump*. The boat rocked back and forth, splashing water up higher on Patrick's legs. He howled curses at the sky.

"You're a motherless scant of a whore pup!" he cried, hopping out of the water and back onto the beach.

"Grab the shovel on your way back in, will you? We're going to need that."

Patrick swiped the spade off the sand and lobbed it at the boat. Ben yelped and ducked. The blade missed his head by six inches and splashed into the ocean. Ben reached over and drew it in. "You coming, or what?" he asked, using the spade to row away from the shore.

Patrick grumbled under his breath. The boat was floating farther and farther away. "I hate you, Ben Fogelvee," he called out over the lapping waves. Ben smiled and waved back at him. Patrick took a deep breath, steeled his innards, and rushed like a madman into the frigid surf.

After Patrick had pulled himself into the boat and shaken off as much water as he could, the pair found the ship to be a bit of a tight squeeze. Between the mast, their backpacks, the spade, the hammer, the baton, the machete, the wrench, the trowel, and the two mariners, there wasn't much space to loll around. But as close as it was, the boat floated marvelously, and they were both soon in high spirits. "See? Isn't this nice?" Patrick asked as he paddled.

"I have to admit, it's pretty good," Ben said, nodding approvingly. "I mean, I don't want to say you were right. Because I would never say that. But we're 50 feet from shore, and we haven't drowned yet."

"And the sun is shining," Patrick pointed out.

"The sun is shining," Ben conceded.

"The water is smooth."

"The water isn't awful."

"And we won't stop for anything."

"Not for anything?" Ben asked, cautiously hopeful.

"Not for anything," Patrick said. "I tell you, when this boat stops, we'll be at the Florida coast or the bottom of the sea." They shook on it. "And the wind! Oh, the wind, she is a-blowin'! A little bit farther, and we'll unfurl the sail."

The farther they paddled from land, the happier Ben felt. The sea breeze was really clearing his mind. "Man," he said as they sliced through the water. "We should've done this from day one."

"Yes," Patrick agreed, pushing the water with the spade. "We should have taken one of those land boats."

"We should've skipped Memphis and taken that speedboat all the way to the Gulf."

"Aye, in hindsight, that would have gotten us here sooner. But think of all the fun we would've missed!"

"True. It was really fun to watch your hand get drilled by a railroad spike."

"I hope you'll recall my stoic bravery when you write the story of my life." He estimated that they were now far enough from land to unfurl the sail. He hauled in the spade and secured it against the side of the boat. "All right!" he said, rubbing his hands together. "Time to move! Benjamin, please remove your feet from the bow."

"Which end is the bow?" Ben asked, puzzled.

Patrick stared blankly at him. "Which end is the bow? The end with your feet in it, which need to be removed, you clod."

"Hey, shut up," Ben fussed, curling his feet back into the left ventricle. "It's early. And there's no coffee."

"Don't you dare talk about coffee," Patrick warned. "Don't you dare." He scooted clumsily toward the front of the boat and began working on the sail.

"Why do they call it the bow, anyway? Why don't they just call it the front?"

"Such things are not for us to question," Patrick said, unhooking the rolled banner from one of the bungee cords. "It is simply the seafarer's way."

"Well, I got news for the seafarers. They're dead. *Everyone's* dead. The end of the world happened, and we're still following the same old rules."

"The world didn't technically end," Patrick said. "The world still exists."

"Whatever. Semantics. The apocalypse happened, and we still kowtow to the old ways. You know what, Pat? We've been lazy survivors. We've been doing too much loafing and not enough remaking the world in our own image. Who cares if the front of a boat used to be a bow, or if the back of a boat was the brim?"

"Stern," Patrick corrected. "Weren't you ever a Boy Scout?"

"Whatever, who cares! That's my point! There are only two people left on the entire planet who still discuss the right words for the ends of a boat, and only one of them knows the proper terminology. That's only 50%. That's not even a majority. I say to hell with tradition. I beat the apocalypse, so I get the right to rename the parts of a boat. That," he said, leveling a finger at the front of the boat, "is now called 'the point.'"

"The point of the boat?" Patrick asked, a little less than convinced.

"And the back is forthwith to be called 'the ass.'"

"That is a horrible name."

"Quiet. I'm nestling against the ass."

Patrick finished rigging the sail and hauled it up with another bungee cord. It rose smoothly and flapped open in the wind. It caught a stiff breeze blowing in the right direction, and the heart tub lurched forward. "Success!" he cried. "We're sailors, Ben! We sail!"

"It is no longer called 'sailing,'" Ben said. "It is now called 'hauling ass.'"

The little boat hauled ass for almost three straight hours, never waning in speed. The wind blew favorably, and the boat skimmed smoothly across the surface of the ocean. "If this wind keeps up, we just might make it by dawn," Patrick said, studying the atlas. Of course, having never aquatically hauled ass before, he had no real idea how quickly they might cover ground. Still, he felt in his heart that with a little luck, they could dock by morning. "As long as the wind holds."

He spent some time explaining the particulars of sailing to Ben, inasmuch as he knew them himself. These particulars basically amounted to raising the sail when the wind blew them forward, lowering the sail and paddling when it didn't, and keeping the shore on the port side of the boat. "That's the Benward side," Ben insisted. "It's on the side of Ben."

The wind still blew toward the east when they broke into their vegetable stores for lunch. "This may be the sea air talking," Ben said, tearing into a head of greens, "but I think I'm actually starting to like cabbage."

"You've gone sea crazy," Patrick said sagely. "The thrall of the open water has you now."

The day's storm came and went without much power. Rain fell heavily into the boat, but not in such great volume that they were in danger of sinking. Patrick pulled down the sail, and they managed to hold the boat steady and more or less on course as the waves rocked and tossed them about. And just as quickly as the little storm gathered, it disappeared. The sun broke back through the clouds and fog, the ocean calmed, and the point of the boat still faced east. They wrung out their clothes, Patrick raised the sail, and they were soon back up to speed.

The conversation drifted as they sailed on. They talked about Disney World, and pudding cups, and the medical benefits of ingesting embalming fluid.

"How fitting that it was those very chemicals that saved our lives!" Patrick decided. "It's almost poetic."

Ben groaned. "Don't talk about it. I think I'm going to be sick," he said, leaning over the edge of the Love Boat.

"It's okay," Patrick said, patting his back. "Seasickness is a natural part of life. It's nothing to be ashamed of. But it's also disgusting, so I'm going to have to push you overboard."

Ben swatted him away and managed to keep his food in his stomach where it belonged. He leaned back against the Benward ventricle and closed his eyes and tried not to think about swallowing cadaver juices.

The boat sped on, the coastline slipped by, and despite the chill in the air, it was really a pleasant day. The tall banner flapped heavily in the wind. "*Jabalem twoja matkai,*" Patrick waved to the fish that splashed out of the water. "*Jabalem twoja matkai* to you all!"

And so they sailed through the Gulf, raising the sail when there was wind, paddling when there wasn't, and closing the gap between them and the Magic Kingdom. Eventually, the sea air helped Ben forget about embalming fluid, and about their friends at Fort Doom, and by the time it was dark, he even found himself able to sleep.

21.

Ben awoke with a start when the boat slammed into the beach. "Wakey, wakey!" Patrick cried, leaping out of his ventricle. He splashed into the shallow water and pulled the boat onto the beach. Ben struggled to sit up and blinked sleepily at the world before him. They were docked on a mostly deserted beach, presumably somewhere in Florida. The glow of the sun was just breaking somewhere behind the eastern fog.

"Holy shit," Ben yawned. "We're alive. This stupid idea was actually not that stupid of an idea."

Patrick gave him a low bow. "A-thank you."

"Did we make it? Where are we?"

"An excellent question." Patrick turned toward a man who was either sleeping or dead farther down the beach. "Excuse me! Sir!" he called out. The figure stirred and sat up. "What's the name of this town?"

"Hudson. Hudson, Florida," called out the bewildered looking man. He had a thick eastern European accent. "You—you come here by boat?" he asked, confused.

"We do! We are in search of Disney World. Where might we find it?"

The man pointed toward the hazy morning sun. "One day's walk," he said.

"Huzzah!" Patrick exclaimed. "Thank you for your help. *Jabalem twoja matkai!*"

The man leapt to his feet and made an obscene hand gesture. "Fuck you!" he said in a thick Eastern European accent. Then he stormed off down the beach.

Patrick turned to Ben and shrugged. "I guess he doesn't want safe travels."

"He didn't sound like he was from the Midwest, either," Ben blenched. "He drinks dead people juices."

After a quick breakfast of carrots and pearl onions, they gathered up their few belongings and bid farewell to the trusty sea craft. They hiked up the beach and into the town of Hudson, bearing due east.

The road to Disney World was unsettlingly quiet. After the man on the beach, they didn't see a single other soul as they plunged into the heart of Florida. They picked their way through entire cities that showed no signs of life. The air was still, and the only sound was the occasional scrabble of rats against the rubble. The farther they walked from the water, the more thickly the Monkey fog settled back onto the earth. By the time they reached the city limit sign of Ardmore Gardens, they found themselves once again walking through the old familiar yellow blind.

The Florida landscape was different than any they'd yet encountered. The ground was marshy and wet, dotted with lakes and creeks and little swamps. The unsettling combination of wetlands and human desertion had a quieting effect on the two travelers. They talked little as they pushed deeper and deeper into the state, when by all rights they should have been growing more and more excited.

"I'm just going to say it," Ben said after a few hours of near silence. "Florida is creepy as shit."

"God, tell me about it," said Patrick. "Why did anyone want to retire here?"

They were still walking when night fell. They had just crawled out the far end of a large swamp and entered a small, empty town. "What do you think? Camp here for the night? I mean, God knows how much farther we have to go. Want to call it for now?" Ben asked. "Patrick? Pat?" But when he turned, Patrick's eyes were glazed over, sparkling with teardrops.

"I know how much farther we have to go," he whispered. He pointed up at the highway, toward a battered road sign. WALT DISNEY WORLD NEXT 5 EXITS.

"Ho-ly shit," Ben breathed. "We made it."

Patrick shoved him playfully. "We made it."

He shoved back. "We made it."

"We made it."

"*We made it.*"

"*We made it.*"

"We made it!"

"We made it!" Then bounced around the highway shoulder, laughing and dancing like idiots. They howled at the growing darkness, their excitement reverberating off the overpass and shaking the deserted buildings around them. They skipped around, delirious, until Patrick stumbled in a pothole and fell into the guardrail, shoulder-first. "Ow."

"And that's how Patrick died. Three feet from his destination."

"Shut up."

"You gonna lay there all night, or are we gonna go to Disney World?"

Patrick rolled to his feet. "To Disney World!" he cried, pumping his fist in the air.

"To Disney World," said Ben. "Which park?"

Patrick stopped, his arms frozen out at awkward angles. "Come again?"

"Which park are we going to?"

"What do you mean, which park? We're going to Disney World. *That* park."

Ben shook his head. "You are the single worst planner anyone has ever followed blindly into a post-apocalyptic situation."

"That reflects more poorly on you than it does me," Patrick pointed out.

"You still have those maps from the zombie whisperer?"

"Maybe." Patrick dropped his knapsack and dug through the pockets. "Ah! Yes. Here they are."

"Right. *They.* Four of them. Four maps, four parks. Which one do you want to go to?"

Patrick frowned. He stared at the maps in his hand and tried to let the Spirit of the Illinois guide his decision. The Epcot map had a rocket ship on the cover, and he hated flying. So that one was out. The map for Hollywood Studios showed some doofus singing on an American Idol stage, so that one was *definitely* out. He tossed it over his shoulder. "This one looks promising," he said, holding up the Animal Kingdom map with a huge, pissed off lion on the front.

"The lions are dead," Ben reminded him. "The Animal Kingdom is an animal graveyard."

"Right," Patrick said. "Hm." He stared down at the last map. The cover just showed a big, circular something-or-other with the words "Disney's Electrical Parade" written in light bulbs. It didn't exactly scream excitement. "You're letting me down, Great Spirit," he said. "Oh! I know! Hold on, let me see if I can get anything from this." He produced the folded piece of paper from his back pocket and examined it closely. The tip of his tongue poked out the corner of his mouth while he read. "Yeah, no, nothing," he finally decided. He folded it back up and returned it to its hiding place. He crossed his arms and cupped his chin in his hand. "Okay, Ben. So if you were a man--"

"I am a man."

"--And you had to pick one park to see--"

"Complete with burned out baby skeletons."

"--Complete with burned out baby skeletons, which would it be?"

"The one with the castle. Obviously."

"The castle!" Patrick cried, snapping his fingers. "Of course! *Neuschwanstein!*"

"Neuschan-what?"

"*Neuschwanstein.* It's the real castle that the Disney castle was modeled after. In Germany."

"Seriously? It was designed after a real castle?"

"It was."

"I don't believe you. Google it for me."

"I can't."

"Because you don't have a data plan?"

"Because I have no idea how to spell it. German is hard. And that word is a holocaust of vowels." Ben squinted at Patrick. Patrick squinted back. "Mm-hmm. I said it."

Ben shook his head. "Okay. So Magic Kingdom."

"Magic Kingdom!" Patrick leafed through the map, but it only gave the layout of the park itself, not the location of the park in the larger scheme of Disney World. "Okay, look. I know you're bad at this sort of thing, but you've been here before, so I ask you. Can you get us to this Magic Kingdom? Despite your complete and utter ineptitude when it comes to cardinal direction?"

"Yes, ass. I think I can."

Patrick placed his hands on Ben's shoulders. "And here, at the final stretch, you begin to prove your worth at last."

"When I write your life's story, every chapter's going to start with a reminder of how much of an ass you are."

"I *knew* you were writing my life story!"

They hiked up to the overpass and entered Disney property. Ben led them along the highway, stopping to read each purple and red road sign that hadn't given up in the fight against neglect. It was slow going in the dark, made even slower, in Ben's estimation, by Patrick's self-imposed (and self-accepted) challenge to concoct at least 50 Disney-themed innuendos before they reached the park (starting with "My pants are a magical kingdom," "I'd like to tinker with her bell," and "Those aren't mouse ears"). But at last they came to a junction with a sign that read MAGIC KINGDOM NEXT LEFT. "That is where we find the castle. And without looking at a stolen atlas for help," Ben said proudly. Then he added, "Suck it."

They turned onto World Drive and began hiking the last stretch of road to their destination. As they walked, Ben was stricken by how little everything had changed, all things considered. Tall trees still lined the roads and masked the many secrets of the park. The entryway to Hollywood Studios, though empty and covered with debris, looked like it was one good sweeping away from being open for business. The fog and the darkness made it hard to see much, but Ben could still picture the Hollywood Tower Hotel looming above the trees in the distance.

The monorail track appeared alongside the road. It loomed starkly over them, floating in and out of view as the dark fog swirled above. Some sections had cracked and broken away, leaving mountains of concrete and steel along the roadway. They crossed over the shimmering lake, smooth as obsidian in the night, and passed the clean outline of the Contemporary Resort on the right. "If memory serves, the Magic Kingdom is just over yonder," Ben said, pointing ahead and to the left.

"Yonder close?" Patrick asked.

"Yonder close," Ben confirmed.

They turned down the drive that led to the parking lot. As they approached the park, Ben noticed something glimmering in the distance. Patrick saw it too. "Look at that. They turned the lights on for us," he said, furrowing his brow. Ben peered into the brownish yellow evening fog. There was a second glimmer, and a third. Then more and more, until Ben counted eight points of light in the distance. They flickered and flashed in the air.

"Torches?" Ben suggested.

"Looks like it. Maybe they *are* still in business."

Ben stopped walking. "I don't like this. It's not right."

"No," Patrick agreed. "It's probably not."

"Think we should wait 'til it's light out?" There was no mistaking the fear in his voice. "There's still one more peril before we're done. Bombastic Tom and--"

Patrick started. "*Ubasti* Tom," he said.

"Come again?"

"Ubasti Tom. That's what the old lady said. I don't know why it just registered. Ubasti Tom and the Hollow Man."

"What's an Ubasti?"

"I have no idea."

Ben frowned. "It doesn't sound pleasant."

"No, it doesn't," Patrick admitted.

An invisible hand of ice closed around Ben's chest. "The old lady said we would make it to Disney World," he realized aloud. "But she didn't say we'd survive all the perils, did she? Specifically?"

"No," Patrick said gravely. "That tricky minx, she did not. I had assumed we'd face all the perils *before* getting here, but..."

Ben shifted uneasily from one foot to the other. "What do you want to do?"

Patrick's face became hard and unmoving, uncharacteristic and impossible to read. "She was right about everything. She'll be right about this. Whether we go now or we go tomorrow, whatever's gonna happen is gonna happen."

"It doesn't have to," Ben insisted. "This isn't *The Time Traveler's Wife*. This is Disney World. We're here; we made it. This is it. Hooray! Now we can turn around and go. Right now. Make your peace here, or hell, we'll go to friggin' Epcot. We don't have to do this."

"We didn't come here to make a stand in the parking lot," Patrick said, shaking his head. "*She* wouldn't have just stood in the parking lot."

"No," Ben sighed. "She wouldn't have."

Patrick took a deep breath. The words of the fortuneteller rang in his head. *The bulldog or the mouse hunter must fall. You will choose.* "Ben--" he began, but Ben held up a hand and cut him off.

"Save it. I know."

"No," Patrick insisted, "you don't."

Ben gritted his teeth. "Well, let's just say, if I don't know, then I don't care. This is the part of the story where you say something sentimental or heart-wrenching or some bullshit, thinking maybe I'll go and let you go on alone to face the doom of a dozen sentient torches in the night. Right?"

"Well. Yeah. Something like that."

"I'm not leaving. And anything you say can only make me regret not having the sense to leave, so save it."

Patrick shook his head sadly. "If you were a superhero, your power would be loyalty."

"I *am* a superhero," Ben said, gritting his teeth. "And don't no one forget it."

They crossed into the grass and approached the line of torches, Patrick pulling the machete from its scabbard, Ben grasping the wrench. What the dark night's fog couldn't hide, the brilliant flames shining into their eyes did. "Oo-we," called a voice from the darkness behind the row of light. "What do we have here?" *Wait,* Patrick thought. *I know that voice.* He stepped through the line of torches stuck into the grass and crossed onto the pavement. He squinted into the mist. A burly figure emerged from the darkness.

"Calico?" Patrick said. Bloom's henchman gave him a smart little salute.

"Don't sound so surprised, Yank," he said, grinning his horrible grin. "I told ya I'd be comin' for ya."

"Technically, you wrote it," Patrick pointed out.

"Oh, come on," Ben groaned, his heart falling like a lead weight. "You tracked us all the way to Disney World? From Illinois? Are you fucking *crazy?*"

"Not crazy. Just determined," came a low, even voice from the gloom. Patrick's eyes were adjusting to the light of the torches, and at the edge of their halo he noticed a second man sitting on the asphalt. The man stood and walked toward the torches. "You cost me something very dear." The man stepped into the light. Patrick gasped involuntarily. He recognized the cold, hollow eyes instantly.

"Bloom," he whispered.

The left side of Bloom's face was wrinkled and scarred. He noticed Patrick staring at it. "Gravel burn," he explained, tracing a finger down the side of his face. "I wanted to thank you for that. And for the experience of drowning. That was new to me."

"You look dry enough now," Patrick said.

"I make a hell of a lifeguard," Calico grinned.

Patrick swallowed. "Yes. Well. The scars look totally natural. A little concealer, and you'll be fine. Nice catching up, but we should be going." He grabbed Ben's arm and turned on his heels, but Calico leapt forward, quick as a snake, and grabbed Patrick by the scruff of his neck.

"Don't think so," he grinned. He whirled Patrick around easily and shoved him over toward Bloom. Patrick stumbled and fell to his knees on the cold, hard blacktop. The machete flew from his hands and went clattering across the asphalt. He looked up just in time to see Ben leveling the wrench at Calico, keeping a distance as he crept his way toward his fallen friend.

"Pat, you okay?"

"I'm daisies," Patrick said.

Bloom kicked the machete across the parking lot, into the darkness. Then he picked up a bottle from the ground and took a thoughtful sip. "I was dead for almost four whole minutes before Calico gave me the breath of life. Think about that. Four whole minutes. The human body is a wonder." He tipped the bottle toward Patrick. "Care for a drink?"

Patrick examined the bottle. *Whiskey? Rum?* "I'm not thirsty just now," he said.

Bloom shrugged. "Suit yourself." He set the bottle on the ground. "Calico, call the others." Calico dug into his pocket and produced a little whistle. He blew into it, one loud, sharp, shrill note that rang off into the distance. He waited expectantly. Five seconds later, they heard another

313

whistle, the same sharp note, from beyond the trees.

"Them boys is gonna be happy as pigs in shit when they come back'n find yer two sorry asses dead on the ground." Calico pocketed the whistle and drew out a dagger. He hauled back and threw a hard kick at Patrick's ribs. Patrick rolled to avoid it, but not quickly enough. The toe of Calico's boot caught him in the stomach. The air blasted out of his lungs like helium from a popped balloon. When he opened his eyes, he saw Ben charging, wrench raised high. He swung it down at Calico's head, but the man whirled deftly to the left, threw a hard punch into Ben's stomach, and tossed him aside into the gravel. Patrick watched miserably. Ben would just keep coming until they put him down for good. *Goddammit.*

Bloom looked on disinterestedly as Calico tightened his grip on his dagger and squatted down next to Patrick. "You owe us a train, boy. Guess I'll take the payment out in pounds of flesh." He flicked the knife forward, digging the point into Patrick's shoulder. Pat grunted in pain and reached out with his other hand, grabbed the whiskey bottle by the neck, turned, and swung it up at Calico's face, exploding it against his temple. Calico screamed and clutched at his eye, brown liquor and blood pouring down his face. Patrick pushed himself to his feet and awkwardly dodged a blind swing of Calico's dagger. He grabbed one of the torches at the edge of the asphalt and yanked it out of the grass. Calico charged him, blade brandished. Patrick lowered the torch and shoved the flame into Calico's face. The whiskey roared to life, blazing hot yellow and blue flames across his face. He screamed and screamed, dropping his knife and swinging his fists blindly in the air. He fell to his knees, scrabbling at the fire until his hands blistered and his skin peeled and popped. He spewed vicious obscenities into the night, his legs kicking wildly, his entire body writhing in pain. Soon the whiskey burned off and the flames subsided. Calico sobbed and clutched at his face. It was black and melted, and already scarring over through the bubbles.

"Jesus, Pat," Ben breathed, steadying himself to his feet. "What did you do?"

Bloom approached the fallen Red Cap quietly. He knelt by Calico's side and took stock of the damage. He sighed heavily. "That is disappointing." He drew his the sabre from his hip and slid it across Calico's throat. The screams stopped instantly. A strip of steaming blood spurted open across his neck. A river of red soaked his coat, and with one final flap of his legs, Calico was dead. Patrick watched in open-mouthed horror, stunned by his own actions as much as by Bloom's. Bloom slid the sabre back into its sheath. He rose to his feet just as Ben charged again.

"Ben, don't!" Patrick yelled. But he was already swinging the wrench. Bloom ducked the blow easily. Ben spun, off balance. Bloom grabbed him by the throat and, with his free hand, landed a hard jab to the nose. The bones crunched under the force, and Ben went down a second time.

"Leave him alone!" Patrick yelled. "I threw you off the train; this is about you and me!"

"It is," Bloom admitted, shaking out his hand. "I admit, when Calico was so hell bent on tracking you down, I was more than happy to let him off the leash." He removed his cap and ran a hand over his shaved head. "I don't begrudge you what you did. You chose a side, and you followed through. I respect that. I would have done the same. But you understand, Mr. Deen, that there are consequences for every action. Even after the world has been destroyed, there must still be balance. Order. Do you understand that?"

Patrick nodded. "Sure. I understand. I mean, where I'm from, we call it petty vengeance, but whatever. Tomato, to-mah-to," he said evenly, despite the hammering in his chest. His blood was really pumping now, and his shoulder throbbed with pain.

Bloom gave a wan little smile. "Well. Vengeance isn't so petty." He moved like water. His hand flew to his sword, and he drew it in one smooth motion. He glided forward like a man on ice. Patrick tried to dodge, but Bloom was too fast. He buried the blade deep into Patrick's belly.

Patrick looked down, stunned, at the pool of black blood spreading through his shirt.

So close, he thought as darkness began to settle over his eyes. *We are so goddamned close.*

He heard Ben yelling thinly, as if he were hearing him through a storm. He felt Bloom's blade slide back out of his gut. He closed his eyes and sank to the ground. He moved his hand to the wound and felt a warm spill running through his fingers. He opened his eyes one last time and saw Bloom's face returned to its normal placidity. "And so order is restored," he said simply.

You could have just gravel burned my face, Patrick thought.

22.

The world rang with silence as Ben watched Bloom shove the sword into Patrick's stomach. "*Noooooooo!*" he screamed. His mind scrambled, and he was choking. He couldn't breathe. He saw Patrick's eyes gloss over as he fell to the ground.

I'm in shock, Ben thought dully as he pulled himself to his feet. His skin tingled with numbness, and suddenly the scramble faded, and he could think clearly. Logically. He walked calmly over to the machete in the shadows and picked it up. Bloom flicked Patick's blood from his sword. Ben stepped up behind him as the man bent down and whispered, "And so order is restored." And, very calmly, Ben raised the machete and hacked the blade down on Bloom's neck.

When Ben came to his senses, he was cradling Patrick's limp body near the torches. How much time had passed? He turned and saw Bloom's body splayed out on the ground to the left. His head was somewhere nearby.

Ben turned back to Patrick, hot tears stinging his down his cheeks. Pat was still breathing, but shallowly. "Goddammit, Pat," Ben said, his voice thick with mucus. "I told you we should just leave."

Patrick coughed a weak laugh. "Fighting was a good idea. At the time."

"Shut up," Ben choked.

"Hey." Patrick grabbed Ben's sleeve with a blood-soaked hand. "You gotta get out of here."

Ben shook his head. "Bloom's dead."

But Patrick persisted. "More coming. The whistle. Go. Now."

Ben grimaced. He felt more tears choking their way up his throat. "I'm not leaving you like this, goddammit," he said through gritted teeth. He could feel his face flushing hotly. "I am *not* leaving you like this."

"Didn't come all this way so *both* of us could die," Patrick rasped. He smiled thinly through the pain. "They catch you here, they'll kill you."

"I'm not leaving," Ben insisted.

"Think I'm beyond repair," he said, choking out another little laugh. "Ben. Go. Back to Fort Doom. Be with friends. Learn how to talk to that girl. Rebuild a world, remake a life, or whatever dumb stuff normal people do after the apocalypse."

Ben wiped a string of mucus from his nose. "It's not dumb," he said.

Patrick tried to shrug. "It's pretty schlocky."

Ben heard men shouting from off in the distance, back the way they'd come. "Shit," he swore. "They're coming."

Patrick nodded. "Go."

"No." Ben wiped his nose with his sleeve, then slid his hands under Patrick's shoulders. "You're coming with me." He heaved backward, dragging Patrick across the asphalt. Patrick cried out in agony.

"Stop!" he gasped, shrinking into himself. "God, please, stop."

Ben released his hold and fell to his knees, hot tears dripping from his cheeks. Patrick whimpered and grasped at his gut wound. "Go," he said again. "Please, Ben. Go."

Ben's chest heaved with labored breath. He shook his head and clapped his hand awkwardly over Patrick's shoulder. "I'm sorry we didn't make it," he whispered.

Patrick patted his hand reassuringly. "We did," he said. "We did make it." Then he closed his eyes, and Patrick was gone.

Ben screwed up his face and scrubbed his eyes with his sleeve. He wanted to scream, to pick up the torches and smash them to bits and burn goddamn Disney World to the ground, but that would bring the other men all the faster. His chest heaved with silent sobs as he pulled himself to his feet. He grabbed Patrick's bag and dug through it, frantically pushing aside weapons and cans of food. Near the bottom, he found the little cup of butterscotch pudding. With the world swimming through a sheen of tears, he set the Snack Pack next to Patrick's pale form. "This stays with you," he murmured. Then he cleared his throat, shouldered Patrick's bag, grabbed his own, whispered a shaky goodbye, and turned and ran away from the lot.

By his best guess, he was heading west.

23.

Patrick opened one eye and watched Ben tear across the parking lot. He smiled wanly. *I'd like to thank the Academy.* He struggled slowly to his feet. He'd lost quite a bit of blood, and he was woozy, though he wasn't quite as bad off as he'd let on. From what he could tell, Bloom had miraculously missed all major organs. Hell, if he could stop the bleeding, he could probably even survive the injury. Under other circumstances, of course. Circumstances that involved emergency rooms, peroxide, stitches, and gallons and gallons of morphine.

He would've loved to have gone with Ben. He'd been looking forward to starting over, *really* starting over, with the gang in Alabama. They were good people. Ben would do well there.

As for Patrick, well, he'd given a bit of a white lie when he told Ben that they'd made it. *Close, but no cigar,* as his grandpa used to say. He still had a little farther to go. He reached down, wincing with pain, and grabbed the little pudding cup. *Thanks for this one, Benny Boy,* he thought.

He moved forward toward the turnstiles of the Magic Kingdom. The voices were getting louder behind him, so he picked up the pace. He hopped painfully over one of the metal gates and struggled up the mall.

He had no idea where to find the castle, but he figured he was bound to stumble across it, even in the dark. It was the hallmark of the friggin' place, right? They probably weren't hiding it.

A wide path opened up before him, bisecting two rows of shops, now in various stages of decay and dismay. It looked like a main pathway, so he dragged himself along it, one hand pressed firmly to the hole in his belly. As he stumbled up the road, the mist around him began to glow a soft yellow, and he knew the sun was rising. *That'll help things a bit*, he thought. Light filtered down through the Monkey Fog, and suddenly, there it was, looming straight ahead-—the dark outline of Cinderella's Castle.

From the sound of things, the Red Caps in the parking lot had just found the two dead bodies. There was a lot of shouting, and someone was giving orders. Patrick looked down at the path behind him. He was leaving a pretty unmistakable trail of blood. A blind detective could follow that. He quickened his pace and hurried toward the castle.

The stairs proved to be more difficult than he expected. His light-headedness increased with every flight, and several times he had to stop on a landing and wait for the stairwell to stop spinning. The steps were utility stairs, made of cold iron and shut up in a dark section of the castle. Undoubtedly, there had been some "magical" elevator that whisked guests up and down in the time before. But the castle wasn't as tall as it looked from the outside, and before long he stumbled his way to the top floor. He burst through and found himself in a small hallway. There was another door straight ahead. He pushed through it and practically fell into Cinderella's bedroom.

"Oo-wee," he said, letting out a low whistle. The room was extravagant, even in ruin. The walls and ceiling were dark wood with what looked to have once been gold paint. There were beautiful stained glass windows set into the walls, some of them even intact. Majestic doorways separated the rooms of the suite. Patrick stalked through them, admiring the detail of each piece of furniture as the world grew brighter outside and cast more light on the castle.

At the far end, he found a window that had been broken out completely. He poked his head out and looked down. He was standing at the front of the castle, looking down the long, main Magic Kingdom walkway. Through the fog, he could see shadows of Red Caps sprinting up the path. He had ten, maybe fifteen minutes before they made their way up the stairs.

Perfect.

He kicked out the little points of glass that remained in the window edge and climbed onto the sill. He was deathly afraid of heights-—for some reason, high places always seized him with the illogical thought of, *Oh my God, what if I jump?*--but he forced himself to straddle the sill, one leg in, one leg out. Cinderella's room on his left, Disney World spread before him on his right. It was a good place to be.

He looked down and admired the Snack Pack in his hand. That stupid little pudding cup that he'd carried and kept safe for 1,500 miles. His heart swelled in his chest, threatening to burst. "And me without a spoon," he said.

He peeled back the foil lid and dipped two fingers into the butterscotch goo. After so many months of vegetables and beans, the sweetness of the pudding took him by surprise, exploding in his mouth in a wonderful, sickly symphony of sugar. In four scoops, the Snack Pack was empty. He held up the little plastic container and kissed it. "We made it, pudding cup."

He set it down on the ledge and reached into his back pocket, ignoring the pain in his gut that flamed to life when he shifted his weight. He pulled out the letter and unfolded it, gingerly and for the last time. Tears stung his eyes as he moved his fingers over the familiar scrawl. The letters were sharp and uneven, the careful scribble of a child.

My summer vacation, it said across the top. *Isabella Deen, age 6.* Patrick wiped a tear from his cheek and blinked hard as he read the words he knew so well.

This summer I will go to Disney World. I am iksited. Daddy says I can be a princess like Cinderella. Mommy likes Mulan becus she is a good rore model, but I like Cinderella. Mommy says magic things happen at Disney World. It is our first vacayshun. Daddy never went to Disney World and I never went too. Daddy says our first time will be together and that makes it speshul. I am so happy to be going to Disney World.

Patrick folded the letter and held it to his lips. He breathed in the musty smell of the worn paper, remembering the scent of baby powder and Annie's lavender lotion.

He looked down and saw the last of the Red Caps disappearing into the castle. He thought he could hear the rattle of their footfalls on the metal staircase. He clutched the letter tightly in his hand and turned to face the rising sun. A gust of wind blustered up from the east and pushed the yellow fog swirling away. The wan yellow disc appeared on the horizon, bathing the park in its glow. Cinderella's Castle sparkled in the light.

"We made it, Izzy," he sighed with a smile. "I am so happy to be at Disney World with you." Then he closed his eyes and waited for the end of the world.

About the Author

Photo by Emily Rose Studios

Clayton Smith is a sometimes-writer, sometimes-napper based in Chicago, where he uses neither his bachelor's in journalism nor his master's in arts management. He is often calamitous, and good at bacon. He lives with his impressively tolerant wife.

Clayton's previous works include *Pants on Fire: A Collection of Lies* and the comedic play *Death and McCootie*, which debuted at the 2013 New York International Fringe Festival.

www.StateOfClayton.com

 @Claytonsaurus

facebook.com/Claytonsaurus

Made in the USA
San Bernardino, CA
02 April 2017